Blue Bay

Maria del Mar

ISBN 978-1-961017-25-2 (Paperback)
ISBN 978-1-961017-26-9 (Ebook)

Inquiries and Book Orders should be addressed to:

Leavitt Peak Press
17901 Pioneer Blvd Ste L #298, Artesia, California 90701
Phone #: 2092191548

"No way!"

"Way…"

"I'll be right there!"

Snapping the cellular phone shut, the man smiled.

Pablo Aguilar faced the ocean as he stood at the top of the cliff. Sunlight pulsed steadily on his skin, coating it as thick as if it were honey. Warding off the slowly increasing heat a steady breeze tickled his senses, keeping him cool and alert. Just the way he needed to be for what awaited them.

Finally they arrived. The homeowners stood next to their visitors staring at the entrance. Everyone smiled.

The pirate stepped up to his new in-laws. "You have done well for yourself, Pablito." He laughed as his eyes scanned the white walls and tiled roofs. There were spacious wide arches and iron balconies with elaborate scroll work. Bunches of bougainvillea accentuated the façade, its riotous colors ranging from purple to bright orange-pink. "This is a nice place you have here."

Shane came up behind them as his sons walked by and entered through the big gates carrying Marina's chest between them. Marina was Pablo's firstborn and only child. And the chest belonging to her consisted of pirate treasure, hence needing two men to carry it. *"Amigos!"* he exclaimed happily. "Welcome to the *Hacienda Aguilar-Banks*!"

"Hacienda…" repeated María Isabel dreamily as they all drifted behind Shane Butler and his sons.

A few minutes later found them sitting around the kitchen island, toasting with chilled champagne the total success of their voyage.

The lawyer turned respectfully towards the pirate. "I do not wish to overload you on your arrival. There's plenty of time before the next storm," he chuckled slyly, "if you ever want to go back, that is."

Don Carlos shrugged. "Anything is possible, *licenciado*." His eyes twinkled devilishly even though there was only a ghost of a smile on the handsome face. In his fifties but with the strength and stamina of a much younger man, Don Carlos Gaitano was a female fantasy incarnate. A true pirate, his skin was dark from the sun, his hair still rich black but shot with occasional silver strands, graying in a breathtaking way. His eyes were gray, sometimes the color of silver, sometimes that of storm clouds. A shadow highlighted his face at the moment, making him even more handsome. Standing tall and strong, excited at his new adventure, the pirate seemed to radiate energy inspiring trust and confidence in those around him. He was the man you would follow without a doubt in your heart or hesitation in your mind. The man you would gladly offer allegiance to because he would protect you, respect you and take care of you in return.

Shane acknowledged him with a nod. "I will let you get settled in first. Get your bearings. Relax," he winked at the stranger. "Call me when you're ready."

Pablo laughed, clapping his friend on the back as he turned to leave. "We will, *amigo*. A few history lessons will put them both up to date."

"As much as possible," Joe added with a laugh. His light brown eyes twinkled, the stud in his ear sparkled, and the gold wedding band on his left hand shone as he ran his hands over his cornrows.

"Well, we can't present them in public until they don't give themselves away," their lawyer reminded them with a wry smile, adjusting the ultra modern rimless glasses on his face. "You'll need all the help you can get."

"You're right," Shayla agreed. Shayla was Joe Banks' wife and mother of Jackson and Salomé Banks, the older pair of the trio of children. Said children had been raised together equally with two fathers and two mothers, and two older cousins in the house, more like older brothers. Everyone was very close and it made for very interesting situations. Shayla herself was biracial, black on her mother's side and Native American on her father's side. It tickled her that Salomé had ended up with Indio Gaitano, the pirate's adopted Native American son. It was her parents' love story all over again.

"Okay," Sloane jumped in, cool and smooth as into a pool, "so here's what we do. Why don't you go with your boys and take a break, get us all some food. Get extra! Give us time enough to settle in a little bit, and come right back. I'll call the order in at Rico's, and all you have to do is pick it up." Sloane Aguilar, formerly Gaynes, was Pablo's wife and Marina's birth mother, although by the time that happened she had the experience of helping out with rowdy teenage twins before going on to helping raise and care for Jackson and Salomé co-parenting equally with Shayla. She was a transplanted California surfer girl with the golden tan and the straight as glass sun bleached hair, eyes the turquoise color of the Caribbean Sea, teen model turned catwalk darling and finally fashion designer. Now she had her own business consisting of a modeling agency where Salomé was her partner and prize model, and Xaira, Marina's stunningly beautiful Oriental charge starred. But her best role was that of being one of the mothers of the Aguilar-Banks crew. Her most prized photograph was of herself strutting down the catwalk in a shimmery twenties inspired shamelessly short black sheath with long black fringe and glittery black stilettos, Pave diamond hoops in her ears and bangles on her wrists, straight blond hair flowing like a cloud behind her. On her hip a year-old Jackson, head tilted back looking up at her in adoration, a smile spilling around the pacifier in his mouth, naked but for a blindingly white diaper wrapped around his little black bottom.

"Cool. I might as well pick Heather up while we're at it. She'll get the kick of her life," Shane smiled. They had made their way outside and now all agreed, bonding as they stood around in the cobblestone courtyard.

"See you in about an hour, I guess," Shayla smiled, waving at him.

"Oh! One more thing!" The lawyer turned back suddenly as he began walking away. "Expect a visit from the twins." He sighed, the slightest frown glinting in his eyes even as they sparkled with humor. "The Blue Cat's this side of ballistic."

Joe stepped forward, his frown taking over his whole face, his body language tense. He arched an eyebrow at the blond man in front of him. His question, when it came, was soft but deadly serious. "Is that right?" His hands went to his hips and he rocked on his heels, pressing his lips together thoughtfully.

"What's up with St. Jacques now?" Pablo asked quietly. Latin in every single aspect, Pablo Aguilar was a very macho, breathtakingly gorgeous older Hispanic male, strong and romantic, tender and stern. His hair echoed the pirate's, still black and slightly streaked with silver. A shadow also graced his face, and his dark eyes, usually sparkling with humor, now glittered with darker thoughts.

Shane sighed. "The boys tell me that Cat's been dreaming about Marina." Shayla interrupted with a sound of disgust, shaking her head impatiently. "Those two are too connected, I tell you."

"He thinks she's still five!" Sloane agreed.

Joe sighed. "What's he saying?"

Derek stepped up clearing his throat. His blond hair curled around his head like a halo, blue eyes intense with the seriousness of the conversation. "It's both of them." All eyes turned from him to his sibling for confirmation.

Tyler backed his brother. In contrast, his hair was cut short in a sleek style that accentuated his classically handsome face, his eyes as amused as his father's. His smile flashed quick, making him even more handsome. He nodded. "Deveraux's raging."

"They're both going crazy," explained Shane. "They know something's going down."

Pablo rubbed his eyes with a sigh. "What are they saying?"

"What else?" the lawyer laughed. *Where are our kids?*

The couples smiled as they looked at each other across the round table. Fanatics of medieval times, both Pablo Aguilar and Joe Banks had been inspired when it came to decorating their common spaces. Therefore their dining room possessed a round table, the likes of which would have made King Arthur proud. The room was made of stone, tastefully decorated with incredible ceiling to floor tapestry panels depicting castles and medieval life. Crossbows and assorted scary weapons hung on the walls. Among these were huge mirrors, beautifully framed in elaborately carved wooden pieces of art, flanked by torches. The mesmerizing music of monks chanting was piped into the room by hidden speakers. The murmur of voices along with the clink of glass and silverware contributed to an intimate environment.

Pablo tapped his gleaming steak knife on the side of his wine glass to get their attention. "I would like to say something." He stood up, raising his wine glass in a ritualistic gesture. He smiled as his companions joined him. "I have never, for all my traveling, embarked on such an incredible, dangerous, mysterious journey." His eyes twinkled, even as they crinkled at the corners. "I never realized I was so dashing and brave." He grinned as they laughed, his heart expanding in his chest. "As our children would say," his voice pitched lower with emotion, "you guys rock," he informed his family, his heart in his eyes, "and *you*," he turned to the Gaitanos, "are the most extraordinary friends I have ever had." Tears filled his eyes. Then tears filled everybody's eyes. They touched glasses and sat back down.

Joe laughed. Candlelight rippled in his cornrows at the same time it sparked off his earrings. His handsome black face fell in relaxed lines, brown eyes warm, showing his happiness. "It sure feels good to be home, though. It will be exciting to show you around, Carlos."

Don Carlos Gaitano nodded his dark head at his friend across the table. The two couldn't be more different. Grey eyes, the color of storm clouds, looked out of his tanned face. The same laugh lines graced their corners. "I shall be a most willing pupil, Joe, a most eager scholar," he laughed.

Next to him, his beautiful wife rolled her eyes in amusement. María Isabel Sandoval de Gaitano was the epitome of the Spanish woman to whom so many ballads had been devoutly written throughout the centuries. Her rich gypsy heritage was evident in both her personality and her looks. Eyes the color of sea foam laughed out of a lightly tanned face. Her skin was flawless, her laughing mouth wide and generous, her still dark hair rich and luxurious as it tumbled over her shoulders. "He thinks he is a boy," she announced happily, looking into her husband's eyes. Suddenly, she saw them flicker warily, looking beyond her, although the smile never left his face.

Don Carlos laughed again. "I, personally, feel so comfortable, it reminds me of home." His eyes swept the mirror behind his beautiful wife. Yes. Definitely. There was somebody there. He had an impression of dark skin and dark hair hanging in ropes. If the person meant well, why the stealth? He quickly scanned the walls around him, assessing what was available to him. "Marisa," he crooned, making her look sharply at him. "Do you remember the events that unfolded at the port of Carey?" he inquired softly.

María Isabel stared, breath caught in her chest. Her sea green eyes followed him as he stood and moved around the table. She shook the hair out of her face but she didn't hesitate. Standing, she mirrored his movements. "Right now, *querido*?" she murmured, excitement at the unknown overpowering her.

Don Carlos smiled at the telltale note of anticipation in her voice. "Right now, *mi amor*."

Their hosts just looked at each other. They had grown accustomed to their adventurous guest during their recent stay in Encantada where their roles had been reversed. And because they had come to know their guests very well, Pablo and Joe found themselves looking at each other, pulses racing. In silent agreement they noiselessly slid their chairs back from the table, making it easier for them to get to their feet as quickly as possible if necessary. So, they watched with smiles on their faces until the pirate moved. Suddenly, everything changed.

Don Carlos Gaitano felt behind him and turned, reaching for the weapons on the wall. With a minimum of movements, he took the dirk and tossed it. María Isabel snatched it out of mid-air as it reached her, immediately slipping it out of its scabbard. As she did so, her husband was already taking down the sword closest to him and pressing his back against the wall, glancing at the arched stone entrance next to him. Then, it happened.

All hell broke loose.

A man stepped into the room. In the same instance Don Carlos had him sighted down the cold steel blade of his weapon. The dreadlocked man locked luminous green eyes, striking in the dark face, with eyes the color of the steel it caressed. In reflex he took a couple of steps back. Suddenly he stopped and smiled slowly at the pirate. The Aguilars and the Banks flew to their feet.

Joe roared. ***"Oh, hell, no!"***

The dreadlocked man calmly reached behind his back and drew out a gun, pointing it steadily at the traveler with both hands. In arrogant male provocation he raised an eyebrow, even as his voice came out low with the barest hint of mocking amusement. "Now what?" he taunted.

Shayla gasped. "*Catamaran!*"

María Isabel took only one step forward as she was immediately stopped in her tracks with a single look from her husband. Pouting beautifully, she murmured a protest. "Oh, please, let *me* take care of him." Eyes glinting dangerously, she went to move between the two men who were now laughing at each other but was once more detained by another look from her husband.

Pablo stepped between the men swiftly, holding his hands stretched out like a referee. "*Caballeros*," he laughed, deeply amused. "Dramatic as this encounter may be, you are both of my extreme confidence." He turned to the younger man of the two. Cocking his head to one side, he smiled affectionately. "*Gato?*"

The younger man's eyes flashed at him for an instant even as he made the gun disappear. "*Tío*," he murmured, letting himself be pulled into a hug.

Pablo embraced him, kissing his cheek fondly, and patted him on the back. Then he stepped back to look at him and the guest. The weapons had somehow made it back to their places on the stone wall before anybody realized it. The pirate never ceased to amaze him. "Don Carlos Gaitano is our guest here, as is his beautiful wife, María Isabel Sandoval."

The young man held out his hand, eyes still suspicious. Smiling, he introduced himself. "Catamaran St. Jacques."

A second man appeared, although these couples weren't surprised by anything anymore. This one was identical to the first; except for his hairstyle of choice, neat stylish cornrows. Like Jackson they both were, but not quite. Not exactly like Joe either, but similar.

Sloane smiled affectionately at the new intruder. "Blue…"

This one introduced himself, his voice just as low. "Deveraux St. Jacques." The twins looked at Pablo. Deveraux held a hand out towards him in apology. "Sorry, Tío…"

Pablo dismissed the apology away with a shrug and a wave of his hand. Smiling just as affectionately at this one, he pulled him in for a hug and a kiss. "*No es nada, Azulito.*"

"Where is Marina?" Everyone but his brother turned to look at Catamaran. Then they turned to look at Deveraux.

Deveraux looked back. "Where are our kids?"

Silence fell on them suddenly, everyone at a loss for words. The pirate and the dread looked at each other still, chests rising and falling with their quiet breathing. In through the arch Deveraux had just entered came a man, two more, and a woman.

Shane Butler stopped in his tracks and took in the scene. The air was extremely charged and nobody was moving. A smile spread on his face. "No! I just missed it, didn't I?" he chuckled, shaking his head at himself.

"Now, Shane," Heather, his wife scolded in a soft, musical voice, "don't you go adding wood to somebody else's fire…" she murmured. Tossing her brown curls and smiling brightly at everyone she made her way to the table, bringing out their lunch. "Are you making trouble, boys?" she inquired sweetly, quickly displaying containers with steaming pasta, and crisp green salads. Her sons looked at each other and smiled.

Deveraux chuckled. "Answer your mother, boys."

Derek grinned back at him. "She's not talking to *us*, dude."

Tyler clapped Deveraux on the shoulder as he pulled out a chair for himself. "Yeah, dude, she's talking to *you boys*."

Pablo and Joe looked around them for a moment. "Everybody's ready…" Pablo murmured frowning slightly, "… but…"

"I have a feeling we're missing something major," Joe told him under his breath, glancing from one twin to the other. All of a sudden a door slammed somewhere in the house, followed by a scream.

"Papi!"

The men looked at each other again in startled recognition. Pablo's frown grew deeper, worry clouding the expression in his eyes. *"Xaira!"*

Joe groaned. "I knew we were missing something…"

"Xaira?" gasped Shayla, eyes wide in her beautiful dark face.

Sloane buried her face in her hands. "How could we forget Xaira?" she moaned, shaking her head.

María Isabel glanced around her, gauging the different reactions to the exquisitely exotic name. *"Xaira?"* she murmured with a smile. The name rolled off her tongue, the accent contributing to the perfect pronunciation, sounding like XA-eera. The Butlers stood around smiling as if they hadn't missed the show after all.

The screaming got louder as it got closer. *"Papi!"* The voice broke as if the person were crying.

Don Carlos frowned with sudden concern. "Who is Xaira?"

Catamaran tossed his dreads back as he answered with a laugh. "Marina's pet."

Deveraux dug an elbow into his brother's side in warning. "Cat…" he began, but the voice finally reached them.

"Papi!" In through the recently busy archway stepped a vision in the form of a teenage girl. The young woman came to a halt in front of the homeowners. All dressed in black, her movements were sleek and graceful like a cat's. Black jeans faded to gray enclosed slim hips and strong thighs like a glove. Slung low, they displayed a tiny silver belly ring and framed a tribal tattoo on her lower back. Her tan was not natural but carefully sought from the sun, bringing radiance to her skin. Long flowing hair, black as night, straight as glass, was tied in a single careless braid down her back, held by a bandana at the end. High cheekbones graced an exquisitely flawless face of breathtaking beauty. Brimming with tears were slanted almond eyes, so dark they were almost black, giving away her Oriental heritage. She was a stunning creature which distress made seem years younger at the moment. *"Papi!"* Gasping, she stood in front of Pablo. *"I can't find her!"* she howled. Except for the twins, the whole family took a step forward reaching out towards her if not physically, mentally.

Pablo, sensing the near hysterics, pulled her closer by one hand and took her in his arms. "Come here, *nena*," he crooned as if to a child. "It's okay, baby." Holding her closer, he stroked her back as the young woman poured her heart out, sobbing against him, words muffled between gasps.

"I can't find her!" Xaira wailed. "I've been looking, and looking, and…"

"It's okay, baby," Joe reassured, stroking her head, trying to comfort her.

"…I just can't find her!"

Catamaran stepped closer, circling like a shark. "I thought you were with her," he charged, soft voice accusing.

Xaira wrapped her arms around Pablo in a silent plea. "I was," she sniffed, tears beading her eyelashes.

"So, how'd you lose her?" Deveraux asked smoothly.

"Don't pick on her," Shayla drawled in warning. This was their baby.

Slanted eyes squinted like an evil empress Xaira turned them on the twins, a cold fire burning in their depths. "Don't mess with me," she said softly.

Catamaran smiled. "Or what?" he taunted gently.

Xaira licked her lips, catching the tears at the corners of her mouth. "Not *what*," she said, her voice dripping icicles. *"Who…"* Around her, eyebrows raised in amusement at the implication of a nasty word left unsaid.

Catamaran softened on the inside although you could never tell on the outside. He held nothing but deep affection and complete admiration for Xaira, but he wouldn't allow himself to show her this, disguising his sentiment with gruffness instead. He smiled wider at her challenge. "Alright, who…?"

"Me." The voice reached them before the figure appeared. This one, dressed in black, was totally male, looking like a dark version of the Marlboro man complete with cowboy hat and boots. The Gaitanos kept silent as the Butlers laughed happily and everybody else exclaimed in delight.

"Jesse!"

The man's mouth twitched with a ghost of a smile. Joe pulled him into a bear hug and kissed him fondly on the cheek. Turning to the pirate he left his arm around the newcomer's shoulders. "Carlos!" he exclaimed happily, "María Isabel," he turned his head towards her, "please meet one of the scariest people in my world. This is my brother-in-law, Jesse Coltrane." Squeezing the new arrival, he finished the introduction. "These are our guests, Don Carlos Gaitano and María Isabel Sandoval de Gaitano."

The pirate looked into the stranger's eyes for a moment before stretching out his hand. "Don Carlos Gaitano. At your service."

Jesse nodded and shook his hand, his features softening for a fraction. "Snake. At yours."

María Isabel laughed with delight. Being an incredibly good judge of character she knew that there was a story here somewhere. It would be a pleasure to hear it. "Snake," she repeated slowly, savoring the word. Glancing at Catamaran, her eyes sparkled mischievously even as they avoided her husband's amused gaze. Offering her hand, she met Jesse's eyes as he took it and kissed it, his features relaxing into a soft smile for the incredibly beautiful woman before him. "Are you a venomous viper, Mister Coltrane?"

"No, ma'am," he protested quickly in a very deep soft voice, squeezing her hand gently as he let it go. "I'm tame as a kitten." This made the twins cough, choking on their laughter.

"Yeah, right!" exclaimed Blue.

"A black panther kitten," added Cat.

María Isabel ignored them although the corners of her mouth twitched. "Or are you a sneaky sly individual?" she asked almost as if to herself, cocking her head to one side and studying him closely. Her eyes didn't linger as they found the scar that carved his face from his temple to his jaw almost slicing his left cheek. Clearly old, but plainly visible, there would be time to get to know this man, she decided, and ask about it later.

"No, ma'am," Jesse drawled again. "I'm actually slick but shy, and I do tend snakes…" he shrugged. "Most people call me Uncle Jesse." At her raised eyebrows, he elaborated. "These people tend to either be children or act like them," he added, glancing at the twins.

"Enough!" Sloane protested. Taking both the beautiful Xaira and the menacing Uncle Jesse by the hand, she cocked her head to the twins. "There's plenty of food for everyone."

"Don Carlos!" All heads turned as Caribe burst into the room, as excited as a child on Christmas morning. "Have you seen…" Catching himself, he skidded to a stop. Solemnly, he returned gaze for gaze. Silently, he went to stand beside the pirate and his wife.

Shayla waved her fingers at him, eyes twinkling with laughter. "Hi, baby, how're you doing? Making yourself at home yet?"

Caribe nodded, warily eyeing the twins. "Yes, thank you. I think I found Jackson's room."

Pablo smiled. "Are you sure?"

Caribe nodded again. "Yes."

Joe grinned. "How can you tell?"

Caribe grinned back. "There are naked girls on the walls."

Shane laughed. "That would be it."

Sloane smiled at him. "You're welcome to use it until he gets back, honey." She began the introductions with Shane's family. Then she turned to the twins. "These," she told the islander, "are our nephews Deveraux Azure and Catamaran. We call them Blue and Cat."

She waited for the two men to greet the younger one. Then she continued. "This doll is Xaira, Marina's best friend and our youngest. She works for me at my shop and is a black belt instructor at Pablo and Joe's school." She smiled as his eyebrows raised, his interest piqued. "And this scary fellow is our very own Uncle Jesse. He's married to Joe's baby sister, Rain." Everyone smiled.

"The tattoo artist." Caribe told him with a smile. "Marina mentions you,"

Uncle Jesse was curious. "Oh, yeah? What does she say?"

Caribe shrugged. "She adores you." Satisfied, Uncle Jesse nodded.

"What about me?" Xaira wanted to know.

Caribe turned to look at her thoughtfully, nodding slowly. "She adores you too. She said you're like her younger sister." *She said if we were to meet, you will fall in love with me before we both know it.* But this he kept quiet. He trusted Marina's judgment and Xaira was so beautiful.

"I am," the girl replied.

"This is Caribe," Sloane finally explained. "He came over with Don Carlos and María Isabel, and will also be staying with us for a while. He's a very good friend of Jackson's and the girls."

Caribe grinned once more. "Very nice to meet all of you. I'm very excited to be here."

The twins fixed him steadily with their gaze. Cat shook the dreads out of his face. "Where are our kids?"

Caribe gazed back steadily at him. "They're back home. On the island," he answered carefully.

Shayla motioned him to join them. "You pay them no mind, Caribe," she advised him gently. "They can be mean and scary but right now, they're just jealous." They all gathered around the table and sat down. Grace was said, and in short time they were eating, exclaiming at the richness of their fare. Spirits lifted as friends and strangers eased into an agreeable level of comfort amongst themselves. "The twins," Shayla explained to their guests, "think the girls are theirs, with Jackson thrown in as an extra bonus."

Caribe grinned. "Well, the girls seem to think *I* am theirs."

"You are, son," Joe agreed.

"Most definitely theirs," Pablo conceded.

"Relax, baby," Sloane told him. "The Blue Cat can wait until after lunch."

Don Carlos quietly studied the strangers. The lawyer and his family were relaxed, obviously comfortable with their company. The twins were also relaxed, all tension drained from their big strong bodies, but their eyes remained watchful, intense. Sighing to himself, he decided there was only one way he was going to find out things. His eyes searched, met and held Pablo's. "I thought they were *your* children?"

Pablo grinned at the seemingly innocent question. "So did I," he sighed, taking another sip of wine. He glanced at the now scowling twins. Patience had never been one of their virtues. He looked back at the amused pirate sitting across from him at the full round table. "Truth is, they are *our* kids."

Don Carlos raised his own glass to his lips and drank. "How so?" he asked, genuinely curious. His eyes twinkled with mischief. "There seems to be a difference of opinions."

Joe laughed as the twins scowled even more fiercely. "Let's start at the beginning," he announced happily. "Allow me to formally introduce the boys. Catamaran and Deveraux Azure, as you can see, are identical twins. They were born to my older sister Lisa on a dark, stormy summer night in Jamaica. A few weeks later, she, along with her husband Jean Luc, the twins' father, lost their lives in the middle of a hurricane." His dark eyes glistened for a moment with unshed tears before smiling brightly at them. "*God giveth and God taketh away*," he told them shakily. "I lost a brat sister…"

"Whom you adored," Shayla reminded him softly.

Joe nodded. "Still do," he admitted. Then he sighed. "And I got two brat baby boys."

"We were starting high school," Pablo explained. He stopped, frowning for a moment. "Mid teens," he added for the pirate's benefit. "With his dad gone working all day and just his mom at home Joe was thrown into the role of dad before his time. His baby sister Rain was way too young to be of any real assistance, almost a baby herself. I was automatically recruited to help out."

María Isabel smiled at him knowingly. "Any regrets?"

"None," both Pablo and Joe answered at the same time.

"As you can see," explained Joe, "they are identical on the outside, except for their hairstyle. Well, when they were babies their eyes were just gray until the real color set in." He shrugged. "We could only tell them apart by their personalities. Then they began walking and talking. Once they were mobile we just called them the Blue Cat."

Don Carlos nodded slowly. "So they in turn are about the same age as you were with them when you have your own children."

"Actually, a few years younger," Joe explained. "The twins were eight when Jackson was born, nine for Salomé and ten for Marina."

The pirate nodded again. "I see clearly now." He looked around. "Is anyone anybody's godfather? Any christenings involved?"

"Well, that's the interesting part," Pablo told him. "The four of us," he said, waving his hand in a circle between his wife and himself, Joe and Shayla, "we baptized each other's children. But each kid got somebody else as backup," he finished with a wink.

Shane's hand shot up. "We got Jackson," he said, pointing to his wife and himself. "The firstborn went to the grown adults," he grinned.

Don Carlos smiled as they all laughed. "Who got the girls?"

"I baptized Salomé," Deveraux informed him. "First twin got the first girl."

"Order is important," conceded Don Carlos before turning to his brother.

"I am Marina's godfather," Catamaran admitted slowly. "I am also her mentor, one of her best friends," he glanced at Xaira, "and her boss."

Jesse smiled as the pirates glanced at him. "Lisa and I confirmed everybody's asses," he sighed dramatically, going to adjust the cowboy hat that was no longer on his head before letting it drop again, making his company laugh softly.

María Isabel turned back to the twins and smiled. "So, of course they are your kids," she sympathized. "It makes all the sense in the world." She laughed at her husband. "It's almost like Max being Marina's."

Don Carlos chuckled. "Max is more the Lair's than Marina's."

"Oh, that's not true, Carlos," Shayla laughed. "You know Marina would kill for…" her voice ended in a strangled whisper and all eyes turned to her tear-filled ones, "…Max."

The Butlers looked at their friends in alarm for a moment, but waited for the explanation in silence along with their sons and the rest. Innocent as the expression was by itself, people said it all the time and it meant nothing to them. But seeing Shayla's reaction took their breath away. Sloane and Shayla blinked back tears. The twins looked at their uncles suspiciously. Jesse and Xaira kept quiet. Carlos and Joe glanced at each other in silent understanding.

Pablo scowled fiercely, even as he laughed. "Marina has already killed for Max."

Shane looked at his wife as she frowned, puzzled. He shook his head in warning at her before she could say anything and she subsided. Tyler and Derek shot questions at each other with their eyes.

Catamaran studied his wine glass for a moment before taking a long drink. He couldn't stand it anymore. "Who's Max?"

"Where's Marina?" Deveraux insisted.

"With Jackson and Salome," Joe informed him. "Now, let us finish here, and you'll hear all about it."

With that, they all settled down again and finished their fabulous meal.

Leaving the incredible dining hall behind once done they all moved to another of the house's common areas. This particular one consisted of a nice, spacious private movie theater where the children had entertained when they were younger and was now currently left for family nights. It wasn't very large, just comfortable. The seats were soft and roomy, arranged just like in the theaters, in three rows. The carpet under their feet was thick and soft, framing a perimeter around the seating area. Movie posters, old and recent, hung on the walls, subtly lighted so they seemed to glow. A real Coke machine stood in a corner humming invitingly, bright and familiar, its days of dispensing actual Coca-Cola long gone. Now it held nothing but bottled water. Next to that was an old-style popcorn maker, now dark and silent. Bottles of water were passed around as everyone made themselves comfortable.

Shifting around in his seat while everything was set up, Catamaran pulled out his cell phone, his thumb seeming to caress the pads as he pressed the numbers. "Baby. Come on in. I'm at Tío's. Call you later." Flipping the phone shut he slipped it out of sight again.

Caribe marveled at the workings of the overhead projector the Butler men had set up for him. It was primitive by today's standards, almost obsolete in a world where you could scan anything and use a computer. But they hadn't had time for that, having just arrived. So the contraption was unearthed from a hidden closet used for storage and presented to Caribe for his use. He wanted to stop and caress the metal, smoothing out the cord for as long as it stretched, peer into the lens, and marvel at the light. Instead he bit his lip in an effort to contain his excitement and smiled as the Butler brothers set it up for him, passing his hands over his dreads. The room dimmed suddenly and an image appeared on the dark screen. Nobody spoke for a moment. Caribe's heart swelled with love. "Marina-Salomé," he sighed. He turned to the other dreadlocked man. "Cat." Glowing green eyes turned to him. "I dream about them too."

Cat nodded. "When and where did you meet them?"

"Funny, how they never mentioned you," Deveraux added.

Caribe shrugged. "Maybe because they hadn't met me yet." He glanced at the Gaitanos for reassurance. "It happened in Encantada. I hadn't met them yet either, when I drew this picture." He smiled at the memory. "I saw them in a dream."

"I'm sorry," Deveraux interrupted, "but what does this Encantada place have to do with Spring Break and a picnic?" He shook his handsome head in exasperation. "There are pieces missing here."

"Permit me," Shane cleared his throat. "There's nothing to a good story like the beginning." He grinned. Turning back to the twins, he thought for a moment. "You are right. It all starts with Spring Break and a picnic. Jackson and the girls go to Crescent Cove, get a room together by the beach, and hang out. A picnic appears in the picture and the girls disappear."

The twins looked at each other, eyes flashing alarm signals although their outsides remained calm. Cat rubbed his eyes, gaining time as he gathered his thoughts, his heart heavy in his chest, a small roar beginning in his head. He turned his feline eyes on his uncles. "When, where and how?"

Blue ran his hands over his cornrows in a strong family resemblance to Joe. His eyes were accusing. "When did you hear of this?"

Shane lifted a gentle hand at his friends, his eyes invoking a calming gesture. "Not until much later. You see, Jackson was supposed to go with them but couldn't make it. By the time Jax figured out what was going on, it was too late. The girls were gone."

"Gone where?" Blue insisted.

"Well, they seem to have taken a boat and gone to a small island a few miles offshore. The boys that took them there thought it would be fun to indulge in a little date rape..."

All eyes turned to him, none wider than Xaira's. "They were *raped*?" Her eyes flashed back to Pablo as he took her hand and kissed the back in a fatherly gesture, shaking his head at her in reassurance.

"No, no," assured Shane, "of course not. They found some driftwood to defend themselves and threatened the boys instead." He shrugged apologetically. "I guess one of them is psychotic and he opted for abandoning them."

"So they got stranded?" Blue asked. "But if you knew all that, why couldn't Jackson just bring them?"

"Jackson did go get them," explained Shane. "He actually stayed for a couple of days, looking for them."

"A couple of days?" Blue expressed the astonishment and outrage they were all feeling. "Did somebody get to them before he got there?"

"No, *nobody* got to them. But there was a storm. A big storm. The girls found shelter in a cave up in a cliff. But when they woke up the next morning, it seems," he looked around at the faces enthralled with his story, "that the storm is an atmospherical phenomenon that creates a time warp. It opened a portal."

The room fell silent for a moment. On the screen, the picture had changed to a view of the docks in Encantada, the many-masted ships seeming to bob on the water. Drawing after drawing, the viewers were treated to scenes of island life.

Shaking his head as if in shock, Blue expressed what they were all thinking. "You mean to tell me that they *time traveled*?" He frowned. "That's *possible*?" He looked accusingly at Caribe. "I don't know *who* you are---"

"*Azulito...*" Pablo's voice was soft in warning.

Caribe picked up the story where Shane had left off. "I meet them there. To us, my mother and myself, they're just the latest of a number of *visitors* that have come to the island over the years, from different moments in time. Some try to stay, but most don't make it. Too afraid. But because of their visits, we have seen glimpses of evolving history. Marina and Salomé came to us at a moment when the island needed help. New people with fresh ideas and different perspectives, education, experiences..." he trailed off, registering the shock in the younger faces of the people around him. One by one, he showed portraits of the key people in the girls' lives. "This is Leila, my mother," he explained, smiling at the familiar lines in the woman's face. "She is the…" He struggled for a word until he found one, "liaison, so to speak." His hands drew patterns in the air as he spoke. "I dream of the visitors, so I get to draw their faces. Leila is the contact person. She explains what's going on, eases the way for them."

Derek was the first one to speak, breaking into all their thoughts. "Have you met many time travelers? What do you call them, *visitors*?"

Caribe shook his head. "I never expected to, either. Leila had only once before, when she was a little girl. And then, just a few more throughout her lifetime. I'm not sure if she had given up hope of ever meeting anyone else." The next drawing made everyone go quiet. The man in it seemed carved from stone, his features finely chiseled, his face in light and shadows. "This is Indio." Silence settled over them for a moment.

"He looks like an Indian," Cat conceded.

"He *is* an Indian," agreed Don Carlos.

"He is Gaitano's second," Caribe explained.

"What does that mean?" Tyler wondered out loud.

"Indio's in charge of the island when Gaitano's away," Caribe explained.

"What Gaitano?" Cat demanded, looking at the pirate. "You, Gaitano?"

Don Carlos shook his head, chuckling. "No, not me. I wish," he added ruefully. Silver eyes met green cat eyes. "My other son."

"Other?" Blue asked, curious.

"Indio is my son like you are Joe and Pablo's sons. He too, lost his parents in a storm. Theirs hit them while on a ship out at sea. We were taking care of him for them," he explained, reaching out absently for his wife's hand, "because we had Carlitos, and one more was no problem. Since then, we've had two sons."

"Equally?" Blue was even more curious.

Don Carlos sighed. "Are you less of a son to Joe and Shayla than Jackson? Does Marina have more rights as far as Pablo and Sloane are concerned, than you? Do they treat either of you differently than

Salomé? What about Xaira? Given the age and sex and individual differences…"

"No. You're right," Blue admitted. "To the parents we're all the same, whether they gave birth to us or not."

"In that way, Indio is as much our son as Carlitos is. God gave us one of them, but he also gave us to the other one."

"So what do you do in Encantada…" Blue's voice trailed off as he caught sight of the next drawing. This one was of the crew of La Gitana. All eyes stared and all mouths stayed quiet as they studied the faces.

Xaira gasped as the realization hit her. *"Pirates!"*

"Pirates?" echoed Heather. *"Real* pirates?" She turned to Shane. "You *knew* about this?"

Shane nodded. "I've known since Jackson came back to get his parents."

"Came back?" demanded Blue, incredulous. "Jackson already went there and came back to go back there? What's he got, a free boarding pass?"

"What happened?" Cat asked quietly, eyes flashing with the thoughts raging inside his head.

"Meet the crew of *La Gitana*," Joe began. "When the girls end up in Encantada, La Gitana is out at sea with everyone except Indio, who happened to be left behind while Gaitano is on his voyage. Solomon, Giancarlo---"

Impatiently, Blue pointed at the central figure on the paper. "This must be your other son," he said. "Looks just like you," he added with a fleeting smile.

Don Carlos grinned. "Thank you. That is the son I gave life to, Carlos Juan Miguel Gaitano y Sandoval."

"If you're both Carlos…" Derek wondered.

"For family, I'm Carlos and he's Carlitos. For Encantada, I'm Don Carlos and he's Gaitano," Don Carlos explained. "The island is his."

"Things must be good, when we get to own a whole island," Cat mused out loud.

"Things got better," answered the pirate, "when the girls and their brother show up on the island, and Carlitos doesn't end up losing it."

"Better, how?" Jesse asked quietly.

"First," continued Caribe, "Salomé hooks up with Indio." Passing the papers, he showed them a portrait of the couple.

Heather gasped. "Oh, my God!" Her eyes flew to Shayla's, hand reaching out to her friend. "Such a beautiful couple," she whispered.

Shayla nodded, tears stinging her eyes. "They are," she agreed softly, "and so good together."

"My opinion," María Isabel added gently, "is that they're absolutely made for one another." She looked around at her companions.

Don Carlos' voice rumbled as he agreed. "Indio seems to have come to life since meeting Salomé. He used to be a shadow before in comparison."

"Indio treats Salomé like a queen but respects her like his equal," Joe agreed.

Pablo nodded. "It's a good match."

"What is it exactly Indio does, again?" Blue asked, genuinely curious.

"Indio is Gaitano's second," Caribe repeated. "He's the QuarterMaster. If Gaitano's sailing and doesn't take him, Indio's in charge of the island. On this occasion he stayed taking care of the Lair."

"What lair?" asked Blue.

"The Sirens' Lair. It's a place where pirates go to get a drink and a girl." Caribe smiled as every male in the room grinned. The females rolled their eyes.

"So, it's a whorehouse?" Derek asked.

"Not exactly," Joe explained. "More like a saloon with a nautical theme and an upstairs with rooms with girls."

"Does Gaitano own it?" Tyler wanted to know.

"No. The Lair belongs to Giancarlo Ilarraza." Caribe put back the paper of the crew of La Gitana and pointed him out. "This is Gaitano's Sailing Master and one of his best friends."

"What do the girls do all this time?" Heather was curious.

"Well, Salomé ends up working at a dress shop," Caribe explained, showing more pictures.

"What did she do there?" Xaira expressed her curiosity quietly.

"She draws," Caribe frowned for a moment before smiling. "She designs," he corrected himself, flashing a look at Sloane who smiled at him encouragingly, "clothes for the women."

Heather laughed. "She must've created a sensation."

Shayla snapped her fingers in the air in a zigzag fashion. "Anywhere my baby goes…"

"What about Marina?" Heather asked.

Caribe grinned. "That's where Max comes in." He showed them a drawing of the general store. "Meet the Klines. John, Larissa, and Maximillian." The room fell silent as portrait after portrait passed before their eyes.

Cat grunted in disbelief. "Max is a baby?"

"Oh, and such a cute baby," Shayla laughed.

"Max is *the* baby in this story," Caribe continued. "When Gaitano gets back from his voyage, he finds things running pretty smoothly. Indio is absorbed with Salomé, and the Klines' store is better organized and producing more than ever before because Marina has Max out of their way. Everything is going good except that Gaitano has come home to discover not only strangers in their midst, but that things are off with his books."

"Books?" Blue wondered. "What kind of books?"

"Accounting books," Caribe answered absently, keeping the flow of pictures on the screen.

"Accounting?" echoed Blue thoughtfully, running his hands over his cornrows. He threw the pirate a glance and frowned. "Since when do pirates keep books?"

Don Carlos returned his gaze and smiled. "Since they can hide their piracy by being sea merchants."

Cat grunted again. "So, what's Gaitano? Pirate or sea merchant?" Everyone looked at the screen where the crew of La Gitana looked back at them once more. Nobody spoke for a moment as they studied the man in question.

Xaira glanced at Don Carlos, playing absently with the bandana holding her braid in place. "Gaitano's a pirate…"

Don Carlos' eyes shone, but he gave nothing away. Looking away from her, he turned to her companion. "What about you, Snake?"

"Pirate," Jesse answered, not thinking about it. He turned from the screen to the man addressing him. "Gaitano's a pirate."

Cat shook his head. "No. More."

"More?" Blue asked his brother, frowning.

"More," Cat repeated. "Dude owns an island, he has a crew, so he must have ships, plural," he said absently, glancing at the pirate couple for confirmation. "But to keep an island of whatever size running, he must have a flow. Not knowing anything about piracy, I can only assume that it is a trade, mostly dependent on luck, maybe a little intel. Luck is random, however." He hesitated, shaking the dreadlocks out of his face for a moment. "So, in order to keep this island…" he trailed off and looked at the guests. "I assume it has inhabitants. I mean, Caribe is not a pirate, are you?" he asked the young islander.

Caribe laughed. "No. Not me. I am just their…" he shrugged. "For their last trip they ended up taking me, to keep track of their activities and to make the girls feel safer."

Cat nodded. "So, he has people to take care of, which means he needs businesses, hence the Klines' store, and the Lair, which means he needs supplies…" He trailed off and shook his head again. When he looked up, his cat eyes met silver ones. "Your son, Carlitos, is a full on sea merchant. Hence the books." He sighed deeply. "But if I were to bet, I'd say he's both. Sea merchant *and* pirate."

Don Carlos laughed. "You must be the business end of the Blue Cat."

Cat grinned. "I am." He turned back to the screen. "So Gaitano comes home to find things are a little different, a little better, except for his books. Then…"

"Then," continued Caribe, "he finds Marina in his pool."

Shayla touched Heather's hand and confided quietly. "It's really *her* pool."

Heather smiled and winked at her with a shrug. "If he wasn't in it when she got there…"

"That's right," agreed Sloane, as quiet as Shayla. "Finders, keepers…"

The women laughed at Don Carlos as he shook his head with a sigh and mock disgust complete with an eye roll. "It's still Gaitano's island," he rumbled, playing along with the beautiful women surrounding him. Then he laughed. "Carlitos comes home to find his brother infatuated to the point of distraction over the beautiful Salomé," he winked at Shayla, "and discovers Marina in *his* pool. Once they begin talking, he finds her an educated woman, and the books come up. He immediately hires her."

"Okay, wait a moment," Derek interrupted gently. "I was under the impression that the men of your time have no respect for women." He paused, as the pirate looked at him steadily. "So, you're telling us that when Gaitano comes home and finds Marina in his pool, he actually…" he hesitated, shaking his head.

"I know what you mean," his brother continued. Tyler frowned as he also turned to the pirate. "Gaitano just gets off a ship, and talks to Marina instead of…" he trailed off as he struggled for a word, "ravishing her?" He also shook his head. "That doesn't go with the impression we have of pirates."

"We're not all rapists." Don Carlos shrugged in good humor. "What can I say? Gaitano is an educated man," his eyes twinkled, "with good taste." He chuckled to himself as his friends laughed.

"Carlos has a point," Joe pointed out. "These boys," he waved a hand at the crew of La Gitana back on screen, "are all educated men."

"We made sure they were," María Isabel added smoothly. "Carlos and his brothers provided every privilege, advantage, and every connection they had to make sure of the boys' education." She paused for a moment. "Giancarlo's parents collaborated with them so that Gian could have the same opportunities. So, the three of them have been making mischief together since they were very young. Solomon just joined them recently, a couple of years ago."

"Well, if Gaitano, Indio, and Giancarlo are so tight from being together for so long, what's so special about Solomon that he got in so close to them?" Blue asked.

"Solomon," the pirate informed them, "saved Carlitos' life." He held up his hand slowly, showing them two fingers. He mouthed the word. "Twice."

Blue sighed. "That would just about do it for me, too."

"So, what's going on with Gaitano's books?" Cat asked.

The men hesitated. Joe sighed and looked sternly at their company. "You realize that this is now private pirate affairs." Catching the twins exchange amused glances, he scowled. "Gaitano's books are none of our business, except for the fact that he approached Marina, hired her to do a job, and she did it for him. What happens with that is strictly between Carlitos and Marina."

Cat waved a hand at him. "All right, okay, we're sorry. No disrespect. But whatever it was, it must have been pretty bad if a pirate is going to accept," he shook his head, "no, *ask* for help from a female?" He turned to the female pyrate for support. "Am I right?"

María Isabel nodded, putting a hand on his arm to appease him, smiling when the dreadlocked young man relaxed under her gentle touch. "You are absolutely right, Cat," she agreed. "Just keep in mind, your goddaughters'," she touched Blue's shoulder to include him, "arrival at Encantada not only changed Encantada and island life, it also transformed my boys' lives and the Gaitanos in general as well."

Cat sighed deeply in frustration. "What did she find?"

The men hesitated again. Pablo nodded. It was his turn to speak. "When I got there, Marina said to me that they were in trouble. Some merchandise missing, some guns being smuggled," he waved a hand in the air. "Marina's exact words if I recall, were, '*Papi, they're taking everything but the nails on the cross*.'"

"And were they?" Blue asked.

The pirate scowled for a moment at the thought. "Yes!" he said passionately. Leaning forward in his seat, he waved a hand at his son's crew on the screen. "There is something you must know. All activity on these waters is monitored by a committee that operates out of an island called Carey. That is where I do business along with my older brother, Don Miguel Gaitano." He paused.

Joe laughed and turned to his friends. "Huge, scary dude, scarier than Jesse," he said, shaking his head, "thunder in his voice. This guy was the real thing." He sighed. "Scared the shit out of us," he confided, glancing at Pablo for confirmation.

"Did Gaitano have to report his findings?" Jesse was curious.

Pablo nodded. "Absolutely. Marina told Carlitos that he had to clean house."

"So did the committee go to Encantada?" Blue wondered.

"No," Caribe drawled. "Gaitano had to go to Carey." He sighed. "And that's where Jackson comes in."

"Wait," Xaira said, shaking her head. "You're confusing me. I thought Jackson was already there."

"Well, he was," Caribe told her. "But that's why Jackson came back here to get his parents."

"But why would Jax care whether Gaitano went to Carey or not?" Xaira insisted.

The parents laughed softly. Sloane and Shayla looked at each other and smiled.

Catamaran reached over and gently tugged on the bandana in her hair. "Pet's right. Jackson shouldn't be caring about what a pirate does or where he goes."

"Don't call me that!" Xaira hissed at him, slapping his hand away.

Cat grinned and grabbed her hand, raising it to his lips. He pulled her towards him. "I'm sorry, I forgot. Come here, give me a kiss.

"Cat!" Xaira glared at him, exasperated. She swore softly, the f word under her breath. "Hell!" she whispered. She smooched him on the lips and angrily shoved him away from her, making the twins laugh.

"Leave her alone," Joe growled in warning.

Caribe sighed. "I haven't known Jackson very long, but we're good friends. So you must know better than I that ordinarily he wouldn't have cared."

"So why does he care now?" Cat demanded.

"What's so special about this particular trip to Carey?" Blue asked. "I mean, besides the presentation to the committee?"

The parents laughed again.

Shane shook his head and sighed. Laughing softly, he locked fingers with his wife and kissed her hand. He winked at her. "I'm not touching this one."

Blue frowned. "What?" He looked around at the parents. He was greeted with silence. Looking at his twin, their eyes met. He saw something flicker in Cat's eyes. "What?"

Cat's eyes glowed as realization dawned on him. He shook his head. His heart felt gripped all of a sudden in something dark, cold, and not very nice, before it was released again to try and pound out of his chest. He swore softly, like Xaira before him. "You're kidding me!"

Blue stared at him, his heart also hammering. "No…" The twins turned to stare accusingly at the pirate.

Don Carlos met their gaze and smiled slowly, his true pirate heart showing in his eyes. He shrugged. "Gaitano took Marina."

"No…" It was Blue's turn to swear softly.

Xaira buried her face in her hands and Jesse gave a low whistle as he readjusted his cowboy hat now back on his head.

"He just *took* her?" Cat demanded.

"Nice," Blue added, sarcasm dripping from his voice.

Joe stopped them with a look. "I'm not justifying Gaitano and his methods. I've seen the guy in action. But you need to understand that at this moment in time their relationship is still that of boss and employee."

"Still?" Xaira's voice was a whisper.

"He needed to present the findings to the committee, just because they were related to things that went on mostly while he was away at sea."

"As far as Carlitos was concerned, it was nothing more than a business trip. Their friendship was solid enough that he felt she would forgive him," Pablo told them. "As a matter of fact, if I understand correctly, Marina didn't even know Carlitos was Gaitano until he had her on board La Gitana." He shrugged. "She thought he was just a sailor."

"So he's a liar," Cat suggested, raising an eyebrow at the pirate.

Sloane and Shayla and Heather gasped at the same time. *"Cat!"* Xaira laughed silently at him.

Don Carlos chuckled. "No, not a liar. He just hadn't told her yet."

"When the girls got to the island we were expecting him soon," Caribe explained, "so Marina was hearing his name all the time." It was his turn to shrug. "Some people hate him, others are afraid of him, but most are just jealous of him. She just convinced herself that something bad would happen if he learned of her presence on the island."

Blue laughed a short angry explosion of sound. "I guess she was right, huh?"

"Azulito," laughed Don Carlos, playing on his uncles' affectionate nickname, "my son was lost from the moment he set eyes on her. Put yourself in his place for one moment. Would you have told her you were *Gaitano?*"

"No, I guess not," Blue admitted hunching his shoulders in defeat, head hanging down, elbows on his thighs, hands between his knees.

"Marina must have freaked," Cat sighed, shaking his head.

Caribe nodded sadly. "She lost it," he sighed. "But they worked it out."

"Where was Salomé throughout all this?" Tyler asked, curious.

Caribe glanced at him, concentrating on the images he was showing them of the ship out at sea. "Gaitano told her that he was taking Marina whether she went with them or not. He gave her a choice to accompany them or stay. Salomé went. Marina was terrified that they would get stuck in our time and never come back to this place and time. The girls didn't know yet that they could come back on a storm. Besides, Indio was going on this trip. Only Jackson got left behind. Gaitano thought he would be more trouble than help."

Derek nodded his head in understanding. "And where were you?"

Caribe laughed. "I wasn't given a choice either." He shook his head at the memory. "I had to go help calm the girls."

The picture changed on the screen. They all stared fascinated at a whole different group of people.

Xaira gasped. "Oh, my God!" she exclaimed softly, sliding forward in her seat until she was leaning over the empty one in front of her. "It's like a movie…"

"I would love to see a movie," Caribe said.

She turned her head to look at him for a moment before turning back to the screen. "I'll take you some day," she offered absently, impatiently, making him grin.

"That's the committee?" Derek asked.

"That's them," Caribe answered. He pointed them out one by one, as if he were introducing them. "The samurai is Jai-Ling. He's from the Orient, obviously. Suleiman comes from the Mediterranean. Sultan's from Africa, like Solomon. These two are redheads and cousins. Jack and Rouge."

"Rouge?" Xaira exclaimed. "There are *lady pirates*?" Her head turned back to look at María Isabel as the Gaitanos laughed. Her eyes narrowed suspiciously on her. "Are you one of them?"

María Isabel smiled gently at her and shrugged with good humor. "Not really. I am Don Carlos' wife. I am known as the mother of Gaitano and Indio. I am a gypsy. But," she added with a musical laugh, "I must admit I have participated in a few episodes of my men's lives." Looking back at the screen, she let her eyes caress the beloved familiar faces. "Rouge actually grew up in Encantada with Gian and the boys. As soon as her training was complete, her family gifted her with her own ship and carted her off to Carey."

Xaira frowned. "Why?"

"Giancarlo," answered Don Carlos. "Rouge and Gian, like your girls and our boys, are destined to be together. Individually, they are each very rich and extremely powerful." He sighed. "Together they are going to be indestructible. It would send just about every pirate out there into a frenzy. Their lives would be threatened…"

"I get it," Xaira nodded. "I imagine that a child out of that union would be in constant danger for as long as it lived." She glanced back at the screen. "So, are they together now or not?"

"Yes and no. For now, Rouge is in Carey. But they do get together whenever possible," Don Carlos explained.

María Isabel smiled. "Soon. Especially after seeing Carlitos and Indio." She shook her head with a laugh. "They'll get together soon." The group fell silent for a moment, all eyes on the screen.

Caribe pointed out the last pirate. "And this formidable fellow---"

"Let me guess," Blue interrupted. "Don Miguel Gaitano." He sighed deeply, rubbing his eyes. "Marina must have wanted to die."

Caribe nodded. "She did. They all made her check their own books."

Cat turned to look at him. "Was shit going on with them too?"

"A couple," Caribe admitted. "But they were all very grateful for her findings. They sent Gaitano back to Encantada to take care of business."

"And did he?" Blue asked.

Caribe nodded. "Sure." He smiled mysteriously. "After *El Baile del Luto*."

It was the Butler boys' turn to frown and look at each other. Derek turned to Pablo. "Isn't *luto* mourning?" He shook his head as Pablo nodded with a smile.

"There's a mourning dance?" Tyler demanded. "No way…"

Caribe laughed. "It's not really a dance and they're not mourning. It's more like a pirate party."

Xaira eyed him curiously. "So, why's it called that?"

The islander grinned. "They all wear black." Passing the pictures slowly, he explained the scenes to them. "Marina thought it would be a good idea to gather information from every pirate she met."

"What kind of information?" Jesse asked.

"Where they were on the ocean on which dates," Caribe shrugged. "Stuff like that."

"And did they give her the information?" Blue asked.

Cat glared at him. "A stranger in their midst?"

Caribe nodded. "Are you kidding? Gladly. Marina Aguilar is Gaitano's accountant." He shrugged again. "Why wouldn't they?"

"Oh, look!" Heather exclaimed. "Look at Salomé and Indio!" She sighed happily. "They are stunning!"

María Isabel smiled proudly. "They were."

Heather stared at her, eyes wide with wonder. "You were there that night?"

María Isabel nodded happily. "We got there a little later, but just in time."

"Just in time for what?" Blue demanded.

"The show."

"What show?"

Her eyes shone at the memory. "You'll see."

"Marina looks beautiful," Xaira sighed dreamily. Then she moaned softly as she caught sight of the young pirate. "God, Gaitano's gorgeous," she whispered, making the women laugh appreciatively. "But who's that?" she asked, pointing out the figure of a woman.

Don Carlos smacked his lips and laughed. "Lo-la..."

"An old ex-girlfriend of Carlitos'," Shayla scoffed, making them laugh.

"Ex-girlfriend," Xaira giggled. Then she grew serious as the picture changed. "And who's *that*?" she frowned at the next one.

"Lucifer," answered Don Carlos, making fear strike in the young woman's heart suddenly. "His name is Xavier."

It was the twins' turn to lean forward in their seats, eyes intense. "Damn…" Blue murmured, shaking his head.

"So, what happens?" Cat wanted to know.

Caribe laughed. "Marina meets Lola…"

The Butler boys grinned. "Must have put Gaitano on the spot," Derek laughed.

"You should've been there," Caribe agreed. "Lola didn't appreciate that Gaitano was there with a…," he frowned, searching for the correct word.

"Date," Shayla offered.

Caribe nodded. "Yes. Date."

It was Tyler's turn to laugh. "She got pissed off he took another woman to *El Luto*?" He laughed again.

"Exactly. She wanted to dance for him."

"Dance?" Jesse asked.

"Lola is a very talented flamenco dancer," Don Carlos explained.

"Why do I get the feeling something happened with this Xavier fellow?" Shane inquired.

"Xavier wanted to buy Marina," Caribe explained. The twins swore.

A muscle twitched in Jesse's face as he froze. His voice dropped lower. "So, what happens next?"

Caribe chuckled mysteriously. "Watch." Carefully, he passed the pictures as if they were frames in slow motion. Mesmerized, all eyes remained glued to the screen as the story unfolded.

They all saw Lola's dance and Gaitano's indifference. They watched as Salomé enticed the musicians. When they saw Marina next, Xaira gasped.

"She gave Gaitano a lap dance? Okay. Now I'm jealous."

Before their eyes, Marina bewitched the pirate in front of his brethren. Next thing they knew, the flamenco dancer was flying at Marina.

"What happened there?" Heather asked in surprise.

"Bitch called Marina a *puta*," Shayla explained.

"She called her a *whore*? *Why*?" Heather cried, indignant. "Because Marina took her man? Too bad! Marina's the one Gaitano took to El Luto!"

María Isabel laughed softly. "Carlitos was never Lola's man. She was just someone he had an experience with."

"Lola appreciated the Gaitano part of him more than she ever cared about the Carlitos part," the pirate explained.

"*Oh!*" the men exclaimed suddenly at the next frame. They laughed as they watched a beautiful rendition of Marina's hair flying around her face as she slapped the flamenco dancer into submission.

Heather gasped. "Oh, no, she didn't!"

Sloane nodded, eyes fixed on her baby. "Oh, yes, she did!"

Cat grinned. "That's my girl!"

Xaira held her hands up. "Marina in a cat fight? That's it! She must be crazy about Gaitano," she said, wonder in her voice.

"Oh, she adores him," María Isabel agreed softly. "And Carlitos absolutely cherishes her."

They watched as Marina continued slapping the flamenco dancer until the woman was on the ground. Before their eyes, the story continued unfolding. Xavier steps in, laughing, mocking. Gaitano draws his sword. Then all the pirates draw their swords.

Heather gasped again. "They fought over her?"

"No, no," Caribe assured her hurriedly. "It didn't get that far."

"It's that guy!" Xaira exclaimed. "It's Xavier, isn't it?" She shook her head. "He make trouble for Gaitano?"

Don Carlos laughed. "He tried."

Catamaran turned to look at the pirate. "He *tried*?" He waved an angry hand at the screen. "That looks like a standoff to me, so I assume some lives were threatened?" he asked, raising a sarcastic eyebrow.

Don Carlos nodded, eyes glittering. "Only one."

"Whose?" Cat demanded. "Marina's?"

"No," María Isabel said, once again putting a soothing hand on his shoulder. "Xavier's." Everyone fell quiet as they saw Carlos walking away, his men on either side of him with swords still drawn. The young pirate was carrying Marina, who had both her arms and legs wrapped around him like a velcro monkey. Her eyes looked haunted and furious at the same time and her hands were held out behind him.

Jesse laughed. "Let me guess. She's flipping out both Xavier and the bitch."

Caribe nodded in agreement. "Yes."

Jesse laughed again. "That's my girl." And he fell silent once more.

The images changed. Caribe took them through their voyage home from Carey back to Encantada and the family's reunion as daughters were met at the docks by Jackson and the parents. From there, they were quickly taken through the island's cleanup and the Pirates' Convention Expo.

Blue turned his head to look astounded at his uncles. "You guys took part in these raids?"

Joe laughed. "Of course! What did you think? We were just going to sit around while our children's friends needed help?"

"No, of course not. I just thought that you had gone to pull the girls out," Blue explained.

"Azulito," Sloane called him gently, smiling when his eyes met hers. "Once we got there, there was no pulling the girls *out*. Things got set in motion that are beyond our control and comprehension, and we just got kind of sucked in." She tossed her beautiful blonde head and looked at each of them. "I believe, the same as Leila, that the girls arrived at Encantada because they had a mission. The proof is right here," she added, gesturing at the pirate couple.

María Isabel nodded in agreement. "God only knows what would have happened."

Shane frowned. "Well, besides losing Encantada, what else could've happened to your son?" he asked Don Carlos. "I mean, they wouldn't have killed him, right? Not if he was the one being cheated and robbed?"

The pirate's laugh sent a chill along their spines. "There are worse things than death, *licenciado*."

It was Jesse's turn to smile. "Ain't that the truth."

Don Carlos smiled at him before turning back to the lawyer. "What price do you put on a man's honor? His integrity? His word? Carlitos' losing Encantada would have made him the laughingstock of the Caribbean. He would have lost men, ships, his whole life as he knows it would have been irrevocably changed." He took a deep breath, stretching his arms high in the air and letting them fall slowly, running his fingers through his hair with a sigh. "The accountant, Marina Aguilar," he smiled. "Your goddaughter, daughter, friend, employee, sister?" he paused, tweaking Xaira's braid, making her nod and smile shyly at him. "This accountant, Marina Aguilar, saved our son's name, his fortune, his life…" He shrugged. "Do you blame him for keeping her?"

Startled eyes turned to him. Cat's seemed to glow. "He's *keeping* her?"

The pirate shrugged again. "I told you he had good taste."

"Oh, my God," Xaira gasped, making all eyes turn back to the screen. "Is that Max?" In front of them was an image of the baby. It was a close-up of Max in someone's lap, gurgling, reaching. Caribe sighed as he showed the second frame. It seemed as if he had zoomed out and they looked on in horror at the knife in the person's hand. "That's Xavier," Xaira hissed. "I swear it is." Nobody spoke, but they all looked at Caribe. When the third frame came to view, tears came to Xaira's eyes. "I knew it!" she muttered under her breath. Everyone stayed silent for a moment, shock not letting them do anything but shake their heads.

Blue turned to look at the women. "Mami, were you there?" he asked quietly.

Sloane shook her head. "No, Azulito, not *there*."

Shayla shook her head also as he turned to look at her. "We were together at the docks," she said softly.

"We knew nothing," María Isabel confirmed.

"This has to do with Marina, doesn't it?" Xaira asked.

Caribe nodded. "Yes." He sighed again. "This happened at the Lair. All the men were there and Xavier shows up with Max."

Xaira shook her head. "He couldn't get Marina otherwise, huh?"

Jesse smiled slowly. It never reached his eyes. "Holding a baby as hostage. What a concept."

The Butlers were horrified. Shane turned his head to look at the pirate, eyes wide behind his glasses. "What was everybody else doing? I mean, who got Marina?"

Caribe's voice was quiet. "I did." He frowned and pressed his lips together at the memory. "She freaked."

"Of course," Tyler said.

"Where was the mom?" Derek asked, eyes staring at the scene.

"Xavier wouldn't give her the baby. Only Marina," Joe answered, running his hands over his cornrows.

"What were *you* doing?" Blue demanded.

"We were actually having a good time," his uncle started answering.

"Playing drums," Pablo interrupted.

Blue stared at him for a moment, and then shook his head. "I'm not even going to ask, Tío," he murmured.

"What about Jackson?" Xaira wanted to know.

Joe gave a short laugh. "Fit to be tied."

The pirate smiled. "He called her Houston."

Blue shook his head, dazed, unable to tear his eyes from the screen, where the picture changed. Evident now was the room where pirates were divided in opposite sides, leaving Xavier alone with Max in the middle of the room. In the background, Joe and Pablo could be seen sitting with some drums while Jackson scowled next to them. Blue barely glanced at the pirate next to him. "What?"

"Jackson called Marina, Houston," he explained. "When she came in the room, he yelled, *Houston!*"

"*We have a problem!*," a chorus of voices around him completed the phrase.

"We'll explain later," Shane assured him.

The picture changed again, and Caribe continued his narrative. "We reached town and got Larissa. Outside the Lair, Marina stopped to pray. Then she smacked the hell out of the pirate that was posted outside the door."

"Why? What happened?" Heather asked.

Caribe smiled. "She asked him if he knew who she was. He went, '*The accountant…*'" he told them in the same fateful *ooh-la-lah* tone the pirate had used before being struck by lightning. Caribe snickered.

"There you go," Shane told his wife with a grin. "That would do it for me too, I'm telling you," he sighed, shaking his head.

Caribe shrugged with a smile as Xaira gave a soft laugh. "He got cute with her. She didn't appreciate it."

"Who's that huge pirate next to her?" Heather asked in a hushed tone. "Is that your other brother?" she asked the pirate close to her.

Don Carlos shook his head. "No, that's not Juan, but he is the law in our waters."

They all watched enthralled as Marina entered the scene and Xavier readily gave up Max to her. Soon, she was on his lap. Don

Carlos observed the twins sit up straight and take notice. By the time Xavier was kissing Marina, they were all murmuring.

Xaira's sharp mind wouldn't let her be still. She put a hand on the pirate's arm, making him turn his head and look into her eyes. "Did Xavier really like Marina, or…?" she drifted off, letting the thought catch in his mind.

Don Carlos smiled. "How did someone so young get to be so smart?" he murmured. Then he sighed. "You're right." He looked back at the screen, eyes flashing steel like a sword. "Xavier was just going out of his way to make Carlitos miserable. It turns out, we came to discover, that he just wanted everything that was his."

"So the accountant was just a possession?" Blue asked.

Don Carlos nodded. "Yes."

Horrified, they looked on. Before long, swords were drawn, and Xavier was skewered, pinned to his chair, Marina's hand on the handle of the sword.

Xaira began to cry. "Oh, my God…" she whimpered.

Stunned, nobody spoke for a moment. The visual was graphic, explicit in its details. The expressions in the different faces were priceless. Laughter in Xavier's, even in death, outrage in Marina's, and fury in Gaitano's. Everyone else around them looked as much in shock as those that were now seeing the illustration.

Shayla and Sloane lunged at one another, arms wrapping tightly around each other. Sloane moaned, the sound coming from deep in her soul.

"We never saw this!" Shayla cried out, tears choking her voice.

"Xavier must've said something," Xaira said, tossing her head angrily. She turned to glare at the men that had been present. "What did he say?"

The pirate met her furious eyes. "Xavier dared to threaten a future child of Carlitos and Marina's with sexual assault…"

Heather reached out to her friends, murmuring. "Oh, honey…"

María Isabel wrapped her arms around both women, blinking back hot tears that threatened to spill. "I am so sorry, *mis corazones*," she whispered.

A collective sigh ensued at the next illustration. It was of Pablo Aguilar and Joe Banks tearing out of the Lair with their three children in tow. Nobody spoke another word for a while as Caribe changed the scenery. The rest of the illustrations were of Marina and Carlos together, happy, working, dancing, laughing, evolving as a couple. Finally, the ceremony at the cay called *Arrecife*.

Cat sighed audibly. "So Gaitano married Marina." It was a statement.

The pirate nodded. "That, Gato, is why he's keeping her"

Cat shook his head in disbelief. "Marina got married without me?"

Joe patted his shoulder. "Chill, Catamaran," he urged gently. "Baby girl can't drop off the face of the earth. They have to come back. Bring their pirates with them." He sighed, rubbing his eyes. "And when they do, we'll make them get married all over again, just for you." Pressing his lips together, Cat could only nod.

Trying to ease the silence, Shane turned to the now silent Xaira. "I understand why you would miss them," he said softly, "living together and all. I'm sorry I couldn't tell you what was happening." He shrugged. "I was sworn to secrecy and it was too incredible..." He shook his head and turned to Jesse, a puzzled frown on his face. "But how did *you* come to miss her?"

Jesse sighed and stretched, arching his body away from the back of the chair. "We go out once a week."

At this, Shayla frowned. "*Every* week?" She looked at Sloane. "Did you know Marina and Jesse were getting together every week?"

Sloane blinked back tears and shook her head slowly. "No. I knew they went out a couple of times to that cowboy dive on Front Street to shoot some pool..."

"They line dance," Xaira explained softly, sniffling. "Marina got hooked..." It was her turn to shrug.

"Rain goes out with the girls," Jesse explained. "I pick Marina up. We have a couple of beers, talk about school and work, dance and shoot pool. It's become a ritual." He smiled. "Sometimes Rain and the girls even join us."

Sloane shook her head again. "Marina mentioned that you would miss her, but I didn't realize…" Frustrated, she clenched her fists and flung her head back. "*God!*" Eyes burning with blue fire, she raked them over her companions, steel determination in her voice. "I don't care that she's a grown woman with a man of her own! I'll be damned if I ever lose track of my baby again!"

Pablo took his wife's hand in his, easing it open, rubbing his face against it before kissing it. "*Suave, mami,*" he murmured.

Xaira began crying again. "Oh, God, Uncle Jesse," she sobbed softly. "Now Marina's part of *El Duelo*!" she wailed.

Jesse could only nod. "I know, baby," he said quietly.

The twins groaned.

Cat screamed at the ceiling.

Blue just shook his head. "I can't believe it!"

Don Carlos frowned. "What's *El Duelo*?"

Pablo shook his head, shocked. His brown eyes opened wide as he pushed back his own tears. His mouth opened, but no sound came out. He closed it again.

Joe groaned. "It's a club," he finally managed, dazed. "A very particular, special, damn club for people who have killed someone."

Surprised, Don Carlos looked around him. "Are you in it?" Everyone shook their heads but Xaira who motioned silently at Jesse, who was nodding, and herself. Enlightened, the pirate nodded slowly. "What do you do?" he asked softly.

Jesse turned pain filled eyes to him. "Talk about our feelings. Repent. Do random acts of kindness. Commit to doing good…" He shrugged. "Spread the Word. Talk about God…"

The pirate reached for his wife's hand and kissed it absently without taking his eyes off the pair. "Snake," he called softly, getting Jesse's attention back to the present. "May my wife, Marisa and I, join *El Duelo*?"

Xaira began to cry harder. Standing up suddenly, she flung herself away from the seat. "I can't take this, you guys, I'm sorry."

"I need a drink," Blue said as the twins joined her.

"I need to think," Cat announced.

"Wait, you guys!" Tyler stopped them, startled. "We have to plan."

"Let's talk," Derek agreed.

"Our place," Xaira said suddenly.

"Let's go," Blue agreed.

Catamaran turned to the parents. "We'll see you later."

Jesse also stood up. "I need to relax."

Turning away, the Butler boys, the St. Jacques twins, an uncle called Snake, and the Oriental young woman as beautiful as a China doll, all began filing out. Stopping suddenly as one, they all turned back to look at the people they were leaving behind.

"Yo! Island boy!" Xaira called out, wiping the tears from her face.

María Isabel smiled as their companion just stared at them, surprised. "I think she means you, Caribe," she said softly.

He frowned. "Me?"

"You got any kids?" Xaira asked, exasperated, making him shake his head hurriedly.

"Neither do we," Jesse explained. "You get to come with us."

"Move your butt or get left behind," Xaira sang out. Looking at the pirates, she smiled sadly. "Welcome to Blue Bay." Then she turned away, the rest on her heels.

Island boy looked at the pirates, who nodded encouragingly. Relieved, Caribe followed after the six, making seven. The parents sighed.

Outside Caribe looked up, filling his lungs with clean air. He could smell the ocean from where they were, although he couldn't see it for the walls that surrounded the Hacienda's courtyard. A lone seagull cried once as it glided overhead and continued on its way. There was an assortment of vehicles in the Hacienda's driveway by now; a couple of these only had two wheels. Caribe watched quietly as both Jesse and Xaira each got on one and took off, engines rumbling in the afternoon stillness. Before them was a very large vehicle, black paint gleaming in the sun, shining like brand new.

"Come on, Cat," Tyler was almost begging. "You've gotta let me drive, man."

Catamaran shook his dreads back with a wicked laugh. "Sure, man." He tossed him the keys. "I love to be driven around."

Derek laughed. "I drive back here."

"Whatever, y'all, let's just get out of here," Blue drawled.

Four doors opened, and all five men got inside. Catamaran rode shotgun in his own vehicle. Caribe struggled to contain his excitement as he found himself sitting between Derek and Blue. Tyler started the engine expertly, his laugh happy as he adjusted sunglasses on his face and a cap on his head. Overhead a glass moved, purring as it let real daylight in. Catamaran adjusted the passenger seat until it was leaning back more a couple of notches. Their windows remained up giving them certain anonymity behind their barely legal tinted glass. Music seemed to surround them suddenly, enveloping them in an overpowering beat. Tyler put the car in gear and followed the fading motorcycles. Caribe looked at his companions. The music coming over the speakers was like nothing he had ever had before but apparently they all liked it. Their faces held smiles as their heads bounced in rhythm. "This is nice," he finally said.

They all glanced at him before going back to what they were looking at. "It is," Blue reassured him.

"It's only gonna get nicer, island boy," laughed Cat.

Soon, they were in town. Caribe watched closely, trying to take it all in. It was too much. Nothing in his young life had ever prepared him for this. The sights and sounds were overwhelming to the senses. Finally he gave up, closing his eyes and leaning back, letting the music distract him. He opened his eyes slowly as he felt their vehicle glide to a crawl. They found themselves in front of a nondescript building. Old, it was a few stories tall and made out of brick. It seemed to be a warehouse with nothing outstanding to distinguish it from its neighboring buildings. On the ground floor were a few businesses, their signs the only indication of life in them, their storefronts attractive, sharply contrasting with their drab background. A comfortable park bench ran along the wall between a barber/beauty shop named Sea Side Styles and a place called **Rain Dance**. An older black man lounged on the weathered slats, a newspaper in his hands. The color of his skin was that of dark worn leather and his hair was long gone, his bare head making him look timeless. His still athletic body was enclosed in jeans, and a light *guayabera*. The light cotton shirt had four pockets, two at chest level and two at waist level on either side of his body with tiny pleats running down vertically through the center of each, connecting them, parallel to the buttons. This one was white with black embroidery. It was just like those worn in Cuba, the Dominican Republic, and Puerto Rico. Next to him resting against the scrolled ironwork of the bench lay a medium-to-large sized mongrel. Its hair was long, its coloring splotched in gray ombré with black spots that seemed to blend into its luxurious coat. Both man and beast looked up, one's eyes dark like strong coffee, the other's eyes blue like faded jeans, startling against all the dark fur. The man's chin went up in greeting before his face disappeared behind the newspaper once again. Next was a space where the plate glass window just said TAE KWON DO. A few yards away was another beautiful plate glass window with black lettering highlighted in silver, indicating it was ***SNAKE'S TATTOOS***. All around the window, snakes and serpents crawled and writhed in beautiful bright colors. Caribe had to look twice. Lounging between the window and the door was a beautiful young woman like none he had ever seen before. She was dressed in black leather from head to foot. Brilliant colors marred her soft white skin from one bare shoulder to mid arm. Her outfit was tight and eye-catching as it displayed cleavage and long legs enclosed in dark hose. One foot was on the ground, and a beautiful black cat, barely visible but for his movement and his green eyes, paced on the sidewalk, snaking around her leg, rubbing itself against the black leather boot. Her other boot enclosed foot was on the wall she was leaning on, her knee pointing straight out to the street. In spite of the odds you couldn't see her panties, but the thought of almost tugged at his imagination. One arm wrapped around her middle propping her opposite elbow, hand close to her face which was framed by expertly layered blue black hair. A cigarette dangled almost forgotten between long pale fingers, smoke rising slowly before being snatched away by the gentle breeze. It seemed to Caribe as if hoop earrings cascaded from one ear, graduating in size from the smallest at the top of her lobe, to the largest dangling at the bottom. From her other ear a long thin silver chain dangled with a large tear shaped crystal at the end swinging like a pendulum. His companions rolled down their windows calling her name, whistling and blowing kisses at her. The young woman looked up and smiled at them, bright blue eyes contrasting dramatically against her dark makeup, blinking through her straight bangs, and blew kisses back at them. Next to him Blue groaned softly before chuckling. They joined him. She was beautiful in a scary way, Caribe decided. At the corner of the building were a set of electronic gates. Tyler reached up to the car's visor where a plastic device was clipped and pressed a button. A whirring noise filled the air as the gates glided open. They drove in and down into the basement of the building. It was nothing more than an old parking garage. In it was a beautiful black Mustang convertible with the words SLOANE'S BABY on the license plates, a bright red Jeep, a turquoise colored Ford Ranger Splash edition with surf stickers all over the back window and a couple of surfboards sticking out from the bed, and the two motorcycles Jesse and Xaira had ridden away on. The men all got out of the car and headed across the floor to a small cargo elevator in a corner.

Derek turned to Caribe. "Come on, man. We won't bite," he assured him.

"Not yet," Cat leered at him.

"Not us," Blue added. They laughed.

Laughing with them, Caribe joined them. "What is this place?"

"It's where we live," Derek explained as they stepped into the elevator. Slamming the gates shut, he pressed a button. There was a clang and a thump, feeling as if something struck the elevator from the bottom. Then it started rising. The men laughed at Caribe's expression.

"Don't be afraid, man," Tyler assured him. "This is how we get to the floors above us."

Caribe grimaced. "Where I come from we use stairs." The men laughed again. "Do you all live here?"

They shook their heads. "Not us," Catamaran explained, "we live nearby."

"This place has four stories and a roof," Derek told him. "The first floor, as you saw, is occupied by a few businesses. Tyler and I live on the second, Salomé and Jackson on the third, Xaira and Marina on the top floor. You'll see."

The elevator glided to a stop and the cage opened once more. Caribe froze. In front of them, sitting as still as statues, were two huge dogs, the likes of which he had never seen before.

"Don't move," cautioned Tyler needlessly. "They are part of our security system. Let them feel you out. Relax."

Caribe swallowed. "I can't breathe," he admitted in a whisper.

"It's okay, guys," Derek said, in a tone used for children.

"These are rottweilers," Blue told him, as the beasts stood and approached Caribe, their sleek black hides reflecting light as their massive muscles flexed. They sniffed at his feet, his pants, his hands, his arms.

"They'll eat you, as soon as they'll look at you," Cat grinned.

Caribe swallowed a moan as one of them stood on its hind legs, placing his huge front paws on his chest, making him stumble. "Good puppy," he gasped, looking into the dog's eyes. Convinced, the beast proceeded to lick him. Not to be outdone, its companion joined him in the welcome. The men laughed.

"Come on, man," urged Blue, stepping out.

The space beyond was enormous, running for almost the entire length of the building. At the very end, was a large Sacred Heart picture contained in an antique frame, overlooking the place. The roof here was dotted with strategically placed sky lights, being the top floor. Great panes of ceiling to floor glass had been placed at intervals in the walls, bringing daylight unto the whole floor and the outside in. The space was open, not exactly divided by walls, except for one enclosed section where the guest bathroom was, and two others on opposite sides of the building where the bedrooms were, Xaira's by the elevator and Marina's under the Sacred Heart. The rest of the floor was divided in different kinds of arrangements. Towards the street side of the building was a kitchen area with modern conveniences. The predominant color was blue with bright yellow and acid green accents. A small 10-gallon fish tank sat on one end of the black granite counter gurgling nicely, complimenting the sea food theme. Fish magnets swam on a sea of stainless steel on the refrigerator, and an old drugstore booth had been restored and placed next to the window overlooking the town with paper fish mobiles hanging over it. Next to that were beautiful standing rice paper screens. This dining area behind them was strictly Oriental with a low table surrounded by floor cushions, and live bamboo growing in huge ceramic pots decorated with cranes and koi fish. A large brass Buddha smiled serenely at the small stone fountain gurgling in front of it, while incense burned on either side of it. Another area contained some sort of equipment, the likes of which Caribe had never seen before. Later, he was to find out it was for exercising. There were standing bookshelves with lamps and assorted armchairs and rocking chairs. Most of the areas were tastefully divided by different height walls made out of glass blocks. Half of one wall on the ocean side contained canvases and assorted painting materials. Here Caribe hesitated, wanting to stop and look through the different pictures. "Who paints?" he asked casually.

Tyler threw him a smile. "Xaira. She's pretty good. Ask her to show you some time."

Up ahead were Jesse and Xaira already waiting for them in a sitting area next to a magnificent view of the shore. Beautiful heavy wooden furniture upholstered in blue denim with assorted pillows made out of Navajo blankets surrounded a low coffee table made of glass framed with the same rustic wood. Tastefully arranged on the table were assorted fashion and surfing magazines mixed in with large hardcover books of Time Life photographs. As Caribe drew nearer he could see the ocean. It was closer to them here than it was to the warehouses on the dock back in Encantada. He couldn't help but smile. In front of him on a far brick wall was a big screen similar to the one where he had shown his pictures but different. On it images and words flickered indicating it was playing urban music on Music Choice. The music was piped via hidden speakers throughout the whole floor. Xaira and Jesse were already waiting for them, heads bouncing to the song playing at the moment. Caribe stood and watched for a moment, he was too excited to sit down. Blue and Cat strolled casually to the majestic picture windows facing the ocean so they could talk quietly among themselves, occasionally glancing at him. Derek and Tyler went to one of two tables in the center of the floor. They began an avid game that consisted of sliding a small circular object across the table, trying to put it in the opponent's space at the same time they impeded their opponent from doing the same. The dogs sat to one side, watching them with interest. The next table was larger, more elaborate. Wooden balls chased each other across a beautiful royal blue background, trying to go in pockets in the sides as Jesse and Xaira jabbed at them, poked them, and pushed them around with long wooden sticks. The table itself was of rich heavy dark wood, hand carved, the legs resting on lion's claws. Suspended over it was a beautiful Tiffany overhead lamp, advertising a Puerto Rican light beer named Medalla in beautiful golden tones against an ebony black background. After a while of watching, he went and stood next to them. Beside him was a free-standing wall. It held a large aquarium, at least five hundred gallons. Inside was part of an ocean reef, spectacularly colorful salt water fish prominently displayed by hidden lighting. It was a piece of art by itself. On the lid an army of dollar store mermaid figurines lined the perimeter, each one beautiful in its own individual way. He turned to the girl. "One of the boys said that you share this floor with Marina."

Xaira ignored him for a moment as she focused on her shot. The ball went into a corner pocket, making her grin at Jesse. He bowed his head, waving his hand over the table. It was her turn again. "We do," she spoke quietly.

Caribe nodded slowly. "You must miss her."

At that, tears stung the back of her eyes. She stopped what she was doing and faced him squarely. "I miss Marina so much," she choked out, "I feel like I want to die right now." Anger flared in her eyes. "Can you understand that?"

Caribe nodded again. "Marina misses you just as much."

Xaira tossed her head and turned back to her game. "Oh, yeah? So why did she stay?"

Caribe laughed softly. Spreading his hands helplessly, he shook the dreads out of his face. "She married Gaitano. What was she supposed to do?"

Xaira didn't think. "Come back and bring him with her." Pocketing another ball she went around the table for her next shot. "We need her here."

Caribe laughed again as the rest of the males in the room stopped what they were doing and joined them. "Gaitano needs her there."

"She has a job here," Xaira shot back.

Caribe walked around the table in the opposite direction so he was facing her. He looked away from her, for a moment distracted by the gorgeous fish swimming behind her. Turning back to Xaira, he focused. "Marina has a job in Encantada," he countered casually.

"Marina works for *me*, island boy," Cat informed him, green eyes boring into him.

Caribe turned to face him. "No, Marina works as the accountant for La Gitana of Carlos Gaitano y Sandoval." Shaking his head, he laughed. "No! Wait! I take it back." He looked at each of them, as they were all now facing him. "Last I heard, Marina was working for Don Carlos."

"How can that be?" Blue demanded. "Don Carlos is over here now. Marina is still there."

Caribe shrugged, meeting his glare head on. "Bring it up with Don Carlos, if you want." He shook his head again. "You will just have to ask Marina yourself now, won't you?"

Breaking off from the group for a moment, Derek went to rummage in the refrigerator. "You know," he called from across the room, "there has to be something to this Encantada." He came back with beers for everyone. Handing them around, he waited until they were all open and tasted. "It's not just Marina who stayed," he pointed out. He smiled as Xaira rolled her eyes at him. "Salomé and Jackson stayed also."

Tyler turned to his brother. "No kidding, genius. The question is how do we get them back?"

Xaira narrowed her eyes wickedly at them. "Yeah! It sucks being alone in the building with you guys. I can hear you all the way up here."

Caribe laughed at them. "What makes you think they *want* to come back," he teased. "After all, they did stay…" Around him everyone took in and let out assorted deep breaths and sighs.

Xaira shook her head in disgust, her slit eyes glinting with determination. "They'll want to come back," she announced. "Don't you worry about that."

Caribe laughed again. "Oh, I'm not worried. I'm the one that came over." He looked around at them. "By the way, how does one get along in your world?"

Blue laughed. "Very carefully."

"We can't let you out on the street yet," Tyler warned him.

"No," Derek agreed. "You would give yourself away in a heartbeat."

"Caribe," Jesse told him in a soft warning voice, "you have to be very careful in our world. In our times."

Caribe grinned. "I grew up around pirates, remember?"

Jesse nodded, readjusting the cowboy hat on his head. He tilted his head back and drank from his beer. Smacking his lips, he looked steadily at the native once again. "We have worse."

Caribe nodded solemnly. "So, where do we start?"

"Can you read and write?" Cat asked, curiously.

Caribe snorted in disgust, offended by the question. "Of course I can read and write." He thought about it for a moment. "Well, I see why you would ask." He faced the twins. "*I* can read and write."

"That will help." Blue turned to his companions. "We need to school island boy here."

"That will take days," Tyler nodded.

Derek snorted. "That may take weeks."

Blue shrugged. "Whatever it takes."

Cat nodded in agreement. "First things first." He held his beer in one hand, absently scraping the label off with his thumbnail. "We need to get all of you I.D. cards, to begin with."

Caribe snorted at the notion. His time travel sense that allowed him to communicate with the visitors, now his hosts, told him what I.D. Cards were. "We do have names."

"Yes," Cat countered smoothly, "but we have to move up your birth dates by three hundred and fifty years, island boy." He grinned. "Do you have anything to say now? I didn't think so."

Caribe chuckled. "Are you always this bossy? No wonder Marina would rather work for the Gaitanos." Everyone laughed around them in good humor.

Catamaran shook his dreadlocks. "Let's see who she ends up with, island boy."

Caribe laughed. "Good luck."

Cat grinned back. "Yeah, yeah, whatever." Turning away from him, he turned to the lawyer's sons. "Okay, guys. Who do we have that can do this for us? We need to hook up the three of them for starters."

Tyler crossed his arms over his chest and took a deep breath. "Real identification cards, well, that would be Khan."

Derek nodded. "Khan," he agreed.

Cat sighed. "That's my man too." He turned to his brother. "Once we get that out of the way, we need to school our guests on the third millennium."

Tyler nodded, pointing at his brother and himself. "We can do that."

Blue held out his hand. "They need to have these identifications established. What are they going to do while they're here?"

Caribe laughed. "I came here to learn. Don Carlos, however, can do whatever he wants. He has money." He smiled to himself as they all turned to look at him. "Lots of money."

"So he can hide behind a legitimate business," Blue said. "That's good."

Jesse nodded. "Sounds like a plan, boys. We should ask these people what their preferences are."

"So, let's do it. Have another beer first, play a game, and let's go back." They all agreed.

Xaira turned to Caribe thoughtfully. "What did you come to learn?"

"About your world," he responded automatically. He turned his head slowly to look at her. "About art."

The young woman's eyes crinkled almost shut, her smile transforming her whole face. "Have you come to the right place." She nodded at him. "I got you." Lifting her hand, she put it in front of him.

Caribe smiled as he slid her some skin. "And I got your back."

Derek drove them on this occasion. This time their heads bounced to some *reggaeton*. The music invaded them. Jesse and Xaira followed them back. The parents were waiting for them in the courtyard in the center of the property. They were basking in the sun next to a beautiful inviting swimming pool, a tin tub full of ice and bottles of water beside them. A pair of very large German Shepherds sat flanking the chaise lounge chair Don Carlos was reclining in. The pirate was grinning from ear to ear.

"*Muchachos*!" he greeted the younger people. "Did you have a good meeting?"

Caribe laughed. "Yes, Don Carlos. We will be getting real identifications," he said, rolling his eyes at the pirate.

Don Carlos laughed. "I see. And who will be in charge of this?"

"We have a friend named Khan," Tyler answered, going to sit at the foot of his mother's chair.

Shane took his glasses off with a sigh, rubbing his hand over his hair before dragging it over his face. "My son, the connected guy."

Joe took a deep breath. "Khan may not do everything legal, but…" He shrugged.

Pablo nodded, rubbing his chin thoughtfully. "He's the best there is. Also, it helps he's on Gato's payroll." The women murmured in agreement.

Don Carlos smiled. "Well, you are all on my payroll," he announced to the surprised group assembled in front of him. "And because this is so, I will have your stories."

Blue laughed. "We shall have yours."

Don Carlos inclined his head towards him. "And so you shall." Seeing them stir, he stopped them with his hands in the air. "Not right now." He sighed dramatically. "This old man has come from a place far, far away." He grinned as they laughed. "Soon."

"What are you thinking of, *muñeca*?"

They were sitting on the deck that surrounded their lighthouse. Shirtless, his back was against the wall. Cutoff pants enclosed his strong thighs, long legs stretched out in front of him, bare feet in space, ankles firmly anchored on the edge of the deck. The sun beat down on them, a soft breeze ruffling his black hair, curls blowing around his head. His large hands were busy as Marina lay with her head on his lap, his fingers combing her hair in a soothing hypnotizing movement. She wore a beautiful bright sarong she had fashioned herself, the colors rich and vibrant against her dark tan. She wore shells on her ears, wrists, and ankles. A much beloved string of turquoises graced her left arm, accompanied by a plain silver band on her wedding finger. A small cross, also of turquoises inlaid in silver, nestled on her chest, suspended from a black cord. She sighed, burrowing her head deeper into his lap, making him smile. She loved it when he called her a doll. "Nothing…"

Now he grinned. "Nothing?" He chuckled. "Surely something. This isn't you, *mami.* " His fingertips massaged her head. "What's wrong?"

Tears stung her eyes, but she couldn't lie. Not about this. Actually not about anything. Not to him. "I miss my parents." Pushing herself off his lap, she sat sideways so she could look at him. "I miss *your* parents."

Fascinated he took some hair that was blowing in the wind and held it between his fingers twirling it, watching as it sparked rays from the sun, making the shades of color seem to melt and blend and contrast. "But they just left last night," he teased. There was no response. Then he took a deep breath. "I know," he sighed. "*I* miss my parents, and I haven't since I was a teenager." He shook his head ruefully. "I have been taking them for granted. It took me seeing you with yours to realize what I have been missing out on with mine." Letting go of her hair he took a different bunch of strands and did the same, enjoying the play of light and color. "What do you want to do about it?" he asked quietly.

Marina's hazel eyes searched his wildly. She closed her eyes. Her throat stung, making it hard to swallow. She took in a shaky breath and shook her head slowly. Her voice was a ragged whisper. "I don't know." Looking away she brushed angrily at her tears, eyes searching over the horizon. "I am *never* going to outgrow my parents. Besides being some of the coolest people I know, they're my best friends," she admitted sadly. Helpless, her hands fell back in her lap. "I wouldn't have life, and I can't live without them. I've got my own place, I don't live with them, but I can't live *without* them." She frowned at her own thoughts. "Do you know what I mean?"

The young pirate nodded although his eyes were also lost at sea, matching its color, seeking whatever it was she was trying to say. His voice was still quiet. "What do you want to do about it?"

She shrugged. "Not think about it, for one." Turning her head to look at him again, she took his face between her hands, looking deep into his eyes. "I am never going to leave you," she whispered passionately. Her next thought she couldn't express out loud. *And I pray to God you never leave me.* Pulling him closer she pressed her lips against his, just for a moment, and then let him go. The ocean caught her attention again. "I'm just waiting for the next storm, I guess."

"That's in a couple of weeks."

"I know." Her voice was quiet.

Carlos nodded. Taking her hand in his, he locked fingers with her and raised it to his lips. "We have time, Marina," he reassured her. "Meanwhile, would you like to go on a voyage?"

Marina turned to look at him again, her smile chasing away her tears. "When?"

The pirate grinned. "Ship's ready to sail…"

It was Marina's turn to raise his hand to her lips. "Let's go," she whispered.

This time they took *Tiburón* which was lighter and faster than *La Gitana* and they could sail on their own. Gaitano didn't leave anyone behind. He took his whole crew. Jackson and Storm tagged along. For the most part it was quite an uneventful voyage. They stopped at Arrecife for a break, arriving in the late morning hours.

Jackson stood by the ropes, surveying the cay with a critical eye. "Is this it?" he asked. "Is this what you guys rave about?" He grunted, amusement making his eyes shine. "It looks even smaller than I remember from the wedding."

"So, what are you saying?" laughed Salomé. Putting her hand on his shoulder to steady herself, she perched on the side of the boat, reaching up for the ropes with the other.

"Too small for you?" Marina taunted, balancing herself on Salomé's other side.

"Sure," Jackson laughed, placing himself between them. "Give me a bigger island anytime." For a moment, the three of them stood as if suspended in time, and then they dove in perfect synchronicity.

Behind them the pirates sighed.

Storm shook her head. "I've never seen brother and sisters like these." Her amber eyes squinted as the wind blew her hair about her face. "It's like you have to pry them apart or something," she waved a hand in frustration at the three heads appearing suddenly as they swam away.

The men grinned.

"We know," rumbled Indio, "we've tried."

The Captain laughed. Climbing up on the side of the ship he balanced himself holding on to the ropes. "And the thing is," he declared in mock dismay, "if you're not on them all the time, they tend to disappear."

Indio followed him. "They do," he chuckled at Storm. Both men held their hands out waiting for the beautiful pyrate to join them. Sighing deeply she let them pull her up between them. And just like the three before them, they dove in and swam to shore.

Once on the beach the mandatory laps were run around the cay before the couples fell on the sand, breathing hard and smiling at each other.

"So, where are we going?" Marina demanded.

Carlos grinned as only a husband humoring his wife will. "It's a surprise."

"Oh, come on," chided Salomé, green eyes luminous in the bright midday sun. "What more of a surprise than this trip?" She turned to look at the brave next to her.

Indio chuckled and shook his head. "Don't look at me, I love surprises. I'm not saying. I don't know."

"You lie," laughed Salomé.

"Yes," he admitted with a grin. "But I'm still not saying."

All eyes turned to Storm, making her squirm. Jackson took a wet lock of hair and tugged at it gently. "You are honor bound to Rouge, right? Not to these two thugs?" he asked hopefully.

Storm grinned. "I'm surprised I'm even here." She laughed as he flung the lock of hair across her face in mock disgust.

The brother and sisters smiled strangely at them and stood, stretching. The pirates watched as they gathered a few shells and bits of coral for a while, tying them in a bundle. Without any warning, the three of them raced into the water with whoops of joy, and began to swim back to the boat.

The pirates shook their heads ruefully and laughed, following in their wake, swimming right behind them.

"Xaira…" Don Carlos murmured. "What about her?"

Pablo and Joe turned to follow his gaze. They were in an upstairs balcony of their common property, overlooking the courtyard. Downstairs below them, one long plank, a yard wide, crossed the width of the swimming pool. Xaira and Caribe fought on it, using long bamboo sticks. They jabbed, kicked, twisted and turned, all the while trying not to fall in. The homeowners looked at each other and sighed.

"We acquired Xaira by chance," Joe answered. "Certainly not planning on it," he smiled. Raising the long sweating glass in front of him full of ice cold beer, he lifted it in a silent toast of the young woman in question.

Pablo chuckled, joining him in the toast. "No, there was no stopping Xaira," he agreed.

"Why does Catamaran call her Marina's pet?" Don Carlos wondered.

Joe threw back his head and laughed, earrings sparkling in the sun. Rays of sunlight reflected off the blackness of his sunglasses as he moved. "'Cause he's a brat!"

"Marina found her," Pablo began slowly. He turned to Joe. "Do you remember that day, *papi*? We were all at the dinner table, and Marina begins talking about this little oriental girl she had met? Whom she thought was in trouble?"

"Yeah," Joe drawled, "I do. She thought this little girl was being forced to prostitute and take drugs against her will." The men fell silent for a moment, all eyes focused on the girl before them.

Don Carlos took a deep breath. "Was it true?" He shook his head as the men next to him nodded theirs slowly.

"To make a long story short, Marina won her trust. Explained to the girl that she did not have to lead the life she was living," Joe explained.

"How old is she?"

"She's seventeen now, but she was thirteen when Marina found her."

"Was there a man controlling her life?"

Joe nodded his head, his cornrows rippling in the sun. "Oh, yeah. Absolutely. Big man. Not in size, like Jai Ling or Jimmy. In stature. As in name, reputation. Power." He turned his dark gaze on the pirate. "The man liked little girls. And he didn't mind sharing with other men that liked little girls."

"In order to keep the little girl calm, he needed her drugged," Pablo continued. He turned his aviator glasses on his guest. "Little girl had enough one day."

The pirate turned to look at him, his gaze steady. "What happened?"

Pablo looked back at the pair below them thoughtfully, rubbing his chin absently. "Marina had been working on her for a while. Spoke to her about the law, sexual abuse, children's rights, women's rights." He waved a hand in the air as if to indicate the vast range of topics discussed by his daughter. "It must have all sunk in. One day, out of nowhere, it just happened. A motive and an opportunity." He shrugged. "Little girl killed one of those men that liked little girls."

The pirate chuckled. "Of course. That is why she is part of El Duelo." He shook his head in admiration of the beautiful oriental vision that seemed to dance in air. "Then what happened?"

"Little girl ran away, scared out of her mind, and found Marina." Pablo met the pirate's eyes. "Man came looking for her."

"So what did you do?"

Joe sighed. "We couldn't have that. She needed protection and we were able to provide it. Marina was freaking out like we had never seen her before. There was no way we were going to allow that. So we did the only thing we could." He turned to look at the pirate. "We gave the man an offer he couldn't refuse."

"Which was?"

"Free the little girl, and get out of town."

Don Carlos nodded in agreement. "Good. What else?"

"We made him clean up his own mess, give some explanations, hand us the little girl with papers, and leave her independently wealthy," Pablo laughed.

Don Carlos frowned. "That easy?"

Joe laughed. "No, of course not. You see, once *we* have the little girl, she becomes a liability. Xaira was not only incredibly smart for her age, she had also learned to be sly. After Marina convinced her of her tragedy, she compiled evidence against her…" He frowned, searching for the correct word. "…owner, so to speak. Besides illicit drugs, a veritable opium den, and being a gang lord, the man was also dabbling in slavery, selling children for sex."

Pablo took a deep breath, letting it out slowly. "That is when we discovered we are not above blackmail. So we convinced him to do what we wanted. Free the little girl and get out of town. Of course, we also convinced him to leave her all set for life. God knows he could afford it."

The pirate thought about it for a moment. "So, Marina brings her home, but is very young herself."

"We all agreed to become legal guardians for Xaira. The four of us," Joe explained.

"But we made Marina take full responsibility for the girl," Pablo made clear. "When Shane, Joe and I bought the old abandoned building downtown, we let all five of our kids live in it. We fixed it up, and made them sign leases. They rent to own. Shane's boys get a floor, Jackson and Salomé went in together just out of habit from living under the same roof, and Marina…"

"Takes Xaira with her," guessed the pirate. The men next to him nodded. He pushed the sunglasses up his nose. It was taking him time to get used to them, but it sure beat squinting in the sun all the time. It gave him fewer headaches. Taking a sip of his beer, he set the sweating glass down, stopping the track of a drop with his thumb. He grabbed a hold of the tail of his T-shirt, taking the time to clean his sunglasses before putting them back on. He sighed. "Did you legally adopt her?"

Now they shook their heads. "No. She wouldn't have it. Said it was enough that we had to split our lives with the twins, besides our own kids. She believed that if we did, we would be spreading ourselves too thin," Joe explained. He shook his head at the memory. He whistled under his breath. "Baby girl will be taken care of by us, don't worry. All our children will gladly share."

"Xaira is very wealthy," Pablo confided. "All she needs until she is legally an adult are guardians." He blew the clueless girl a silent kiss and placed his hand over his heart.

"When will this take place?"

"Her birthday is in a few weeks."

"Do you have complete and absolute trust in her?" Don Carlos inquired.

Both men next to him nodded again. "Absolutely," Joe answered. "Baby girl would give her life for us."

"Baby girl would kill for us," Pablo looked at him over his shades.

Don Carlos nodded. "That is exactly what I need. A little warrior. I should include her in my inner circle also…" he wondered.

"Yes," Pablo urged. "Absolutely."

"No doubt," added Joe.

The pirate smiled. "So it shall be."

The rest of the voyage was uneventful. They kept busy with helping the crew do their chores, and doing their forms on deck. On their second day they threw anchor. Night had fallen, dropping on them suddenly, leaving them exposed under a black velvet canopy full of stars. The pirates invited their guests up on deck to join them. They laughed, they sang, they played drums and chanted, and just had a good old time. After a while the sailors drifted off to wherever it was they went to sleep, leaving the main crew of *La Gitana* with the Aguilar-Banks brother and sisters.

Salomé sighed happily as she stretched long and hard, standing on the tip of her toes, fingernails scratching at the sky. Relaxing, she dropped her heels back on the deck and smiled. "Where are we?"

Indio grinned. "The middle of the ocean."

"Not," all three siblings chorused.

The brothers Gaitano laughed.

"Now how can you tell?" the Captain challenged. "It is pitch black out here."

"Not," the siblings repeated.

"Look at all this starlight," Salomé retorted. "You can see plenty."

"So, what do you see?" Indio asked.

"Wait a moment. Moonrise will be in a few minutes," Salomé grinned. The pirates stood to one side. They watched their guests curiously, containing their amusement until they couldn't hold it any more. They exploded with laughter.

Giancarlo slapped Indio on the back. "She's smarter than you, my friend."

"That's cheating," Solomon smiled.

"What do you see now?" Indio insisted.

Brother and sisters stood together, turning slowly, searching deep in the darkness. They conferred, whispering in hushed tones before turning back to the pirates.

"Okay," Jackson finally said. "Open water's right behind us. But over there," he pointed in front of them, finger scanning in a long horizontal line, "is land."

"We can barely make them out but it seems to us that there are the outlines of mountains," Marina explained.

Following her gaze, the pirates saw what she was seeing.

Carlos chuckled proudly at his wife. "Good job, *divina*. How did you learn so much?"

She shrugged, smiling shyly at him. "Papi and Dad. They taught us to watch out for things you never see."

Suddenly Salomé gasped softly. "And how could you miss those bonfires?"

Storm laughed. "That's excellent. Now turn around," she suggested softly. They did as she said and gasped. "Here it comes," she laughed softly.

The ocean had changed while they had been talking, no longer a lake of black ink. The horizon seemed to shrink as the full moon began announcing itself. Distant clouds glowed underneath with the force of the white light. The top edge appeared like neon, slowly showing more. They watched in awed silence as their world filled with night light. Slow as the ascent appeared it was gradual and steady until the orb seemed to jump out of the water, creating a long golden path in front of it. And just like that they could see everything.

"Now turn around," Giancarlo instructed them.

They turned around. They saw. They sighed, wonder in their faces. Indeed, in front of them were the outlines of mountains. The distant beaches glowed white in the full moonlight, interrupted only by the bonfires they had already spied. The darkness was relieved by shapes and shadows of more and less darkness, hinting at jungles, forests and hills.

"Now, what do you see?" Solomon asked.

"Definitely land," Marina answered softly. "You can practically see from end to end, so it must be an island."

"Which island?" Jackson asked curiously. "Carey?"

Indio laughed, shaking his head. "You will see in the morning."

They stood around for a few minutes longer, and then went below to rest.

"What about you?" the pirate asked suddenly.

Jesse held up his wine glass against the light, twirling the stem between his fingers for a moment, watching the rich burgundy color slide against the crystal. Sipping from it he smacked his lips, raising his eyebrow in sign of appreciation. Setting the glass down, he looked back steadily at the pirate. "What about me?"

"What is your story?" Don Carlos raised his hand and shook his head as Jesse started to shrug him off. "Every man," he told him, "and every woman, for that matter, has a story to tell."

Jesse reached up with one hand and smoothed his hair back on his head. "I killed a man once."

Don Carlos shrugged. "So have I. A few, actually," he added, frowning to himself. The pirate had to wait a while, but the story came.

"I have known Rain, Joe's younger sister, since we were in school together. She was my best friend, smart, talented, funny, and very cute. I loved her even then. I set my heart on her and decided to win her over. When I finally did, I brought her home to meet my mother." Jesse stopped for a moment, caught up in the distant memory of his own narrative. Everyone leaned closer over the table, the better to hear Jesse, half forgotten beers held loosely between wet palms. Pablo and Joe exchanged glances. They knew something had happened once but they had never known what. It seemed like they were going to hear about it now. "I didn't realize," Jesse continued slowly, carefully, "that my father was coming home. Unexpectedly." He stopped suddenly, caught up in something only he could see.

Don Carlos held silent for a moment, until he could no longer. "I gather this wasn't a good thing," he said quietly.

Jesse laughed a harsh sound in the quiet dining hall. "My daddy belongs to a club, Don Carlos. A very private, exclusive club. They have a very special symbol. It is three K's." He stopped once again, at the collective gasps around him. They were all hearing about this now. The only one who didn't understand was Caribe. "My daddy, Don Carlos, is a white man who doesn't like black folks." Once more, his laugh was short and bitter. "He saw Rain, and he lost it."

No one spoke. No one dared. The pirate, however, was overcome by curiosity. "How so?"

Jesse smiled a slow, death smile. "His goons overpowered us. They held us down. Some of them began to help themselves to Rain." A muscle twitched in his cheek as he fought to keep from looking at Joe. "Every time I made a move towards her they wailed on me. After a while, they had to hold me up. They let me crawl to her, and hold her head, while…" His eyes scanned coldly all their faces, absorbed as they were by his words. "…they raped her." His hand went up automatically to readjust the cowboy hat that wasn't on his head right now. "And all the while, she squeezed her eyes shut, and told me how much she loved me, and how they could force her body, but they could not change her heart or capture her soul." He sighed wearily, dragging both hands down his face. He frowned for a moment. "Actually, it took Change longer to get over it, than it did Rain. My younger brother," he added for the pirates' benefit. "We've always been close. He came to participate in Rain and my mother finally meeting each other. He adores her. It was supposed to be a celebration. He walked in on what was happening, right in the middle of it. They held him back also. He was just sixteen at the time. Saw the whole thing. Cried the whole time, screaming and wailing as if they were killing him. I tried to help him. Got my face carved for my efforts. Shock lasted for days." Jesse nodded to himself. "Only scars on Rain now are inside. She can never have a baby." He sighed deeply. "But you know what? Rain is stronger than me. I thought these animals would ruin her forever. I didn't know how to touch her at the beginning. But she convinced me that the fastest…" He hesitated, shaking his head. "No, the *only* way she was ever going to get over it was if I made love to her to erase what happened. Rain is smarter than me, too. I don't believe she has completely forgotten, because we do live childless, but she is over it. She's thriving. Our sex life is good, normal, healthy… actually, quite spectacular," he admitted with a faint smile.

Joe gasped, overcome by tears. "Jesse…" he choked out. But words left him. He turned blindly to the twins. Tears ran down their faces also as their eyes sought each other.

Snake Coltrane turned back to the pirate. "The men took turns. So occupied were they with what they were doing, that they got careless. I slipped away unnoticed at one point, and came back with Daddy's shotgun." He smiled absently at something only he could see. "Blew away whoever it was on top of her at the time. Never cared to know who it was. I was only sorry I got so much blood on her, but she cleaned up just fine. And eventually, so did her mind. My mother walked in on this. See, she wasn't anything like my daddy. Savannah absolutely adored Rain, sight unseen. Still does. Even more after having met her, and known her for these past few years." He sighed. "So Savannah walks in on all of this, and doesn't ask a single question. Didn't need to. All she saw was a mess that needed some serious cleaning up. Daddy's own goons took care of the body. Savannah had a long talk with Daddy behind closed doors, and next thing I knew, I was out of the house in my own place with Rain. Marquez took care of us."

Pablo wiped at his own tears. "We remember. We just didn't know what happened, *papi*."

Jesse glared at them. "And if Rain gets wind that you know now, she will leave me, no questions asked."

Joe shook his head, anger replacing his shock. "Come on, Jesse! You know us better than that." The men fell silent for a while, as Jesse organized his thoughts, the memories as painful as ever.

"I took Change with us."

Don Carlos frowned. "Change? So the three of you left."

Jesse nodded. "I don't know how my mother did it, but Daddy never came looking." He sighed. "We all finished school, went on to college, pursued our own interests. The whole time, under Marquez' care. Eventually, Rain and I got married, and just couldn't have any children." A bark of laughter escaped him suddenly. "Except for Change. He's a regular baby making machine." At the pirate's puzzled look, he held his hand out. "He has five. And, one on the way."

Don Carlos smiled and nodded. This man would also be of his inner circle. "How would you like to work for me, Snake?"

Jesse's eyes slit, mischief making them sparkle. "I have my own business, Don Carlos. I don't have to work for anyone. I own a tattoo parlor, play with snakes as a hobby, providing serum for their venom, and I am also into the recovery of wayward children and runaways with my best friend." He smiled. "Can you afford me?"

Don Carlos closed his eyes and nodded solemnly. "Yes."

Jesse nodded, ignoring the shuddering aftermath his story had left on his family and friends. "It will be my pleasure." He held up his hand.

The pirate smiled. "The pleasure will be mine." He slid the cowboy some skin.

Salomé sat up suddenly, Indio's arm heavy across her hips. Something had woken her straight out of a dream.

"*Salomé!*" The hiss was followed by a soft rap on the door.

Sliding out of bed, she left the warmth at Indio's side, and threw on the man's shirt draped over the chair by the door. Wrapping it tightly around her, she quickly opened the door before it got knocked on again. "Marina!" she hissed back. "What time is it?"

"Time to get up," Marina grinned.

"No," moaned Salomé softly. "It's still dark." She eyed her sister warily.

"Not really. Sunrise is in a few minutes. It's getting light, baby," she sang out. Marina looked not as tired as Salomé was sure she felt, and seemed very excited in a contained way. She was practically crackling with energy, and her eyes sparkled with all the excitement.

Salomé's eyes slit with suspicion as she studied her sister. "What are you up to?"

Marina's response was automatic. "Wouldn't you like to know?" Then she shook her head, laughing softly. "Get ready and come on deck."

"No…"

"Yes!" Marina insisted firmly.

"Why?" Salomé demanded as her sister began to turn away.

Marina looked over her shoulder with a mysterious smile. "Because I know where we are." And she was gone.

A few minutes later Salomé ran into her brother outside her cabin. She grinned. "She got to you too, huh?"

Jackson grinned back. "Of course. Just like Christmas morning at home." Laughing, they quickly climbed up the steps to join their sister.

It was getting light. The sky had turned gray and getting lighter by the minute. Over the horizon, a streak of intense orange pink grew bigger and brighter. Behind it pushing at the slash of color, the sun. Like the moon the night before, its ascent was also gradual and steady but instead of creating a path of light before it, it opened the world wider, slashing at the clear blue sky. Mesmerized, they soaked in the silence of the morning quiet, but for the sound of the water lapping at the ship's sides. Faces turned towards the sun, they felt the first heat wash over them gently. Standing between them, almost bursting from excitement, Marina sang softly.

"I know where we a-are, I know where we a-are…"

"Where?"

Startled, the three of them turned around and faced the pirate crew.

"Finally!" Jackson laughed. "I thought no one was coming to rescue me."

Marina practically danced around them. "I know where we are," she told her husband, deep satisfaction evident in her voice. "But they don't."

"And how would you know, anyway?" Salomé demanded. She glanced suspiciously at their Captain. "Did you tell her last night?"

Raising an eyebrow, Gaitano glanced at her, amusement sparkling deep in his eyes. "Actually, we have better things to do…" he let his voice trail off, the insinuation clear as the man chuckled.

Disgusted, Salomé turned away. "You are such a boy!" she murmured under her breath.

"Tell us, Marina," Jackson demanded, "or I'll throw you overboard."

"Well, come look," she invited, "and if you can guess, I'll save you the throw and jump myself." Grabbing them each by the hand, she dragged them to the other side of the ship, facing land. The sun at their backs now, they gazed silently at the view before them. Sunlight made the topography stand out with crystal clear preciseness. "Look,"

Marina whispered to them. Pointing a finger, she scanned the shore-line. "A river comes out there, and there."

"How do you know?" Salomé asked, frustrated.

"You know they do," Marina answered, mysterious once more.

Jackson shook his head. "I don't see any rivers."

"Well, you're not going to see them from here," Marina rolled her eyes at him.

"All I see is beaches, groves of pine trees, and the mountains behind them," Jackson insisted.

Fascinated, the crew of La Gitana drew closer, absorbing every word.

"What are we looking for, Marina?" Salomé asked.

Marina sighed, exasperated. "You guys have got to trust me." Standing between them, she took a deep breath. "Look with the eyes of your heart, not with the eyes of your mind."

"Explain," Jackson demanded.

Sighing again, Marina rolled her eyes once more, in amuse-ment. "Jax! Come on, man! How would I know where we are?"

"You're psychic or psycho," Salomé announced. "The jury's still out."

Next to them, Solomon smiled. "I am betting on psycho," he teased.

"I will take that bet," offered Giancarlo.

The pirates laughed. Their guests ignored them.

"How about," Marina suggested softly, "maybe we've been here in our time, instead of this one?"

"What do you mean, Marina?" Salomé demanded softly. "Things change, people and places change in two or three hundred years."

"Sure they do. But it takes thousands and millions to change a mountain or a rock, don't you think?" Marina challenged.

Jackson nodded his head slowly. "I see what you're getting at," he conceded. "So, if you know where we're at, what does this look like in our time?" The pirates moved even closer, until they were right next to them.

Marina took another deep breath and smiled. "Okay." She began pointing out different places in front of them. "In our time, there are radio towers over there, and up there. People live there, there, and there. Over that way, behind that point, is a marina with really nice boats. Over on the other side, behind that other point, lies one of the world's most beautiful beaches." She paused as she felt her brother's and sister's growing excitement next to her.

"You have got to be kidding me!" Salomé exclaimed.

Jackson whistled softly. "No way!"

"Way," Marina answered happily. "There are two towers on that rock you can barely see, straight ahead in front of us, which means that there are three more condominium towers just down the beach."

Salomé gasped. "Oh, my God, Jackson," she whispered, reaching out blindly and clinging to her brother.

"Over here, way on this side is Dracula's castle."

The pirates frowned. "There is a castle there in your time?" Indio asked out of curiosity.

Jackson almost choked on his laughter. "No, dude. Not a real castle. It is just a very large hotel that took over the neighborhood, and we used to call it that because it seems to loom over everything around it. She's just playing." He shook his head slowly and wrapped his arms around his sister. "I can't believe it," he breathed.

Salomé's voice came out in a strangled whisper. "I know where we are."

"We surf there, right in front of us, and down the beach away from civilization, in the jungle, in the Northeastern Ecological Corridor." Marina sighed. "But best of all, look at the mountain behind everything. The island's major rainforest. And it's going to be nice and windy today."

"How can you tell?" Storm asked softly, not wanting to break their spell.

"Look," Marina instructed her. "You see all those shiny spots on the mountain, like silver?" She felt the pyrate nod next to her. "They are leaves," she explained softly. "Big leaves. The tops are brown, and the undersides are silver. When the breeze blows in from the ocean, it lifts them, so the mountain sparkles. When the leaves dry up and fall, the edges curl. We used to use them as umbrellas when we were children."

"*Yagrumo*," Salomé whispered. "This is *Boriken*."

The pirates' eyes never left their guests.

Jackson's eyes shone with tears, and more tears ran down the girls' faces. "This is our town, dude," Jackson choked out.

"Papi was born here," Marina explained, turning to her husband.

"Do we get to stop and play?" Salomé demanded.

"I'm going at least body surfing," Jackson muttered, taking off his shirt.

"No. Not yet," Indio told them.

"We will come back tomorrow," Giancarlo reassured them before their faces fell.

"We have to see someone first," Storm explained.

"So, where are we going?" Jackson demanded.

"The city," their Captain rumbled next to them, making them all turn towards him. "San Juan."

The siblings sighed, visibly moved, their emotions raw, expressed in their eyes and their faces.

Salomé choked on a laugh. "In our time, we call it *Old* San Juan." The pirates smiled.

Jackson turned his face for a moment into Salomé's hair before lifting it to look at his brothers-in-law. "Thank you, man. Thanks for bringing us home. Papi's gonna freak when he finds out. We will remember this as long as we live."

One by one, the Aguilar-Banks embraced and kissed their pirate friends in gratitude. Then they drifted off together by themselves to express their joy and wonder.

Indio turned to his brother. The two men searched each other's eyes for a moment, before falling into an embrace themselves. "This was really good, Carlitos," Indio whispered in his brother's ear.

"I guess so," Carlos whispered back. Smiling, they let go. Gaitano laughed, happy at the gift he had just presented to his wife and her family. "*Tiburón*! San Juan!"

They sailed as close to the shoreline as they possibly could. Excited, the travelers named the places they knew in their own time. It was breathtaking. Bright sunshine washed over the land, bringing everything to light. They took turns looking through spyglasses, calling out to each other. Once they got to a place they knew in modern times as Piñones, the anchor got thrown once more. It was barely the middle of the day and the sun beat down fiercely on their heads. The pirates and their guests faced off in the middle of Tiburón's deck.

"We're not moving," Marina told her husband, a frown beginning to crease her brow. "I thought we were going to San Juan."

"We are, Marina," Gaitano explained patiently. "We are just not going to *sail* into San Juan." He smiled at her. "We go on shore here and ride horses the rest of the way. Do not forget the whole city is a fortress. They are constantly looking out for the likes of us."

Marina pressed her lips together and nodded her head. She tried smiling back at him, but it never reached her eyes. "Okay, so we ride in," she agreed softly.

The pirate snatched her hand and pulled her towards him before she could walk away. "Wait a moment. What's wrong?" Shaking her head she tried pulling away. He just held her closer. "Talk to me. You were ecstatic a couple of hours ago. Why are you doubting now?" He frowned as she shook her head again, straining out of his grasp, reaching for her siblings in a totally theatrical fashion. If he weren't so confused, he would laugh.

Over to the side, Jackson was beckoning. "Dude!"

Taking a deep breath, the pirate squeezed his wife's hand and went to join them, his crew right at his side. "Jackson…"

"Houston!" Salomé cut in. Frustrated, she shook her head, her long black hair flying about her face, clouding her distress.

"Salomé," answered Gaitano carefully. "What is the problem?"

Salomé paced for a moment in front of them, before finally shaking her hair out of her face. "What is the political and socio-economic status of the island at this moment in time?"

Confused, it was the pirates' turn to shake their heads. "What?" Solomon asked, absolutely puzzled at the change in their guests.

Giancarlo smiled gently. "Those are very big words for such a pretty girl." He grinned as Salomé rolled her eyes at him. "Explain to us, simple folks, what it is that you want."

"What she means," Jackson explained, "is, what is going on around here these days?"

"What year is it?" Salomé asked. As mouths opened to answer, she threw her hands in the air to stop them. "No! Wait! I don't want to know!"

Marina pulled her hand away from her husband's grasp and hugged her sister. "We really don't want to know," she agreed softly.

Giancarlo smiled, puzzled. "*Muchachos*," he called to them in an effort to ease the tension. "What does it matter, what year it is?" All eyes turned to look at him.

"If you haven't noticed," Salomé informed them, "Jackson and I, and Marina to some extent for that matter, are racially challenged."

"We're black," Jackson explained quickly at their puzzled frowns.

"Slavery is abolished on this island in the year 1873," Marina said quietly.

The crew fell silent for a moment, understanding dawning on their faces. Storm shook her head, hands reaching out for Jackson's. "It hasn't happened yet," she told them sadly.

"So, we are worth nothing on this rock?" Salomé asked mournfully.

Indio chuckled as he pulled her closer to him, away from Marina, wrapping his huge arms around her. "Salomé," he crooned, pressing a kiss on the top of her head, "you will never be worth nothing here or anywhere else you go on this planet. Anytime." He laughed softly, the sound rolling inside his chest. "*Nena*, it doesn't matter what the political socio-economic status is," he teased gently. "Besides, take a look around you. We are all racially challenged, as you say."

"Yeah, but as slaves?" she asked, tears beginning to sting the backs of her eyes.

"Salo," the Captain distracted her, "where is your sense of adventure? Where is the woman who single-handedly orchestrated a lap dance in Carey a few weeks ago?"

"This is different," Salomé pouted beautifully. "Race was not an issue on that occasion."

"And it's not an issue now, *preciosa*," Gaitano reassured her. "Imagine Solomon if it were."

"Yeah, but he's a pirate. He's a free man," she protested.

"And you are a free woman," he insisted. "Relax. Solomon gets along here just fine." He chuckled. "As far as everybody who knows us here is concerned, I'm a sea merchant, nephew to Don Juan Gaitano. These are my sailors," he laughed as he waved a hand to include his crew. "Don't worry," he assured her. "We have clothes for you to wear. While we are out in public, be smart. Keep your eyes and your ears open, and your mouth closed." He grinned as Salomé rolled her eyes at him. "You learn more that way. Trust us. You'll be fine. Besides, where we are taking you it doesn't matter, *mami*, it just does not matter."

Taking a deep breath, Salomé finally relaxed. "Okay," she nodded, "I trust you." Pulling free from Indio, she wiped at her tears. Pushing Marina to one side, she fell into the pirate's arms. "I'm sorry I'm such a baby, Carlitos," she whispered.

"It's okay," he reassured her, his low voice soothing.

"I do trust you, you know, it's just that this gets so scary at times."

"I understand."

"You are so absolutely cool, and so awesome for Marina, dude. I adore you," she confessed.

The pirate sighed, happiness washing over him like a wave. It was at moments like this that he was convinced he had been directed by a higher force. "Cool," he answered. "I'm crazy about you too." He hugged her, squeezing her tight for a moment, his eyes meeting his brother's over her shoulder. Dropping a kiss on top of her head and another on her upturned face, he finally let her go. "I suggest we all get our things and prepare to go ashore. Let's move, guys, San Juan..."

They were spellbound. The village of Loíza had one of the largest concentrations of African slaves on the island, and it was quite evident as they made their way. The Aguilar-Banks realized that they couldn't rightfully describe the changes a few centuries make to an environment, especially if most of the environment includes population explosions, and man made structures. No, they really couldn't describe it, so they didn't even try. It was too difficult. Their raging feelings inside barely let them assimilate what their eyes were seeing and communicating to them. It was exciting and disturbing at the same time. Complete areas of the city that they knew to be well populated in their time, teeming with local and foreign tourists, were yet to be established and seemed desolate to them in comparison.

Soon they were in the city. It was busier than every other place they just left behind them. People milled around the streets, voices calling in different tongues, but predominantly Spanish. As they strolled the cobble stoned streets of San Juan, they pointed out landmarks they recognized, and old buildings that were still brand new. They were not nervous anymore, not really. The pirates watched with curiosity as they stood on different street corners, discussing in hushed tones as they pointed to different buildings.

"Gaitanos!"

They all looked up as a group of men approached them.

"*Oficial!*" The men responded in greeting, eyes twinkling. There was no end to their amusement. Their real identities were solidly hidden and they had fun fooling the local law. The men greeted each other.

"Haven't seen you in a while!" one of them exclaimed stepping forward to vigorously shake hands. There were two more hanging back, watching the girls.

Following their gaze, Gaitano stepped up. "*Caballeros, mi esposa, Marina Aguilar de Gaitano,*" he said, formally introducing her as his wife.

The men's eyes widened even as they visibly retreated. They took turns bending low over Marina's hand. Then they turned their attention to her sister.

"Indio," the officer said thoughtfully, "would you happen to know of anyone I could hire as a housekeeper?"

Indio grunted, putting a possessive arm around her shoulders. "The free woman, Salomé, is my woman," he informed them, "so, no," raising an eyebrow at them.

The men laughed, glancing at the remaining female.

Storm shook her head, laughing at them. "Uh-uh! Do not even think about it! I know your wives!" Hooking her arm through Jackson's, she pressed her body against his. "Besides, I now belong to Jackson Banks."

The leader beamed in approval as if he were a proud father. "Congratulations and best wishes to all of you! Enjoy your stay in San Juan!" And they parted ways.

The pirate and his crew shuffled up and down cobble stoned streets until they reached an arch in a wall with a scrolled iron gate. The sun was setting behind the city, and its rays slanted in the courtyard beyond. Giancarlo pushed his way to the front of the group. The Captain stopped him with a look. "Tío Juan!" he called into the building.

"Carlitos!" The prompt reply came from somewhere inside. The man himself made an appearance, his welcoming smile bright in his handsome face. It hadn't been so long since the last time they saw each other, Carlos and Marina's wedding having taken place barely a few days earlier. His shirt billowed as he strode towards them, framing a gold cross hanging from a black cord around his neck. The boots on his feet were worn and soft, quiet as he approached. Clanging some keys he quickly unlocked the gate and ushered them in. "Come in! Come in!" He stayed to lock the gate again and followed them inside. In the middle of the courtyard they met with the Council.

Salomé laughed. "You guys are everywhere!"

The pirates laughed with her. Sultan stepped up, his pants cut off like a regular sailor's, a tiger skin vest adorning his torso, a lion's claw set in gold rolling on his bare black chest. Gold hoops graced his ears and his nipples. His head was bare and smooth, making him look like an older version of Solomon. Or Mr. Clean. "So are you, Salomé," he teased. "You have become a good pyrate."

Salomé nodded, acting coy as she teased him back. "Well, you know, have to keep up with the boys."

Jai-Ling turned to Marina. She would never stop being in awe of this bare-chested samurai. Her eyes stung as she thought of Xaira back home. Regardless of the sword strapped to his back, the imposing Asian commanded respect and exuded confidence. At the moment, his black almond eyes became glittering slits from amusement. "Are you still fighting Solomon?" he demanded.

Both Marina and Solomon looked at each other and laughed. "Always," they admitted at the same time.

"I can't stop them," Carlos said, shaking his head mournfully.

Suleiman clapped him on the shoulder. The turban on his head and the crescent sword at his hip as familiar to them as the attire of the pirates they frequented on a daily basis. His teeth flashed white against his dark face as he laughed. "You cannot stop what is in their hearts."

Carlos lifted his hands in mock defeat. "I give up."

"Aguilar-Banks!" The voice seemed to roll towards them in the same manner as when distant thunder grows closer. The time traveling trio sighed with pleasure at the sight of the man with the voice. Don Miguel Gaitano rolled as he strode towards them, his size being quite larger than just about everybody else's present in the courtyard. Black hair was streaked with gray, gold hoops graced his ears, and a large smile illuminated his face. The scar was still there, running from ear to chin. The potential for terrifying and stopping grown men in their tracks was still there. They had discovered that the pirate had a certain power, an invisible energy that he displayed at will, capable of making a person tremble from fear or wanting to cry. They had witnessed it with their own eyes, besides the fact that their dads had experienced it firsthand. Pablo and Joe had actually had to hold back tears as fear struck their hearts when they had caught a glimpse into the pirate's true heart during the taking of *La Diosa del Mar*, to which they had been invited. But this wasn't Blackbeard. It was Don Miguel, the legendary Captain of *La Gaviota*. Their new uncle. The one their parents wished had been around while they had been growing up to help keep them in line. "My daughters," he exclaimed happily, opening his arms wide and scooping both Marina and Salome against his chest. Squeezing them until they squealed, he laughed heartily and kissed them on the cheek, on their foreheads, on the top of their heads, one after another. Finally, he rubbed noses with each of them before letting them go, before turning to Jackson. "My son," he said affectionately, running his hand along the black corn rows. Looking deep into the tiger eyes, he embraced the girls' brother, kissing him on the cheek affectionately. A final hug and he released him. "How was your trip over?"

Jackson grinned at the pirate. "I can't believe we are here. Last time we visited it looked much different," he laughed.

Tío Miguel laughed with him. "I'll bet."

"Gian!"

"Rouge!" They all turned to look. Everyone's favorite lady pyrate came flying through the courtyard, flinging herself into the Sailing Master's arms. Giancarlo caught her against him, closing his eyes as she smothered him with kisses, her fiery locks mixing with his own ebony curls. Her name tore from his throat with a moan. "Rouge…"

Throwing her head back, Rouge laughed, even as tears streamed from her eyes. "Giancarlo Ilarraza," she finally gasped. Holding his handsome face between her hands, she smiled at him through her tears. "I have missed you so much…"

"Later," Jack laughed, his own fiery curls confirming his blood relation to the beautiful lady pyrate. First cousins, they were, always looking out for each other, although they commanded their own ships and crews. "La Gitana," he greeted his friends respectfully, as they all moved further inside the building. "All is well, I trust."

The men nodded. Moments later, they found themselves sitting on the far side of the courtyard, amidst potted palm trees, next to a fountain. Huge, tall elaborate cages contained exquisite tropical birds in bright, beautiful radiant colors. Servants moved around quietly, lighting torches and pouring wine, while they were serenaded by the tiny tree frogs typical of the island.

Carlos took a sip of his wine and held the glass loosely in one hand, swirling the liquid inside, while reaching for Marina's hand with the other. He turned to look at her for a moment as they locked fingers, and winked at her, knowing quite well what the gesture usually did to her. She smiled at him, and he looked back at their hosts.

"So, here we are," he said, a hint of amusement in his voice. "The Council *and* Tío Juan. It must be serious."

The younger of his uncles leaned forward, elbows on his knees, his own wine glass between his hands. "It is, Carlitos. Very serious."

Indio's voice rumbled as usual from next to his brother. "We must be in trouble. How much?"

Juan laughed without humor. "Plenty."

"Actually," Tío Miguel corrected. "Not you, boys. But your girls are." Shocked silence immediately followed his words. It didn't last long.

"No way!" Jackson exclaimed, fighting to not jump to his feet.

"Way," Jack said solemnly.

Jackson frowned, thinking for a moment. "This is about Xavier, isn't it?"

"It is," Juan Gaitano confirmed. Once again, they all fell silent.

Xavier had been an issue for the pirates for most of their lives. They had grown up together as teenagers on the island of Encantada, a young crew of pirates in training. The young man had removed himself from their lives, thanks to Indio, following a rape he had committed against a young woman in their group. The young woman had mysteriously disappeared, however, never to be heard from again. Throughout the years they had encountered the dashing young man sporadically. Being all pirates sailing the same waters, they tended to run into each other now and then. Just recently they had discovered that the suave young man, as smooth as he was handsome, was just as evil. They had also learned that he was much more in their lives than they had ever imagined possible. Actually, they had been absolutely clueless. But once Marina and Salomé had come into their lives, courtesy of the freak storms that created the time warp creating the portal bridgeing their different worlds, the truth had come out. Xavier had not only had a secret vendetta against the younger Gaitano brothers, but he had also exhibited the worst psychotic behavior they had ever personally experienced. Xavier had turned out to be the mystical elusive figure known as the White Ghost, single handedly extinguishing whole communities of natives along their islands, just as the conquistadors had before him when they came to the New World. Marina had uncovered the truth slowly and painfully, thanks to a combination of process of elimination, and good old twenty-first century deduction. It turned out that, as she had expressed to the young pirates on a few occasions, Xavier wanted anything and everything that was theirs. Especially anything that was Carlos Gaitano's. It turned out to be personal. The stakes had risen when Carlitos claimed her in a cave full of pirates at the notorious annual pirate's ball called *El Baile del Luto*, or the Mourning Dance, which had taken place in Carey, the local pirates' headquarters barely more than a month ago. On that particular occasion the event had almost ended in a blood bath but thankfully had not. Recently Xavier had reappeared once more in their lives just a few weeks before. The encounter had ended in his own demise at the hands of the accountant of La Gitana, Marina Aguilar.

Salomé's voice broke in the growing shadows. "They want revenge, don't they? Xavier's men? They want revenge for the death of Xavier…" her voice trailed off, choking her. Her hand reached blindly for Indio's, at the same time the young brave's sought hers.

Marina's eyes stung with sudden tears, her throat almost closing up on her. Her words came out in a strangled whisper. "Fucking Xavier!" Someone was calling her from far, far away.

"Marina…" She looked up into Jack's sad eyes. It seemed to her as if each time he said her name lately it was with heart breaking pity. "Marina," he repeated when he got her attention. "Xavier isn't coming, darling, you took care of that. But his men are." He took a deep breath and nodded solemnly. "In force." He spread his hands, seeking confirmation.

Marina looked around at the rest of the Council. Rouge nodded sadly, tears in her own eyes.

"It is true," Jai-Ling informed her. "But you are a mighty warrior, Aguilar. You shall be well taken care of."

"To the best of our ability, Marina," Suleiman confirmed, his sword winking in the candlelight.

Sultan thought for a moment. He was barely visible but for the flickering light dancing on his skin. Finally, the familiar lion's claw rolled on his bare chest as he flexed his powerful muscles. "There have been rumors, and we can only speculate." Marina tore her swimming eyes away from his for a moment and glanced at Jack, who nodded again. She took a deep shuddery breath. Jack had been right last time, also, as much as she denied it, and he would never joke or lie about something like that. She looked back at the mighty African. "You have saved our trade, so to speak," he smiled wickedly, "in these Caribbean waters."

"What he means, is," Rouge called out softly, "we will do anything for you, baby."

"Anything?" Jackson wondered out loud.

"Anything!" Jack answered passionately.

This time, it was Tío Miguel's voice that rumbled in the creeping dark. "I suppose what we are trying to say, Marina, is that we will protect you with our lives if necessary. However, you have a choice. You already come from another world." He sighed, turning to his nephews. "Maybe it's time you boys cashed in, so to speak, and went exploring. Other worlds, other times…" He shrugged his massive shoulders. The suggestion suspended in the air, floating in their minds along with the tiny tree frogs' song. "Storm also," the older pirate continued, stroking his scar thoughtfully, turning to the young woman next to Jackson. "You are too smart and beautiful to stay on a ship full of females. Besides, I would be disappointed if you were to leave Jackson."

Storm shook her head quickly. "Never!" she declared passionately.

Tío Miguel nodded. "Jackson is not of our world, however," he pointed out. "Entertaining and enlightening as he is, he does not belong here. Neither do his sisters."

Carlos glowered at his uncle, his heart thundering in his chest. "Marina is my wife," he growled.

Tío Miguel shrugged again. "So you go with her. All of you. Go."

Juan nodded solemnly from his seat. He took a drink of his wine and smacked his lips quietly. "I agree with Miguel. Carlos and María Isabel are already gone into their world. Go, boys. Do not tempt fate. Wait for Xavier's men to catch up with you, face them and get out."

Giancarlo moved restlessly, looking at Rouge before turning back to the men. "If Carlitos, who is our Captain, and Indio, the Quartermaster leave, what happens to us?" he asked. "What happens to La Gitana?"

The older Gaitano brothers looked at each other silently before turning back to their nephews and their crew. "You are wealthy enough to disappear. To drop off the face of the earth. We suggest you do just that," Tío Miguel told him.

"The Council is willing to buy you out," Rouge explained quietly. "Completely. We are talking about *La Gitana*," she began counting the younger Gaitanos' ships with her fingers, "*Star Fish*, *Tiburon*, *Poseidon…*" She stopped to shake the hair out of her face, turning her soft brown eyes to Indio. "Even *La Diosa del Mar*," she added, referring to the Spanish galleon they had recently captured, whose precious cargo had consisted of African slaves, diamonds, and gold.

"How would you explain our disappearance?" Indio challenged his uncles. He had been in charge of the capture of the galleon, and most of the treasure had gone to him.

Tío Miguel shrugged with a laugh. "Ships sink…" His words hung in the air, making the young time travelers shudder.

Rouge turned to Giancarlo. "Let's go with them, baby," she urged softly.

Giancarlo turned startled eyes on her. "You would do that?"

"I would follow you anywhere," she declared passionately. Her chest rose with a deep breath. "That would mean, the Council would take on the *Sea Gypsy* also," she added quietly, referring to her own ship.

"*I* would take the *Sea Gypsy*," Jack said. "Keep it in the family."

"What about me?" a quiet voice interrupted them. Everyone turned to look at Solomon, who had held his silence even as his thoughts raged inside him. He hadn't known the younger Gaitano brothers since teenagers, as had Giancarlo, Rouge, and Jack. But he was a member of the crew of La Gitana. He was the Boatswain, and his position was as important as each of theirs. Besides, he had saved his Captain's life. Twice. *And*, he thought to himself, *Marina needs me to fight with.*

Tío Miguel laughed, eerily reading his thoughts. "I suppose you would have to go also. After all, you are part of the crew. And Marina's pet," he added wickedly.

"No doubt," Jackson said, his laugh sounding hollow even to himself.

Carlos squeezed his wife's hand, even as his eyes sought his brother's. "This is something we need to discuss," he said slowly.

Indio nodded in agreement, tossing his head, making his long hair billow like a cloud around his shoulders. "We need to talk about this."

Juan smiled. "You have a choice. But you are smart men. We trust you to make the right one."

"Take your time and think about it," Tío Miguel advised them, "but don't think too much. You do not have all the time in the world. Your father said he would be back on the next storm. That is in a few days. You have until just before then to make up your minds in order for us to take care of matters should you decide to leave." He waited as his nephews exchanged long silent looks. "Now enough said. Who's hungry? We have been expecting you. For tonight you are our honored guests."

Eat, drink, and be merry. That's what they did. Or at least, what they tried to do. Their meal was light but satisfying. Somehow, nobody had much of an appetite. The place they were at turned out to be Juan's. Being the man in charge of transporting prisoners back and forth in the seas, he needed headquarters in San Juan. There were two stories, with beautiful arched and tiled hallways, where mosaics graced the walls and scrolled iron was used as decoration. Villa Azul back in Encantada, Don Carlos and María Isabel's home, was an echo of this place. At the moment, he had the whole Council staying with him while they cleared up the situation that had come up, and now the crew of La Gitana. Once their meal was over, the dessert consisted of a peace pipe which was passed around once, before it disappeared. Although night had completely fallen on them no one was sleepy. The sky over the courtyard showed off its canopy of stars, the still full moon creeping along its course.

The pirates watched their visitors closely. Jackson sat cradling Storm in his lap, the two of them speaking quietly and urgently. Every once in a while he would stop to kiss her deeply. She in turn would hold on to him, distress evident in her body language as she wrapped her arms around him, clinging to him with all her might. Marina and Salomé stood to one side, moving towards and away from each other, in an old ritual they grew up watching their mothers do whenever there was something to think about and figure out. They paced in opposite directions, turned, walked towards each other, passed, and turned again. Over and over in a nervous dance, once in a while stopping to exchange words in hushed voices. All the pirates could detect was the desperation and frustration in their tones.

Marina fought the tears that were threatening to overwhelm her. Reaching out, she stopped her sister as they were about to pass each other once more. "Salo! I fucked up, didn't I?"

Salomé shook her head, her hair flying about her face. "No, baby! No! Don't say that!" She hissed at her sister, not wanting to be overheard, and not wanting her to stumble after they had come so far. "You did what you had to do. What was going to happen anyways. It just so happened to be at your hands." She peered deep into the hazel eyes she loved so well.

Marina bit her lip before finally nodding. "You are right," she whispered. "Carlos would have done it, if I hadn't."

Salomé nodded. "There you go. Chill, baby," she cautioned softly. Their eyes locked for a moment. Then turning away from each other, they continued their pacing.

Close by, Carlos and Indio sat facing each other, heads close together.

"Indio," Carlos said softly in the dark. "We are going to have to decide. Fast." He frowned, shaking his head. "This isn't looking good for us."

Indio nodded, his voice rumbling deep in his chest. "It doesn't, I agree. But are we ready to give up our lives, all we have known forever, to go into this foreign place, this future world?"

"Scared?"

"Yes."

"Me too," Carlos sighed.

"But I am even more scared of us losing the girls," Indio confessed in a hushed tone.

Carlos took a deep breath, raking a hand through his thick curls. "So am I."

To one side, the rest of the pirates were watching what was going on with their guests.

Juan sighed, crossing his arms over his chest and stretching his long legs in front of him. "They all seem a bit upset," he observed.

"Were you expecting otherwise?" his brother asked.

Juan shook his head ruefully. "No, I suppose not."

"Marina can barely contain herself," Giancarlo pointed out, playing with Rouge's hair absently.

Jack snorted softly. "How would you feel if Xavier's men were after you?"

"I would be terrified," Rouge admitted softly, "and I pride myself of not being scared of anything. Or at least, not of much."

"Marina is freaking out," Solomon observed. As everybody turned to look at him, he shrugged. "That is what *they* call it."

"If she is freaking out, as you say," Sultan responded quietly, "she will not be able to think clearly now, will she?"

"It is not for us to make light of the matter," Suleiman told them. "We are not in their position."

"Agreed," Jai-Ling conceded, "but all that nervous energy should be directed elsewhere. What would it take to distract her, right now?"

The older Gaitano brothers looked at each other and laughed softly. Juan shook his head at the Asian man. "You called her a mighty warrior. What do you think?"

Tío Miguel shook as his own laughter rolled in his chest. "Only one thing, right now. Only one person." He called out to the beautiful young woman his nephew had taken as his life partner. "Marina!" Getting her attention, he beamed at her. "Why don't you play with Solomon?" He grinned wickedly. "We would be privileged to watch you kick his ass."

Carlos' head shot up. "No!" He protested. "He has gotten much better. He hurts her."

Marina rushed to the pirates. "Oh, but it hurts so good!" she declared with a grin, distracted already. Turning her head to look at her husband, she met his eyes. "Yes." Then she shrugged in a flirtatious manner. "I'll let you fix me up afterwards."

Her husband grinned back. "Solomon!" he called out to his Boatswain. "If you would please, fight my wife…" He rolled his eyes in defeat.

Solomon smiled slowly, moving backwards to the center of the courtyard. "The pleasure will be all mine." Standing straight, he slapped his hands to his sides and bowed deeply. "Marina," he sang out softly, in the accustomed way that had become a ritual to them, "come out and play…"

They fought. Carlos had given up long ago on the notion of keeping his wife and Boatswain away from each other. They had gone into huge, lengthy discussions about it, and he could never seem to convince her that fighting the young African was hazardous to her health. Actually, she thrived on it. And so did the young man. The Boatswain absolutely adored his wife, and had found meaning to his life in their physical relationship. He had grown harder and stronger, and she had become quicker and meaner. Savages, the both of them. But Carlos respected their need for exercise and their mutual joy in physical pain. It was something he couldn't give his wife, and yet he couldn't deny her. Instead, he had ended up accepting that she had a dark side that, although it had come out strong after they met and she found herself in the company of pirates, he couldn't really control. In his own dark heart, he did not want to. He absolutely loved her darkness. It matched his own. And she really wasn't hurting anyone, since Solomon had gotten so good at Tae Kwon Do. If you didn't count Xavier, that is. Marina had absolutely killed him.

Indio grunted. "They make it look so…"

"Cool!" Jackson laughed. "Come on, dog, you and me."

Indio accepted, getting to his feet. He quickly braided his hair and followed his brother-in-law. "I have been wanting to kick your ass for a long time," he teased.

Jackson snorted in disgust. "In your dreams."

Salomé turned to her brother's girl. "That leaves you and me, baby. Let's go." Beckoning, she went to join the fighting men.

"Sure," Storm shrugged. "But I don't have much practice."

"That's okay," Salomé told her. "I promise not to hurt you." She smiled slyly. "Much." Her eyes slit fiercely, green fire glowing from within. "I'll give you a taste of what will happen to you…" she whispered, "…if you ever hurt my brother." She laughed throatily. "I promise."

Storm turned to look at Jackson's sister, to see if she meant it. Her skin prickled and the hair stirred on the back of her neck. "Yes," she breathed, knowing Salomé meant what she said. They may get along, but Salomé and Jackson shared blood and genes.

The courtyard filled with the sounds of fighting, as the three pairs danced around each other.

Don Miguel Gaitano spread his hands. "And that," he informed his companions, "is how you distract the Aguilar-Banks."

Later that night, Carlos and Marina found themselves alone in their guest bedroom. His uncles had convinced him to stop watching, and prepare for her instead. He had balms and ointments ready for her on a tray, and next to the beautiful four-poster bed was a deep tub with claw feet filled with water he had heated himself while he waited for her to finish playing with Solomon. He ended up joining her in it, and what was supposed to be nice and relaxing became a water fight instead. Did he mention she was a savage? Candles burned about the room, the occasional one sizzling as it got splashed. Marina screamed with laughter as he threatened to dunk her into the bubbles he had so lovingly put in her bath water, quickly covering her mouth as she remembered where they were. Her husband just smiled wickedly. Finally he stopped teasing her and approached her with a large sponge. She smiled in contentment and sat up, knelt, and stood up accordingly, giving him access to her body, the better to clean her. Finally they were dried and sitting on the bed, he in clean cut-off pants, and she, just wearing his shirt. By candlelight, he offered the creams to her, before beginning the process of healing. She was bruised just a little this time, but he knew it was just this time. One of his secret concerns was that one of them, either his wife or his Boatswain, would kill the other without meaning to one day. He prayed it never happened, and if it were ever to come to that, he prayed he would be there to stop it from happening. A soft knock sounded on their door, interrupting his thoughts.

"Come in," he called out, smiling at his wife's expression.

A middle-aged woman peered around the door, her beautiful dark face highlighted by the candle she was holding in one hand, the white fabric wrapped around her head covering her hair shining in the light. "I am sorry to interrupt, Carlitos," she grinned. Rolling her eyes comically, she sighed dramatically. "Tío Juan sent me."

Carlos grinned back, beckoning her to come inside. "It's okay. Marina, this is my uncle's housekeeper, Ana. She's been with him ever since he got this place. Her husband and children are also employed by the Gaitanos."

Bustling inside, she walked right by them towards the now cool bathtub. They saw that she had a stack of sheets held in her free arm. Grinning, she put her candle down on the table next to them, and proceeded to throw the sheets on the floor around the tub. These rapidly got soaked as they absorbed all the water they had splashed. "Actually, Juanito wanted me to make sure you hadn't drowned Marina." Going back to them, she laughed softly as she caught the young woman's embarrassment. Picking up the candle once more, she nodded encouragingly at them. "Now. Drown her with your love, Carlitos," she advised with a wink. Walking away, she chuckled softly. "That is what she really needs."

Once the door closed behind her Marina moaned, covering her face with her hands. Her husband laughed, taking her hands away, and kissed away any shame she felt. Getting back to the ointments, he rubbed her sore muscles. Once that was out of the way, he proceeded to obey and do just what the very wise Ana suggested. Marina was delighted.

They were up before the sun. The Council saw them off under a canopy of morning stars. The moon had completed its course and had gone to rest behind the distant mountains.

The older Gaitano brothers turned to their nephews. "What are your plans, boys?" Juan wanted to know.

Carlos sighed. "We will go back to Encantada, but it is only fair that the Aguilar-Banks see Boriken as it is now, before they leave."

Indio agreed. "Dawn is still a few hours away. If we go right now, it will still be early morning by the time we reach the big river. It would be nice to take them up to the mountains for a little while."

"Then we need to take them to the beach at Pablo's home town. They caught a glimpse of it yesterday morning as we were coming in. They would never forgive us if we didn't make it there," Carlos explained.

Tío Miguel nodded. "Very well. We will give you a couple of days, and then we will set sail right behind you." He waved his hand at the Council. "All of us. We will wait for your father to come back and you decide what to do. If you haven't made up your mind by then, I am sure he will assist you." He smiled lovingly at the young people before them. "God bless and Godspeed. See you soon."

A round of goodbyes, accompanied by a loving expression from Rouge towards Giancarlo, and the crew of La Gitana was gone.

"Khan!"

"Master!" Khan bowed and shook his hand, in the way of Tae Kwon Do.

"Nice to see you, son. Come in." Pablo smiled at the young man and ushered him inside. "How are things? Your family doing good?"

"Yes, sir." They walked through the house to the inner courtyard. The days were getting progressively warmer and nicer, making swimming pools more inviting than in the recent weeks. "We missed your classes this past month." The classes he was referring to were the ones Pablo and Joe gave at their own Tae Kwon Do academy.

"Yeah, well, sorry about that. Something incredibly unexpected came up."

Pablo steered his guest to the far side where a beautiful wrought iron table with a glass top could be found next to some potted palms. A brightly colored umbrella decorated with a bright coral starfish with neon green and yellow accents draped over a stunning royal blue background kept them in the shade. The sun filtered through the nylon fabric, making the colors glow on the inside, creating a cool effect on the table.

Turning to Joe, Khan saluted. "Master…"

Joe saluted back. "Khan…"

Pablo grinned. "How were classes with Derek and Tyler?"

Khan laughed, a deep throaty sound that rumbled in his broad chest. "Fine. Just not the same."

"You're spoiled," Joe teased.

"Yeah, whatever. I still rather continue my classes with you guys."

"Not classes anymore, since Derek and Tyler are instructors. You missed your private lessons. Like I said, spoiled."

"Like I said, whatever."

Pablo chuckled. "Come, meet my guests." Stopping at the table, he proceeded to introduce his in-laws. "Don Carlos Gaitano and María Isabel Sandoval."

"Don Carlos," Khan greeted politely, reaching out to shake hands. When the woman stretched out hers, he hesitated. She was absolutely beautiful in an exotic way he couldn't describe, stunning for her age. Definitely in the ranks of Sloane, and Shayla, and his own mother. Instead of shaking her hand, he found himself doing something he had never done before in his life. He bowed, and kissed her hand instead. "María Isabel."

A fifth chair was drawn to the table and they all sat down. Bottles of cold water were passed around and they all leaned back and look at one another. The pirate and the young man studied each other for a moment. Khan was tall and muscular, like a basketball player. His skin was dark, partly from the sun, mostly from his Mediterranean heritage. Black hair clung to his scalp in tight waves, large brown eyes with long lashes held both intelligence and curiosity. His face was finely chiseled with high cheekbones and a firm jaw. Beautiful strong teeth flashed bright as he smiled. "How is the little sister?"

Pablo nodded with a smile. "Marina is just fine, thank you."

The pirate frowned. "Little sister?" He turned to his host, motioning to the young man. "Another child of yours?"

Pablo laughed. "No, no, not like that. Khan and his brothers work for Cat. Actually, Marina used to hang with the youngest of them, a few years ago."

Khan turned to look at the pirate, a ghost of his smile gracing his face. "His name was Sheik. He was one of Jackson's best friends and Marina's boyfriend. He was killed."

Don Carlos hid his shock as well as he could. "I am sorry for your loss."

Khan shrugged at the unspoken question. "Sheik was at the wrong place at the wrong time." He sighed. "He knew better."

"Marina is now married to Don Carlos' son, Carlitos," Joe put in quickly, before any unwanted sadness filled the air. At Khan's surprised expression, he laughed. "I know, I know, it happened very quickly."

Khan nodded thoughtfully. "Is it good?"

Everyone nodded. Pablo put a hand over his heart. "Yes. It is a very good thing."

The young man frowned. "Forgive my surprise. I hadn't heard."

"Don't worry," Joe assured him, "no one has. Yet."

Khan nodded slowly and turned to the pirate. "Marina is a fabulous girl. Your son is very lucky."

Don Carlos nodded back, smiling. "Yes, he is. They both are."

Khan took a sip of his water and laughed softly. He turned to his masters. "What can I do for you?"

"We need your services."

He grinned. "Which would those be?"

"Oh, I don't know," Joe teased him. "Maybe some of that underground work you do in that fantastic basement of yours."

Khan nodded slowly, turning curiously to the pirate and his wife. "I suppose this has to do with you."

Don Carlos spread his hands. "I understand I can afford you."

María Isabel, quiet until now, smiled at him. "We would be very grateful if you would help us, Khan. We hear you are the best at what you do."

"I am." He thought for a moment. "What do you need?"

The pirates turned to their hosts. Joe moved forward, putting his arms on the table, rolling the water bottle between his hands. "We need ID's."

Khan nodded. "Just the two of you?"

"No," María Isabel answered, "there are three of us."

"I see. Who's the third?"

"He is a young man named Caribe. You'll like him. He's hanging out with Xaira right now," Pablo explained.

"Okay," Khan replied slowly. He turned to the pirate once again. "I hope you don't mind me asking you a few questions, Don

Carlos. I am very particular about who I take on as my clients. It is the secret of my success," he explained.

The pirate laughed and spread his hands. "Go ahead."

"Where are you originally from?"

"The Caribbean."

"Why don't you have an ID already?"

"They don't have them where I come from."

Stunned, Khan just looked at him. "I must say, I haven't heard that one yet." He studied the pirate more carefully. "You understand most of the people I deal with are criminals of some kind or another."

Don Carlos nodded. "I understand. We are."

"How so?"

"We are pirates."

"Pirates?" Khan laughed. "I thought most modern day pirates, were mainly drug runners. Either that, or Somalian pirates preying on passing ships."

"No, we don't run drugs," Don Carlos said thoughtfully. "And we are not modern day pirates from Somalia."

"So, what kind of pirates are you?"

"The original kind."

Khan sighed deeply and turned to his hosts. "Explain."

Pablo and Joe looked at each other. "Should we?" Joe asked.

It was Pablo's turn to sigh. "I think we should."

Joe turned back to Khan. "Salomé and Marina got a little lost during Spring Break. They did a little time traveling," he said carefully, looking him in the eyes. "Landed themselves in the Golden Age of Piracy."

"They are still there," Pablo added, "and no, there is no way for us to prove it, except to say that we couldn't make this up if we tried. Carlos and María Isabel came back and brought Caribe with them. We can't let them give themselves away, until they are well schooled in our world. In our time. They have the means of establishing new lives for themselves. All we need is your help."

Khan just stared. He wanted to accuse them of playing with him. But he couldn't. There was something in their eyes. "Excuse me." His chair made a scraping noise on the rough tiles as he stood up from the table. He began a slow walk around the pool. Drinking water from his bottle, looking up at the sky, petting the resident German shepherds absently as he walked by, his thoughts raged inside him. He replayed the conversation slowly to himself, so he could be sure of what had just been said. He thought he had just heard something he wished he hadn't heard. It could be a hoax, he thought. It could be Candid Camera time. But these were his masters. Besides, tricks were for kids. He concluded that he had heard correctly. Coming back to the table after a couple of laps around the pool, he sat back down with a sigh. "Is there anything else I can help you with?"

Don Carlos smiled. "You will do it?" At the young man's nod, he laughed with relief, his hand reaching out to squeeze his wife's. "I understand you could also help us take care of some things we brought over."

"Things?" Khan asked, curiosity getting the better of him.

Pablo nodded. "Wait." He turned to Joe. "Let's show him." They excused themselves and went into the main house, coming back with Marina's chest, her gift from the Council between them. "Who would help us with something like this?" Tilting the umbrella, he flooded the table with light. Opening the lid, he allowed Khan to get his fill of what was inside.

Khan was speechless for a moment. The sun shone straight down on them and everything in the chest sparkled. He couldn't believe what his eyes confirmed. In front of him was a treasure like nothing he had ever seen before. He turned to the pirate, fighting not to drool. "This belongs to you?"

Don Carlos laughed, shaking his head. "Oh, no, not mine. That is Marina's."

"Marina's?" Khan repeated in wonder. "Little sister has done good for herself." He turned to his masters. "May I?" At their nod his hand dove into the chest and came back out with a handful of gold coins, and ropes of gold strung between his fingers. Letting everything go, he dove in again and came back out with precious jewels. Shaking his head, he dropped everything back inside and turned to the pirates. "I suppose you have more of this."

Don Carlos nodded. "We do. Much more. But not here. Not right now. I can go get some, though. In a few days." He looked steadily into the younger man's eyes. "Can you move it?"

"Yes." Khan pressed his lips together and nodded slowly. "I can. It may take a little time, so while you get the merchandise, I will look around for buyers. Meanwhile, you should categorize it and create an inventory to get started." He took a deep breath and let it out shakily. "Would that be it? Is there anything else I can do for you?" he asked softly.

The pirate and his wife looked at each other. María Isabel flashed him a smile. "No, Khan. That would be all for now."

"All right, then. All I need from you for now will be your full names, birthdays, and your ages. And Caribe's. I will do the rest."

They nodded. Don Carlos waited as he reached inside his jean pocket for a scrap of paper and a pen. "Carlos Gaitano y Mendoza, May eighth, fifty-five. María Isabel Sandoval de Gaitano, December fifteen, forty-five. Caribe Lacroix, September twenty-first, nineteen."

"Thank you." He grinned. "I guess I'll have to adjust your birthdates by like three and a half centuries or so." He rolled his eyes. Standing, he shook hands with the pirate and once again, kissed his wife's hand. "I will take care of everything. So very nice to meet you. It will be my pleasure doing business with you."

Everyone relaxed and smiled. "We'll see you out," Joe offered, standing with Pablo to join him.

Khan turned back for a moment. "Oh, I almost forgot. Don Carlos." He met the pirate's eyes. "Will your son, Carlitos, be joining us?" What he didn't ask was if Marina would be staying wherever it was she was supposed to be at the moment.

Don Carlos looked at his wife again. They locked eyes, communing silently. Turning back to him, he nodded slowly. "I believe he will. Soon enough." He smiled. "So will our other son, Indio. That would be Salomé's boyfriend," he added with a laugh.

Schooling his features, Khan smiled back. "Of course."

Outside, he turned to his masters. They saluted each other, and just stood around for a moment, listening to the breeze ruffle the bougainvillea in their driveway. They all looked at each other for a while. "Thanks for coming, Khan."

Khan smiled. "Needless to say, this stays between us." Shaking his head he stared at them, almost accusingly. "You could have knocked me over with a feather. But I'm hooked now. I'll be in touch." He laughed softly. "Nobody would ever believe me."

Pablo laughed. "Nobody."

The young man hesitated. "This is for real, huh?"

Sadly, Pablo nodded. "I'm afraid it is, Khan. It's one of those things that Life just throws at you and you have to receive with blind faith."

"Blind faith…" Khan shook his head. "I'll be damned. Who else knows about this besides you guys?"

Joe sighed and bent down to pick up a pebble. Aiming carefully, he sent it sailing over the wall that surrounded the property. "Shane and his family, the Blue Cat, Xaira and Snake." He sighed. "We didn't ask for this."

Khan nodded. "I hear you. Nobody would." He gave them a smile. "I'll get everybody's pictures later." He hesitated. "You realize I need to tell my own family, right?" he asked and sighed with relief when they nodded. The homeowners embraced Khan, and he was gone.

The Aguilar-Banks were stoked. They felt as if they were out on a field trip, which in a sense they were. It had been a quick ride on horseback in the dark back to where the ship was. From there, a short sail up the coast retracing their previous route until they reached the big river. Anchoring the ship they left Giancarlo there and rowed up the wide waterway, snaking among a few scattered villages inhabited by sleeping slaves, natives and landowners, as dawn began announcing itself. They could smell the morning before they saw it. Their senses were invaded by the sights and sounds that accompanied the transition from dark to light. The tree frogs had grown quiet and the birds had grown louder. At one of the villages they docked the rowboat and continued on horseback. Solomon chose to stay with the natives, among whom he had friends and acquaintances. Now they found themselves up on the side of a mountain surrounded by rolling hills. They had come out of a dense forest where they tied the three horses they had shared, leaving them grazing, and walked unto a clearing bathed by bright sunshine. It was the beginning of June by now, Spring Break far behind them. Trees heavy with fruit adorned the lush grass, and fabulous African tulip trees known as *flamboya-nes* displayed a riot of color, seeming to burst into flames. Delicate yellow butterflies dipped and dove in the air before them. A grove of bamboos creaked, indicating there was running water nearby. A crop of rocks marked an embankment where the mountain sloped gently out of sight before dropping steeply. Patches of banana and plantain trees dotted the mountain they were on and the hills at a distance like scattered emeralds. The air was clear and clean, the steady breeze upending the *yagrumo* leaves of the trees surrounding them so they sparkled silver like glitter. Life was good. Yes, indeed, the Aguilar-Banks were quite stoked.

"Hey, Gaitano!"

"Jackson?" The pirate turned to look up at his brother-in-law.

Jackson had found himself a tree dripping with fruit and with even more, some ripening and some rotting, at the base. He was now half hidden in its branches, making himself comfortable on a big bough. Sitting next to him and leaning against the trunk was his lady love, Storm. They were busily munching on beautiful large mangoes with yellow and fuchsia skins. "Have some breakfast, man!"

Carlos nodded. He raised his hands and caught two mangoes that were thrown at him, one after the other. Offering one to Marina, he pulled her down beside him on a blanket he had laid out for them. He grinned. "Thanks, Jax!"

"No problem, dude." He munched on his mango for a while, before calling out again, this time to his other brother-in-law. "Hey, Indio!"

Indio rumbled from his own blanket. "Don't want any!" He had taken the romantic approach, laying Salomé down and stretching out on top of her, the better to kiss and nuzzle her, whispering promises in her ear. Salomé, absolutely loving it, wrapped her arms around the brave's neck and sighed contentedly, closing her eyes as she turned her face to the sun.

Jackson shrugged. They fell silent for a while, everyone absorbing the morning in their own personal way. Those that were enjoying the fruit finished and wiped the juices off their faces, rinsing off with water they had brought along.

Storm grinned at her man. "I love being up here with you. It's like when you are a child, and you hide where you can see everything, but no one can see you."

Jackson grinned back at her. "That's exactly what it's like, isn't it?" He dropped suddenly, making her squeal, and hung from the bough upside down by his knees. "Makes you feel like a kid again."

Marina called out from her place next to the pirate. "Don't let him fool you, girl, he's still a kid."

Storm laughed. "Yeah, I know. Boy's got a lot of growing up to do."

Laughing with them, Jackson grabbed hold of his perch and, muscles straining, hoisted himself up to his original position. "Yeah, yeah, whatever." He smiled wickedly at Storm. "That's not what you say when…"

"Jackson!" she gasped. They all laughed. Jackson leaned towards her. Smiling, Storm met him halfway. They closed their eyes and their mouths met, dissolving in a kiss.

Suddenly Marina couldn't help herself. Grinning from ear to ear, she gave in to her impulse and began singing softly. *"Jackson and Storm, sitting in a tree, k-i-s-s-i-n-g…"*

"First comes love," Salomé giggled from the next blanket over. *"Then comes marriage, and then comes Jax pushing a baby carriage."*

Storm's heart began beating faster. Pulling back, her eyes locked with Jackson's. "No marriage…"

Stealing a kiss, he hushed her, his eyes never leaving hers. "It's just a kids' song, baby, no one's talking about marriage," he said quietly, his heart also beating faster. "Don't be scared," he smiled. Storm nodded, swallowing her heart and blinking back tears. Settling down they all fell silent again.

Marina turned her face up to the sun, closing her eyes, soaking its rays with true devotion. It wasn't every day that they got to hang out with nothing to do. She felt Carlos' fingers in her hair, tucking loose strands behind her ear. Almost purring, she rubbed her cheek against his big hand. He kept it there for a moment before beginning a slow, luxurious caress. The air filled with a distant sound, faint at first, slowly getting louder. Her eyes flew open and searched her husband's. She saw that he was listening intently. "Someone is singing," she whispered. Looking next to them she noticed that Salomé and Indio had broken their embrace and were now sitting up, also searching the area around them carefully. A quick look confirmed that Jackson and Storm had fallen silent also. They all waited in silent expectation. Quietly, the three pirates amongst them reached for their swords. Marina threw her energy out the way she had done when they had first gotten stranded on the island that fateful day, oh,

God, so long ago, it was nothing more than a distant memory now. It was her way of scanning. But she couldn't detect any danger. All she felt was mild curiosity. And still, the singing grew louder and closer. Suddenly the source came into view. Everyone froze.

In their clearing, stood a beautiful girl. Shocked, her eyes widened with surprise and then curiosity as she spotted the two couples on the blankets in the grass. The breeze blew the hair around her face for a moment and she tossed her head, getting it out of her eyes. The pirates slowly raised their hands in greeting, being careful not to scare her. Marina and Salomé did the same, smiling at her. The girl smiled back. She was barely more than a teenager. Her skin was deep bronze, her hair thick, black as coal and loose around her shoulders. Straight bangs reached her eyebrows, framing beautiful large brown eyes. Tribal markings graced her features in swirls and slashes in red and black. Shells hung from her ears and her neck, matching more shells on her wrists and ankles. Her feet were bare but her body was clothed in light cotton, the top low and sleeveless, the skirt falling to the top of her knees. In her arms, cradled against her chest was a baby. For the moment all they could see was its brown back with its little butt resting on her forearm, and the back of its head. Done with quiet time the baby squirmed and twisted in the arms holding it, turning around to gaze at them. Now they could see that it was a little boy around Max's age. But that wasn't all. Hanging from around its neck was a large solid gold disc almost covering his whole torso.

Marina gasped. "No way!" Ignoring the girl's puzzled look, she reached for her husband's hand. "That's a *guanín*!"

Understanding, the girl began to panic. Turning the baby away from them again, she started backing up. "No! No!"

Marina stood up. Reaching a hand out towards her, she began to speak hurriedly, not knowing or caring if the girl understood her. "Oh, no, I'm sorry, it's okay, really!" She brought her other hand to her own chest. "I'm Marina, and this is *El Capitán Pirata*," she explained hurriedly, introducing her husband as the pirate Captain.

Saving the moment, Gaitano stood up slowly. "No, no, no," he laughed, rolling his eyes. "Carlos." The girl still looked startled, but at least she stopped moving.

Following the lead, Indio also stood, helping his girlfriend to her feet. "*Indio pirata*," he chuckled.

"Salomé," Marina's sister called out, bending at the waist and waving at the baby who was craning his neck.

"*Tormenta*," Storm sang out from the tree, giving the translation of her name in Spanish. Startled, the girl looked up meeting identical twin grins. The pyrate pointed to her chest, nodding her head encouragingly. "*Pirata*."

"Jackson." He shook his head in mock disgust. "No *pirata*." He beamed when the girl giggled and offered her some fruit. "Mango for the baby?"

The girl hesitated but finally nodded, smiling shyly, and the ice was broken. Thus began a long sweet exchange as they communicated in spite of the barrier between them, slowly deciding on broken Spanish, their gestures more expressive and eloquent than their words.

"Sing for us," Marina encouraged. "How do you keep your son so calm?"

The girl smiled, seriously considering her answer. "It's about contact while I sing to him. I hold him. Close. I embrace him. He feels the vibrations of the notes I sing. The rhythm of my chants." She sang for them. It was a nonsense verse, like a lullaby. Whatever it was, it seemed to be a tranquilizer for the baby. In a few minutes, Salomé, Marina and Storm had learned the verse.

They convinced her to join them and got her story. She wouldn't give them her name but admitted she was a *taína* of Arawak ancestry. She became spooked suddenly, looking over her shoulder and all around her. Slowly, she calmed down again. The baby called her *Toa* in his baby babble, letting them know she was his mother.

Carlos questioned her gently. "I thought there weren't any *taínos* left."

She smiled, shaking her head sadly. "There aren't, not really." Making herself comfortable on Indio and Salomé's blanket, she adjusted the baby on her lap as he munched on the mango Jackson provided, both little hands holding the colorful fruit, smearing his face with sweet, sticky yellow pulp. "There are very few of us left.

The Spaniards are still after us, so we pretend to be of mixed blood already." Breathing a big sigh she dropped an absent kiss on top of the baby's head. "They want our gold," she hissed in a savage whisper, "and our blood."

"Do Spaniards bother you? Your people?" Carlos wondered, reaching out to take the mango pit from the baby as he expressed that he was done with it, and wiped his face gently.

She nodded this time. "What people? I have no one left. They killed my whole family. My whole village. It was just me and…" She hesitated, blinking back tears. "They killed his father." Sighing, she admitted the truth to them. "One Spaniard. *Don Gerardo*," she choked on the name, almost spitting it out.

Marina thought for a moment. "The baby's a *cacique*, isn't he?" she wondered out loud, using the term for the chief of the taíno Indians.

"The last in these parts," the girl admitted reluctantly. "Maybe the very last."

"So do you usually have to hide the *guanín?*" Jackson asked, curious, referring to the gold disc on the baby's chest. It was what had distinguished the *caciques* from the regular *taínos*, the same way some American Indian chiefs were told apart from the rest of the braves by their long elaborate headdresses made from eagle feathers. "It must be worth a lot to the Spaniards," he pointed out.

"Yes," she confirmed, "they would kill him for it and for who he is." She sighed again. "I have to hide the whole baby."

"So you have to hide his heritage to save his life," Indio concluded, shaking his head sadly.

"I have to hide everything. The Spaniards are not above taking from a baby." She thought for a moment, looking at each of them in turn, and seemed to come to a decision. "Would you like to see?" At their nods she smiled, offering the baby. "Hold my *cacique*," she requested shyly, her face beaming with justified pride.

Marina immediately held out her arms, making everyone laugh. "Come here," she crooned, looking into the beautiful brown baby eyes, "*tesoro, precioso…*" The baby, as fascinated with the natural highlights in her hair as her husband usually was, gurgled contentedly.

The girl stood up gracefully and headed towards the crop of rocks nearby. Making her way carefully over them, she disappeared around a huge boulder. They could see her movements as she backed out from behind it a few times, bent over at the waist as if she were pulling things out from somewhere. Finally, she came back towards them carrying something in her arms. Reaching them she set it carefully in the ground among them. The pirates and their company stared, unbelieving.

Before them was a *dujo*. This was a type of small bench close to the ground, carved from stone with a curved seat and a curved back rest. The caciques were the only ones to have them, in the same way that kings were the only ones to sit on thrones. On the seat she had put an array of primitive gold armbands, much like Indio's leather ones, and assorted jewelry made of gold, shells, feather and stone. Among them, carved pieces of stone called *cemís*, representing the gods the *taínos* believed in. Beautiful, elaborate pieces of art. The riches of a primitive chief. The young women gasped in wonder while the men expressed their awe. The girl smiled with pride.

"¡Mujer!"

Everyone looked up, startled, in the same way impalas look up from what they are doing when a lion is sensed. The voice was still far away but it was unmistakable. Someone was calling for the baby's mother.

The girl froze, startled out of her mind. She looked at them, her eyes filling with sheer terror. *"Don Gerardo,"* she whispered, fear almost choking her. Everyone jumped to their feet, joining her. Scrambling quickly, she grabbed the *dujo*.

"¡Mujer!" The voice was still distant, but noticeably closer, the sing-song tone mocking.

Flinging the stone seat into Jackson's arms, she began ushering them behind the rocks. *"Hide the baby! Please! Don't let him find my son!"*

Taking command, Storm spun her around to face her. *"¡Tranquila!"* she ordered, willing the girl to calm down. "We will go over there, and they," she told her, gesturing at the men, "will go up there," she motioned back at the mango tree. Facing Jackson, she took the stone bench and gave him her sword.

"*¡Mujer!*" The voice was much closer, making everybody scramble to their positions, suddenly leaving the girl alone in the clearing.

Taking a deep breath, the girl smoothed the skirt over her thighs. Schooling her features, she bent down and began to pick dandelions, twirling them between her fingers. She sneaked a peek at the boulders by the embankment where the females were. Marina had the baby's face pressed against her chest, Storm was quietly guarding the treasure, there was no time to hide it without calling the Spaniard's attention to them, and Salomé stood with their blankets in her arms. The girl widened her eyes at them, cautioning them to silence. Glancing at the tree she made out the three men, still as stone, swords in readiness.

"*¡Mujer!*" Finally the arrogant Spaniard came into view. They couldn't tell whether he knew her name or not. It was quite evident to them that he delighted in calling the girl *Woman* just as if she were an object. Throwing back his head, he laughed wickedly as he caught sight of her, almost falling off his horse as he dismounted. The man was drunk. "*¡Mujer!*" He mocked her in the tone one used when finding a long lost friend. "Where have you been? I have been looking everywhere for you."

"Don Gerardo!" the girl cried, pretending to be woken from a reverie. "I didn't hear you…"

"Aaaah," he laughed, wagging his finger at her, scolding her as you would a child. Stumbling across the grass he reached her side. The hidden visitors studied him closely. He was young still, maybe in his thirties. Certainly old enough to know better than to be stalking a teenager. But they were in a world where females achieved womanhood with their first period. His hair gleamed in the sun, the color of brass. He reminded them of Don Luis Vega y Ramos, former Quartermaster of La Diosa del Mar, the Spanish galleon captured by Indio. Except for the eyes. Don Gerardo's were a startling blue, striking in his pale face, darkened by the shadow of a beard. The shirt he wore was dingy and his trousers dirty. The boots on his feet were well worn. "I have been looking all over for you." His words slurred.

Carefully, the girl side stepped around him, trying to stay out of reach. She shrugged, keeping a wary eye on him and a smile glued on her lips. "I just got here."

"No, no, no," he laughed, stumbling behind her. "I have been looking for a very long time." Suddenly his hand snaked out, grabbing her wrist. He laughed as the girl cried out, yanking her towards him. Everyone around them held their breath. The man's demeanor changed suddenly. He was still laughing but his features scowled at the girl he had captured. A cloud passed over the sun, dimming the light on the hillside. "Where is the baby?" he demanded.

The girl looked at him steadily. "What baby?" she asked him, trying to get free. Her voice carried to them loudly, and the message was clear. Don Gerardo must not find the baby. "What baby?" she repeated, anger getting the best of her now. "The one I lost?" With a final yank, she pulled free from the unsteady Spaniard. "You know it died at birth. There is no baby, sir!" she informed him.

"Oh, but you lie," he laughed, reaching for her again. "You think I am a fool, but I know all your tricks. You have been hiding him from me, quite successfully until now," he acknowledged bowing his head mockingly at her. "But I will have your child," he informed her, his voice falling to a threatening growl, "just as I had its father." Capturing her between his arms, he pulled her close against him. "As I will now have its mother."

Not being able to hide the disgust that crossed her features, the baby's mother pushed against the Spaniard with all her might. "There is no baby!" she panted. Managing to get him at arm's length, she freed one hand and slapped him as hard as she could. The sound of her hand connecting with his face sounded loud, almost echoing off the hillside. *"There is no baby!"* she screamed at him, stepping back, chest heaving from the effort. In Marina's arms, the baby squirmed at the sound of his mother's voice. Marina held him tighter, breathing into its mouth to distract him, forcing him to not cry out loud. It worked. The baby took a deep breath, looking up at Marina and smiled, gurgling softly once again.

Don Gerardo put a hand to his face where the imprint of her hand was rapidly making an appearance. There was death in his eyes.

"¡Puta!" he sneered at her. Reaching for her with both hands he put them on either side of her head and with one vicious twist, snapped her neck. Without a sound the girl crumpled to the ground. Behind the rocks the girls gasped, terror striking their hearts. Up in the tree, the men fought to not give themselves away, a roar in their ears. The Spaniard looked down at the broken girl in the grass, a glazed expression passing over his eyes. Emotions raged inside him, distorting his features. Finally he stood over the girl, trembling with fury. *"Now look at what you made me do!"* he screamed at her at the top of his lungs, his voice a roar in the still morning. Pulling one foot back, he kicked the dead girl in the head with all his might. Walking away from her, he started pacing in a circle around the body. Finally, he stopped. Smiling slowly, he went back to her, his eyes glazed over. "Now, I will have you," he laughed.

Behind the rocks nobody moved, terror paralyzing them. But from the tree, the three men dropped silently like ninjas, the swords in their hands gleaming as the cloud in the sky finished its path, and the sun shone bright again, bathing the hill in its light once again.

"Don Gerardo!" The Captain of La Gitana advanced towards the Spaniard, murder in his own eyes.

Startled, the man backed away from the girl, guilty as sin, looking at them as if they were ghosts. "Who are you?" he stammered, his alcohol induced brain not letting him think clearly nor react quickly.

"Your death," Carlos informed him. Throwing his sword to the side, he kept advancing on him. Following his movements, on either side of him, Indio and Jackson did the same.

The man gasped, stepping back. "No," he cried out choking on his own terror, "no, I didn't mean it."

"Now we will have you," Indio's voice rumbled deep in his chest. They had reached him by now, the three of them dispersing until they were surrounding him.

"There is no baby," Jackson told him.

"Jackson!" Carlos said suddenly, getting his attention. "You don't want to do this," he cautioned.

"Get out, Jackson," Indio growled, circling the Spaniard, "you don't need this." Jackson hesitated.

"Jackson!" Carlos turned to him, death in his eye. Swallowing, Jackson froze and nodded, leaving the brothers alone.Simultaneously, they advanced on the man with no more weapons than their fists. From their hiding place, the girls stopped looking. They couldn't watch. They didn't have to see any longer. The hillside was filled now with the sounds of a man being beaten to death.

The ride back down the mountain for them was grim and silent. The horses made their way down the hill carefully, their muscles straining as they were urged wordlessly. Business as usual for the pirates, the visitors were in shock, however. Nobody spoke, they had no words. Storm and Jackson had wrapped up the girl's treasure in their blankets. Indio cradled the stone bench on his thighs as he rode. Behind him, Salomé pressed herself tightly against his back, her arms wrapped around him, making sure the dujo didn't fall. On the third horse, Carlos rode with Marina in front of him. In her arms, cradled like a hammock in one of the blankets, was a brown baby that the world would never know as the chief he was, his station in life and his family robbed from him before he had a chance to grow.

Detective Jamal Blackmon of the Blue Bay Police Department sighed. Leaning back in the swivel chair at his desk he stretched long and hard, raising his arms over his head. Bringing his hands down, he smoothed them over his shaved head before letting them drop down on his desk once again. He had loosened the tie around his neck, opening the collar of his shirt. The sleeves were rolled up on his muscular forearms. Chocolate brown eyes shone with intelligence out of a beautifully carved face the color of dark wood. The only hair on his head besides his eyebrows and eyelashes consisted of a thin, stylish mustache running down the sides of his mouth and around his chin. The popular style was called a *candado* in Spanish. It meant padlock, referring to the shape. Very popular with the ladies, since that strip of beard assured certain spots of a girl's anatomy could be rubbed in just the right way at just the right time. Something his wife, Maya Hardington, principal of the local elementary school, could testify to. He sighed again and looked across his desk at his nephew, Rashawn Blackmon, recently promoted to CSI in his own precinct. "You are sure of this, Rashawn? No doubt in your mind?" he asked in a deep voice that seemed to come from beyond his chest.

Rashawn sighed, shaking his head. His black hair was styled in neat cornrows. Nice sized cubic zirconias winked from his ears. Tall, he was built like a football player, large like a tank, all solid muscle. It was his day off, so at the moment he was wearing faded jeans, running shoes, and a football jersey. His eyes were the color of cinnamon, skin barely a few shades darker than his uncle's. His voice confirmed the family relationship between them. "I'm sure, man. I thought hard about this because I know y'all are friends since forever and still hang out..." He shook his head thoughtfully. "Summer insists."

Summer had been a cheerleader in college at the time Rashawn had been playing football. Exceptionally beautiful, she was one of Sloane's models. That was her hobby. Her passion was surfing, however. Summer was the typical beach girl with a golden tan, a swimsuit model body, eyes the color of a cloudless sky, and long straight blonde hair down to her tight ass. She had noticed Rashawn because, in her words, he wasn't hitting on her like he should. Rashawn noticed her because, well, she made sure he noticed her when she was cheering. The thing was, when Rashawn got hurt in a game and the doctor recommended he didn't play anymore Summer quit cheering because she would no longer be seeing him. The squad's loss was the young man's gain. She devoted herself to capturing him, mind, heart and soul. The girl was on a mission. She applied herself wholeheartedly to conquering him, surpassing the difference in their backgrounds. First thing she did was become BFF, best friends forever, with his mother and sisters. It took them convincing him to take her out for the first time. Not wanting to scare him away, Summer proceeded slowly and cautiously, letting him discover her little by little. When he found out the truth about her, which was that her intelligence far surpassed her looks, he was hooked. Summer was funny, compassionate, emotional, talented, and real. Eventually, they couldn't hide from the truth. They were soul mates. Now, they were together. And it seemed as if it were going to be forever.

"Where is your girlfriend getting her sources from?" his uncle asked.

"The university. They left for Spring Break and then never made it back. They haven't dropped out and they haven't shown up. It's as if they disappeared off the face of the earth."

The older detective pressed his nephew for details. "Tell me more."

Rashawn leaned forward in his seat. "Well, it seems they were last seen by two young men from campus, Quentin Matthews and Todd Lowell. Quentin is actually friends with Jackson. Summer tried speaking to him, but he's tight mouthed. All she could get out of him was that he hasn't seen him since Spring Break. Todd plays stupid however. He's not talking and Summer says he creeps her out."

Jamal nodded thoughtfully. "Good old female intuition." He waved his hand for the younger man to continue. "Go on."

"The thing is, some friends of these guys have been worried and some rumors got started. I've been trying to reach them, Jamal. Jackson won't pick up. It's been days since I've been trying, but the truth of the matter is I haven't seen any of them myself, for weeks. I can't reach Salomé or Marina, either. Derek and Tyler act like they don't know anything, and when I approached Xaira she almost burst into tears, you know how emotional she is over Marina. Deep inside my heart tells me she doesn't know anything, although we both know she wouldn't talk if she knew." He frowned, no longer being able to hide his immense concern. "You need to see these." He slid some papers across the desk at his uncle, who covered them with his big hands without immediately looking at them. "Summer thought she better talk to me about it before the shit hits the fan. She remembers me mentioning their parents in relation to you." He shook his head, frowning at his thoughts. "I'm really glad she did. She's being pressured to investigate. I convinced her to put a lid on it until I spoke to you."

The older Detective Blackmon nodded thoughtfully. "Thank you, Rashawn, you did good. Now, you are positive of this?" he insisted. "Absolutely no doubt?"

Rashawn knew better than to get frustrated at his Uncle Jamal's interrogation. They were both investigators at heart. "None, dude. It's your friends' kids. My own friends." He looked at his uncle straight in the eye. "Jackson Banks, Salomé Banks, and Marina Aguilar."

The crew of La Gitana was quiet as they lifted anchor and began to sail away. The ride down the mountain had been silent, each one of their party lost in their own thoughts. Solomon had stared when they finally got to him. Their expressions were solemn as they loaded the rowboat with the articles they had taken. The baby looked at him with curiosity, but had not had a cause to complain or cry. Everything was still new to him. He had not seen his mother's murder, or the man who committed it, they had made sure of that, and so far he had felt safe. Besides, the girls did a good job of keeping him content as they sang to him and chanted. Solomon had looked at his Captain with a million questions in his eyes, but Gaitano had just shaken his head in warning. The expression on his face alone was enough to make the Boatswain go quiet.

Indio took it upon himself to ease the tension a little. "How did it go, Solomon? Did you get to catch up with both your girlfriends?"

Solomon laughed. "Actually, I did. All three of them." The two pirates looked at each other and grinned.

Now they were heading back up the coast once more. Giancarlo also had been excellent about keeping his thoughts to himself. Instead of saying anything he had helped them load everything unto the ship. The baby had been handed to him from the rowboat and he had held it to his shoulder, the instinct of fatherhood kicking in naturally.

The pirates had gotten together away from the Aguilar-Banks, clueing Giancarlo and Solomon in on what had happened. Jackson hadn't said a word since they came down the mountain. Going off by himself, he went to a coil of rope that was on deck. Lying down on the planks, he folded his arms, pillowing his head, and stared up at the bright late spring sky.

Storm had been affected the most, knowing the impact the experience would have on the family. She wouldn't cry in front of the pirates, but they all knew she wanted to. Tears she would never cry for herself. All they could do was offer her unconditional support. After a while, she shook herself and faced the men. "I need to show him what it was worth." They didn't ask what she was talking about. They knew exactly what she meant. Without saying another word, Storm took the baby from Giancarlo and strode across the deck to her man. Dropping to her knees she placed the now sleeping baby on top of him. The baby stirred, unable to wake up yet, and stretched like a starfish, sprawling on Jackson's chest, facing the sun, and sighed deeply. Its little mouth made tiny sucking movements. Jackson sighed, holding him close. Storm lay down next to them and threw her arm over both, her head pillowed on Jackson's shoulder. In a few minutes, they too were also asleep.

No words were spoken by the rest of the party. Instead, they all turned to do their chores automatically. By the time the sun was straight overhead, they had reached their destination. The hometown of Pablo Aguilar.

"Joe!"

"Hey, Jamal! What's up, man?"

"Long time no see, dude. What have you been up to?"

"Nothing much, dog. Had to leave town for a few weeks, but that's been about it."

"Oh, yeah? Taking time away from the family?" The detective smiled, hearing the familiar chuckle on the other end of the line.

"Nah, man. Never like that. We were all together. And now we're back."

"Cool. You up for a little game?"

"Always," Joe laughed. "How about this evening?"

"You're on. Tell Jackson I am going to beat his ass."

"Sorry, dog. Jackson's still out of town. You're gonna have to settle for just Pablo and I."

"Nah," the detective rumbled. "Let's raise the stakes. Get Shane and the boys…"

"Why? Am I going to need a lawyer?"

"Maybe, after I'm through with you."

"Then maybe I should get the Blue Cat for backup."

"Definitely. I'll bring Rashawn and you just have to get yourself an extra man."

"How about Snake?"

"The more ass to kick, the better."

"You're on. See you later."

"Gator." Ending the phone call, Detective Jamal Blackmon turned to his nephew. "We're on. Court at the Hacienda. We usually play around six. Everybody's done for the day."

Rashawn shook his head, even more admiration than he originally felt for his uncle filling his eyes. "You are one slick dick,
Detective. I'll be there."

"Aguilar!"

"Gaitano!" Looking across the deck, they grinned at each other.

"Where are we?" he teased.

"Home, Capitán," she responded with a laugh, brimming with excitement.

"Would you like to go to the beach?"

"Please, Capitán!"

"What's it worth to you?"

Marina smiled at him. "Take me to the beach, and I'll show you later…"

Her husband raised an eyebrow at her. "Promise?" At her nod, he laughed. "Giancarlo! We are going to the beach!"

Giancarlo laughed back at his Captain and proceeded to sail the ship as close to the coastline as he could. They threw anchor when they couldn't get any closer. This time they all went ashore, Solomon maneuvering their rowboat carefully between the cays until they arrived at a small lagoon. Before they reached the sand, Jackson and his sisters jumped off. Laughing and shouting, they splashed like children. Feeling left out, Storm joined them, contributing to the screams of laughter.

Marina wiped the water off her face, smoothing the hair back on her head. She turned to the men that were still on the rowboat. "Gian! Throw the baby!"

Offended, the Sailing Master held the baby closer against his chest and stared at her. Surely the accountant had gone mad. "What? No." He shook his head. The Aguilar-Banks trio laughed.

"Don't be afraid," Salomé called out. "How do you think babies learn to swim, anyway?"

Giancarlo kept shaking his head. "No."

Storm laughed softly. "I'm staying out of this one."

"Come on, Gian! It's all good, man!" Jackson called to him, stretching his arms out.

"No."

The brother and two sisters began to chant. "Throw the ba-by! Throw the ba-by! Throw the ba-by!"

Giancarlo turned to Gaitano for support. "Captain…"

Carlos shrugged with a laugh. "It has been my experience that the Aguilar-Banks crew usually knows what they're talking about.

Indio smiled. "You might as well throw the baby, Giancarlo."

Solomon grinned. "Before they come and get it."

The Sailing Master wasn't convinced. "Carlos, is this absolutely necessary?"

Gaitano nodded encouragingly. "Throw the baby."

Disgusted, Giancarlo scowled at them. "Savages. All of you," he muttered. And he threw the baby.

They cheered. The baby flew through the air and landed with a splash. Moving as a pack, Marina, Jackson and Salomé swam to where the baby had gone under. The pirates watched expectantly, and Giancarlo held his breath. The water sparkled in the bright sunlight. They could see the little brown body under the surface, a trail of bubbles in its wake. As the bubbles dwindled, the small native rose, bobbing to the surface, rolling on its back, legs kicking, coughing, screwing up its little face. The Aguilar-Banks crew cheered. The baby howled.

Laughing, Jackson grabbed it under its arms and lifted him out of the water. "Again. One, two, three." Looking right into its squinty eyes, he took in a big breath of air and dunked him again. Once more, the trail of bubbles. This time, when the baby came back up, he didn't howl as much as he sputtered. Jackson did the same thing once more. "Again. One, two, three." The baby sank, and they could see his little arms and legs moving. It came back up, blinking. When Jackson held him up to dunk him again, at the count of three, the baby gasped and held his breath. They cheered once again. The pirates looked at each other.

Giancarlo just shook his head, a ghost of a smile tugging at the corners of his mouth. "You're right, Carlos. They do know what they're doing," he said softly, wonder in his voice.

Salomé smiled. "See, Gian? We would never hurt a baby." Taking him from Jackson, she turned him on his stomach, skimming him over the water as she turned in circles. Seeing the baby taking in air, she weaved him in and out of the water, making him look like a little dolphin. The baby began squealing with laughter.

"My turn!" Marina cried, waving for Salomé to give it up to her. Laughing, her sister relinquished him. She squealed at the baby. "Cacique! Come on, baby boy!" Turning him over on his back, she floated him. The baby blinked up at the sky. Marina glanced at what he was looking at. She gasped at him, her sing-song voice soft. "See the pretty bird? That's an alcatraz. Look! It's fishing!" The baby turned his head, following the path of the majestic sea bird, a sleek gray missile, as it dive bombed into the water with a splash, as professional as an Olympic diver. A few seconds later it popped back out, long beak in the air as it threw its head back. A flash of scales, and the fish was gone, the alcatraz happily gulping. The bird bobbed on the water for a few moments, and then soared back into the sky. "*¿Viste eso, mi amor?*" she breathed into his ear with a soft gasp, making the moment magic. "See that?" The baby turned his head to look at Marina hovering over him. "All gone," she sang, smiling at him. The baby gurgled back.

The pirates shook their heads and jumped into the water with a smile.

"That," the pirate told his crew softly, a mixture of wonder, awe, and pride in his voice, "is the mother of my children."

"If you ever change your mind," Solomon teased, "she can be the mother of mine." Gaitano splashed him. The Boatswain laughed. He was determined to make sure the Captain never took the accountant for granted. They hauled the rowboat out of the water and tied it to a palm tree. Those in the water joined them soon after, looking around them curiously.

"Does any of this look familiar to you?" Indio asked.

Jackson laughed. "No, man. This is complete jungle right now. In our time, there are cement houses here." Turning around, he thought out loud. "If the point is behind us, over there," he signaled behind them, "we want to go in the other direction." They all began walking down the beach, the combination of cool wind and hot sun quickly drying them. The baby shivered but didn't complain, looking around him with wide-eyed wonder. Jackson slid a glance at his sisters. "Run?"

Indio reached for the baby. "I'll take Cacique now." Taking him from Marina's arms, he put him on his shoulders, holding his little hands for balance. In a moment, the brother and sisters were running down the beach.

Storm sighed. "There they go again."

"Always," Giancarlo agreed. The pirates laughed.

By the time they got to where they were going, the visitors were already back in the water. This time, however, they were riding the waves. The pirates watched with interest as they screamed and yelled, sliding down small walls of water, over and over again. The process seemed easy. They swam out to a certain point, and tread water, waiting. The wave would come, and they began to swim back to shore. At the crest of the wave they would kick hard, one closed fist extended before them as they maneuvered with the other hand. Then they would slide down the face of the wave in a diagonal motion, momentarily disappearing in the tube before popping back out in the white water close to the shore. They did this time and time again. The pirates studied them carefully.

Giancarlo shook his head. "They make it look so easy."

"It must be, to them," Solomon observed. "It should be, to us." He smiled.

"It looks like fun," Indio added.

Carlos agreed. "I can do this."

Storm rolled her eyes. "Give me the baby," she told Indio, reaching for him. The pirates stood and headed towards the water. The baby gurgled, holding her face between his little hands. "Hi, Cacique," she said softly. "It's just you and me, baby boy." Turning him around in her arms so that his back was to her, she sat him between her legs. The sun had already dried the ocean water on his skin, leaving a film of salt. Gently, she brushed the sand off him. The baby relaxed and watched with interest. After a while, a long while, actually, they all came out and joined her on the sand.

Jackson smiled at his girlfriend, offering her his hand. "Come with me, Storm. I'll show you how to body surf."

She smiled up at him. "Is that what you call it?"

"Yeah." He motioned with his head. "Come on."

Solomon reached for the baby. "Cacique," he called softly. "My turn, baby." And so the baby changed hands again as the female pyrate went into the water with her man. Those left on shore waited until she got her fill, and then they headed back.

The sun had moved in the sky, casting longer shadows on the sand. They walked back slowly, taking their time, enjoying the balmy trade winds. Halfway to their rowboat, they stopped and looked out across the bay.

Marina scanned the far shoreline with her finger until she reached the end. "In our time, there's a lighthouse on that point," she told her husband. "And in front of us, the waves come in sets of three."

Gaitano hesitated and counted. Smiling, he turned to her. "Indeed they do. I believe you have been here before, centuries from now," he teased.

Marina smiled at him, tears of love filling her eyes. "Thank you for bringing us here, baby."

"My pleasure," he replied.

Moving closer to them, Salomé hugged him around the waist impulsively. "No, the pleasure is all ours."

Jackson agreed. "Yeah, man, thanks a lot." Shaking his head, he looked at his sisters. "Wait till we tell Papi."

Soon afterwards, they were back on the ship. The day remained just as beautiful to the very end. They sailed out on the open water, leaving Boriken and the sunset behind them. In front of them, stars began to appear as the sky got darker. Now they were headed home where they had to weigh their choices, and their combined fates would be decided. The baby yawned, whimpered, squirmed and howled. *"¡Toa!"* The plaintive cry for his mother broke their hearts. Standing in a circle they passed him around, from arms to arms. Each one of them had their own personal style in attempting to console the child. They rocked him, sang to him, danced with him, chanted at him, and howled with him. At the end they achieved their shared goal when the baby *taíno's* eyes filled with defeat so sudden and exhausted it couldn't disguise his deep understanding of what had happened. Sighing deeply, Cacique cried himself to sleep. Still they passed him from arms to arms, now with prayers and lullabies. Finally they could breathe. They were going back to Encantada, with new experiences, and a baby native taíno chief whom destiny had thrown at them, and whom they called Cacique.

That night, the pirate sighed happily as the still full moon spilled into his cabin. His wife was expressing her gratitude as only a woman in love could. And as he held her in his arms, deep inside her, her fingernails gently raking his back, he basked in the knowledge that Marina was crazy about him. How did he know? Carlos groaned, feeling himself soak in her desire. He was just as crazy about her.

The men stood around looking at each other. They were ready to go.

Pablo smiled at the assembly. "There are ten of us. Let's make this easy," he laughed wickedly. "Young people against the *viejos*."

Deveraux laughed. "That would be six against four, Tío."

"You are right. But since Snake's the oldest of you, we get him." Joe smiled as they all groaned.

"That's not fair," Cat shook his head, grinning.

"It's all good," Jesse laughed at them. "They could use the help."

They divided into two teams. The younger team consisted of Deveraux and Catamaran, Derek, Tyler and Rashawn. On the team of the older folks were Pablo and Joe, Shane, Jamal and Jesse. And they played.

They played long and they played hard. Basketball was a passion for all of them, and they liked nothing better than getting together on the court until they were all dripping with sweat, muscles screaming, like any red-blooded guy. Since they were at the Hacienda, and hadn't been all together in so long, they decided to hang out after the game. The place to be was poolside, where it was nice and cool as the evening progressed. They put together a couple of tables, brought out bottles of water, and sat around to talk.

"Where are the kids?" Jamal asked, not wasting any time.

"They're out of town," Joe answered smoothly, "hanging out with some friends."

"Haven't seen them in a while," Rashawn added thoughtfully.

"We were just with them. They're doing fine," Pablo told them. "Actually, Marina just got married. We were at her wedding."

"Is that right?" Jamal asked. "Do we know the young man?"

"No, I'm afraid not," Joe answered. "Boy's not from around here." He stole a look at the twins, who were leaning back now, increasingly amused at the turn of events.

"Well," Jamal drawled, "the truth of the matter is, something has come up. I need to get in touch with them."

"Not possible," Joe told him. He exchanged a look with Pablo.

Pretending not to see the men trade glances, Rashawn spoke up. "Why not?"

"There is no signal where they are at." Joe frowned, increasingly disturbed at the course the conversation was taking. Everyone else kept quiet, waiting to see where this thing was going.

The detectives exchanged glances this time. Jamal took a deep breath. "They must be far, if there's no signal."

Pablo raised his hands, halting all conversation at that moment, pointing at the men in front of him for a moment before letting his hands sink back slowly to the table. He looked at the pair of detectives steadily for a moment, his eyes hard and steady, taking time to gather his thoughts. Finally, he took a deep breath. "Jamal, I know you are fond of our children, as we are of Rashawn. But this conversation is beginning to sound like an interrogation." He locked eyes with the older detective. "Is there anything you want to say?"

Jamal sighed. "Off the record?" He waited for Pablo to nod. "Your children are being investigated."

Catamaran laughed. Reaching for his cell phone, he interrupted gently. "Excuse me, I have to make a call." Everyone fell silent as he did so. They waited as he connected and someone picked up at the other end. "Xaira. Hey, baby girl. I think you better bring in the pirates and Island Boy. Now. 911 kind of right now. Yes, you may use Marina's Mustang. I'll take full responsibility. Don't worry about it, the insurance covers you. Get over here now. Right now. We'll wait for you." He blew her a kiss, ending the conversation. Snapping the phone shut, he waved it at the men with a wicked grin. "As you were."

"Why are our children being investigated?" Joe frowned, puzzled.

Shane interrupted, adjusting the glasses on his face. "Why don't you start at the beginning, Jamal?"

The older detective sighed, stroking the padlock of hair on his face. "I'll let Rashawn tell you."

Rashawn sighed as all eyes turned to him. "I wish Summer was here. She could explain it better."

Derek frowned. "What does Summer have to do with it?"

Tyler looked just as puzzled. "I took a class with Summer. She's very smart."

"I thought she became a private investigator," Shane said.

Jamal nodded. "She did."

"Summer?" Joe asked.

"Good choice," Shane commented. "Studies reveal that people open up more to people who are beautiful." He shrugged. "Human nature."

"How's she doing?" Blue asked.

"Very well, thank you," Rashawn acknowledged.

Joe shook his head. "What does Summer have to do with this?"

"Well, Summer actually comes in on this on two sides. For one, there's a lot of rumors going on in school. Kids are talking…"

"Talking?" Jesse asked.

Rashawn shook his head. "Speculating. It seems that no one has seen them, any of them, since Spring Break. Not Jackson, nor the girls." He looked around at the faces looking back at him.

Jamal looked at the parents. "But *you* have seen them, however."

Pablo nodded. "Absolutely. We know *exactly* where our children are."

"Where?" Jamal asked.

Shane held up his hand, cautioning his friends. "Why do you want to know?"

"It's more than want, Shane," Jamal answered. "We *need* to know."

"Hold on," Jesse said, leaning forward in his chair. "What's the other side? What does this have to do with Summer?"

"Summer has been recently employed by an insurance company," Rashawn answered. "She checks out things for them." He sighed, and looked at his uncle.

Jamal picked up a backpack that was on the ground by his chair. Reaching inside, he drew out some papers. He slid them over the table to the homeowners. "You better take a look at these."

Shane intercepted them. "*I* better take a look at these." Holding them up, he scanned them quickly, silently. The color drained from his face.

"*Licenciado?*" Pablo frowned, concerned at his lawyer's reaction.

"What are they?" Joe asked.

Shane looked up, dazed. "Insurance policies." He shook his head.

"Insurance policies?" Jesse asked. "Whose?"

Rashawn snorted. "Who are we talking about? Jackson, Salomé, and Marina's."

"No," Joe said, shaking his head. "That's not possible. They don't have any insurance policies. The only insurance our kids have is car insurance on their vehicles."

"Wrong," Jamal said softly. He gestured at the papers still in their lawyer's hands. "Check them out for yourself. Why do you think Summer got involved?"

"This can't be," Joe muttered, snatching the papers from Shane. He, too, scanned them. His expression became one of shock. He passed them to Pablo.

Pablo took a deep breath and looked at them. "Life insurance? *One million dollars?*" His voice rose. "Surely these aren't real."

"But they are," Jamal insisted, taking the papers from his friend, and putting them away again. "*One million dollars. Each.* Making the four parents the beneficiaries." He sighed. "By your reaction, I realize you didn't know anything about this."

"We didn't!" Joe glared at him.

Pablo arched an eyebrow at Shane. "*Licenciado?*"

Shane held his hands up, shaking his head. "Don't look at me, I didn't know anything about this, either."

"But why would our children do this? Who would help them do something like this?" Joe wondered. Everyone fell silent for a moment, then they all turned to look at the twins.

Pablo squeezed his water bottle, making the plastic crackle and pop under his crushing fingers. When he finally spoke, he addressed Deveraux, his voice dangerously low. "*Azulito?*" He paused, waiting for the young man to look at him. "Would you happen to know anything about this?"

Deveraux Azure looked up at his uncles as if in a daze. "I do." He choked on the words and coughed. When he tried again, his voice came out stronger. "I do."

Joe leaned forward, his eyes boring into his nephew's. "Talk to us, Blue."

Deveraux sighed. He scrubbed his hands over his face and looked back at them. "They came to me. The three of them." He hesitated.

"When was this?" Joe prompted.

"When Marina turned twenty-one. They wanted to give back to you, for everything you have ever done for them. You are their world."

"What do you mean they wanted to give back to us?" Joe demanded. "We are their parents!"

Deveraux spread his hands in helplessness. "Exactly. So they wanted to give you back their lives. This is the only way they thought they could do it."

"But they are so young!" Pablo exclaimed, glowering at him. "What were you thinking of?"

The young man shrugged, trying to defend himself. "Young people die, too! That was their reasoning. And I helped them. I thought they were being smart. That they were right." He sighed. "Crime can be random. They could be coming out of Cat's club and be assaulted because of who they are. They could get jacked. They could have an accident…"

"Okay, okay, we get the picture," Joe waved a hand at him. "Why didn't you tell us?"

Deveraux looked straight at him. "I am their lawyer. They are my clients. They knew you would get like this. React this way."

The group fell silent for a moment, everyone lost in their own thoughts.

Shane cleared his throat. He turned to the detectives amongst them. "As you can see, Pablo and Joe knew nothing about this."

Jamal nodded. "Oh, I can see that. No way you could fake this."

"Then what's the problem?" Joe asked.

"The problem is, where are the kids?" Jamal retorted.

"Summer got pulled into this as a precautionary measure," Rashawn explained.

"How's that?" Jesse wondered.

The detectives looked at each other, eyes communicating silently for a moment. Rashawn spoke up again. "The insurance company heard about the kids disappearing during Spring Break. They want to make sure that you, the parents, as beneficiaries to these millions didn't... haven't..."

"They think we murdered our own children?" Pablo roared. His fist came crashing down on the table, making all the other water bottles jump and topple over. "Over life insurance policies we knew *nothing* about?" Now his voice was low, shaking with emotion.

Joe gasped. "My God..." He covered his face with his hands for a moment, scrubbing it before running them over his cornrows. His heart felt like it would pound out of his chest. He turned to the older detective. "*You*," he said slowly, his voice hoarse with emotion, "have known us for years. Do you believe, that we would..."

"No!" Jamal cut him off, holding his hand up before he finished expressing what was so obviously and painfully not the case. "Of course not," he hissed, glaring at him. Like a cop. "But in this state, there doesn't have to be a body, for there to be a murder..."

Pablo nodded. "We get it."

Joe agreed. "At the kids being gone..."

"Where are the kids?" Jamal asked.

"They are safe," Pablo answered carefully.

"May I see them?" Rashawn asked. "It would help if Summer could talk to them and report back to the insurance company."

Shane shook his head sadly. "I'm afraid that's not possible right now."

"Well, can you prove they're alive?" Rashawn frowned, puzzled by the parents' reaction. "They *are* alive, aren't they?"

"Yes. They were alive last time we saw them." Joe looked at Pablo, his eyes crinkling at the corners. He chuckled, then, at a private joke. "You will have to go to them."

Pablo glanced at Joe and shook his head, the smile on his face growing wider. "But first we have a story to tell." He took a deep breath, and laughed. "How would you like to stay for dinner?" He turned to Derek and Tyler. "Call Rico's and order for us. Dinner for fourteen." He handed them his cell phone.

Distracted, Rashawn frowned. "Fourteen? There are only ten of us." He was puzzled at the sudden light mood he felt in everyone. Suddenly, there was a commotion from inside the house.

"*Papi!*"

Catamaran laughed. "Not anymore."

Xaira burst in, trailed by the pirates and Caribe. She stopped in front of Catamaran and glared at him. "Okay, Cat. It sounded like life or death."

Jesse reached for her hand and squeezed it with a laugh. "It is, baby girl."

Joe stood to make the introductions. At the sight of the ladies, all the men got to their feet also. "Jamal, Rashawn, meet our houseguests."

Pablo laughed. "Caribe is staying with us. He is our children's friend. And these are our in-laws. Don Carlos Gaitano and María Isabel Sandoval."

Jamal Blackmon swore under his breath. It seemed to him as if he'd been at the Hacienda for days instead of hours. He felt as if he were having an out-of-body experience. They'd had dinner from Rico's in the medieval dining room, and then had progressed from there to the family's movie theater. There, a story like none he had ever heard before had unfolded. He felt like Khan had, when his services had been solicited. There must be cameras somewhere, and people snickering behind the scenes, for real. But these were his friends. It was too elaborate a hoax. And there was no motive. If it hadn't been for Summer they wouldn't have even stumbled unto this. Certainly neither Pablo nor Joe had any reason to play such a trick on them. He dragged his hands down his face and looked at his friends. "Now, what?"

"Do you believe us?" Joe asked.

The detective met his eyes. "I don't know. Are you lying to me?"

Joe got upset. "What the hell do you think?"

Pablo put a hand on his arm, restraining him. He turned to the younger detective. "What about you?"

Rashawn shook his head. "I really don't want to…"

"Because…" prompted Shane.

"Because this can't be real," he protested.

"But…" Jesse encouraged him.

Rashawn sighed. "My instincts tell me that it is." He looked at the pirate. "It's all real, isn't it? The storm, Encantada…" He glanced at María Isabel. "Jackson, Salomé and Marina are really on that island, aren't they? They are actually there with your sons…"

María Isabel smiled sadly. "My sons are good men, Rashawn. Jackson and the girls are safe. And actually, quite happy. We realize they are not of our world, in the same manner we are not of yours. That we decided to merge, so to speak, was purely because it was the only practical thing to do," she added with a soft laugh. Both uncle and nephew were mesmerized with her speech. "Marina and Carlitos married, because they could not be one without the other any longer. The wedding took place when it did so that the Aguilars and the Banks could come back knowing that their daughter was well taken care of. The only reason they did not come back with us was because they wanted to hang out, as they say, in our world a little longer. The impact that these particular time travelers have had on our island has been immeasurable. Not only have they had effect on the local economy, but they have saved lives, and made some rich and aspiring pirates much wealthier. They have armies of men at their disposal. Men that would gladly give their lives for these sisters and brother. Do you think that these men would let anything happen to these young people after all they have achieved because of them?" She shook her head, laughing softly at the enthralled detectives. "They are pirates, gentlemen, not heathens. They are educated men. Jackson, Salomé and Marina made a conscious choice to remain a little longer. They will return, and they will not come back alone. I guarantee it. When they do arrive back at Blue Bay, they will be, not only wealthier than when they left, but richer from the experience alone."

"And you can prove this?" Jamal demanded for the third time since they had finished their fantastic tale.

Pablo rolled his eyes in exasperation. He turned to the twins. "*Muchachos*, would you be so kind as to show the detectives Marina's chest?" The twins disappeared and came back with the requested box between them. Pablo put his hands on the lid and looked at his friend straight in his eyes. "Now, keep in mind. This isn't ours. We are keeping it safe for our daughter. She earned it. It was an extravagant gift from some very grateful people as a token of their appreciation for services rendered." Raising an eyebrow, he waited until he nodded. Lifting the lid slowly, he revealed the contents. "How the hell do you think we could make this up?"

Jamal's eyes widened in much the same way Khan's had. Then he scowled ferociously. "What the hell do you call that?" he demanded.

"Pirate's treasure," Pablo growled back. "What the hell do you think I call it?"

"Or booty, if you'd rather," Joe shrugged.

Next to him, Rashawn swore under his breath. He turned to look at Pablo as he slammed the lid shut. "What are you going to do with that?"

Joe chuckled. "Nothing. It's not ours. Khan is working on moving Carlos' own bounty when he brings it over." He shrugged. "We'll soon know."

The pirate, quiet until now, stirred. He had kept silent throughout the whole thing. Had said nothing while Pablo and Joe told the story, during the slide show and even when the twins, the lawyer and his sons, Jesse and Xaira had expressed their unconditional support. Now he felt the need to defend his friends. "Have these people ever lied to you, Detective?" He smiled as the man shook his head.

"Why would they do so now? Why," he asked slowly, choosing his words carefully, "would they lie to you now, when they stand to lose everything? When they could be accused of the murder of their own children?"

"It doesn't make sense," Rashawn admitted.

"No, it doesn't," Jamal agreed. Taking a deep breath, he let it out in a long sigh. "When is the next storm?"

The pirate grinned. "Actually, in a couple of days." He laughed, teasing the men. "Care for some adventure, *caballeros*?"

"I have to see this with my own eyes," Jamal said firmly. He glanced at his friends. "If this is a hoax, I'm gonna kill you."

Joe smiled. "We know that."

Pablo clapped him on the shoulder. "We are not stupid, Detective." He laughed. "You are in for the adventure of your life."

Jamal glanced at the drawings that were still in his hand. "May I borrow these for a while? I would like to study them a little bit further."

"I'll get you copies," Pablo offered. Then he grinned. "We are keeping the originals. Caribe will be famous some day."

Don Carlos laughed in delight. "Anybody else care to join the party?"

Shane hurriedly shook his head. "Not me. I'm good. I believe them. I spoke to Jackson myself. He wasn't faking."

"I'm going," Cat announced suddenly. "I want to see our kids for myself."

Jesse nodded. "You couldn't keep me away if you killed me."

Rashawn shook his head. "Summer would strangle me with her bare hands if I didn't go." He laughed. "She knows these guys. Not only would she believe it in a heartbeat, but she's capable of having me bring her back a souvenir."

Don Carlos nodded, as nobody else volunteered. "It's decided, then. In a couple more days, we catch a storm to Encantada."

"What are we going to do with him?" Salomé sighed. Nobody said anything for a while. They were sitting around in a circle, legs crossed, heads together as they thought hard. The object of their attention sat on Jackson's lap, his little back against the hard bare torso. He grabbed Salomé's finger and brought it to his mouth, sucking eagerly. His beautiful brown eyes crinkled at the corners as he looked back at them smiling.

"Well, we're taking him with us right now," Jackson pointed out.

"We couldn't just leave him," Marina agreed.

The Captain sighed, wondering where this was all leading to. "We could keep him," he offered. All eyes turned to stare at him.

"No." Marina's voice was firm as she shook her head. Her eyes met her husband's. "No, Carlos. I love babies, but we don't need a ready made family. We need time to work on our own. We just got married," she reminded him, rolling her eyes with a smile. "We get to make our own baby."

Gaitano breathed a silent sigh of relief. He never knew quite what to expect from his woman. "All right, *mi amor*."

"So what happens with this baby?" Indio wondered.

Salomé flashed him a look. "Don't even think about it," she warned him. "We're certainly not keeping him. We're not even married."

Indio turned to look at her. "Will you marry me?"

Salomé gazed at the brave, oblivious of all eyes on her. "Yes."

He frowned, chest rising, trying to get his galloping heart under control again. "I have witnesses. You can't back down."

"I know," she breathed. "I won't."

"This isn't going away," he warned her. "If you are going to accept me, Indio, as your husband, and become a Gaitano like Marina, you better mean it."

Green fire seemed to burn deep inside her eyes. "Oh, I mean it, alright, baby. What about you, though? You're asking me to be your wife. Can you hang with the Aguilar-Banks?"

Smiling slowly, Indio locked eyes with her. "Yes," he answered, nodding once slowly. He lifted his hand in front of his face. His girl slid him some skin.

Jackson let out a sigh, breaking their spell. "Well, I'm not ready. I'm personally still reeling from Marina and Carlitos' wedding."

Storm nudged him with her elbow. "Nobody's asking you," she hissed at him with a smile.

Jackson grinned. "We're talking about Cacique here." Turning serious, he got back to the question at hand. "What are we going to do with him?"

"Well, I'm keeping him, but not for us," Marina answered, glancing at her husband.

"What do you mean not for us?" Gaitano demanded. "Who are you keeping him for?"

"I know someone who needs a baby right now much more than we do." She turned her head to look at her siblings. "I want Cacique for Jesse and Rain."

Salomé's eyes lit up, glowing with green fire. "Uncle Jesse!" she gasped. "Perfect!"

Jackson shook his head with admiration at his sister. "Rain is going to die."

"Either that or kill us," Salomé agreed.

"So you agree, it's a good idea?" Marina asked anxiously.

"It's an excellent idea, boo," her sister confirmed.

Jackson nodded. "Done. Cacique for Jesse. And God deliver us from Rain." They laughed softly, continuing to love the baby as the ship sailed steadily on, back to Encantada.

"So, this is it?" Jamal wondered, turning around in a circle.

"Yeah, it is. Sorry for the accommodations," Joe laughed. "We tried to get you a five-star hotel, but they were all booked."

"Surely you are not scared, Detective," Pablo teased. "This is nothing but a humble cave," he shrugged, spreading his hands wide.

"It is not the cave I'm worried about," Jamal grumbled.

"Not much of a cave," Catamaran observed.

"It's not the cave itself, what's important," Jesse pointed out.

"Well, we're here, now," Rashawn sighed.

Shane looked around and rubbed his hands. "Gentlemen!" he announced. "You are about to embark on an incredible journey. I wish you the best of luck," he stepped to the side as his sons moved around him, placing bags of clothes against the far wall.

Jamal jerked his head towards them. "Looks like there will be more of us coming back, than there are of us going." He turned to look at the pirate.

Don Carlos chuckled, anticipation gleaming in his eyes. "It is my and my wife's fervent hope, Detective, that you may be right."

The detective shook his head. "I don't know about this," he grumbled.

"Well, I know that I'm getting out of here," Blue said. He turned to his twin. "Good luck, man." They embraced before stepping back to look at each other. "Bring back our kids."

Catamaran nodded, winking at him. "That's the whole idea, man. Hold down the fort for me."

"How long are we going to be gone again?" Rashawn asked.

His uncle looked at the papers he was holding. "Six days. Starting tomorrow, until the day we get back. So that would leave us five full days and nights in Encantada." He looked at his hosts to confirm. "It shouldn't be more, right?"

Joe shook his head. "No, it shouldn't be. We came on blind faith. That timetable Jackson and Pablo created was right, down to the day." A sudden gust of wind blew through the cave.

Derek turned to the rest of the men. "Sorry to break up this party, guys. But we've got to go." As if agreeing with him, thunder rumbled overhead.

"Yeah, Dad, we've got to get out of here before the storm hits," Tyler agreed. He slapped hands with those that were staying and followed his brother out.

"Tell the kids I'm sorry about this whole mess," Blue called to his brother over his shoulder as he, too, exited the cave.

"I will have all of your cell phones now, if you please," Shane gave them last minute instructions. "I will have them back here fully charged the night before you get back so you can call us. We will be waiting." He turned to the detectives. "We do expect more of you to come back than there are of you going. You realize these kids are not coming back alone. But please, proceed with caution. Carlos will fill you in tonight with any last minute detail he considers relevant for you to know."

"Keep in mind, gentlemen," Pablo advised softly, "our youngest daughter just committed a heinous crime." He turned from one detective to the other as his words sank in. "We would greatly appreciate it if you didn't scare her to death. Her brand new groom might not take it lightly."

"Yes," agreed Joe. "Please, let there be no misunderstandings. We don't want anyone hurt." He turned to his relatives. "This includes you two cowboys. You are going to validate Jamal and Rashawn. Not to abduct our children. Is that clear?"

Jesse tilted his hat back on his head. "I got this."

"Aw, come on, man," Cat grumbled. "We are going as tourists. Nothing more."

"Make sure that's all it is," his uncle insisted. "For your own good." Joe stared at his nephew. "Cat?" He waited for him to look at him and scowled. "Don't fuck with Carlitos," he warned softly. "He's the real deal. They all are."

From outside, they heard the Butler boys calling. "Come on, Dad! It's starting to rain!"

Shane grinned. "We have to go." He shook hands with those who were going. "May you have luck in your journey. I would appreciate it if any of you kept a journal for me. You know, impressions, thoughts, that kind of thing…"

"Dad!"

Shane grinned. "Sorry, got to run. Let's go, *amigos*," he told Joe and Pablo. The men nodded, and followed him out to the mouth of the cave.

"Enjoy yourselves, men," Joe advised. "This is a once in a lifetime experience." He looked at each of the five men and nodded. He embraced each of them and left.

Pablo's eyes locked with the pirate's. "Carlos…"

Carlos Gaitano nodded at the unspoken request. "I will bring them home, Pablito. *Tranquilo, papi.*"

Pablo nodded. "I am counting on you." The men embraced one last time, and parted ways. The five who left were staying. They went down the cliff and swam out to their waiting boat, Shane's *Atlantico*. A few moments later, they were nothing more than a speck jumping on the distant waves. The five who remained were the ones going on the voyage of their lives. Now they all turned to look at each other.

The pirate laughed. "I suggest you make yourselves comfortable, *caballeros*. Storm will be here soon." They didn't move, silently watching the swirling clouds in the darkening sky. Lightning flashed overhead, followed by a loud clap of thunder. The wind picked up speed, beginning to flow in soothing dancing currents inside the cave, high next to the ceiling. The sun had dropped into the ocean long ago. The water churned, already black in contrast to the darkening sky. The men all turned and filed inside the cave. There, they were protected by the direct wind. For a moment, the modern day men just stood there looking at each other. Walking around them, the pirate lit strategically placed candles, making the cave glow softly. "Do not be afraid," he told them without looking at them directly. "This storm does not hurt. In fact, you won't feel a thing." He frowned, thinking for a moment as he kept puttering. "Maybe you do." He shrugged. "I was quite distracted when I came over with María Isabel and Caribe recently. I was embarking on an adventure into a world of which I knew nothing about." He chuckled to himself. "It seems you, gentlemen, have an advantage." Placing some blankets in the middle of the cave, he took a large candle and invited them to join him. They all sat around in a circle. "Now," Don Carlos smiled at them. "Is there anything anyone wants to know?"

Jamal looked steadily at the pirate. He was on high alert. But nothing was going off. No whistles, no bells, no alarms. On the contrary, he was coming to realize that the man before him was one he would trustingly follow in the pirate's world or in his own. He wasn't sure what he was getting into, but there was no turning back. He couldn't smile, though. Instead, he sighed. "I must confess, Don Carlos, I was quite overwhelmed the other day at the Hacienda."

The pirate's eyes began crinkling at the corners slowly. "I imagine you were." He chuckled as the other man shook his head, smiling back. "So, what may I help you with, Detective?"

Jamal grinned, finally, gratitude flooding his eyes. "If there are going to be pirates running amok in my town, I would like to know a little bit about whom they are, and where they come from. That way I can help them better with becoming good citizens of Blue Bay." He took a deep breath. "I would like to know more about the people I am going to meet, Don Carlos. I need to be prepared."

The pirate looked around at the rest of the young men. "Do you all feel the same way?"

They all nodded.

"Actually, I have had time to do a little research, and study these people, so I feel like I actually know these guys, some at least," Cat spoke quietly.

Jesse adjusted the cowboy hat lower over his forehead, shielding his eyes in the steady candle light. "Same here." He glanced up at the roof of the cave as thunder rumbled overhead once more. Drawing up his legs, he dug the heels of his cowboy boots in the sand in front of him. Draping his arms over his knees, one hand grasped the wrist of the other. "But the detectives here haven't had the same chance. Besides," he added, glancing at Catamaran, "it wouldn't hurt to review and have the information fresh."

Rashawn looked at the pirate. Inside the cave, the cubic zirconias in his ears gleamed with the reflection of the candles' flames. "I have to know these men, Don Carlos. These guys are my friends. The girls hang with my girlfriend Summer. They go shopping at the mall together. Jackson and I go way back." Beautifully shaped eyebrows raised in self-humor. "I would love to know what I am getting myself into."

"Aaaahhh," smiled the pirate, eyes sparkling with mischief. "You see, that, Rashawn, I cannot help you with." He shrugged. "Simply because I don't know what's in store for us, besides accomplishing this mission we have. Other than that," he spread his hands out in a helpless gesture, "I can only introduce you to the men you are going to meet."

Jamal handed him the copies of Caribe's drawings. "If you would be so kind, Don Carlos."

The pirate took the papers from him with a smile. "It would be my pleasure, Jamal." He shuffled the papers in his hands silently for a moment, glancing at them. Caribe had even included individual portraits. Taking a deep breath, he began. "This is the crew of La Gitana," he said softly, his voice filling with pride. "Carlos, Indio, Giancarlo, and Solomon." Slipping the paper behind the rest, he began with the individual portraits. "Carlos Juan Miguel Gaitano y Sandoval, twenty-eight. To family and friends, he is Carlitos. To the rest of the world he is Gaitano. Captain of La Gitana, El Tiburon, Starfish, and Poseidon. Commander of the island of Encantada. He is a good, God-respecting young man, Detectives. He is feared by some," he admitted, "he committed a serious mistake in his youth that earned him a name. Since then, he has been a very righteous and successful man. Pirate and sea merchant. What you would call a Robin Hood?" His eyebrows lifted with the question. At their nod, he continued. "Fantastic sense of humor, an even bigger sense of adventure. His men love him, his brother adores him. You can ask them yourselves. And he is as devoted to his uncles, his mother and

I, as we are to him. Recently married to Marina del Sol Aguilar of the Aguilar-Banks of Blue Bay. Now, he has included the Aguilar-Banks in his life and soon, yourselves." He shook his head, chuckling. "The poor boy is absolutely clueless." He sighed and grew thoughtful once again. "He has always been an extraordinary man. But *nothing*," he closed his eyes for emphasis, then opening them again, "*ever*, like the man he has become since meeting Marina."

Jamal nodded. "I have known the Aguilar-Banks for decades. It must be good, for them to approve."

"Oh, yes," agreed the pirate. "You will see for yourself."

"He's that gone, huh?" asked Rashawn.

The pirate grinned, lifting his eyebrows with mischief. "Jackson has led me to believe the term is *whipped*, Detective." The men laughed. The picture changed. "Indio Gaitano, twenty-eight. I have raised him since the age of two, but I have been in his life since years before the day he was born." A finger lovingly traced the feather in the young brave's hair and the hoops in his ears. "He is Carlito's brother and First Mate. His right hand. His companion and best friend. They live and would gladly die for each other. That is why it has been Heaven sent that they end up with sisters like Salomé and Marina who are so close themselves, they can only understand the brothers' relationship. Indio is the Quartermaster of Gaitano's ships. He has never been interested in owning his own ship."

Rashawn frowned. "Why is that?"

Don Carlos chuckled. "He doesn't want the responsibility. Ships, men…" The pirate shook his head. "No, not Indio. Indio has been saving his fortune. Just like his brother. He owns half of El Tiburón, Starfish, and Poseidon. They are equal partners, really, except in one sense. One is Captain and the other is Quartermaster. Indio does not have his own ship or his own crew. The only thing that distinguishes them is that Gaitano owns and is Captain of *La Gitana*." He sighed. "Indio is content to be with his brother. Or he was, until now." He laughed. "Now, he is with Salomé."

"Would he come here to be with her?" Catamaran was curious. His eyes gleamed in the candlelight, his hands going up to hold his dreadlocks away from his face.

"Yes." The pirate looked at him steadily. "Indio was the first one told about this…" His hand waved around at the cave, as more thunder rumbled overhead. "This situation, so to speak." He explained. "Salomé was equally entranced by Indio as he was by her. She wanted to spend more time with him, and decided to tell him the truth, to see if it would affect his feelings for her in any way." He chuckled, shaking his head. "Well, to say my son was delighted at this new adventure would be putting it mildly." He laughed. "He has always been a very serene, contained young man. Now, he seems to crackle with energy, whenever he is around her. He has changed." He nodded, looking at all of the men. "You can expect to see my son Indio in your Blue Bay."

"Indio's position as First Mate and as brother and best friend must be priceless to Gaitano," Jesse observed. He reached up with one hand and adjusted the cowboy hat on his head.

"Absolutely," Don Carlos agreed. "Indio was in charge of the takeover of *La Diosa del Mar.*

Jamal frowned. "Is that a ship?"

The pirate nodded. "A Spanish galleon." The men whistled appreciatively. "Indio could retire on his share and live happily ever after with the beautiful Salomé. As Quartermaster he makes a lot of the decisions. He is also in charge of order at sea and on land. Something like you, detectives." He smiled.

"So, Indio is like Gaitano's partner," Jesse suggested.

The pirate nodded again. "Exactly." He went on to the next portrait. "This man has a lot in common with you, Catamaran." He glanced up at the jewel green eyes. "He is a business man, also." Taking a deep breath, he presented the next pirate. "Giancarlo Ilarraza, also twenty-eight. He has been running with Carlitos and Indio since they were about ten. His parents came from Italy, his father was a merchant. Gian, however, chose to play with the big boys. Once they understood they couldn't dissuade him, they left him in our care. He owns the *Sirens' Lair.* That is our local…" he frowned for a moment, looking for a word, "…bar, you could say. He is Gaitano's Sailing Master. Giancarlo directs the course of the ship. He is in charge of navigation." He slid the portrait behind the last one. "This young man," he frowned, "is Solomon. He is from Africa. Carlitos rescued him from being marooned a few years back. Since then, Solomon has saved his life twice, the last time being at the taking of *La Diosa del Mar*. We don't know much about him, gentlemen, and truthfully, we don't care. We respect his privacy and his pain." He arched an eyebrow at them. "After all, he comes from Africa to the New World…" He spread his hands as if he didn't need any more words. The men in front of him nodded in understanding. "Solomon is the Boatswain. He is in charge of maintenance and supplies. He is also in charge of helping take care of Marina. The girl tends to get a little emotional at times," he grinned, rolling his eyes, making them laugh. "Solomon and Marina fight, gentlemen. It is a thing of beauty to watch. She may be the master, but he has learned fast. Lately, he has hurt her during their fights." He sighed, shaking his head in puzzlement. "It is frightening how she enjoys pain."

"Marina is well trained," Jamal felt the need to defend her. "As well as Jackson and Salomé. They have been fighting since they were in diapers."

Rashawn grinned. "She likes to fight with the boys alright. I know from experience." He nodded at the pirate. "I've fought with Marina."

Jesse chuckled. "I'll bet she's kicked Solomon's ass."

Don Carlos laughed out right. "Many times."

Catamaran waved a hand in the air. "It's all good. It all comes from Blue and me beating her up when she was little." The men laughed, but at the pirate's startled expression Cat had to confess. "It's cool, Don Carlos, I'm just playing."

Shaking his head, the pirate began laying out the portraits. This way the men could absorb the information he was giving them better. "Now, these two women are lady pyrates. This one," he said, tapping the young woman on the left, "is Rouge. She is captain of her own ship, the Sea Gypsy, and responsible for her own crew. Rouge also ran around with the boys, along with her cousin, Jack, until she became a young woman. She is with Giancarlo." He gently laid her portrait on top of his in such a manner their faces were next to each other. They made a stunning couple. "They have fought their love for years, doing their best not to make enemies."

"That's right," Catamaran remembered from the day he met the pirate. "The rest of the pirates are afraid of their power if they get together."

"That is correct," Don Carlos confirmed. "But since Gaitano and Indio met Marina and Salomé…" He shrugged. "They will overcome any obstacles in their way. I agree with María Isabel. They will get together soon. This one," he said, pointing at the other young woman, "is Storm."

The men peered at the picture, studying it closely.

"She is very cute," Rashawn observed.

"Yes," agreed the pirate. "Storm is quite beautiful inside and out. She's also a fierce pyrate," he warned them.

"She good in a fight?" Jamal asked.

"The best," Don Carlos nodded. "Storm is Rouge's Quartermaster." Then he grinned. "Storm is also Jackson's girlfriend."

Rashawn laughed. "Lucky Jackson."

"Yes. They both are." The pirate lay down another paper. "Rouge is part of the Council. So is this young man. Jack is Captain of the Black Mermaid. They both have hair the color of fire." He moved on. "Now, these men are new to our waters. They came looking for trade, and in turn, found a little bit more than they were bargaining for. However, thanks to," he took a deep breath, "Marina Aguilar, accountant of La Gitana at the time, presently of La Sirena, their wealth has increased." He gestured with his hands. "That is why the treasure chest Pablo and Joe are guarding so closely. It was a gift from the Council." He continued. "Jai Ling, Captain of *Ocean Wind*, obviously comes from the Orient. Suleiman is from the Mediterranean, and his ship is the *Chymera*. Sultan, Captain of *Kalahari*, is from Africa. They have all, along with Rouge and Jack, and my brother, have sworn loyalty to Marina Aguilar. And by association and by their own merit, Jackson and Salomé Banks."

"This one looks like you," Jamal said quietly, pointing out the largest pirate in the group.

Don Carlos laughed. "This is my older brother, Miguel. Captain of *La Gaviota*." His face grew sad for a moment. "He lost his family, a wife and an infant daughter, in the same accident Indio lost his parents." His voice dropped to a hushed whisper, his eyes whipping around the men. "It is never spoken about. My sons do not even know. They are all he has." The men nodded solemnly. Clearing his throat, he blinked back his tears and shrugged. "As you can see, he is quite large. His energy is very powerful." Smiling, he seemed to be looking at a distant memory. "Miguel can make a grown man cry with a look alone." He grinned at them. "The girls can tell you." He sighed, waving his hand over the paper. "This is the Council. Gaitano had to present his findings before them, and he took Marina."

"So, that's when he kidnapped her," Jamal said thoughtfully.

"That, Detective," Don Carlos answered softly, "is when they fell in love."

Catamaran snickered, his eyes glowing wickedly. "It don't matter anymore. Hurt as I was that I wasn't present, boy's in the family now."

"Poor guy," Rashawn laughed.

Jesse rocked back and forth, a smile twitching at the corners of his mouth. "Gaitano is a smart man. He'll know better than to hang with the likes of you." They laughed.

The wind picked up then, beginning to howl softly around the ceiling. It seemed to flutter for a moment, like when a small bird flies inside a church, and looks for a way out. Suddenly, the cave was completely illuminated by light as strong as the flash of any camera. The men fell silent for a moment, waiting for the thunder to follow. It did, first rolling, and then crashing and booming into its own echo. The wind lashed around the cave once more, making the flames of the candles brace themselves, shuddering on the wicks. Hands came out, paperweights on Caribe's artwork. The men sighed as the candlelight steadied.

The pirate took a deep breath, anxious now to finish his report. "The only other people you are to concern yourselves with are these." He jabbed at a family portrait. "The Klines own Encantada's only general store. John is part of Gaitano's army, and Larissa is close with the girls. Max is their baby son. Marina is in charge of the baby while the parents work." He frowned for a moment, thinking hard. "I heard them call it *daycare*." The men laughed, making the pirate smile. "Marina also takes care of these babies. Juan and Jaime are twin boys belonging to a couple of natives." He continued throwing papers down. "Padre Ignacio is our local priest." He shook his head, his eyebrows rising with mischief. "He betrayed Marina when he invited her to mass in his church and Solomon abducted her. I don't think she has forgiven him. And Pedro Barbosa is our local sheriff. He had to lock Jackson up in order for Gaitano to sail away with Marina. They are part of Gaitano's army." He sighed. "This is Liana. Carlitos gave her the dress shop he took from Dominique Swan, Xavier's sister. She is promised to Dr. Kyle Richardson, the island medic. These two fellows are also part of Gaitano's army. The old timer is Silas, and the Chinaman is Jimmy. They take care of the Lair while Giancarlo is at sea. At night, they go to the village to watch the natives dance." He rolled his eyes with a smile. "That's where they saw the girls. They told Indio where he could find Salomé." He sighed, shaking his head. Yet another paper. "Manuel and Leila are Caribe's parents." He smiled fondly at the portrait of the couple. "Leila is the liaison between the two worlds." He frowned thoughtfully for a moment. "Seeing as how we are here now, she'll probably dream about us tonight. If she hasn't already," he added.

Catamaran nodded. "The difference being she doesn't have Caribe to do the drawings for her."

The pirate looked at him. "That's right. But that doesn't mean she won't know who you are. Trust me. Leila sees you coming." He chuckled at the thought. There were two papers left. They were each of a different pirate. The first one was of a very large man, almost of the proportions of Don Miguel Gaitano. Caribe had captured him unawares; a brooding expression in his eyes, the rugged face captured in clear detail, from the smile wrinkles around his eyes, to his graying hair ruffling in the wind. "This is John Hawthorne. He is the reason Marina's not in prison at this moment in time. He is the law in our waters." He explained hurriedly before they could voice a question. "John was there when it happened. He actually went into the Lair with Marina when she went looking for Xavier. Witnessed the whole thing." He sighed.

Jamal cleared his throat. "Would your John Hawthorne change his mind?"

The pirate shook his head hurriedly. "No. John, like just about every other pirate that has set eyes on her, believes Marina has been Heaven sent. John was with Marina the whole time she confronted Xavier. I have known him since before our children were born. He has three grown sons around Carlitos and Indio's age. They work together, sort of like you and Rashawn. They are based in Carey, however." He took a deep breath and shook his head slowly. "No, gentlemen. John Hawthorne will not be taking Marina away." He shrugged, dismissing the idea, muttering under his breath. "John is crazy about her." Candlelight flickered again, licking at the hollows and planes of his ruggedly handsome face, the flames mirrored in his eyes. "It is not John Hawthorne Marina has to worry about," he added solemnly.

Catamaran stared at the pirate. "Xavier is dead."

Don Carlos turned his head to look at him. "Yes. His men are not."

Jesse whistled, pushing back the hat on his head. "Are we headed for trouble?"

The pirate shrugged. "There are five of us." The men laughed.

Rashawn pointed to the last portrait. "Who is this other guy?" Caribe had caught a young man, in full pirate attire. A cross hung on his chest; his boots were folded with big silver studs on the sides. His coat seemed to be fluttering in the wind, and the expression on his handsome face was thoughtful and intense. His hair was longish, brushing the tops of his shoulders, and hoops hung from his ears.

Don Carlos frowned, gazing at the young man. He sighed. "I really have no idea why Caribe would include this one. He," he told them, tapping the young man's chest, "is also the law in our waters. He sails *La Prision,* a prison ship that is in charge of taking away our worst criminals. This is my younger brother, Juan Gaitano." He glanced at the detectives. "If we have the luck to run into him, you will all get along just fine." Putting the papers neatly in order, he handed them to Jamal. Smiling wickedly, he turned to them. "Gentlemen," he grinned when he got their attention, his look sinister in the cavelight. "Care to join me outside for a few minutes, and catch a time warp?"

Grinning back, the men joined him.

Heaven and ocean spread out before them. The sky displayed a steady light show, as bolts and flashes of lightning provided enough clarity for them to see every detail. Waves churned with whitecaps. They moved in a circular motion, slowly picking up speed. The clouds above them began a circular motion themselves, but in the opposite direction. Spinning faster, a thin thread appeared out of the ocean, defying gravity, rising to the center of the churning clouds. The sky seemed to create a vacuum effect, suctioning the water until the ocean below it stilled. The men caught their breaths as a flash of lightning held, suspending the moment in time. Far off, a boom sounded across the water, creating a ripple that rushed towards them at frightening speed, making them shudder against the cold wind that hit them, filling the cave behind them and spilling over. Once gone, everything held for a heartbeat. Then the water just dropped out of the sky, splashing heavily down below. The ocean received it excitedly, absorbing the water as a nurturing mother. The sky restarted its light show. The men breathed again.

The pirate grinned, laughing as the fading lightning burst strongly one last time, illuminating his features. The men's heart sped up, there was no mistake. Now they knew without a doubt. This was the real thing. Don Carlos spread out his hands with the abandon of a child. *"Caballeros!"* he boomed, competing with the thunder overhead. *"Welcome to Encantada!"*

Back at the Hacienda Aguilar-Banks, a family gathered at a small poolside table. The umbrella was folded at the moment, giving them a better view of the spectacular storm performing overhead. Pablo and Sloane Aguilar held hands, as did Joe and Shayla Banks. Between them, María Isabel Sandoval de Gaitano, rosary clasped between her hands. Their lips moved in an old ritual, their intentions clear in their minds and in their hearts. They all prayed for the return of their children, the arrival of the young pirates, and the safety of the men who went to get them. And they especially prayed for the pirate orchestrating the whole thing, Don Carlos Gaitano.

Xaira scowled, her beautiful almond eyes glittering. Frustrated, she shook the hair out of her eyes and turned to glare at Caribe. Island Boy glared right back. She huffed at him and then her hair was whipping around her head as she turned and walked away. Caribe looked after her. He couldn't help rolling his eyes with a big sigh. They had been hanging out together almost since they met. Xaira had attached herself to him as if he were a lifeline to her precious Marina. She had taken him to the movies, as promised, spent hours watching TV and at the library, and days at a time on the internet. Caribe was smart and educated, and as absorbent as a thirsty sponge. It had been a wonderful trip until now. They had been discussing art in its many forms, and as enthralled as he was by the masters and other artists, Caribe wasn't interested in trying any of these alternate forms himself. Not oils, not watercolors, not even crayons would make him unfaithful to his beloved sketches. He could if he wanted, it wasn't that. It was just that he simply didn't want to. His sketches were like his children, and he was quite happy. He didn't want anything else in his life. Now he took a deep breath and sighed, pulling his dreads out of his face for a moment before following her. She stopped and stood in front of the enormous picture windows in the apartment she shared with Marina. Outside, lightning flashed over the ocean, clearly marking the line between sky and water. It was dark already, and you really couldn't see much, except for the fact that there was nobody on the beach at this hour. Caribe stood behind her and caught her flinching at another burst of lightning. Sighing, he put his arms around her in a brotherly gesture, pulling her against his chest and dropping his chin on top of her head. For a moment he said nothing, waiting quietly as she relaxed in his arms. He sighed again. "You realize you are being a brat."

Her voice was as quiet as his. "No, *you* are."

Frowning above her, he felt exasperated at his own need to explain himself. "It's not that I don't like everything you are showing me, Xaira. I love it! But it's not me."

"You won't even try!" she accused softly, tears creeping into her voice. "What is it about your sketches that have you so in love with that style of art?"

He let out a slow breath, thankful for the patience he had acquired from his dealings with Marina and Salomé. "The result is immediate."

"It takes you days to complete a sketch," she pointed out.

"Yes," he agreed, "but that's filling in the details real carefully. I can have a recognizable face in a few minutes. I couldn't hope to get the same results painting."

Xaira sniffled. "You need a camera." Then she mumbled. "I can't believe you won't even try."

Caribe scowled and squeezed her, pressing his chin more firmly on top of her head. His voice rumbled in his chest, vibrating along her back. "Okay, okay, I'll try." Pulling back, he spun her around to face him. His heart clenched in his chest as he caught sight of her eyes swimming in tears. It reminded him of pebbles under water as the river gurgles over them. He scowled deeper, upset at himself for making her cry. "I'll try, Xaira. I'll do it just for you, because it's not something I have to do for myself. I can't stand to see you so disappointed in me. I'll do one of everything for you, I promise. I'll even try sculpting and pottery if you want, and you can have one of every one of my tries. But it's not just me." He reached out with a finger and caught a tear on its tip as it spilled from one of her eyes. Without thinking he licked the salty drop, unaware of her heart speeding up. Looking into her eyes, he tried staring into her soul. "There is something else, isn't there? You're not crying just because I won't play with colors, or paint. What's wrong?" His eyebrows rose, stopping her before she began shaking her head. "In the whole time I have known you, you haven't cried because I wouldn't try something. As a matter of fact, we've been spending just about all our time together, and I have never seen you cry," he accused. "What is it? It can't be me."

Xaira shook her head quickly. "It's me," she blurted out. She wiped her tears away with the backs of her hands, like a small child. The gesture tugged at the young native's heart. Now she looked back at him, relaxed with his arms around her. "I'm scared here, Caribe. It's scary at night. I'm tired of waiting for Marina to come home."

Caribe frowned. "Tyler and Derek are right here below you."

"Yeah! Two stories below me!" She shook her head. "And I don't want to bother them, you know? They go out and come home late, and sometimes I'm all alone in this building, all the way up here, with just the dogs…" she gasped, beginning to sob, "and I'm scared to death, I'm not that brave…" She broke off suddenly, burying her face against his chest.

"Why haven't you told Ocean?" he demanded, referring to Change's oldest. "He's your best friend! He would stay here with you."

"Yeah!" she retorted. "But you can't get anything past Jill, she's the dragon mother! And then you have Change and Uncle Jesse involved, and before I know it the whole family is camping here!" She shook her head. "Don't you get it, Caribe?" she pleaded, tears filling her eyes again. "I am really afraid."

He frowned, totally not understanding. "How could you be so scared? Marina, Salomé, and Jackson have been gone for about three months."

"I know," she wailed quietly. "And nothing had been going on, that whole time! It's just been recently," she hiccupped. "Since you guys got into town." She shuddered. "I thought I was imagining it at first, but now sometimes I just know someone's up there, and I have to pretend I don't until he goes away…"

Caribe sighed, holding her tighter, trying to ease her sobbing, and rubbing her back. He crooned in her ear until she was down to sniffles. "Okay, now tell me more. Explain this thing you are saying to me."

Wiping at her tears again, she pulled back to look at him. "Sometimes I feel as if somebody's watching me," she confided quietly. "While I sleep."

Caribe frowned. "How is that possible?"

Xaira lifted a finger, drawing his gaze up. "The skylights," she whispered. "If someone gets on the roof, they could look down at me in my bedroom or Marina's, or out here."

"How could anybody get up there?"

"Fire escape on the street below. If they can reach it, they can get all the way up to the roof."

"What about the dogs?"

"They sleep inside and mostly patrol the stairs between the floors. It's pretty tight inside here," she drew a shaky breath, "but somebody could actually get on the roof."

Caribe thought for a moment, his hands absently rubbing her arms, soothing her. "Who would do something like that?"

Xaira shook her head, hair flying in slow motion. "I have no idea." Her eyes overflowed with tears. "I don't know what's going on."

Caribe nodded. "Take me upstairs."

Xaira took one of his hands and pulled him behind her. She guided him up some spiral stairs to the roof. Unlocking a gate, and opening a door, they finally found themselves outside. The wind whipped around them, making them huddle against it. Lightning flashed in the distance a little faster, clearer without the salt coated glass of the windows. Caribe looked around him in wonder. It was another world up there. It had been designed for cookouts, sunbathing, and private gatherings. Tastefully decorated it boasted a garden, a patio, a hot tub, and even a lap pool for exercise. There were small trees in huge terracotta planters bordering the perimeter of the building. There were different decks for the different activities, all connected with beautiful walkways with large rough tiles. The lighting made it into a beautiful, inviting wonderland. They went to the skylights, one by one, walking around them. Around the edges, where the frames held the bubble down, was the usual debris you would expect to find. Leaves that had curled in the wind and died. Down feathers from pigeons and seagulls. Twigs, sand, and cigarette butts neatly lined up next to each other, wedged into the frame.

Caribe pulled on Xaira's hand and led her back downstairs, making sure to carefully lock the door and gate behind them. "There's nothing up there," he told her.

Xaira nodded miserably. "I know. I told you it was me."

He stared straight into her eyes. "Do you want me to stay with you?"

Without hesitating, she nodded. "Please."

Caribe sighed again, and looked over her head at the stormy night beyond the windows, letting her go to rub his hands up and down her arms. Finally, he looked at her. "Okay. Take me to the Hacienda first."

Pablo looked at Caribe, searching his eyes. Xaira had handed the native boy a cell phone camera, and after showing him how to use it, had left him to his own devices. Once alone, Caribe had sought out Pablo and Joe, expressing what had passed between Xaira and himself. It was evident by their reaction that they took him seriously. "Are you sure?" Pablo asked.

It was Caribe's turn to nod miserably. "Yes. I saw them myself. There were cigarette butts all lined up carefully over their bedrooms and their sitting room where the TV is. It seemed to me as if they were wedged into the frames so they wouldn't roll around on the roof in the wind. They are still there."

Joe rubbed his jaw thoughtfully. "Our kids may smoke the occasional bowl, but they don't smoke cigarettes."

"I know," Caribe looked at him.

"Okay," Pablo said hurriedly, spying the beautiful Xaira headed their way. "Stay with her. Double check every door and window in the place. Do not leave her side. Let the dogs loose." Laughing, he turned to Marina's precious protégé, their own beautiful youngest daughter. "I hear you're having a pajama party, *mamita*! Come on! We're treating you. Hook you up with some popcorn and snacks, a few movies, whatever you need."

Excited, Xaira grasped Caribe's hand. "Cool! I'm doing an experiment with Caribe. Since he's really not interested in anything else," she rolled her eyes, "I want to see what he can do with a camera. I want a couple of disposable cameras, one color and one black and white. I'd also like him to try out a video camera, if that's okay."

"Whatever you want, baby girl," Joe smiled at her.

"What about a regular digital camera?" Pablo suggested. "*I'd* like to see what Caribe can do." Clapping Caribe on the shoulder, he laughed.

The four of them left for the twenty-four hour Wal Mart located on the outskirt of the city, to stock up on the makings of a pajama party for two. When it was time for them to part ways, Pablo looked steadily at Caribe. Caribe nodded quietly, and climbed behind Xaira on her motorcycle.

The rottweilers looked at Caribe, cocking their heads. He had coaxed them to sit in front of the huge fish tank, in the living area. He was down on the floor, pointing a camera up at them, the spectacular fish swimming as a backdrop. He used the cell phone to begin with. Then came the disposable cameras, first the black-and white, followed by the color one. The digital camera was next, and finally the video camera. He intoned quietly, in the manner of big-game hunters recording the stalking of their prey. "This," he rumbled quietly, "is a portrait of the mighty keepers of the Aguilar-Banks and Butler crew. This handsome couple is better known as Samson and Delilah. They are hard-working and fun. Smart and obedient, you will never find a more faithful pair. Home: Marina Aguilar and Xaira Chang. Samson and Delilah: Captured by Caribe." Smiling, he stopped the video and put it down. Getting to his knees, he called the dogs over and hugged them. "Good dogs," he muttered, rubbing their heads briskly. "Awesome animals, you are." The dogs licked him and pawed him for a while, willing him to continue playing with them. He laughed and stood up, letting them go.

"Caribe!" Xaira was calling him from the kitchen. He walked towards her voice, in time to catch her tossing some lettuce into a bowl for a salad. It smelled good. He knew there were steaks cooking. Feeling him behind her, she continued with what she was doing. "Would you like a bubble bath?"

Caribe grinned. "Sure!"

She tossed him a smile over his shoulder. "Go to my bathroom and help yourself. I'll go in and wash your dreads, if you want."

He sighed happily. "That would be really nice."

"See you later." And she continued flitting around the kitchen.

Caribe turned, grabbing the bag from Wal-Mart off the kitchen counter. Pablo and Joe had bought him a complete change of clothes, including underwear. He made his way to the bathroom, biting off price tags, and tossing the garbage in the bag. Wadding it up, he crammed it into the small trash can and shut the door behind him. He piled his clothes on the toilet seat and added a fresh fluffy towel he grabbed from the rack by the sink. Finally, he pulled back the shower curtain and turned on the hot water in the old-fashioned tub. Scanning the plastic bottles on a rack at the end of the hot tub, he reached for an opaque one with yellow duckies on it. Uncapping it, he smelled it and smiled. It would do. He poured a generous amount of the pearly creamy liquid into the steaming stream of water and recapped it, putting it back where it belonged. Stretching, he began undressing, peeling his T-shirt over his head. Reaching for the faucets again, he began cutting the scalding hot water with some cold, so he could bear it. Off came his jeans, and his underwear. Folding everything neatly, he rolled it into a bundle and carefully put it on the floor. Now he was ready. He climbed in carefully, stepping into the cooler stream of water. First one foot, and then the other, he sighed, happily wiggling his toes in the swirling water. Finally, he could sit down. The bubbles rose, much higher than the water, he realized, a little dismayed. So he slowed the water pressure, until he could handle them a little better. A few minutes later, he turned the water off and leaned back, closing his eyes. He sighed with pleasure. A knock sounded on the door. He groaned inside. "Come in."

The door opened, and Xaira peeked her head around the door. Seeing the situation, she began giggling. Caribe was all but obscured by a mountain of glistening white foam. He had created a space around his head, but the only thing visible was his dreads. "Defeated by the bubbles, huh?" She giggled again. Caribe opened one eye and completely cleared the rest of the bubbles from his face, turning his head to look at her. She strode towards him decisively and reached for the modern shower head attached to the wall. Sing-songing nonsense to him, in the same manner Marina would, she sprayed the bubbles down until they were at a more manageable level. Then she soaked his hair. Caribe sat quietly as she diligently shampooed it, rinsed it, conditioned it, let it soak for a while, rinsed it again, and blotted his dreads dry. "There," she told him, twisting his hair into a turban made from the colorful beach towel. Using both hands, she squeezed rhythmically as hard as she could, until the water passed from his hair to the towel. Then she unwrapped his dreads again, dropping the towel on the floor and draping the ropes of his hair around him. "You should get a haircut. You would look awesome."

Caribe nodded without a thought. "Take me to get one. I will try."

She smiled at him. "Okay."

Caribe grinned. "I'm almost done. Are you going to get clean before we eat?"

Xaira nodded, smiling into his beautiful brown eyes, almost amber, so different from hers, almost black. "What did you have in mind?"

Leaning over the side of the tub, Caribe reached for the cell phone on top of his pile of clothes. His eyes never left Xaira's, and when his voice came out, it was husky. "Come here." Intrigued, the girl moved closer. Slipping an arm around her neck, he pulled her closer. She began struggling, laughing, as she realized what his intentions were. Smiling, he raised his eyebrows at her and shushed her, shaking his head gently at her. Pulling her even closer, he hauled her over the edge of the tub and lowered her into the bubbles on his lap. Dissolving into giggles, Xaira wrapped her arms around his neck, already soaked. Caribe dribbled water over her head before wiping it off her face. They grinned at each other. "Now, give me a kiss," he instructed, as he had heard Cat and Blue do so many times.

Xaira pulled herself closer to him and pressed her lips against his. Their hearts beat faster. Pulling back to look at him, Xaira felt shy all of a sudden. "I liked that," she confessed.

Caribe nodded at her, keeping her in his arms, flipping the cell phone open behind her back. He kissed her forehead, lifting his hand, and glanced over her head, getting it on camera mode, and pointed it at their reflection in the mirror on the wall next to the tub. Then he looked into her eyes. "So did I. Now, give me another kiss." Eagerly, Xaira complied, giving him many kisses. Wet, sticky kisses that tied his stomach in knots. Finally, one lingering kiss. Caribe pressed the button under his thumb. The bathroom echoed with a clicking sh-kshh noise. In his arms, Xaira stirred, drawing away slowly, ending the kiss reluctantly. At her puzzled look, he grinned. "Nothing," he reassured her in a whisper. "Just us." He laughed softly. "Captured by Caribe."

Xaira squinted until her eyes were slits and nodded at him. "Oh." She sighed happily. "Now get out. My turn."

Caribe laughed. "As you wish." Maneuvering gently, he got out from under her and climbed out of the tub. Quickly, he wrapped his towel around his body and let himself drip for a moment on her beautiful bathroom rug.

"Go ask Tyler and Derek if they'll join us for dinner and a movie tonight," Xaira called after him, as he left to get dressed. Smiling to herself, she removed her wet clothes and dumped them in the bathroom sink to take care of later. Lowering herself into the still hot bath water, she proceeded to wash her own hair. She couldn't stop smiling.

Derek stared at Caribe. "You actually believe this," he said in wonder. "You're not playing, are you?"

Caribe shook his head sadly. His voice rumbled low in his chest, as he had learned from the pirates. "I don't want Xaira to know. But somebody has been up there."

"Okay," Tyler said hurriedly, spying Xaira setting the table for them. "Let's let out the dogs tonight on the roof for a little while. They love it up there, anyway. We'll go check on the fire escape."

Caribe nodded. "Cool."

They had a most pleasant evening. Dinner was fantastic. Steaks were delicious and the salad was crisp and cold. They shared beers and interesting conversation. The Butler boys were fully supportive of Caribe's pursuit of capturing his vision of the world with photography. Then they offered to do the dishes for Xaira, which she gladly accepted. From the dining/kitchen area, they moved it upstairs to the roof. Dessert was a sweet creamy drink which they shared quietly. The dogs ran around happy in the dark, barking at the storm raging overhead. Playing, Tyler and Derek chased them around the skylights. Coming back to the pair, they met Caribe's eyes over Xaira's head. They had seen what they were supposed to. The wind whipped around them suddenly, forcing them back downstairs. They watched a scary movie, shared popcorn and soda, and had a good time. The young men finally left for their own apartment, determined to double check the whole building, Samson and Delilah at their sides. Caribe and Xaira smooched outside her bedroom door, smiling goodnight into each other's eyes. Caribe left her there and retreated to the living room, where he was supposed to use a futon mattress laid out on top of the pool table. He dimmed the light in the aquarium until the fish were mere flashes of scales in the inky water. Their movements soothed him. Outside of the aquarium you could see the silhouettes of furniture, tables and bookcases, so he wouldn't bump into anything if he needed to get up. Sighing, he laid down and looked straight up through the skylight into the stormy night. Nobody in his right mind would be out tonight. Closing his eyes, he immediately fell asleep.

Caribe opened his eyes, momentarily disoriented. Movement in front of him made him focus, and he finally recognized the aquarium. Taking a deep breath, he let it out slowly. Now he was wide awake. Something was different. Then he realized what it was. Xaira was plastered to his back, spooning him. He chuckled silently, carefully moving away from her and rolled over unto his back.

Xaira stirred, mumbling in her sleep. "I was scared."

Caribe took her hand in his and brought it to his lips, kissing her wrist. "It's okay, baby," he reassured her quietly, moving his arm to slip around her. She snuggled closer to his side, her head on his chest for a little while. He stroked her hair and sighed, glancing up. Caribe froze. His heart stopped and then thundered away. He willed it to slow down, not wanting to wake Xaira up. He immediately stopped stroking her, not wanting to give himself away. An ember glowed over his head. He watched quietly, knowing that the aquarium was dim enough it wouldn't reflect light in his eyes. Just in case, he slit them anyway, until he was peering through his eyelashes. The ember glowed again, from a different spot. Whoever it was, he was walking around the skylight. It happened again, a couple more times. Then he saw the silhouette of the figure behind it, as they laid the cigarette down on the frame. The person moved, and then was gone.

Caribe waited for a moment. Slipping out from under Xaira, he climbed off the pool table and raced to the kitchen. The nightlight provided by the small fish tank on the long counter was enough to allow him to see what he was doing. Flinging drawers open, he finally found what he was looking for. Racing through the apartment, he stopped for a moment to grab his cell phone and quickly made it to the roof. At the skylight over the pool table, a cigarette still glowed next to its companions. As fast as he could, he crouched and took a picture of it. Then Caribe ran to the edge of the roof and looked down. Below him, a figure jumped off the fire escape, letting it clang against the building, and hit the ground running. He snapped another picture at the fleeing figure. Shaking his head, Caribe went back to the skylight. In his hand was a Ziploc baggie. Turning it inside out, he grasped the cigarette butt. He knew what to do. He had been watching a lot of Investigation Discovery lately. He put it out and flipped the bag right side in again. He sealed it. Downstairs, he wrote the place, date and time with a permanent marker and slipped it into the pocket of his folded jeans, before climbing back on the pool table. Turning on his side he sighed as Xaira spooned him again. Taking her hand in his, he kissed it softly over and over, as he dwelled on the events that just took place. It took him a long time to fall asleep. He couldn't stop thinking and wondering at himself and his thoughts. Hanging out with the pirates must have worn off even more than he imagined. His thoughts were dark. Just like a pirate's.

Detective Jamal Blackmon opened his eyes and held his breath. Something was wrong. He wasn't disoriented by any means although you would think he would be after the storm last night. Jamal knew exactly where he was, but there was still something terribly wrong. He let out his breath silently, forcing himself to clear his head. He slid his eyes around at the men who weathered the storm with him. They too were beginning to stir. Quickly, he got to his feet and strode decisively to the mouth of the cave. He rubbed his eyes for a second and blinked. The sun was just now emerging over the horizon, and the day was still soft with dawn. A gentle breeze was beginning to pick up, stirring the trees around the entrance where he stood, and further into the jungle that crept down the cliff to the rocks and sand below. Silhouetted starkly in the gray and pink light was a man. Jamal thought fast as they looked at each other for a moment, scouring his mind for the name to match the face. Then he smiled. "Don Manuel!" he cried, loud enough for his companions to hear him. Sure enough, a mad scramble ensued behind him, making him grin. "You must be the welcoming committee."

The man laughed, shaking his head in amusement. "You must be the law, where you come from."

"I am," Jamal admitted.

Another laugh. "Leila told me all about you." He sighed. "And of course, although she knows better, I was sent here in hopes of finding our son, Caribe."

Jamal nodded in understanding. "No, sir, Caribe did not come on this occasion. I am so sorry. He sends his love, though, and the promise that he'll ride the next storm in."

Don Manuel nodded. "Thank you, sir." Then his eyes drifted to the men joining them. "Carlos!" he cried happily.

"Manuel!" The pirate laughed with pleasure. The men embraced, then stepped back to look at each other. "Leila sent you, huh?" At the other man's nod, they laughed together. "Caribe is a little busy at the moment. He is learning the ways of the new world. And," he added, "he is also keeping company with a very beautiful young woman."

Don Manuel nodded. "Leila told me as much. She has been dreaming about him."

The pirate gestured at the men surrounding him. "Come, meet my new friends. These are Jamal Blackmon and his nephew, Rashawn. They are the law in their world." The men shook hands and nodded at each other. "Catamaran St. Jacques is Marina's godfather, and also her boss, where she comes from."

Don Manuel grinned. "Girl works for a lot of people, doesn't she?"

Catamaran extended his hand with a smile. "Yes, sir, it seems like she does. But not for long," he grinned. "I imagine I can persuade her to stop working for the pirates and come back to me."

At that, Don Manuel laughed out loud. "Good luck to you, sir." He smiled at Catamaran, studying him thoughtfully for a moment. "You look like Jackson, with Salomé's eyes," he observed.

Catamaran nodded. "My mother was Joe's older sister, Lisa. That makes me older cousin to Jackson and Salomé."

Don Manuel nodded again. "The resemblance is definitely there, sir." He glanced at Rashawn. "As is yours with your uncle," he smiled at him. Then he turned quietly to the last member of their party. "Leila dreamt about you, too." He cocked his head to one side, puzzled. "She said she saw you surrounded by snakes." Impressed, the men laughed, shaking their heads.

"I'm Jesse Coltrane," he said, stepping up to shake Don Manuel's hand. His hand went up automatically to adjust the cowboy hat no longer on his head. "They call me Snake," he admitted to the native. "I work with them, getting their venom so we can have antidotes to their bites."

Don Manuel nodded, and then spread out his hands. "Welcome, gentlemen, to Encantada. I hope your stay here is pleasant. I imagine you came to get the Aguilar-Banks." At their nod, he shook his head sadly. "They will be missed very much."

"Are they here?" Cat asked eagerly.

Don Manuel shook his head. "No, sir, not yet." He turned to the pirate. "Right after you left, Gaitano sailed to San Juan. Tiburón should be back some time tonight."

"Excellent!" exclaimed the pirate. "We will surprise them." Turning to his company, he smiled. "Come along, men," he urged. "Welcome to your new adventure!"

The town was quiet as they marched through it in the early morning light. The men looked around them in wonder. It seemed to them as if they were on a movie set. Main Street Encantada was nothing but a dirt road. On either side, brightly painted store fronts decorated the boarded sidewalks, their wares displayed behind sparkling glass windows. The streets were deserted, save for the occasional cat making its way home. The men went right through town and leaving it behind they entered the jungle. The ground was soft beneath their feet, mostly damp sand. The trees loomed tall and dark above them, making a small canopy. The underbrush rustled with the occasional scurrying animal. Birds began twittering as they announced the morning to one another. From above the canopy, seagulls cried as they flew overhead. Then they came to a clearing. Huts dotted the scenery, still quiet and closed against the night. Here, there were indications of life. There were a few people up already. Natives, they were, brightly colored fabrics brilliant against all that dark skin, delighted smiles dazzling in their beaming faces. "Don Carlos!" They called out to the pirate, evidently very happy to see him. The pirate responded to each one by name. Soon, they stopped in front of a particular hut.

Don Manuel held a hand up to halt the men. "Leila!"

A woman appeared in the doorway, a brightly colored piece of fabric holding the dreadlocks away from her beautiful face. Seeds and feathers decorated her ears and her wrists. The rest of her body was clothed in bright white cotton, making her black skin glow. Her eyes shone with recently shed tears, and her lips trembled even as she smiled. A graceful eyebrow arched at the men, and her voice was husky. "Caribe?"

Don Manuel shook his head at his wife. "You were right, Leila. Not this time. He is with the pretty girl you saw." He sighed. "Next time."

Leila lowered her eyes, and for a moment her shoulders slumped. The men felt her immense disappointment at the absence of her son. Then she seemed to shake herself out of it, although her eyes shone with fresh tears when she looked at them. "It is all right. Next time is soon." Not having words the men could only nod. "Come in," she gestured to the men to follow her. "Let us prove to you we are who we claim to be." The men collectively felt chills down their spines as she laughed, along with her husband and the pirate. They had just arrived and already they were thrilled.

They kept busy all day, exploring absolutely everything they could, on foot, on horseback, climbing, diving, swinging, and swimming. It was as if they were all children again. Boys on a rampage. They discovered waterfalls and ruins; they went to the top of a mountain, and back down to Carlitos and Marina's pool. Don Carlos took them to the docks and explained to them the system Salomé and Marina had established at their arrival. They went to the Sirens' Lair and saw the girls who adored Jackson and met Silas and Jimmy, who ran out to get them fresh fried fish, and some fruit. From there, they visited Padre Ignacio and saw the church from where they had taken Marina. And they also visited Pedro Barbosa, striding down the beautiful conch lined path to the office where the lawman took care of business. They sat at a mosaic patio table complete with benches in the amazing rock garden and discussed Xavier's death and its implications for a while. Pedro Barbosa promised to provide Jamal with copies of the papers exonerating Marina, and they left. Liana welcomed them warmly at the dress shop where Salomé worked, and while they were there, Dr. Kyle Richardson, her most eager beaux dropped by. Don Carlos purposefully left the Klines' General Store for the very end. There they ran into the town busybody gossip, Mrs.

Calloway, who made a big show of acting flustered and scared when the men crowded into the shop.

The pirate glared at her until she left, and laughed. "She believes Jackson, Salomé, and Marina, as well as my own sons, are savages and treats them as such." The men nodded in understanding and were then distracted by the beautiful Larissa and the enchanting Max. John Kline joined them, and they exchanged smiles and words. Max lunged for Catamaran, mesmerized by the combination of dreadlocks and green eyes. Cat gurgled right back at him. Larissa watched thoughtfully. And then they left. Down the beach was the lighthouse, which they climbed all the way to the top, to Carlitos and Marina's room, with all the beautiful sketches on the wall.

Rashawn chuckled. "Most definitely whipped." They stood on the balcony and looked out over the ocean, where the ships come in. There was nothing today. Back on the beach, they kept walking along the shore, until they reached Marina's tent. It was a beautiful tent in the middle of nowhere, between two palm trees, with luscious furniture and fabrics inside. They loved it.

"No wonder she went to work for you," Cat told the pirate.

Don Carlos just smiled to himself and continued leading them back into the jungle.

Gaitano's Bat Cave drew exclamations of admiration from the men. Running hot water indeed, they marveled, as the pirate lit tiki torches all around the small cavern, exposing it to the visitors. A small waterfall steamed as it cascaded into a shallow pool with a sandy bottom. In the middle of the rocky room, cradled among stalactites and stalagmites, there was a deeper pool that acted as a hot tub, large enough to accommodate six. The drier walls were hung with beautiful Persian carpets. Exquisite bamboo furniture was graced with exotic Oriental fabrics. There was even a bed, and a mirror.

Jesse approached the sketches around the mirror and studied them closely. They were spectacular. Definitely some of Caribe's finest work. Two were related to him. Gaitano. A portrait of the crew of La Gitana, and a moment caught laughing with his brother at a private joke. Two more were about Marina. A beautiful one with Max and another of her, fighting Solomon. The last three were of them, as a couple. In the first one was proof of their working relationship. Their heads were together over some books. The next one seemed to be a portrait, not exactly formal, more like a prom picture. Obviously at the infamous Baile del Luto. The last, however, established the lust the couple felt for one another. She was straddling his lap, her fingers in his hair, and his head was thrown back in naked desire. Finally, Jesse shook his head and let out a low whistle. He raised his eyebrows at the pirate. "*So whipped*," he laughed.

The pirate nodded in agreement. Turning away, he spied a basket in a corner. Going to it, he peered inside. Then he lifted his head with a smile. "Gentlemen," he called to them. "The day Marina killed Xavier, Carlitos sent the women here to…" he shrugged, "heal, so to speak. John Kline had hooked them up, as you say, with some products." He laughed softly. "Soaps and creams for the body and hair."

Catamaran laughed out loud. "Shampoo and conditioner?"

So they took turns washing up in the waterfall before relaxing a bit in the hot pool, talking, planning, getting organized. Then they left.

Sunset found them at Villa Azúl, Don Carlos and María Isabel's home in Encantada. It was just down the cliff from their son's cave, making the men smile as they heard the story of the young, rebellious teenage pirate. They were sitting in one of the seating arrangements in the tropical courtyard. This one consisted of pillows surrounding a set of small tables, where they had glasses and a couple of bottles of wine.

Jamal looked at the pirate. "You look preoccupied, Don Carlos."

The pirate glanced at him and nodded. "I am, a little."

Rashawn stared at him. "Your sons are coming back, aren't they?"

"Yes, yes," the pirate waved a hand at him, dismissing the question. "It has nothing to do with that."

"So, what is it?" Catamaran asked. The men all looked at him, waiting for an answer.

Don Carlos sighed. "I haven't reached this age for nothing. Piracy is short lived. These bones are telling me something… and I don't know," he shook his head, "I just have a feeling…"

"What kind of feeling?" Jamal asked, leaning forward.

The pirate looked around at them. "I have a feeling that we are about to receive company."

"Have your feelings ever failed you?" Rashawn wondered, mimicking his uncle's movement.

"Never," he shook his head.

"So, you are about to receive company, and…"

The pirate frowned, transforming his features into a sinister mask. "We prepare for them."

"What would be your best case scenario?" Cat asked.

"That the Council show up," he answered. "Juan sails in and you meet him before we have to leave. That would be nice…"

"But…" urged Jamal, but the pirate sighed, shaking his head.

Jesse looked at him thoughtfully. "Let me guess. Worst case scenario would be Xavier's men come looking for Marina…"

The pirate turned to stare at him. "Exactly."

The men turned to look at each other. "So we prepare!" Cat exclaimed viciously. His voice trembled with emotion. "Marina is my goddaughter. I did not come all the way here to not bring her back."

"It is not up to you," Don Carlos reminded him softly.

Catamaran was not listening. "Jackson and Salomé are my cousins!"

"They are my nephew and niece," Jesse added quietly.

"Stop!" Jamal ordered, making them all quiet down. "We are all going to get through this. Gaitano has to sail in first. We will take it from there."

Rashawn looked at the pirate. "I am sure I speak for all of us when I say to you that we will join your sons and their crew in fighting anyone they have to. Nobody will take nor touch Marina, nor Salomé, nor Jackson."

The stars twinkled overhead with bedtime. A crisp wind blew, carrying the sounds of the pounding surf. And with it, the vibrating clang of the fire escape.

"Positions, everyone!"

The young man quickly scrambled up, hauling himself over the edge of the wall, landing quietly on the roof. Stamping his feet silently, he passed his hands over his hair and straightened his dark T-shirt. The men held their breaths in the dark as he approached the first skylight. In what seemed a ceremony, the young man drew out a pack of cigarettes from his jeans back pocket. Tapping one out, he quickly put it between his lips, the pack disappearing into his pocket again. With a minimum of movements he struck a match, facing the wind so it blew the flame right at the cigarette. He inhaled deeply, his features clearly lit before the match went out. Sucking on the cigarette, the ember glowed brightly for a moment putting his features in prominence. A faint whirr and click got snatched by the wind. Then he did a couple of laps around the skylight, puffing like a chimney, blowing the smoke into the night sky, snatched by the wind. Finally he leaned against the skylight peering down. The room below was lit as it usually was at this hour, only the bed was empty.

"Seventeen."

The young man jumped off the skylight as if shocked. In his panic, he dropped the cigarette on his chest, where it instantly got caught on a fold of his T-shirt. Hastily shaking it off, sparks flew from the ember as it fell to the ground, rolling in the wind to land against the frame of the skylight.

"The girl whose bedroom you are looking down at is only seventeen."

"That makes you peeping at a minor," a voice sighed.

Panicked, he backed up to the next skylight, glowing as if beckoning to him. He had been steadily coming up here for a while, and he had never heard voices before.

"Now *that's* my daughter's bedroom. My *newlywed* daughter's bedroom."

"That makes you a sexual predator."

"Smile." A flash and the young man's features were caught, frozen in the dark, for posterity.

Scrambling like a crab, he ran to the next skylight over the pool table and aquarium. More flashes followed him, catching him in freeze frame. His heart wanted to pound out of his chest, and he was gasping for breath. *"What?"* he whispered into the dark, disoriented, and momentarily blinded.

"This is our building and you are trespassing." Figures seemed to emerge out of the dark. All dressed in black, the men presented themselves, surrounding him. As he began to edge towards the fire escape, twin growls rumbled over the roof. He froze. For just a moment.

Advancing with fury, Joe Banks shouted at him. *"Get the fuck off our building!"*

"Todd!" Derek laughed as the young man froze again, turning to the voice who called his name. The Butler boys stood side by side, grinning, no, more like outright laughing in his face.

Tyler held a couple of leashes in the air and raised his eyebrows. "Oops!" He dropped them. Samson and Delilah rushed off, growls rolling like thunder.

Without thinking, the young man grabbed the rail of the fire escape and flung himself over the side in a graceful arc. The dogs snarled and snapped at him as he disappeared, barking ferociously at the ground below. The men joined them at a run, leaning eagerly to look down. They caught the young man practically flinging himself from landing to landing before diving head first into the dumpster below. There was a yelp followed by a moan. He dove out of the trash and flung himself over, hobbling as he ran away, limping and groaning, his breath ragged in his chest as he pushed his body to its limit.

The men pulled back and looked at each other.

Shane Butler grinned. "Cinderella there lost his shoe."

Derek laughed, the wind ruffling his curls. "I'll get it in a moment."

Tyler shook his head, the lines on his face in a deep frown. "That was Todd, Dad."

"That is the psycho that abandoned Marina and Salomé on the island?" Pablo scowled as his lawyer's sons nodded. He turned to Caribe. "You get him?"

Grinning, Caribe showed him the screen on his digital camera. "I did."

"This isn't good," Joe said.

"No," Pablo agreed. "It's not."

"We told him to stay away, Tío, I swear," Tyler told him.

Derek backed his brother. "Yes. We spoke to him when Jackson came back to get you. We didn't even know he knew where we lived."

"Well, it seems like he's been coming up here for a while," Joe muttered.

"Poor Xaira," Pablo said in a deadly voice, "alone this whole time while this little insect monster has been coming up here watching her."

"Whatever happens, we should wait until Jamal and Rashawn get back. And you realize Jackson is not going to like this." Shane shook his head. "Let's go, men. We will figure this out later."

Turning away, they slowly went back downstairs, securing Xaira and Marina's empty apartment. The Butler boys retrieved a sneaker they put in its own plastic bag. Then they went back to Hacienda Aguilar-Banks to plan.

"Marina?"

Marina turned to look at Larissa. They had just sailed in from their impromptu trip to San Juan. The pirates had grumbled in good humor as the Aguilar-Banks crew had taken off running the moment the plank hit the dock. Jackson hauled Storm behind him, eager to reach the Sirens' Lair. Salomé joined him, the baby Cacique snuggled in her arms, Giancarlo and Solomon racing them all. Marina had run for the Klines' store, anxious to see Max with the desperation of one who thought it would be the last time. Now that she had him snuggled in her arms, she turned to his mother, an eyebrow arching in amusement. "Larissa?"

"You know, honey, there were some people in here with Don Carlos yesterday…"

"Don Carlos?" Marina's eyes widened, her heart suddenly pounding in her chest. Max pulled back, sucking at his thumb, to look at her. She switched him over to her other hip and bounced him gently. "Don Carlos is here?" she asked, trying to hide her shock.

Larissa frowned, growing suspicious. "Why, yes, I thought you knew."

Marina tried distracting her by rolling her eyes with a smile. "Well, no, because we just got here, so there is no way of us knowing when Don Carlos got here, so when did he get here?"

Larissa crossed her arms and studied her. "Well, he was here yesterday, so he must have come in sometime during the night with the storm."

Marina nodded, looking away from her at Max, hurriedly grasping at the lifeline. "Now, you see, that makes sense, because we stayed way behind the storm," she cooed at the baby. She glanced at Larissa. "So, who were these people with Don Carlos?"

"There were four of them," Larissa answered, pretending to dismiss the question. "They all have earrings like the pirates. Three Africans and a fourth man, rough, scar down his face," she said, absently tracing the track of Jesse's scar on her own face.

Marina frowned, puzzled. "Three Africans?"

Larissa nodded. "Yes." She stopped to stare at Marina. "One of them looked like Solomon, but a little older, like your parents." she said, waving her hands around her head. "No hair, except…" she frowned for a moment, remembering. "He had hair on his face like this." Then she showed her on her own her face, spreading her thumb and fingers over her upper lip, and drawing them down the sides of her mouth to her chin. She glanced at Marina. "One had his hair like Jackson and Joe's, with big crystals in his ears," she continued, indicating corn rows over her own dark head. "The last one had his hair like Caribe. But he looked like Jackson and his eyes were green…"

Marina let herself lean back against the counter behind her, lest she stumble and fall with Max in her arms. "Like Salomé's," she finished for her.

Larissa smiled in relief. "Yes. You know these men?" she asked.

Marina forced a smile, recovering enough to stand again. "Maybe." Now she grinned. "May I take Max to the Lair for a little while?"

Larissa laughed. "Of course, you may."

"Max!" The Sirens' Lair burst into greeting as the flustered girl burst in with the borrowed baby in her arms.

"Salomé!" Marina signaled her sister with her head. Said sister was sitting on a bar stool, snuggling her own little native baby in her arms. Indio had slipped behind the bar to help Silas and Jimmy with the customers. Gaitano sat at his usual place at the end of the bar, already a line forming. Her brother sat with his girlfriend, surrounded by a sea of sirens. *"Jax!"*

Jackson's head snapped up at the edge of panic that laced Marina's voice. He stood up and cocked an eyebrow at her. *"Houston?"*

Marina swallowed and hurriedly gestured him over. In a moment, the three heads were together in urgent conspiracy. "I have to tell you something Larissa just told me," she sing-sang, bouncing Max on her hip, motioning to Salomé to do the same. "Don Carlos…" she broke off as a commotion ensued at the entrance.

"Don Carlos!" Jackson exclaimed, overjoyed at seeing him. His sisters smiled, just as happy.

They waited patiently as the pirate greeted his sons first, affectionately ruffling their hair before embracing them and kissing their cheeks. They all grinned at each other. Then he went to the Aguilar-Banks crew. Spreading his arms wide, he drew Marina and Salomé in, squeezing them tight against his chest. He closed his eyes, breathing them in deeply before looking into each of their eyes and kissing them. He let them go and gently took Max's face between his hands, looking into the baby's eyes and murmuring to him before he kissed his little forehead. Absently, he reached out to stroke the dark-haired baby's head in Salomé's arms. Then he turned to Jackson, patted him on the face before drawing him into a bear hug. "How are things?" he murmured affectionately in his ear.

Jackson smiled. He loved this man almost as much as his own dads. "Pretty good. Carlos took us to San Juan."

Don Carlos smiled back. "So I heard."

"Are Dad and Papi here?"

"No, they had a lot of work to catch up on, since they took the time off to be here."

"What about Caribe?"

The pirate raised his eyebrows with a grin. "Hanging with Xaira."

"Don Carlos!" Salomé gasped softly. "Look at you! You have been busy, haven't you?" she asked with a laugh, making Indio look up with interest from the glasses he was shining.

"You look different," Marina accused with a smile. "If I didn't know better, I would say you've had a facial." She laughed softly at his nod. "Where have you been?"

"What have you done?" Salomé narrowed her eyes with a smile.

"I am looking at some land in the Heights," the pirate informed them.

They gasped. *"The Heights?"* They laughed. The Heights was one of the best neighborhoods in Blue Bay. Gaitano left his place at the end of the bar to join them.

"What's your favorite place?" Jackson demanded.

The older pirate lifted his eyebrows and smacked his lips. "Victoria's Secret."

Gaitano stared at his father, having been told about the place by his new bride. "You have been there?"

His father grinned. "You boys are going to love it."

"So I hear," Carlos laughed.

Marina handed Max over to her husband. "Don Carlos, I saw Larissa," she gasped, hurrying to get the words out. "She said…"

"I saw Larissa yesterday, yes," he said, smiling at her as if he were humoring a child.

Sensing something, Salomé handed Cacique to Indio over the bar. "What about Larissa?"

Storm watched with interest from the table full of sirens. "What about Larissa?" she echoed quietly.

Another commotion ensued from the entrance again. The doorway darkened with the group of men. The Aguilar-Banks stared. Shocked, they just stared.

Jackson was the first one to react. *"No way!"* he exclaimed quietly. Then his voice rose in excitement. "Oh, man! Oh, man! Oh, man!" Next to him, his sisters just stared for a moment, tears streaming down their faces.

"Uncle Jesse!" Salomé gasped, totally unbelieving. *"Rashawn!"* Her voice broke. *"Jamal!"*

"Gatito!" Marina whispered, moving towards him as if in a dream.

Catamaran met her halfway and caught her in his arms, spinning her around once before crushing her against him. Bending her back, he dipped her, burrowing his face into the side of her neck. Marina clung to him, her arms wrapped around his own neck, his dreadlocks covering them as a curtain. Sensing movement, Catamaran glanced up and caught the young pirate starting towards him. Straightening himself up and Marina, he spun her around until her back was flat against him, his arm tightly crossed over her chest as if she were a hostage. He lifted a finger in warning. "Back off pirate boy, this is *my* baby."

Marina gasped, tears stinging her eyes. *"¡Padrino!"*

Jackson and Salomé cried out in anger. *"Cat!"*

Catamaran hesitated. Marina had stopped calling him Godfather when she turned thirteen. Since then, it had been *Catamaran, Cat, Gato, Gatito,* and *Dude.* Whatever suited her fancy. He shrugged mentally. But never *Padrino.* "Back off," he repeated. Without taking his eyes off the young pirate, he pressed deep kisses to Marina's temple and to her face.

Gaitano raised his eyebrows at him. "Let go," he said slowly, his voice almost purring in warning, "of *my* wife…" In a moment, he was surrounded by his crew. Storm jumped up from her place among the sirens and quickly took Max from him, as the baby's lip started quivering.

Indio scowled at the visitor. "Let her go, man."

Catamaran shook his head, intent on the girl in his arms. "No."

"Yes," Giancarlo smiled, stepping forward.

Solomon joined him. "Let Marina go." The visitors agreed.

"Catamaran…" Jamal's voice was soft with warning.

Rashawn glared at him. "That's her man!"

Gaitano kept his gaze focused on Catamaran. "Listen to your friends," he advised softly.

Don Carlos chuckled, breaking the spell. "Gentlemen," he announced to the visitors, "meet the crew of La Gitana. Carlos Gaitano, Captain; Indio Gaitano, Quartermaster; Giancarlo Ilarraza, Sailing Master; Solomon, Boatswain; and Marina Aguilar de Gaitano, Accountant, although now, she is accountant of La Sirena, my own ship," he winked at the girl in Catamaran's arms. "Of course, you recognize them from Caribe's drawings." He put a hand on his son's shoulder. "Carlitos…" He turned to his other son. "Indio…" He laughed. "Giancarlo, Solomon, permit me to introduce you to my new friends. Visitors, as the Aguilar-Banks before them." He sighed, gesturing to Catamaran. "This most obnoxious of creatures is Catamaran St. Jacques, Marina's godfather, the cat half of the Blue Cat. The blue half, Deveraux Azure, stayed home because he had a lot of work at his law office. He is Salomé's godfather. They are a set of identical twins born to Joe's older sister. Do not let this one get to you. He can be quite difficult." He glanced at Catamaran and caught him grinning. "We met under quite interesting circumstances."

"What did he do?" Carlos asked quietly.

His father grinned. "He pulled a gun on me."

Gaitano cocked an eyebrow at the man retaining his wife. "Tough guy…"

Cat shrugged with insolent indifference. "He pulled a sword on me."

"Too bad that's all he did." He took a step towards them, glowering. "Let her go…"

Catamaran laughed, squeezing Marina tighter. Just to spite the young pirate. *"Fuck you!"* he taunted softly. The sirens gasped.

Gaitano took a step closer locking eyes with Cat. "No," he smiled slowly. "Fuck *you…*" He took a deep breath. His voice was quiet. *"Get off her."*

Marina began squirming in Cat's arms. "He means it, Cat, let me go," she whimpered.

"I'm *family*, man," Cat said in his defense. "I changed her diapers and cleaned her bottom."

The young pirate threw back his head with laughter. He let his eyes roam over Marina appreciatively, as if he owned her. Which he did. When he met her eyes, he smiled. "I am her *husband. I* change her *panties* and f---"

"Carlos!" Marina stopped him in shocked outrage.

Carlos glowered, coming even closer. *"Let… her…. go…!"* He roared, lunging at Catamaran. The older pirate swiftly stepped in and intercepted his son, not letting him pass. The other one just held the girl tighter. At their table, the sirens squealed and scattered, scrambling for cover, turning to glare at Catamaran.

"This other young man," Don Carlos interrupted, "is married to Joe's younger sister, Rain. Boys, meet Uncle Jesse Coltrane, better known as Snake. He works with them," he explained.

"You know who *I* am." Jesse raised his chin at them, and slowly drew Marina out of Catamaran's grasp, and into his arms, looking at Gaitano. "If you are really with Marina, then you have heard of me. I am Jesse."

The young pirate hesitated and nodded. "You go out every Wednesday night. To a cowboy bar. You dance. You marked them all with their family symbol," he added with confidence.

Jesse nodded. "That's right. That's me," he said slowly. "Jesse." Turning to Marina, his dark blue eyes lit up, with relief and love before he began raining kisses all over her face. Gaitano watched closely, and their eyes met over the girl as Jesse held her tight, then finally letting her go to greet the two detectives with them. He, too, never took his eyes off the pirate. His voice was a warning disguised as a soft reminder. "You know who I am." Gaitano nodded, momentarily dismissing him.

"And these," continued Don Carlos, "are Jamal and Rashawn Blackmon, uncle and nephew detectives." The men lifted their hands in greeting.

"Detectives?" Indio asked, drawing closer, the taíno baby in his arms.

"Dudes!" Jackson exclaimed. "How did you even get here?"

"Did Summer come?" Salomé demanded.

Rashawn shook his head at her with a smile. "No, but it's because of her that we are here. I'll explain later," he said, stroking the side of her face affectionately as Salomé smiled into his eyes. Indio also watched closely, but perceived nothing but the love and affectionate camaraderie of lifelong friends.

"Jamal!" Marina turned, almost in a panic, towards the older man. "Did Papi and Dad talk to you? Do you know about Xavier? Did they explain…" she broke off, as the detective held up a hand, shaking his head at her with a smile.

"Chill, baby girl," crooning to her as he had done so many times when she was a child. "We'll talk later." He hooked a hand behind her neck and brought her forehead against his, rubbing noses with her gently before pulling away to smile into her beautiful hazel eyes. "When we are this close," he whispered to her, sending her reeling back through the years to another place and time when the detective had helped build her confidence and self-esteem along with the rest of the males in her life, "we are nothing but all right." Then he kissed her ritualistically three times. Once on the forehead, and once on each cheek. Just like when she was a little girl. Fresh tears came to Marina's eyes.

Turning to Catamaran and Gaitano, Jackson glared at them. "Now, fuck both of you. If you're just going to fight over Marina as if she were an object, then neither of you deserves her. And if you're going to fucking compete, ha!" His laugh was short and hard. "I would say, hands down, Marina is Papi's, Dad's and mine. We are out of here. Fuck y'all…"

Carlos sighed and turned to glare back at Marina's brother, the blood rushing to his knuckles as he clenched and unclenched his fists. His voice was a growl deep in his chest. *"Jackson…"*

Jackson waved a hand in the air and turned his back on them. "Fuck y'all!" he called over his shoulder. "Let's go, guys." Beckoning to his sisters, he strode towards the entrance.

Salomé turned, snatching Cacique out of Indio's arms, hair flying around her head. "Peace out."

Marina agreed sadly. Taking Max from Storm, she followed Jackson. "Ciao." As one, the Aguilar-Banks crew left the Lair.

"Meet us at Villa Azúl!" Don Carlos called after them. Then raising both hands he softly smacked both Carlitos and Catamaran upside the head, as he walked past them towards the bar in disgust. The young men glared at each other as the older man snarled at them. "Nice job, boys!"

"See what you did!" Rashawn growled at them, following his friends.

Jamal shook his head, muttering under his breath. "Idiots!"

Jesse sighed deeply and rubbed his eyes, also muttering under his breath. "Fuck…"

Solomon couldn't hide his alliance. He too sighed deeply. "Now I am going to have to go so Marina can fight me." Snickering, he was gone. Storm took off running behind them.

"Sit down. The both of you." Jamal frowned when both Cat and the pirate turned to look at him as if he had lost his mind. On the inside, he braced himself. On the outside, he rolled his eyes. "Yes. You." Looking from one to the other, he finally scowled. His voice sounded like a shot in the room. *"Now!"* The sirens squealed again, finally chattering in low angry voices. Jamal waved a hand in apology to them. But he didn't care. The two young men moved. The pirate snarled at him but went to obey. He had been taught to respect age. Straddling a chair turned around, Jamal waved his hands in circular movements, indicating them to do the same. They did, facing each other, leaving him between them. Jamal grimaced at the sudden visual in his head. It was of himself, caught between two young raging bulls. Now he tried not to laugh. He deepened his scowl instead. Turning to the pirate sitting at the bar, he went back to matters at hand. "Don Carlos, do we even have time for this?" he asked, waving a hand between Cat and Gaitano. He pretended to be disgusted. It wasn't too hard.

The pirate laughed on the outside but on the inside he must have been pretty pissed off because his eyes seemed to be filled with thunderclouds. "Oh," he assured the detective, raising a glass of wine in a silent toast, "we are *making* time for this."

"Now," Jamal continued briskly, pointing a finger at each of them. "I talk. You listen." Lowering his hands, he crossed them over the chair he was straddling and glared at them. "Like it or not, boys, you both have something in common, and that's that girl that just walked out. Marina would rather be with her brother and sister right now than here, listening to you two behaving like idiots." He took a deep breath and continued. "Let's do this the right way. Catamaran," he said slowly as if to a child, "this is Carlos Gaitano, Don Carlos' son, remember? Carlitos. You know who he is. Pablo and Joe told you all about him. Gaitano. This is the young pirate who married Marina, your goddaughter, your best friend, your baby. This is her *husband*." Now he turned to the young pirate. "Gaitano," he spoke to him just as slowly, which made the young pirate scowl deeper, first at him, then at the dreadlocked troublemaker. "This is Catamaran. He is one of identical twins, nephews of Joe. He raised them with Pablo from the time they were babies, like your dad explained. Of the girls, his is Marina. Ever since she was born when they were about ten, she was *his* baby. And they have this perfect loving bond, all the way up to Spring Break. She also works for him at his club, so he was out an employee. Please forgive him for being so rude, and let's call it *shock*. Now," he continued sternly, "do you have anything you want to say to Marina's husband?" His voice was demanding and his look was steady as he waited for an answer.

Catamaran looked from one to the other, both waiting, and shrugged. "Whatever, man, I mean," he looked at Gaitano, "I'm sorry. I know I can be a pain sometimes, but that's just my thing. Fucking with people is in my nature. And yeah, I *do* want to say something." Now he glared. "I was fucking *hurt* that Marina didn't wait for me to get married."

The young pirate grinned at him insolently. "Sorry you could not make it. We were kind of far." He shrugged back at him. "About three hundred and fifty years away." He laughed.

The older pirate and the detective looked at each other over the space between the two younger men. The father's voice was a soft warning growl, like a panther announcing itself in the dark. *"Hijo…"* But his son didn't listen.

"First of all, it was *Sloane's* idea that we get married before they went back home. We just jumped on it. Pablo and Sloane Aguilar, and Joe and Shayla Banks wanted to leave their youngest daughter, Marina del Sol Aguilar, *married. To me. Carlos Juan Miguel Gaitano y Sandoval, Captain of La Gitana, Tiburón, Poseidón and Starfish.* Commander of the island of Encantada, in the Caribbean Sea. They wanted to leave her *safe*. Not that it's *any* of your business," he growled, slamming his hands down on the back of the chair he was straddling. He was furious. *"Do not disrespect me on my own turf!"* He scowled deeply, matching the rumble in his chest. "Marina and I have been through a lot together." He pointed a finger at Catamaran. "You are so *not* going to mess this up for me."

Catamaran's shoulders slumped a tiny bit, but he tossed his head back suddenly, as if defying defeat. His green eyes sparkled like jewels, so like Salomé's it took the young pirates' breath away. *"I was hurt.* And if you can't accept that, then *fuck you."* Not sparkling anymore, his eyes glittered with pain and rage. "I *know* who you are. I know *all* about you. I hang with your parents. Actually, I love them a lot. Your mom is the best. But you'll have to forgive me if this is going to take some getting used to. I'm sorry I grabbed Marina like that, man. I'm not used to not being able to. You have no idea…" he broke off, shaking his head. "They just disappeared!" Smoothing back the dreads on his head, he looked at the young pirate again. *"You don't know what it's like."*

"I am *not* sorry this happened, Marina is in *my* world now," came the soft warning. "She has a *life.* Friends, family, people who support her."

"You mean, *pirates*," Cat interrupted.

The pirate turned to his father. "How can you *stand* him?" he demanded. "He is worse than Jackson!"

Jesse covered his eyes and Jamal struggled to hide a grin.

Don Carlos shrugged. "Ignore him. You'll get used to it."

Cat leaned forward. "Don't worry. In a couple of weeks you'll be *crazy* about me."

Jamal snorted. "Or *just* crazy."

Gaitano rolled his eyes. "Whatever. Just don't mess with me."

Catamaran laughed. "What could you do?"

Carlitos raised an eyebrow at him. "I am sure you don't want to know."

Cat laughed again. "Try me."

This time, Gaitano laughed with him. "You have to sleep some time," he told him. "Imagine waking up and she's gone. *Just gone,"* he said, nodding at him. Indio and Giancarlo moved closer to him in silent support.

"You can do that?" Catamaran asked.

"I absolutely, most definitely can. Even while you're wide awake."

"You would do that?" There was a different smile on his face.

"In a heartbeat."

"Catamaran," Jamal spoke softly. "Joe warned you…"

The young pirate's eyebrows shot up in delight. "Dad warned you about me?"

"He did," Jesse assured him.

Gaitano laughed. "You should listen to your *tío*."

"*Fuck you*," Catamaran growled at him.

"Imagine, Catamaran," Gaitano retorted mockingly, "how *old* does she get to be? How many *children* does she have? How does she *live*? Does she ever *think* of you? Even *remember* you? How far does she *travel*? What does her *home* look like? *Where* does she even call home, for that matter?" He drifted off, watching Catamaran's expression go from amused to shock.

"*You wouldn't…* "

Gaitano laughed again, shrugging once more. "What do you *really* think?"

"*You wouldn't dare…* "Cat drifted off, uncertain suddenly, when the pirates laughed.

"Want to know how much I dare?" Gaitano taunted softly.

Jamal leaned forward, trying to hide that his heart just skipped a beat. On the inside, he cursed Cat. "Oh, I *really* want to hear the answer to this."

Jesse felt his own heart ice over. "Catamaran…" he growled.

The young pirate obliged. He leaned forward towards them, and lowered his voice to a confiding level. "Which island am I taking her to?" He turned to look from one to the other, rage turning his eyes into stormy pools. "How many storms are you going to ride here looking for her?" Blood rushed into his knuckles as he clenched and unclenched his fists. "I am *not* holding her against her will. Marina is here because she *wants* to be. They *all* are. What is the worst that could happen if Marina, or Salomé and Jackson, for that matter," he thought out loud, "*never* make it back to your world?"

Jamal threw his hand up in front of Catamaran's face, as he opened his mouth to speak. "*That*," he told him, "is why we are here."

Gaitano turned to him and regarded him for a moment. He nodded slowly. Then he turned to Catamaran, and standing up suddenly he overturned his chair, making that one jump to his feet in alarm and Jamal to quickly move and stand between them. He screamed with rage. *"Don't fuck with me!"* Indio and Giancarlo stood at his sides, flanking him. This time the sirens disappeared.

Don Carlos jumped to his feet. *"¡Carlitos!"* Rushing towards him, he grabbed his son by the shoulders, shaking him before patting his face. "When you hear them out, you will understand." His son turned to look him in the eyes, his chest heaving with his anger. "I told you to ignore him." Taking a deep shuddering breath, the son willed his breathing to slow down. His father smiled and nodded. "Trust Papá," he whispered. Turning to the rest of the men, he laughed. "Villa Azúl, gentlemen!"

They had just dropped Max off at his parents' store, and gone marching through the jungle to the tent Don Carlos had given Marina. There, they swam in the pool in front of it, yelling and splashing before taking a break and relaxing. The girls had decided to stay out in the sun with Cacique, leaving them to sprawl in Marina's space inside the tent.

Rashawn grinned. "This ain't bad, yo!" He laughed, looking at Jackson, swinging lazily in his sister's hammock. "Can't blame Marina for getting used to the adoration."

Jackson grinned back from his place in the unique reclining seat inside the tent, his dark skin making the lush turquoise fabric glow. "No, you can't, can you?"

Rashawn chuckled for a moment, shaking his head. "How'd you guys end up getting mixed up in this, anyway?"

Jackson shrugged, turning away to stare out at the girls playing in the sun with the baby by the water. "Freak storm." He glanced at his friend. "Literally."

Rashawn kept quiet for a moment, the cubic zirconia earrings winking in the ray of light coming in through the opening around one of the palm trees on which his hammock hung. He stared thoughtfully at Jackson. "You know you have to go back."

Jackson nodded slowly, sighing deeply. "We know," he said softly. "That's why you're here."

"Yes," Rashawn admitted. "I'd just rather wait until we are all together before I explain anything."

Jackson glanced at him. "Thanks for explaining." He took a deep breath. "We love it here, Rashawn." He spread his hands out helplessly. "But we know deep inside that it can't last, man." He shook his head, muttering under his breath. "Were we to be so lucky."

Rashawn nodded. "We'll talk."

Solomon cleared his throat. He had been minding his own business, quietly listening to the two friends talk from his place on the sand between them. "This may not be my place…" he began respectfully.

Rashawn smiled at him encouragingly. "Go ahead, man."

Solomon nodded. "It has just recently come to our attention that the Aguilar-Banks are not of this world." He frowned, shaking his head at the thought. "But," he continued, meeting Rashawn's gaze, "some things have occurred that have changed matters drastically." He lifted a hand, quietly pointing a finger at the girls outside. "My captain, Carlos Gaitano, has just married his accountant, Marina Aguilar, and there is *nothing*," he frowned, "any of you can do about it." He shook his head again. "Gaitano will not let her go," he warned the young detective softly.

"Then he will have to come into our world, won't he?" Rashawn asked just as quietly.

Solomon just grinned. "I guess you have to talk, don't you?"

Rashawn grinned back. "I guess so. How do you like fighting Marina, Solomon?"

The young African laughed, putting his hands over his heart. "I *love* it," he admitted.

Rashawn nodded. "So do I." Laughing, the men slid hands against each other's.

It was the middle of the day, and the sun was pounding straight down on the courtyard of Don Carlos' jungle castle. The tops of the plants glowed bright green, shading to darker on the underside of the leaves. The lush exotic fabrics on the sitting pillows sparkled with gold and silver threads and tassels. All the windows were thrown open and the breeze circled around the whole area. They had moved it inside, getting ready for a meeting with the rest of the pirates and Jamal and Jesse. At the moment they all lay around, soaking the sun in cutoff pants, the boys shirtless, the girls with flowered fabrics wrapped around their chests.

Rashawn laughed, happy, throwing his arms wide over the back of the rustic sofa he was sitting on. On either side of him, Marina and Salomé snuggled against his chest. "This is life!" he exclaimed.

Jackson chuckled. "That's why we're here."

"It's pretty cool," Salomé murmured.

"Chillin'," agreed Marina softly, closing her eyes and turning her face to the sun.

Rashawn slipped an arm around each of them, kissing first one, then the other. "Makes you think of the good old days, doesn't it?" he chuckled.

"Yes," the girls sighed. They had used to spend a lot of time together, what with Rashawn and Jackson being best friends. Things had changed just recently, when Rashawn had made detective and hooked up with Summer. But still, they managed to hang out at least once a week, like Marina and Jesse did, treating themselves to some major quality time together.

"Now, look at you," Rashawn teased. "You went and got your-selves into some trouble, found yourselves some adventure, and snagged yourselves a couple of men. Pirates, at that!" He chuckled. "Good job, ladies." The girls giggled, snuggling and loving him until he laughed, getting them off him. "Now what?"

Salomé sighed, glancing at her sister. "We stopped thinking about things a while back, Rashawn."

He raised his eyebrows at her, considering her words for a moment, and sighed. "Not very realistic, is it?"

"No," she admitted softly.

"This has been our reality, Rashawn," Marina said softly. "Since Spring Break, this is all we have known. Encantada and pirates." Tears came to her eyes.

"And Jackson," Salomé added, swiping at her own tears. "Jackson, Rashawn, has been the absolute boldest, bravest, best brother we could have ever wished for! The only time he ever left us alone was when Gaitano took Marina to Carey, and I just had to go with her, Indio was going anyway," she rambled on, "and I couldn't leave her alone, you know."

Rashawn smiled gently at her. "I know, Salo," he soothed, "I know all about it, baby." Looking towards the front of the house, they saw the rest of the men entering. "We'll talk now," he said gently.

"This looks like a family meeting," Salomé said softly.

"Yes, it does," agreed Carlos, looking at his dad.

Jackson cut to the chase. "Summer." He stared at Rashawn. "You said you were here because of her."

Rashawn nodded. "We are."

"Why is that?"

"I thought she was getting her P.I. license," Salomé said thoughtfully.

"What's P.I.?" Indio asked quietly.

"Private Investigator," she told him. "Like the Hawthorne scoundrels," she added, referring to some childhood friends of the pirates that they had met recently. He grunted.

"Who is she working for?" Marina was curious.

"Insurance company," Jamal answered quietly.

The Aguilar-Banks crew looked at him and then turned their heads at the same time to look at Rashawn. Jackson got impatient. "What has Summer to do with us?"

"Rumors began flying at the university after Spring Break because you guys vanished into thin air. There were a couple of guys involved. Quentin Matthews and Todd Lowell." Rashawn hesitated, waiting for confirmation. His friends nodded and he continued. "Where Summer comes in," he said hurriedly before Jackson could interrupt again, "is that your disappearance came to the attention of the insurance company she is working for. They launched an investigation, and contracted her to locate you." He took a deep breath. "She told me, I told Jamal."

Salomé stood up, rubbing her arms as if warding off goosebumps. "No." Her hair floated around her head as she shook it from side to side. "No…" There was wonder in her voice.

Marina frowned. "But why are they investigating us?"

"You disappeared," Cat answered.

She shook her head. "But what have we…" she drifted off suddenly, her eyes growing wide in her face. She turned to look at her brother and sister. *Oh, my God!"* Her voice broke, and eyes glazed over swimming in tears. Marina was going into shock. Jackson took her in his arms.

Alarmed, Gaitano also stood. "What is the matter?"

Jackson squeezed Marina, rubbing her back with one hand, drawing Salomé into the circle of his arms with his other hand. "Aw, shit," he groaned. He closed his eyes, shaking his head from side to side. Finally, he threw it back, roaring into the bright blue sky overhead. *"Fuck!"* He blinked back his own tears and soothed his sisters until they calmed down. "There is no discussion. We are out of here. We have to go back," he said. The pirates turned to glare at the visitors.

Don Carlos took a deep breath and let it out in a long sigh. "Let me explain," he told his son and his crew. "When Marina turned twenty-one, the Aguilar-Banks went with their counselor, Blue," he waved a hand absently at Cat, "to an insurance company. There, they insured their lives for one million dollars each, naming their four parents sole beneficiaries, in the event of their deaths." The pirates turned from Don Carlos to the Aguilar-Banks. Jackson, Salomé, and Marina stared right back. The older pirate continued. "Neither

Pablo, nor Sloane, nor Joe, nor Shayla knew anything about it. Not even their own lawyer, Shane Butler, knew about it. Only the twins, and them," he nodded towards them.

"So their disappearance creates a problem for this insurance company," Indio rumbled. His brother kept quiet, steadily looking into his wife's eyes.

"If Jackson, Salomé, and Marina don't show up alive," Rashawn explained, "they could be dead."

"They think they are *dead*?" Giancarlo was shocked. Solomon, like his Captain, also kept quiet.

"Like I said, they don't show up alive," Rashawn repeated.

"Remember, they are just gone," Jesse told them.

"In Blue Bay, where we are from," Jamal explained quietly, "you don't need a body to have a murder."

"Murder?" Now Indio was shocked.

"Pablo and Sloane, and Joe and Shayla are the sole beneficiaries. They stand to gain three million dollars from their children's disappearance. At not showing up alive, they are declared dead after a while." Jamal made eye contact with each of them. "If Jackson, Salomé, and Marina don't go back home, their parents will be accused of their murder."

Gaitano raised his hands before anybody else could say anything. *"That,"* his voice was commanding, "is *not* going to happen. There is nothing else to say. We will go."

Solomon flashed a grin at Rashawn. "I told you he wouldn't let her go."

Rashawn grinned back. "You were right."

Indio stood beside his brother and nodded, glancing at their father. "We will go."

"Marina, don't leave me here," Solomon said softly. His heart was pounding.

"Of course not," she glanced at him, her answer automatic. In truth, she felt as if she were drowning. Everything around her had become fuzzy and blurry, and Solomon's words had managed to pull her out before she passed out.

"We just talked about this on the way back from San Juan," Giancarlo reminded them. "We are all going. Rouge is coming with us."

The visitors looked at each other. "This is going to prove interesting," Cat grinned.

"I'm not staying," Storm spoke up, bouncing Cacique gently in her arms, "if Jackson leaves."

Jackson flashed her a smile. "I'm not leaving you, baby."

"Then it's decided," Jamal said, trying to keep the wonder from his voice, "you are all going back with us. As long as you understand that in our world there are rules and laws you will have to learn in order to get along."

Gaitano nodded. "Aye."

His crew and Storm echoed him. "Aye."

Don Carlos smiled. "It will be fine." He grinned at the young pirates. "You are going to love it," he assured them.

Catamaran laughed at Gaitano. "You're stuck with me now," he grinned.

The young pirate rolled his eyes with a sigh. "Fuck you," he answered absentmindedly. Cat laughed again.

Jesse cleared his throat, distracting everyone from Gaitano and Catamaran who were now circling each other, keeping Marina between them. "We met Maximillian yesterday in the company of his parents. He's an awesome kid. But there is something I don't understand about this time warp thing," he said softly, catching their attention. His expression was puzzled. "Does it mess up the length of time, also? Because if my math is correct," he turned to Marina, "there is *no way* that is *your* baby." All eyes turned to Cacique in Storm's arms. Quickly, the Aguilar-Banks moved as a united front. Giancarlo and Solomon moved closer.

"You know, I am really glad you said something, Jesse," Jackson said hurriedly. "It's like something funny happened to us on the way here..."

"Now, Uncle Jesse, we need you to calm down..." Salomé interjected smoothly, her tone already soothing.

Jesse glanced from one to the other suspiciously, unaware of the young pirates' amusement. "Why do I have to calm down?"

"Because when you calm down, you always remember just how much we love you…"

"Yeah, we're crazy about you," Jackson added seriously.

"And because we love you with all your hearts, it is that we have done what we did," Marina added softly.

Jesse stopped for a moment to rub his eyes. Sighing deeply, he looked at them again. "What did you do?"

"Well, Uncle Jesse," Salomé explained hurriedly, "we have been thinking about you a lot lately."

"We found ourselves under some extenuating circumstances, recently, where this newly orphaned baby, who just lost its mother under tragic circumstances, came to our attention," Jackson said.

Jesse felt shivers run down his spine suddenly. "No way."

"Yes way!" Salomé exclaimed quickly, before he could grasp the implications. "It's going to be perfect, Uncle Jesse! And we promise we'll help you explain to Rain."

Jesse shook his head, his eyes drifting towards the baby. Black eyes regarded him steadily. "No."

Marina put a hand on his arm. She waited until he turned his head to look at her. "Yes." Her eyes pleaded with him. "Jesse, we've had him for a few days. We call him Cacique, because he would have been chief of his tribe. His mother was murdered in front of our eyes." She nodded slowly at the sudden shock in his face. "Just before she died, she taught us his lullaby. We've kept him calm this whole time. We talked to him about you the whole way here, Uncle Jesse," her voice broke as she retorted to his real title once more, just like when she was a little girl. "He knows who you are. Watch," she whispered raggedly. Taking the baby from Storm, she bounced him on her hip for a moment. His eyes crinkled and he smiled around his thumb at her, gurgling softly. "Cacique," she called to him in a sing-song voice, "beautiful *nene*, this is Jesse…" The baby turned to look at Jesse, sucking his thumb faster. He looked back at Marina. "That is *Papi*. Remember?" She crooned to him. "We talked about it on

Tiburón. That is *Papi*. It's Jesse…" She turned to her uncle. "Wanna hold him?"

Jesse stared at her. "You are serious."

Marina reached for his hand and pulled him closer. "Yes." Undaunted, she continued. Pulling his hand to her mouth, she pressed her lips against it and kissed it deeply. Then she sighed, rubbing her face against it. The baby watched, fascinated, along with everyone else. Marina looked at him dreamily. "It's Jesse," she whispered to him. "It's Papi." Nobody spoke for a moment, watching the drama unfold.

Cat finally broke the silence. "Hell, *I'll* take the baby! I'll be Papi, and *you* can be Tío."

"No," Jesse shook his head, bending down to peer into the baby's shiny black eyes. "I'm Jesse," he whispered. "Am I *Papi*?" He smiled at the baby, stretching out a finger, grinning wider when the baby caught it with both hands and brought it to its tiny mouth for a taste. Jesse straightened, and stood looking at him for a moment. Then, slowly, he stretched out his arms. Cacique stared at him for a moment, sucking his thumb steadily, then just as slowly stretched out his own little arms. The two met. "Am I Papi?" Jesse wondered, his heart clenching in his chest as the baby snuggled against it for a moment, tears stinging the backs of his eyes. He turned the baby gently, holding its back to his chest, much in the same way as Cat had just held Marina. "I am Papi," he announced softly in the baby's ear. He snuggled the baby and kissed it on top of its head. Turning to his nephew and nieces, he sighed happily, tears shining in his eyes. His voice was hoarse when he finally spoke. "*You* tell Rain." His kids smiled. "Thank you."

"Captain Coltrane!"

Jesse turned his head to look at the man calling him, amused at the title. "Sailing Master…"

Giancarlo stepped up to him and waved a hand at the Aguilar-Banks crew. "They made me do it!" he exclaimed in mock indignation. "I did not want to do it, but did they listen to me? Nooooo!" He stamped his foot, trying not to look at the rest of the pirates who were laughing silently at him. "No one listens to Giancarlo!" He threw up his hands in the air for added effect.

Jesse smiled slowly, already bonding with his brand new son. "What did they do?"

"They made me do it!" The Sailing Master continued with his mock rage. "*Gian! Throw the baby*, they said! *No*, I said! And then they began. All three of them!" He sighed with feigned exasperation. "*Throw the ba-by! Throw the ba-by!*" He chanted, mocking them. He pounded his chest with his fist. "Me! Giancarlo Ilarraza! To throw the baby!" Pretending to glare at them, he huffed at the Aguilar-Banks crew, now grinning at him.

Jesse smiled. "What did you do, Giancarlo?"

"What did I *do*?" Gian repeated in mock outrage. "What *could* I do? I…" he intoned slowly, "threw the baby!" He pretended to sneer at them. "Savages."

"What did the baby do?" Jesse asked, caught up in the story.

"*It* is as much of a savage as *they* are!" He huffed. "*It is a baby savage!*" he informed them in a stage whisper. "It *swam*!" Giancarlo scowled dramatically.

The pirates chuckled and the detectives grinned. The Aguilar-Banks, well, they just smiled.

Jesse laughed, and stretched out his hand. "Giancarlo, thanks for throwing the baby, man!"

Grinning, Giancarlo slid his hand against his. "It ended up being my pleasure," he confessed.

Don Carlos laughed, rubbing his hands. "I suggest you go and gather whatever belongings you have together, in preparation of your leaving." He waved a hand at them. "Go get your fabrics from Leila, from the dress shop, your drawings from Caribe, anything you have lying around," he urged. "We will stay here and discuss details." He smiled gently at the Aguilar-Banks, and nodded at Rashawn, who indicated he would accompany them. "We may not have much time," he added under his breath, as the Aguilar-Banks nodded and turned to leave, smiling at their friends, leaving the baby Cacique in the arms of his new daddy. The older pirate turned to those remaining. "Gentlemen," he smiled at the lady pyrate, "Storm, we have business to discuss."

The men grinned at each other. "She's back," Joe murmured.

María Isabel waved a hand from her place between them, gently scolding in anticipation. "Boys…"

Pablo nodded. "Xaira?" he called to her. "In here!" They fell silent as Xaira reached them in their medieval times room.

The young girl burst in on them, her face lit up with a beautiful smile. Her eyes glittered with excitement. Wasting no time, she jumped right into what she wanted. "I need something!" she cried happily. "I need something bad, because I have something that will make us a lot of money!"

The men were immediately interested. "What?" they asked at the same time. María Isabel watched with curiosity.

"You know that big billboard sign on our building? I need you to get that going for me, immediately. Before Marina, Jackson, and Salomé get here," she said hurriedly, gasping for breath. "Then those small traffic islands on either side of our block? I want you to fix them. The city will let you do just about anything you want, as long as you pay for it. Then I want you to buy for me, out of my own money, a couple of electronic billboards, like Times Square. One for each island."

The men kept silent for a moment, just staring at her. Joe frowned. "Those are expensive, baby. Why do you want to go and spend your own money on that?"

"It's an investment," she answered. "I've got something!" Her laughter was contagious in its sheer joy. "I want to share with you guys!"

Pablo nodded, spreading his hands out. "Okay, what have you got for us, baby?"

"Look!" she exclaimed, throwing a pack of photographs on top of the table. "Look what I've got!"

The grown-ups looked through the photographs with growing excitement, as Xaira outlined her unique thoughts. When she was finished, María Isabel nodded, her own eyes glowing. "I will invest in this, on behalf of Carlos and myself." She took the Oriental girl's hand in her own, and squeezed it, pride in her eyes. "Xaira, *mi amor*, this is a wonderful idea!"

Joe shook his head ruefully, chuckling. He slid his hands over his cornrows, the movement making his earrings twinkling in the soft lighting. "I agree. I'm in."

Pablo nodded. "So am I." He turned to the girl. "We need to find out---"

"I'm all over it, Papi," she interrupted gently, pushing some papers over the table towards them. "Please help me polish this proposal. You need to do the rest."

Pablo nodded again, scanning the papers in his hands. "Good job, baby. We'll split this. We'll call Shane and see if he wants part of this. Then we'll do it five ways." He looked up at her, smiling with pride. "What do you call this venture?"

Xaira smiled wide, barely containing her excitement. She sighed with happiness. *"Captured by Caribe."*

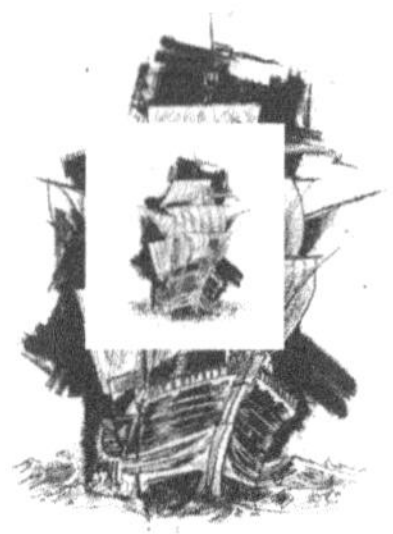

Silas and Jimmy grinned, their heads bouncing to the rhythm of the drums. It had never been so crowded in their hiding spot before. The visitors were mixed in amongst the pirates, except for Gaitano and the one they called Catamaran. These kept Don Carlos and the one they called Jamal between them. The jungle throbbed around them, as the evening sky bled to indigo. Stars multiplied in the dark canopy above them. The brush whirred, croaked, sang and chirped with night creatures. The smell of burning tiki torches carried in the breeze. Happy laughter accompanied chanting and singing. In front of them, the Aguilar-Banks danced with abandon, weaving and swirling among each other, their faces smiling as they gave themselves to the dance.

Jamal couldn't stand it anymore. "I don't know about you guys," he informed his companions, "but I'm going in." In a moment, he was gone. Striding across the space, he jumped into the clearing with a happy yell, joining his friends' children.

"Later, gators," laughed Catamaran, and he too was gone, to appear amidst the spinning dancers.

"I'm going in, too," said Solomon, and was gone, happily joining his friends.

Giancarlo waved a hand at the dancers. "They look so happy…" Laughing, then he was also gone.

"Sorry…" Rashawn mumbled and went with them.

Those who remained sighed and watched. The yells and laughter escalated, indicating the happiness in everyone's hearts. Storm leapt up and went.

Sighing, Silas turned to the remaining visitor. "Go." When the man just looked at him, he held out his arms. "Give me the baby," he said, motioning with his head. "Join your family."

Jesse smiled. "Thanks," he smiled, kissing the sleeping baby on top of his head and passing him. In a moment, he joined his family and friends. The remaining men fell silent for a while, avidly watching the dancers. The young pirates followed their girls amongst them, their hearts beating in rhythm.

"Boys." Both turned to look at their father between them. "There is a storm coming." Don Carlos waited as they glanced briefly at each other over his head, before looking back at him again.

"I don't suppose you mean the storm we are to take into their world," Carlitos said.

His father laughed. "No, that one is no more than wind, rain, and thunder and lightning." He shook his head and made eye contact with each of them. "The storm I see coming is beyond anything I have ever seen before."

Indio laid a hand on the man he called father. "Are we in danger, Papá?" he rumbled quietly.

Don Carlos gazed into his eyes affectionately. "As usual," he answered with a smile. "Actually, more than usual." Sighing, he looked over at the dancers again. "The sequence of events that the accountant has unleashed is unprecedented."

Gaitano felt the need to defend his new wife. "Marina had no idea what she was getting herself and us into, Papá."

"Of course not," the father soothed the son, "but the result is the same." Taking a deep breath, he sighed. "I suggest you boys have fun now." He nodded towards people gyrating and stomping in front of them. "Go dance with your girls. Enjoy the moment." He looked at them. "If my bones don't deceive me, we only have hours. Something is headed this way." The young pirates nodded. Excusing themselves, they went to join their girls and the rest of their group. The pirate took another deep breath and addressed the two remaining men with him. "I believe our time has come, men. I want you to stand by, the next couple of days." He sensed more than saw them nod. "Carlitos and his crew must disappear into the visitors' world.

It is not a bad place," he added noticing their interest, "just different. The Spaniards from La Diosa del Mar will be great assets in order for this change to take place. I suggest you prepare yourselves. We are expecting company." The men grunted in answer, and went back to watching the dancers, Silas rocking the baby. In another moment, the drums overwhelmed them again, transporting them to a place where rhythm and motion soothed them, keeping out the world.

"Watch them." Don Carlos smiled as Catamaran turned his head to look at him when he whispered. They were all back at Villa Azúl, done with the dancing with the natives. They had stopped to cool off at the waterfall first, and then proceeded to come here. Servants milled around, preparing a feast. The air was heavy with competing, mingling scents. Nature provided its own. The flowering bougainvilleas surrounding the courtyard, contrasted with the scent of salt from the ocean. Then there was the aroma of roasting pig and steaming vegetables. Faint, the smells and sounds of the jungle behind them, complimenting the smoking tiki torches that lit the courtyard. Overhead, stars filled the dome of the night sky. "Does Marina love you?" This time Jamal, Rashawn, and Jesse turned to look at him.

Cat scowled, offended. "Of course Marina loves me!"

The pirate chuckled. "Then trust that Marina would make a choice that was good for her and her family that would meet with the approval of all of you." He met the young man's cat eyes with his own silver ones. Firelight flickered in each one's depths. "You've been nothing but a brat to my son since you met him."

Cat sighed. "I know, I'm sorry, I already apologized to him." Then he grinned. "I actually like him, he's pretty cool."

Jamal snorted softly. "He sure got your number." The men laughed.

Jesse agreed, smiling as he held a sleeping Cacique against his chest. "Never seen you move so fast, Cat," he teased his nephew.

Rashawn looked from one to the other. "Sounds like I missed something." A slow smile spread on his face. "What happened? Pirate scare the kitty-cat?"

His uncle grinned. "You could say that."

"It was a sight to see, that's for sure," Jesse rumbled. "Pirate lashed out at the kitty-cat. Game over." The men laughed softly.

"Pirate boy's mean," Cat admitted softly.

Don Carlos patted him gently on the face, as he would his own sons. "Give Carlitos a chance, Catamaran." He turned back to the scene unfolding in front of them, his voice dropping to a whisper again. "Watch them."

"Are you ready for this?" Jackson demanded. He thrummed with pent-up energy, and with excitement at the thought of things to come. Standing in the middle of the group he was part of he felt like a strong and wise leader. "We have to go. No doubt. This whole thing with our life insurance policies is crazy. But to have Dad, Mom, Papi and Mami stand accused of our murder because we'd rather hang here in Encantada is *not* an option!" He looked around the circle, making eye contact with everyone before turning specifically to the pirates. "You have a lot to learn about our world. It is going to be a process. One that Caribe, María Isabel and Don Carlos are obviously well into. But it's your turn to go on an adventure." He grinned. "My best advice to you is to find your niche. Gian," he said, turning to his best friend. "Cat has a club back home called the Blue Cat. Get together with him to hire you as a manager or something. You have experience with the Sirens' Lair." Then he turned to his sisters' men. "You two, I don't really know what you guys could do, figure it out. But if I were you, I'd get myself a boat and do something on the water." Looking at Solomon, he shrugged. "There will definitely be a number of things you can do." Finally, he turned to his girlfriend. "The girls will help you out. Also there are our moms, Xaira and Summer. Talk to María Isabel and see how it is going for her. Although," he added with a laugh, "judging by how Don Carlos is getting along, she must be loving it also." The pirates laughed with him.

"It will be fine," Salomé's soothing voice drifted in the breeze. "We are all smart, grown, capable adults who have just happened to go through a lot together." She grinned as the pirates laughed again.

Hooking her arm through Indio's, she held it close against her, looking at him happily. "We will make your transition into our world as pleasant and painless as possible. Storm sticks to us, and we'll show her how third millennium girls do it. Boys can rely on our dads and Jackson, and of course," she rolled her eyes humorously, "Caribe and Don Carlos, to learn how to get along with all modern conveniences without too many mishaps."

"We promise to provide you with a network of family and friends, to assist you any time you need them," Marina added with a laugh, "we have people back home that will have your back. For that matter, the men who came over with Don Carlos will be of the best help, because they have come here to meet you." She looked up to gaze into her husband's eyes. "I apologize about Catamaran, Carlos," she said softly, "he's a brat. I never thought I would have to warn you about him. He is my godfather and my boss. He's never had to compete," she rolled her eyes with a smile, "with anyone over me before. Don't pay attention to him."

The young pirate just smiled and gazed back at his wife. Hooking an arm around her neck, he brought her close and kissed her forehead. "Don't worry. I already took care of him."

Marina pulled back to gaze at him again, smiling as the pirates chuckled. "Good. It was about time someone did." Laughing softly, she slipped an arm around his waist.

Slowly, they made a circle. Gaitano pulled Indio to his side, and going counterclockwise, Salomé was next. She grabbed Jackson, who had his arm around Storm, by the hand. Giancarlo slipped his arm around Storm also, so that Jackson and he had a hand on each other's shoulder. Solomon stepped in, hand on Giancarlo's other shoulder, and coming up on Marina's other side, slipping his arm around her shoulders, over her husband's, hand resting on her hair. Circle completed, the young people stepped closer towards each other. They took turns, expressing a wish and offering a prayer. Finally they ended chanting, swaying side to side, and stomping their feet. Now the air rang out with the laughter of self-proclaimed lifelong friends.

"What do you see?"

Cat thought about it for a moment. The young pirates were obviously closely connected to his younger cousins. "They're tight."

Don Carlos nodded. "Quite. They have gone through a few adventures together."

"Your son must be a great man, to inspire such loyalty from his crew," Jamal observed.

The pirate laughed softly. "Carlitos *is* a great man. His men respect him *and* love him. There is no greater measure."

Jesse nodded. "I agree. It is evident that he respects and loves them back."

Rashawn chuckled. "Well, they must have a good thing going, because they are following him."

Don Carlos shook his head. "They are, aren't they?" He laughed.

Suddenly, a commotion ensued at the entrance of Villa Azúl. The foyer seemed to spill pirates, coming in from either side of the wall at the front of the house. Startled, the visitors leapt to their feet in alarm. Jamal and Rashawn each reached for nonexistent guns in invisible holsters, out of habit and training. Jesse quickly set the sleeping baby next to him and threw himself in front of it, covering him with his own body, reaching for a knife in a boot that wasn't there. Catamaran swore softly, luminous eyes wide in his dark face, as the pirates reached them. The young pirates and the Aguilar-Banks crew fell silent as they turned to watch. Then a voice carried across the courtyard, clear and shaken.

"Stay away from me, Jack!"

The pirates laughed. The visitors took a step back, senses screaming. Don Carlos swiftly stepped in, quickly making introductions. "Gentlemen!" he announced. "Please meet the Council." Keeping himself between them, he made the introductions. "Suleiman of the Chymera, Sultan of the Kalahari, Jai-Ling of Ocean Wind..." He hesitated as Giancarlo rushed to the group, snatching the female pyrate, and twirling her in his arms. "That is Rouge, Captain of the Sea Gypsy where Storm is Quartermaster. She is with Giancarlo, as you can see." He chuckled. "And this is Marina's tormentor, Captain of the Black Mermaid, Jack."

"Marina's tormentor?" Jamal was curious.

Jack grinned. "Marina believes that if she kills the messenger, the message will change."

"Aaah, got you," Jamal grinned back.

"These are the Aguilar-Banks' family," Don Carlos continued. "Catamaran St. Jacques, Jesse Coltrane, and Jamal and Rashawn Blackmon." He waited as the men shook hands all around. The visitors stood by quietly as their loved ones greeted the pirates with happy enthusiasm.

"You must have been right behind us," Jackson smiled, shaking his head.

"We were," Rouge laughed, letting go of Giancarlo long enough to hug her Quartermaster. Storm smiled happily, squeezing her back. This show of affection had never taken place between them before. Ever since meeting the Aguilar-Banks, however, they had felt freer to express their feelings for one another in the same manner they expressed them to Giancarlo and Jackson.

Cat frowned. "Right behind you?"

Jackson glanced at him, distracted. "Yeah, man, we were just in San Juan a couple of days ago."

"So, what now, Jack?" Gaitano laughed.

Jack rolled his eyes, and grabbed Marina's hand, holding fast as she tried to pull away. "We were sent here to escort you."

Marina froze. She had begun playfully tugging at her hand, trying to pull away from him. Now the only movement in her was her heart pounding in her chest. She gasped, willing herself to start breathing again. "Escort?"

Salomé grabbed her other hand. "Whoa!" She looked at the newly arrived pirates. "Where?"

Rouge rolled her eyes. "The Lair." Turning to the visitors, she smiled shyly. "Nice to meet you." Turning away, she glanced over her shoulder. "Let's go, guys. Right now."

"Victoria!" Don Carlos called out to a young teenage girl bustling about around them. The girl shyly approached them, keeping a wary eye on the newly arrived pirates, and stood in front of her boss. He smiled at her. "Would you please get a basket for the baby? We need to go out and take care of some business. He is down for the night. I would greatly appreciate it if you watched him for us until we get back. We shouldn't be too long, I am sure everyone is hungry." The men laughed in agreement.

"Yes, Don Carlos." The girl smiled back and was gone.

Don Carlos turned to Jesse. "He will still be asleep when we get back," he assured him. In a moment, Victoria was back with the required basket, filled with soft cloths for him. Gently, Jesse picked up his son, pressing a kiss to his forehead and laid him down gently inside the basket. Victoria smiled at him reassuringly and turned away, basket in her arms. The older pirate turned to his company. "Now, let us go."

Catamaran hurried to his side, as they all filed out into the balmy tropical night. "Will there be danger, Don Carlos?" he asked, trying to keep his eyes on the pirates ahead of them, disappearing into the jungle.

Don Carlos laughed. "There just might be, Cat. Let us go and see."

The Sirens' Lair seemed quiet on the outside. There were few pirates milling around, only a few girls on the upstairs balcony. Inside the tavern there were more pirates, some familiar, but most of them unknown. Everyone turned to look as the group entered. From behind the bar, Silas and Jimmy breathed a quiet sigh of relief as they came in.

Pedro Escobar approached the group. "Gaitano." The men nodded at each other and shook hands.

"Pedro," the young pirate said, looking around him. "There seems to be full house tonight."

The lawman laughed. "Yes, sir."

"John!" Marina exclaimed happily as she saw the large pirate surrounded by his sons, the Hawthorne scoundrels, detectives of the seas. Father and sons smiled at her. "Jamal," she called softly, her senses ringing in alarm, "John Hawthorne is the law here." Reaching blindly for his hand, she pulled him to her side, quickly making introductions. "John, scoundrels," she grinned at them, "these are Jamal and Rashawn Blackmon. They are the law where we come from," she explained hastily. The men shook hands, and turned to her. "So, John?"

The pirate cocked an eyebrow at her. "Marina?"

She smiled slowly, sudden fear swimming behind her eyes, her heart beginning to pound in her chest. "Why are we here?"

John frowned. He had caught the fear and could sense her adrenaline speeding up. He needed to defuse this fast. She would be no good scared. "Someone needs to talk to you."

"Do they have a problem with me?" she asked automatically.

He bit back a grin. "Big one."

She narrowed her eyes suspiciously at him. "You don't seem overly concerned, John Hawthorne."

He raised both eyebrows this time. "I am not, Marina Aguilar."

"Gaitano," Carlos grinned.

The Hawthorne scoundrels offered soft congratulations. Their father beamed as if he were their proud parent. "Gaitano." He inclined his head towards her. "After all, you are the master."

Marina frowned, not knowing what he was talking about. "Of what? At what?"

"Head games."

Marina lit up like a Christmas tree. "Head games," she breathed. She nodded, agreeing with him. "I am."

Her family didn't know how to react to the exchange yet, but her husband frowned. "What are you going to do, Marina?"

She turned to him, her smile chasing her fear away and slowing her heart a bit. "I have no idea," she confessed.

"So…" Jackson began, restless already.

"Where is she?" The thunderous voice seemed to roll across the floor, shaking the rafters along the way. The sirens squealed.

Everyone froze. Marina gasped, fear back like an icy drop down her spine. Without thinking, her hand went out. Salomé slapped hers against it, fingers locking automatically. Jackson's hands went down on both their shoulders. The newly arrived visitors stared. Catamaran felt his body begin to thrum. Surely his eyes were deceiving him. Jesse clenched his jaw and his fists. He flowed into stillness, much like Marina's on occasion. This was real. Jamal and Rashawn slid their eyes to each other. If they had any doubt before, it was completely gone now. They were in the middle of a den of pirates. Thank God half of them were their friends. Wordlessly, they drifted away from each other, positioning themselves in opposite sides of the room, across from each other.

"Where is she?" The rolling voice was lower, no longer earth shaking, but all the more ominous. Before them were three pirates. And Charlie. The catalyst between Marina and the late Xavier's demise. The disgusting, sniveling excuse of a man had been the one to facilitate Xavier catching up with Marina a few weeks ago. She had ended it. Now these other pirates were here before her. One of them was red haired like Rouge and Jack. The difference was that instead of flowing, soft hair, his was wiry and thick, hanging in dirty unkempt ropes around his head. His skin was like coffee with a lot of cream, impossibly freckled. His face was also freckled, with a broad nose, and full generous lips. As Marina watched, he sneered, revealing a gold tooth. Her eyes flew to his. They were the color of cinnamon, almost burning in their rage. She looked away to the one next to Charlie. This one was much cleaner and better groomed. He was very handsome, tanned, blond hair tied back with a cord, blue eyes. Actually, vacant blue eyes. Like there was nobody home. He nodded his head at her with a smile. Marina turned away from him and looked at the one in the middle. This one was large. Not solid like John Hawthorne or Don Miguel. Soft instead, like he never outgrew his baby fat. His hair was long, curly and greasy, reflecting the light inside the Lair. His face was completely pockmarked, mostly covered by a thick bushy black beard. Gold earrings sparkled in both his ears, framed by a bright red bandana. His eyes were brown, and blazing. Marina shivered.

Salomé squeezed her hand. "Who?"

The man momentarily turned his attention to her. "The accountant," he growled.

Catamaran drew in his breath. He swore softly.

Salomé tossed her head and flashed her eyes at the man, disguising the fear that threatened to overcome her. "Does this accountant have a name?"

He turned to her with interest, the growl trickling out of his throat. "Marina Aguilar…"

Salomé let go momentarily of Marina's hand and crossed her arms over her chest, framing her breasts, displaying her cleavage to her advantage. As expected, the pirate's eyes drifted, distracting him for a moment. Salomé nodded, satisfied. "That's my younger sister you're talking about, and anything you have to say to her, you can say in front of me."

The pirates laughed, the sound low in their chests, as if they were amused by children. The center one smiled at them, eyes seeming to twinkle. "As you wish."

"There are three of you," Marina observed, waving her hand at them. "There must be three of us." She also, crossed her arms over her chest and nodded with satisfaction. "I want a boy." She pointed at them with her chin. "You got two."

The pirates laughed louder this time. "As you wish," the man repeated. He raised an eyebrow at her. "Which boy do you want?"

"Indio."

"Jackson," Jackson said behind them, squeezing their shoulders.

"Indio!" The name shot out of the mouths of all his loved ones, family and pirates around him, at the same time.

Raising his hands in the air, Jackson backed up slowly. "Okay, okay." He shook his head. "Damn…"

Indio took his place, putting his hands on the girls' shoulders. He squeezed them reassuringly, his voice rumbling in his chest as he faced the pirates. "What do you want, Blake?"

"Your accountant," came the automatic reply, accompanied with a sneer.

Marina shook her head. "I need to know who I'm dealing with." She looked at the pirate straight in the eye. "I don't know who you are," she hesitated, her face lighting up with a smile, "sir…"

Somewhere behind her, her husband chuckled. "Allow me, *querida*." His soft voice rolled over them like a warm wave. "Meet the crew of the *Medusa*."

Marina felt another icy drop roll down her spine. This time all her hairs stood an end. She reached for Salomé's hand and effectuated a death grip on it. Her voice, however, masked successfully her true feelings, projecting only mild curiosity. "*Medusa*?" she murmured. "I do not recognize the name."

"Xavier's ship."

Marina froze, a deathly stillness falling over her like a cloak. "Xavier's ship," she repeated hollowly.

"To your right is James Mallory, the Sailing Master. They call him Crazy Jim," he added, so that she could detect the soft warning in his voice. Marina nodded that she understood. "The mulatto to your left is Blood Red, the Boatswain. And to the center is Captain Edward Blake, the Quartermaster of the Medusa."

Marina nodded, squeezing her sister's fingers rhythmically. "I don't mean to be rude, but what do you want?"

Captain Blake frowned at her for a moment, before offering a seat in front of him. He smiled wickedly. "And your sister, Salomé," he said, smiling at the surprise in their faces at his knowing her name, "and Indio." The three of them sat down, assembling around a table. The pirate didn't waste any time. Putting his hands on the table, he leaned forward, his eyes boring into Marina's. "Is it true?" he rasped in a low voice that seemed to roll inside his chest.

"Is what true?" Marina asked carefully.

"It is! It's true! I saw her myself!" Charlie began screeching, jumping up and down next to Crazy Jim. *"The accountant just killed Xavier!,"* he howled to the rafters.

"Boy!" Salomé glared at him, stopping him with a glint of her jewel bright green eyes. She tossed her hair angrily. "You are starting to sound like a broken record. You said those exact same words a couple of weeks ago." She pointed a finger at him. *"Shut…up…"*

Silently, Jamal and Rashawn moved closer. Next to them, Jackson and Jesse mirrored their steps, leaving all the pirates and the sisters in the middle.

"Charlie," Marina said menacingly, squinting her own hazel eyes at him. "I want to smack you really really bad right now. Don't make me do it," she growled at him, slapping her hands down on the table top.

But did he listen? No, of course he didn't listen. Instead, he was sniveling, tears glistening in his eyes, his lips trembling. But he wasn't backing down. *"She did it",* he screeched. *"Marina Aguilar killed Xavier!"* So caught up was the little man with his tirade, that he didn't notice the Hawthorne brothers move to stand silently behind him.

"Charlie," Salomé said soothingly, in the same tone she had used on her Uncle Jesse just a few hours earlier. "Now calm down…" Behind her, Gaitano began chuckling.

Charlie could not stop. "John was here, and he let her go!"

Captain Blake lifted an eyebrow at the pirate John Hawthorne. "You were here, John?"

John Hawthorne lifted his own eyebrow back at him. "I was, Blake. I sure was. Anything you have to say to me about the way I handled the situation, you are free to do so."

Captain Blake shook his head, even as he kept the scowl on his face. "I would never question you, Hawthorne."

"That's what makes you a smart man," John conceded.

Charlie was fit to be tied, however, spittle running down the sides of his mouth, eyes swimming in tears. He was practically jumping up and down with anxiety, determined to accuse the accountant of what she had so obviously done. "She did it! I saw her!" he screeched, pointing a finger at her. "And then the men took them away!"

"What men?" growled Captain Blake, never taking his eyes off the females in front of him.

"Their fathers! Pablo Aguilar and Joe Banks!" His eyes shone feverishly with rapidly encroaching insanity. Obviously, the smaller pirate was extremely traumatized. They could practically see his mind slipping away from him.

Marina slapped her hands on the table again, this time with much more force. *"No!"*

Salomé stood up, her whole body shaking with anger, pointing a finger at the blubbering man. "Don't you dare mention my daddy and my papi! They are not here to defend themselves!"

"Salomé…" Indio's voice rumbled softly as he pulled her back down to sit next to him.

The pirates smirked, highly amused. "And where are the distinguished masters now?" Blood Red laughed.

"They had to go back home to take care of business," Salomé retorted, "not that it's any of yours."

"So, other than the Gaitanos, you are here by yourselves."

Don Carlos stepped closer. "The accountant has the whole Council behind her, men," he reminded them softly. "These girls are certainly not here by themselves." The men grumbled but looked around them.

Blake smirked. "I had heard about the accountant's penchant for black men but I didn't really believe it, until now."

Marina rolled her eyes. "I was mostly raised by black men," she explained impatiently. She jabbed a thumb behind her. "Jackson Banks is my older brother." Without taking her eyes off the pirate, she pointed a finger around her. "Rashawn Blackmon is our best friend. Jamal Blackmon is his uncle and a major man in my life. Catamaran St. Jacques is my older cousin. And Solomon, our Boatswain," she added, glancing at a very interested and grinning Blood Red, "is my very own fighting partner extraordinaire." Gritting her teeth, she clenched her fists to keep from pounding them on the table. "So fucking what?"

"And Sultan?"

The large African laughed, making the lion's claw roll on his chest with the movement. "I am most honored to be one of the accountant's black men," he offered, winking at her husband.

"What about that prince of yours?"

Exasperated, she shook her head, not knowing what he was talking about. "What prince?" The visitors looked at each other. They didn't know exactly what was going on, but they had an idea. What they didn't understand was why the pirates were all smiling.

Blake frowned, clearly beginning to lose patience with her. "That prince…" he glanced at Charlie for support.

"The prince!" Charlie screeched. "The accountant is with a fresh prince from somewhere called Bel Air!" The visitors glanced at each other, now slightly amused, but still on edge.

Indio smiled. "You mean Will Smith," he offered.

Blood Red licked his lips and grinned, looking into her eyes, no longer glaring. "Would you rather deal with me?" Quickly, he put his huge hand over both of hers on the table.

Marina froze. Her natural impulse was to snatch her hands away out of sudden fear, but she decided that her company was amused enough. Instead, she held his gaze and lifted one knuckle, gently stroking the palm of his hand. "No," she shook her head.

Blood Red chuckled, admiration leaking into his eyes, understanding what her caress had cost her. He winked at her, enjoying the feel of her movement under his hand, allowing her to caress him one last time. "Not black enough, huh?" He squeezed her hand suddenly, grinning when she squeezed back.

Marina's impulse was to flirt, responding with a smile. "That's not why."

"And what about that other captain of yours?" Blake asked suddenly, getting her attention back on him.

Marina frowned, still astounded at herself and her exchange with the Boatswain. "Captain?" she repeated, not sure of what he was talking about.

Salomé squeezed Marina's fingers locked with hers. "What other captain?"

"Jack."

The sisters looked at each other. "Jack?" Everyone turned to look at Jack.

Jack grinned back. His red hair shone around his head in the candlelight like a fiery halo. "Oh, I'm definitely not black enough." The men laughed. The sisters rolled their eyes and turned back to the pirates in front of them.

Charlie was absolutely livid. *"Not the Captain of the Black Mermaid!"* He stamped his foot. *"Not that one! The other Jack!"* he howled at the ceiling, his eyes rolling to the back of his head. *"Captain Jack Sparrow, Commander of the Black Pearl!"*

Jamal and Rashawn looked at each other over the group crowded around the table. Surely they hadn't heard right. Wasn't that Johnny Depp's character in the *Pirates of the Caribbean* series? But then Jackson laughed. They had. Their eyes twinkled with silent laughter.

"Way to go, ladies," Jesse growled, admiration and amusement combined in his voice.

Catamaran chuckled and shaking his head he scolded them gently. "Girls, girls, girls…"

Don Carlos' voice came as a soft warning. "Men…"

"Captain Sparrow is unavailable," Salomé said quickly.

"Yes," Marina smiled. "Jack couldn't make it."

"Forget the Black Pearl then," Captain Blake said decisively. "Is it true?"

"It's true! I saw her myself! John was here! The accountant just killed Xavier!" Charlie screeched, tears streaming down his filthy face, leaving shiny trails on the grime.

"Shut up!" Salomé screamed at him, pounding her free hand on the table.

"I warned you, Charlie," Marina growled at him, moving to stand up. Indio's hand snaked out and grabbed her hair, wrapping it around his wrist and pulling it taut, making her stay in her seat. Blood Red's hand shot out, cupping over hers once again. When their eyes met, he shook his head once at her. Marina whipped her head back at Charlie, as far as Indio allowed it. Charlie was gaping at her, snot running out of his nose, blubbering like a little boy, face soaked in tears. He was pointing a shaking finger at her, his mouth opening and closing like a beached fish. No words came out because he couldn't get enough air into his lungs, gasping instead. Next to him, Crazy Jim smiled at her like an angel, something seeming to spark alive in his eyes for a moment. For just one second. As she watched, true to his name, the Sailing Master did something outrageous. Out of nowhere, his fist shot up in a beautiful arc, backhanded, slamming into the smaller sailor's nose with almost unnatural force. Not only did he break it, sending a spray of blood all over, but he also knocked Charlie out cold. The sirens squealed at the sound of bone meeting cartilage, and then scattered as the sailor finally fell with a sick thud on the floor. "I told you," Marina muttered, relaxing. Blood Red took his hand slowly off hers, watching her warily. Indio let go of her hair. Just a little, though.

Crazy Jim reached over and wiped the back of his hand on Charlie's pant leg. "Forgive me, accountant. Please continue," he said, his voice soft and cultured, almost out of context with the place they were at.

"Thank you, Captain Mallory." Crazy Jim inclined his head at her. She had rightfully called him Captain, recognizing that at their level of Quartermaster, Sailing Master and Boatswain, just like Indio, Giancarlo and Solomon, they were all captains to some extent. Marina turned back to Blake. "Is what true?" Once again, her fingers resumed squeezing Salomé's rhythmically.

Blake fixed her with his gaze for a moment, making sure he had her full attention, Charlie already forgotten. "Did you kill Xavier?" He leaned closer over the table.

Marina leaned towards him. Her voice came out barely a whisper. "Yes."

The Quartermaster slammed his hands down suddenly on the table between them, making Marina jump back in alarm, and Salomé squeal. Storm, startled, glanced at the pirates with her. Jackson's family froze, reacting as a pack. No one moved, trusting Indio to take care of the matter. Everyone seemed to be on high alert.

"*Blake!*" Indio wasn't having it.

"Marina," Don Carlos called, once again stepping in front of his son as he moved towards the group.

"Don Carlos?" she replied, breathless.

"Are you all right, *divina*?" he asked, pushing back against his son until Giancarlo and Solomon took him away to stand by the Council.

"*Sí.*"

"What have you done about the accountant?" the angry pirate roared at John Hawthorne. He turned to Pedro Escobar. "And you? You just let her walk free?"

Pedro Escobar stepped up. "I can't hold her."

John Hawthorne shrugged. "I couldn't find her guilty. You realize Xavier was the *White Ghost*, don't you?" The three crew members of the Medusa seemed to turn to stone. The *White Ghost* had been notorious in their waters for the past months, known for his massacres on poor unsuspecting native islanders. John smiled. "That's what I thought."

Jamal stepped up, the scowl on his face fierce. "Detective Rashawn Blackmon and I have come all the way from Blue Bay to extradite Marina Aguilar, and with her, her brother Jackson Banks, and her sister Salomé Banks."

The crew of the Medusa turned to look at him. "Aren't you two related?" Blake asked impatiently.

"Yes." This time Rashawn stepped up, looking just as fierce as the older detective. The pirates turned their heads to look at him.

"My uncle Jamal and I work together, just like John Hawthorne and his sons."

Blood Red grinned. "You are extraditing the three of them?"

Crazy Jim's eyes glowed. "What did they do?"

"That," Jamal said firmly, "is a personal matter between the Aguilar-Banks and the law in Blue Bay." He stared the pirate down. "Pedro Escobar and John Hawthorne will be drawing the papers for Rashawn and myself so that we can take them home."

Captain Blake grinned. "So I guess Juan Gaitano will be picking them up."

Jamal and Rashawn froze. Their bluff was about to be called.

Don Carlos Gaitano came to the rescue. He knew his younger brother Juan just about better than anyone on the planet, except for their older brother Miguel, maybe. And he just had this feeling that he couldn't shake. "Yes. Juan will be here soon to help take care of the Aguilar-Banks children."

The visitors let out a silent sigh of relief.

The pirates turned their attention back to the girls in front of them and Indio. The Quartermaster looked at Marina. "Why?"

Marina glared at him, her heart still pounding from the scare he had given her, willing her tears to not well in her eyes. "Why what?"

This time, it was he who rolled his eyes. Impatiently, he leaned over the table again and motioned her with his head. His voice dropped. "Why did you kill Xavier?"

Marina leaned towards him, never breaking eye contact. "Xavier said something to me I didn't like."

Blake seemed to think it over. "But you *danced* for him," he finally accused in a whisper. As one, the other four leaned over the table also, making a huddle. Now what was said was just between the six of them.

Jackson threw his hands in the air in disgust. "Oh, come on!"

Storm slid an arm around his waist, stopping him before he did anything. Her voice was soothing in his ear. "Jackson!"

"I danced for him, too," Salomé whispered, "and so did Storm."

The Quartermaster rolled his eyes impatiently, once more. "You didn't sit on his lap." He looked accusingly at Marina again. "*You* sat on his lap."

Marina nodded. "Xavier made me."

Blake pressed his lips together for a moment. "What else did he make you do?"

"Dude, his hands were all over her," Salomé hissed at him.

"They were," rumbled Indio. He looked steadily at the Quartermaster. "He touched her chest and nuzzled her neck." He didn't move as he felt Salomé and Marina stare at him. "He squeezed her breasts a few times." They looked back at Blake. Indio never did or said anything without a reason.

The Quartermaster's scowl grew deeper. "He touched you like that?"

Marina wasn't sure where this was headed, but she was intrigued. She nodded slowly, thoughtfully. "I was on his lap, and he had his hands on me doing like this," she told him. Cupping her own breasts, she squeezed them and massaged them deeply for a moment, distantly amused at all their eyes on her. She stopped and put one hand back on the table, and locked fingers with Salomé again with the other one. "It didn't feel good," she confessed. "He only did it to mess with Gaitano."

A growl trickled out of the man's throat. "Gaitano." His hands formed fists on the table. "Your boss. Your boyfriend?" he asked, raising an eyebrow at her.

Marina swallowed and nodded. "My boss and my boyfriend."

His eyes bore into hers. "Your lover?"

Nodding again slowly, she went for it. "My lover and my husband."

Blood Red's eyebrows shot up in understanding. "That's why." He smiled when Marina nodded at him.

The Quartermaster inclined his head in congratulations. "The whelp does not know just how lucky he is." Curious, the sisters exchanged glances with Indio.

"Why is that?" Salomé asked softly.

"Xavier was completely obsessed with Carlos Gaitano, Captain of La Gitana," Blake hissed.

"Why?" Indio demanded softly.

The Quartermaster hesitated, measuring the brave in front of him, looking him up and down. "You, he was afraid of."

Marina rolled her eyes impatiently. "I knew that. Why did he have it in for Gaitano, though?" she asked, curiously.

The crew of the Medusa fell silent for a moment.

Suddenly, Crazy Jim began chuckling softly. "And people think *I* am crazy."

Blood Red put his fist to his face, biting back a laugh. Over his huge hand, his eyes twinkled. "Gaitano was his driving force."

The Quartermaster hesitated again, returning gaze for gaze on him. "Some people are driven by greed, some by love, more by money, and many by sex." His voice rolled over them like a quiet wave. "But power," he continued, weaving his words, painting a picture in their minds, "is the most seductive force of all. Because once you achieve power," he explained, "you get all the rest." He took a deep breath, his fists clenching and unclenching on the table. "Carlos Gaitano is the most powerful pirate in these waters."

Indio smiled slowly, belying the deadly fierceness in his eyes. It was his brother they were talking about. His heart surged with love and pride for Carlitos. "And it was just killing Xavier," he chuckled, basically mocking the men in front of him.

Marina was getting spooked. "Xavier told me that he would do anything to fuck with Gaitano."

The Quartermaster's eyes flew to hers, as the Sailing Master and Boatswain exchanged looks. It seemed to Marina as if tears were swimming in the depths of Blake's eyes. "Xavier told you that?" Unbelievably his voice broke.

Marina nodded. She was beginning to get a suspicion. "Xavier was very special to you."

"He was my Captain." The man almost hissed in her face.

"Was he your friend?"

One nod.

"Is the Medusa a large ship?"

One shake of the head.

"Were you sharing a cabin?"

Another nod.

"So you really miss him." Her hand crept on the table toward his. His jumped back as if zapped when she finally touched him. He scowled at her, but his tears were swimming closer to the surface. He put his hand back where it had been, letting her lay hers softly on top of it. "Were you lovers?" she whispered. Everyone at the table waited for the answer with held breath.

The Quartermaster seemed to think about it. "Lovers? Naaaaah," he frowned, remembering. "Xavier didn't love anybody. He just loved what the Gaitanos had." He shrugged. "We shared a berth on occasion." He hesitated, frowning. "We had sex, yes, while we were at sea." His eyes met each of theirs, challenging them to pass judgment on him. "While we were on land, he was wild about women. But at sea, it was *me*," he whispered passionately. "Look at me!" he demanded. "No woman will have me! Xavier made me forget!"

Caught up in the man's story, the sisters glanced at each other and looked back at him. "Xavier was very sexy," Salomé conceded.

"Very," Marina nodded, feeling a thrill at the memory of her one and only physical encounter with the pirate before she had to kill him. "He was a good kisser, too."

The Quartermaster Edward Blake was outraged. His lips trembled, and a tear slipped out. "He *kissed* you?"

Marina bit her lip and nodded slowly again. "Xavier was a *very* good kisser." Shrugging, she squeezed Blake's hand. "But he didn't want *me*, Captain Blake; he just wanted to mess with Gaitano because I was his girlfriend." She hesitated. "Xavier was very sick. It was more than his being the White Ghost," she whispered raggedly, tears swimming in her own eyes.

The pirates stared at her for a moment. Earrings sparkled in the moving candlelight that flickered in their eyes. Finally, the Quartermaster needed to know. "What did Xavier say to you?"

Everyone huddled closer, so that all six heads were touching in a circle. In a slow, broken whisper, Marina told them all Xavier had said.

The crew of the Medusa drew back in shock. The Quartermaster was the first one to react. "Xavier said that?" His hands shook. Blinking back his tears furiously, he took a deep breath. "I had no idea. Xavier loved children."

Indio growled. "We know he did. But even if he didn't mean what he said, it takes a very vicious distorted man to say something like that."

"Xavier was very sick," Salomé reminded them.

"You are better off without him," Marina said decisively. "Besides, with Xavier being gone, now you are the Captain and you get it all."

The Quartermaster nodded. "I will take Xavier's place as the Captain of the Medusa, but the White Ghost is dead and gone." He sighed. "Now we are free," he confessed.

The Boatswain looked at his new Captain. "I am not sleeping or having sex with you," he growled.

Crazy Jim snickered. "I may do things most people don't agree with, but I'm not insane. You are not touching me."

Blake made a sound of disgust. "As if I would go anywhere near either of you scallywags," he huffed, scowling until he realized his mates were teasing him. "I do like women, you know."

The sisters rolled their eyes and smiled.

"We are going to hook you up," Salomé offered

"We are going to treat you to a siren, that is going to make you forget all about Xavier," Marina grinned. "The three of you. Get together with our brother, Jackson Banks before we leave. This meeting is over."

The six of them stood up. Each of the men shook hands with Indio. Then they turned to the girls. These, held up their hands. When the pirates did the same, they met their palms with theirs in high fives. The men smiled and turned to Jackson. The pirates laughed. Carlos Gaitano shook his head, his eyes meeting his brother's. The visitors sighed in relief.

Don Carlos laughed. "*Medusa!* Good luck to you and safe voyage!" Turning to the Council and the Hawthornes, he exclaimed happily. "Caballeros! Come join us! *Villa Azúl!*" Happily, they all left.

"Dudes, I am so in!" Shane Butler, Esquire couldn't disguise the awe in his voice. His clients, partners and best friends, Pablo Aguilar and Joe Banks, had just made him a business proposition. He couldn't refuse. He liked it. Very much. They were sitting around the round table in their regular meeting place. Sloane and Shayla had gone out of the house in a long due alone time girls' night out. With the men sat María Isabel, looking very modern and quite spectacular in blue jeans and a crisp white T-shirt. The rubies dripping from her ears, throat and wrist, however, gave her away as the pirate's wife. Now she turned to him with a beaming smile.

"Aren't these young people so wonderfully talented?" she asked, awe and pride in her own voice.

Shane nodded at her, basking in the radiance of her smile. "They sure are, Marisabel," he agreed, using the easier shorter form of her name. "And smart." He looked back at the photos in front of them. "Who is in on this?"

Joe laughed, shaking his head. "Just us, man. Our building, our gig."

Shane nodded again. "I like that." He thought for a moment. "Timing couldn't be better. City Hall is making noises about fixing up the town and making it attractive for tourists. There's a lot of oceanfront realty wasted for lack of maintenance. The projects are falling apart, and the economy's not the best at the moment." Turning to his friends, he grinned. "This would be the exact thing this town needs to get started. I'll call Mark and swing it by him."

María Isabel turned to him, puzzled. "Who is Mark? Is he a friend of the children?"

The men grinned. "No," Pablo laughed, "he is a friend of ours."

"Mark Ross is the mayor of Blue Bay," Shane explained. "This is a small town, and we all went to school together. He's the guy who is going to let us do all this."

"Will he have a problem with any of it?"

"Nah," Shane shook his head. "As long as it's not pornography or hate propaganda we're displaying, he's not going to care. Besides, we're buying." He nodded with satisfaction at the thought. "Mark will give us a green light on this one." He turned to his friends and partners once more. "How far is this developed, anyway?"

Pablo smiled. "Caribe has all the equipment he needs at the moment. Xaira is fervently working on advertising. We hooked her up with a cell phone to run her business from."

"So it's the two of them," Shane observed.

"Yes," Joe confirmed. "Caribe takes the photos, and Xaira manages him."

The lawyer laughed. "They're getting along quite well, aren't they?"

María Isabel rolled her eyes with amusement. "They are inseparable."

"What else have we got?" Shane asked.

"Well, when Xaira approached us, she had already done all the research," Joe told him. "She got quotes on painting our building, contacted the billboard company and priced new ones, and also got a list of prices on the electronic ones. Everything was kind of rough so she got Pablo to polish the proposal for her."

Pablo took a deep breath, glancing at the papers in his hand. "Xaira also wants us to spruce the islands on either side of our block, and went everywhere she could think of. She has a couple of designs for us to look at, so we can decide on what we like best."

Shane grinned. "It seems that a call to Mark won't be enough. Maybe we should run these papers by him."

"Will he have time to see us?" Joe asked.

The lawyer laughed. "Are you kidding? With all the stuff he deals with on a daily basis, he will be more than happy to see us. I guarantee it." Holding up a finger, he reached inside his pocket and pulled out his cell phone. Quickly pressing buttons, he held it to his ear and waited. "Hey, Mark! How're you doing, man? Good, good, same here. Hey, I'm just calling to see what your schedule looks like." His eyebrows shot up and he grinned at his friends. "Same old, different day, huh? Well, Pablo, Joe and I are just chilling here at the Hacienda, hanging with our new BFF, and we got a proposal for you. Tomorrow morning? What time? Ten?" He glanced at his company as they all shook their heads at him. "No, man, we all work. Besides, it's too late. Morning's half gone, by then. How about breakfast, instead? Where?" He hesitated. Joe and Pablo gestured at him. "How about the Hacienda? You haven't been here forever. All right, man, you're on. Seven o'clock. See you then, dude. Take care." Flipping the cell phone shut, he smiled at his company. "We are on. He's coming to breakfast tomorrow morning."

María Isabel bit her lip. "This is a good thing, isn't it, guys?"

Joe passed his hands over his cornrows, before lacing his fingers and putting his hands on top of his head. He leaned back and grinned. "This is an excellent thing, Marisabel," he reassured her.

Shane nodded at her. "We'll get Caribe and Xaira to come, and she can make her presentation herself. Mark will love it."

"And the best part is," Pablo added, "that if we hurry, it will be done in time for our children to see when they get back."

"That fast?" María Isabel wondered. "Just a few days…"

"Just watch," Joe said. "Blue Bay hasn't seen anything like it. It's going to take off just like the Pirates' Convention Expo." Grinning, they all raised their glasses in a silent toast and sat back, smiling at the thought and at each other.

Don Carlos Gaitano took a deep breath and sighed. Standing by himself in one of the upper balconies of Villa Azúl, he had a great view of the courtyard below. Divided as it was into different areas, it provided room for everyone. At the moment, it was bustling with activity. Servants were everywhere, cleaning up all traces of the dinner they had all just shared. On one side, among cushions and pillows, the council and the two captured sailors of *La Diosa del Mar* were quietly discussing the fate of the younger Gaitano brothers. Across the walk from them, the crew of La Gitana sat, heads close together as they, in turn, discussed their own fate. Towards the back, the new visitors were happily talking with the Aguilar-Banks trio. Storm stood quietly to one side, watching with a smile on her face, enthralled with the Blackmon detectives, and the antics of Cat and Snake. The night air rang with laughter, the firelight of the tiki torches licking their happy faces. As he watched, Don Carlos took quick inventory. The meeting of Catamaran and Carlitos: check. Telling them why the Aguilar-Banks had to go back home: check. Their agreeing to join them in the New World: check. Xavier's men came after Marina: check. Marina taking care of it: check. So, why did he have the feeling that the storm wasn't over? Something kept nagging at the back of his mind. He had the feeling that something had happened while he was gone, that he had yet to be told about. His skin prickled. Something…

For the second time that evening, there was a commotion at the entrance of Villa Azúl. Hands spread wide on the railing in front of him, Don Carlos leaned over to get a closer look. Bursting in like they owned the place, two pirates strode in. And, of course, all hell broke loose.

"Carlitos!"

All of his guests, from their different corners of the courtyard, craned their necks and turned towards the commotion. They looked like a colony of meerkats.

"Carlitos!"

Don Carlos flung himself down the hall and ran down the stairs, intent on getting to the scene before anyone else. As his boots hit the tiles below, he saw the crew of La Gitana stand as one. He ran to catch his brothers before they caught his son. Not sure what was going on, he only knew it couldn't be good.

"Carlitos!"

"Juan!" Don Carlos reached them, smoothly standing between the two pairs of men closest to him. "Miguel!" He laughed, quickly scanning his brothers' eyes for any sign of trouble. "Glad you could make it!" He clapped his hands and rubbed them together in a characteristic gesture meant to distract. His brothers embraced him in greeting.

"Tío Miguel!" Salomé and Marina came flying down the walkway, flinging themselves at his older brother.

Miguel Gaitano, Captain of La Gaviota, spread his arms wide, catching the laughing girls in his arms. He smiled, chuckled, rumbled and laughed, squeezing and kissing the captured girls, one after the other. *"Niñas!"* He smoothed his hands down their hair and grinned at them, looking into each of their eyes. "Always so glad to see me. How is that possible?" He shook his head.

Jackson stepped up, clapping the pirate on the back. "Hey, Tío Miguel, didn't expect to see you so soon."

"What brings you, Juan?" Don Carlos couldn't hide his concern any longer. "You look upset."

Glaring, Juan Gaitano glanced at him for a moment before turning back to his nephew. "Carlitos," he growled. Taking a deep breath, he addressed his brothers. "It seems young pup here left his mark on the island on his last trip to San Juan."

Carlos Gaitano froze and faced his uncle. The age difference between them wasn't generational, being merely ten years apart. When much younger, Juan would tease him, always competing for his father's attention since his older brothers were all he had. As men, the teasing never stopped. Don Carlos had found himself standing between his brother and son quite a few times. This time seemed like it may require just that. "What did I do now, Tío?" Curious to hear the answer, everyone quietly moved closer.

The captain of La Prisión took a deep breath. "It seems that there was a very important Spaniard missing from the region of the big river. He was in charge of keeping the peace among the natives and the slaves, and of establishing colonies along its banks." He stopped, glaring at his nephew. Quietly, the visitors moved to stand behind the crew of La Gitana in silent support.

Carlos kept silent for a moment, rocking back on his heels. He met his brother's eyes, and looked back at his uncle. "And?"

Don Carlos shot him a warning look before turning back to his brother. "Who is this Spaniard, Juan, and what does he have to do with Carlitos?"

"A few days ago, the same day La Gitana left San Juan, Don Gerardo Berríos y García was reported missing. A search party was sent out. He was found."

Impatiently, Don Carlos felt the need to defend his son. "So what is the problem?"

"He was found up on a hillside, beaten to death," Juan growled, eyes clashing with his older brother's stormy ones. Clenching his fists, he stepped closer to his nephew, just to be stopped in his tracks by his brother. His voice when it came was deathly quiet. "The crew of La Gitana had been observed at the big river." His eyes were challenging. "The Sailing Master stayed aboard the ship, the Boatswain visited his girlfriends at the village, and the Captain and the Quartermaster were spied on horseback with their girlfriends, the brother, and the Quartermaster of the Sea Gypsy."

Don Carlos turned to look at his son. "Is this true, Carlitos?" he asked softly.

Insolently, his son shrugged. "Is what true? That this Spaniard was found or that we were there?" Before his father could growl at him, he took a deep breath. "Sorry, Papá, yes, we did go to the big river and took horses up the mountain." Everyone looked at him expectantly, but he wouldn't say anymore.

Indio couldn't keep quiet any longer. "Tío Juan," he said, getting the other pirate's attention on him. "Are we being accused?"

Impatiently, his uncle turned to him. "Do you know anything about this?"

Indio frowned. "I know we were up the mountain, with horses. What were you told about this Spaniard?"

Stepping in before his brother killed his sons, Don Carlos turned to him. "What happened?"

Defensively, and as insolent as his brother, Indio shrugged. He pressed his lips together and shook his head. Everyone went silent. The sisters left their Tío Miguel's side, to go stand by their men. Nobody spoke for a moment. Storm turned blindly towards Jackson as he stepped forward. He flung his arm around her neck and held her close.

Jackson faced Juan Gaitano. "I can tell you what happened, man." He took a deep breath. "We were there. It was beautiful. Just like when you skip school and don't go to class and hang out playing outside for a few hours instead. Indio's making out with Salomé on the grass, Carlos and Marina are just talking, and Storm and I are up in a tree. Mangoes for breakfast, fresh breeze, butterflies, birds, shade, you name it. And there's this singing. So here comes this girl. This beautiful native girl with markings on her face, and a baby in her arms. We never get her name, but the baby called her *Toa* so we knew she was its mother. She showed the girls what must be an ancient Arawak lullaby to keep him calm. This girl ends up talking, and mentions your Don Gerardo. She describes a man that has wiped out everyone in her village, in her family, the baby's daddy. No reason but genocide. She said it was so bad, that they had to pretend to be of mixed blood already because the Spaniards were trying to get their gold. So she shows us some things, and here comes this guy yelling for her. He called her *Mujer*. We hide because she doesn't want him to see the baby. Left her alone in the middle of that clearing. And wouldn't you know that the baby was exactly what he wanted? He asked her about him, she denied it, and then he puts his hands on her like this." Trembling with anger, Jackson slowly raised his hands in the air. All eyes were on him. Suddenly, with a violent gesture, he snapped the air between them and looked down at the ground. "And down she goes," he told them, meeting their eyes. Taking another deep breath, he continued. "Want to know what the worst part was? He decided to have sex with her then." He shrugged at the sudden horror in their eyes. "Spaniard was drunk, girl was dead, I don't know…" He shook his head. "Maybe he liked it like that." He ended his story. "Carlos, Indio and I dropped out of the tree like fruit, while the girls kept the baby quiet. We just taught Don Gerardo you don't treat girls like that." Saying no more, he held Juan Gaitano's gaze.

The pirate sighed deeply and met his nephew's steady gaze once again. "So you did do it…"

"I did it too." It was Indio. Distracted, his uncle turned to look at him.

Uncle Jesse put a hand on Jackson's shoulder. "You too, papi?" he demanded softly. "Like Marina, *El Duelo*?"

Angrily, Jackson blinked back his tears. "Yeah," he muttered. "As accessory, I guess, they wouldn't let me near him," he gestured angrily at his brothers-in-law.

"Fuck!" Catamaran swore softly, rubbing his eyes.

Salomé tossed her head angrily, eyes flashing, and slid her arm through Indio's. "Don't look at me," she muttered. "I haven't killed anyone. I'm not doing no fucking El Duelo."

Carlos held his uncle's gaze, a ghost of a smile playing around his mouth. "I assume you weren't notified about that poor beautiful native taína girl found dead by his side." He shrugged. "That's too bad."

"How do I know you are not lying to me?" his uncle demanded angrily, stepping closer towards him. "How do I know that you are not all in on this?" he challenged, looking at each of them.

"*Juan!*" Tío Miguel protested. His voice was low and harsh, cracking like a whip at his youngest brother.

But Juan wasn't listening. Stubbornness and hotheadedness was genetic among the Gaitano men. "And what about the supposed baby?" he demanded.

Carlos Gaitano threw back his head and laughed. His crew snickered. The Aguilar-Banks crew smiled. The young pirate widened his eyes at his uncle. "*Supposed* baby?" he asked, laughing again. He turned to his father.

Don Carlos grinned. "*Victoria!*" he yelled, startling the poor girl and making her squeal, since she happened to be passing nearby at that moment. "If you would be so kind," he smiled at her. Smiling back, she curtsied for him and disappeared. A moment later she was back with a basket in her arms. Murmuring his thanks at her, he smiled into her eyes and took it. Bouncing the basket gently in his own arms, he cooed at the bundle inside. "Here you go, Juan, the *supposed* baby," he told him raising an eyebrow at him.

Outraged, Juan stepped closer to his nephew. "*You took the baby?!*"

"*What* baby?" Carlos growled back. "The *supposed* baby that doesn't exist?" Disgusted, he gestured with his hand. "Or would you rather we should have left him up on the mountainside next to his dead mother and the Spaniard Don Gerardo?" Glaring at his uncle, he turned away angrily.

"What's so special about this baby?" Juan demanded.

"This baby," Salomé said quietly, shaking with anger herself, "is a *cacique*." Her eyes clashed with his.

"What's your proof?" he retorted.

This time it was Jackson who snorted. "He came equipped with a *guanín*, a *dujo*, *cemís* and the cacique's jewelry. What did you expect?" Then he too, turned away, Storm clinging to his hand. The rest of the crew of La Gitana followed them, leaving Indio standing alone with Marina and Salomé.

"*Juan…*" Miguel Gaitano's voice growled in warning again, this time much softer, not harsh at all.

The captain of La Prisión raised his hands and scrubbed his face for a moment, before smoothing them over his head and down his hair with a big sigh. He looked sadly at his remaining nephew. "Why did you keep the baby?" he asked softly. "Talk to me, papi."

Indio nodded. "What else were we supposed to do?" His voice was just as soft.

Marina stepped forward, taking Tío Juan's hand in hers. "*I decided to keep him.*"

The pirate squeezed her hand before she let his go. "For yourselves?"

She shook her head with a sad smile. "No. For my Uncle Jesse."

Jesse spoke up at his puzzled look. "That would be me."

Juan Gaitano turned to look at him. His eyes wandered over Catamaran, and the Blackmon detectives. "You are all visitors?" he asked quietly.

"Yes." Catamaran couldn't keep quiet anymore. "We are family to the Aguilar-Banks."

"We came to take them back," Rashawn nodded.

Now Juan Gaitano was very interested. "Are they in trouble?"

Don Carlos answered before anyone else could. "Sort of. I will explain later." Smiling, he handed the basket with the sleeping baby taíno to Jesse.

This one turned to his younger brother. "Are you taking him away from me?"

Don Carlos and Tío Miguel answered as one, even as Juan shook his head. "No."

Nodding slowly, Jesse held the basket closer and backed away quietly, Catamaran next to him. The Blackmons followed, leaving the sisters alone with the pirates. Quietly, the girls and Indio turned away, to join the captain of La Gitana. The rest of the pirates dispersed, leaving the older Gaitano brothers alone to talk.

"So the boys are leaving?" Juan asked. "They are going, for real…" He drifted off, shaking his head at the thought.

Miguel turned to him. "Isn't that what we wanted?"

Juan nodded. "Yes. They need to get out of here." His eyes drifted to his nephews. "I am really going to miss them," he admitted with a sigh.

"Then make sure you tell them before they go, Juanito. I am sorry about what happened," Don Carlos said, "but I believe them. I hadn't heard the story yet about how they came about the baby. Not with details," he said thoughtfully. "But I was there when the kids presented the baby to their uncle and told them that its mother had been killed in front of them, so I know they didn't just make that part up." He took a deep breath and sighed. "Besides, obviously they have proof. Just because I haven't seen yet the guanín or the dujo or the jewelry, it does not mean they do not exist. It's a matter of asking to see it and Jackson would produce it in a moment, you know he wouldn't claim to have it otherwise." He looked at his youngest brother. "What now?"

Juan sighed again deeply, making the gold cross on his chest catch and reflect the light from the tiki torches next to them. "Now I will have to face the Spaniards." He turned to his brothers, not being able to disguise the worry and pain in his eyes. "How much time do we have?"

Don Carlos looked at them, a wicked smile slowly filling his eyes before spreading on his face. "Muchachos, in two more days the crew of La Gitana along with their girls, and the beautiful princesses of the Sea Gypsy, Rouge and Storm, will be reported as missing at sea." The three men looked at each other and throwing their heads back, laughed.

"Carlitos…"

Carlos Gaitano turned his head to look at his brother. They sat close together by themselves, apart from the rest of the crowd hanging at Villa Azúl that night. They had sneaked off to the cave up the hill for a while and shared a peace pipe, the only place they could be alone. Now they were back in Villa Azúl, feeling ultra relaxed, sitting close together, speaking softly.

Indio met his eyes. "Marina can't take her eyes off you, papi," he rumbled. "Not even Solomon can distract her."

Chuckling, his brother raised his eyebrows at him. "I guess she must like me."

Indio smiled back. "Yes. I think she really does."

"Then I suppose I should go…" He hesitated, searching for a word. He frowned. "What do they call it?"

Indio grinned. "Hang."

Carlos smiled. "I really should go hang with her for a while."

"That would be a good idea."

"We'll continue this conversation tomorrow."

Indio grunted. Standing, they went to join their crew.

Carlos walked straight towards Marina. Around them, everyone else dispersed, leaving them alone. Feeling warm inside, he smiled as her eyes lit up with adoration. Reaching her, he took her face between his hands and pressed his lips against hers. As she yielded, he drew back. Smiling into her eyes, he tousled her hair. Marina responded by slipping her arms around his neck. Holding him close, she closed her eyes and breathed deeply, pressing herself against his chest, her fingers lost in his black locks. "You are tense, papi," she murmured. "You always let Tío Juan get to you."

He sighed, rubbing his face against hers. "I know, I know."

"What can I do to help you relax?" she offered softly.

The young pirate was just a guy like any other. Pulling back, he made her look at him. His eyebrows raised, his eyes twinkling with mischief. "Blow me," he murmured.

Shocked, Marina widened her eyes at him, until he chuckled. Then she narrowed them and licked her lips. "Baby," she whispered huskily, "I will blow you dry."

Her husband bit back a moan as he thrilled at her words. His hairs stood on end, and he was slowly but surely rising to the occasion. Without a word, he took Marina's face between his hands again and proceeded to eat her mouth. Over and over, he kissed her, over and over again. He stopped only when she was breathless. His eyes were smoldering and his own voice was husky when he could finally speak. "Cave or lighthouse?"

Marina didn't hesitate, nor could she hide her grin. "Tent. It's closer."

Carlos laughed and stole another kiss. Groaning, he ate her mouth again for a little while longer. Then he proceeded to grab her hand and drag her behind him, down the middle of Villa Azúl, and on outside towards the dark beach.

Carlos smiled. He had stuck the tiki torch he had grabbed for them to see the way with in the sand next to the tent. Not in front of it because it wasn't meant to display what lay inside, which in a moment would be them, but near enough where they had access to it. The full moon of a couple of nights ago in Boriken was already waning. Still large and bright however, it bathed the tent and its surroundings in a soft silvery glow. Inside, there was just barely enough light for them to see where they were and what they were doing. He chuckled as she warbled softly about the flap of the tent being open and anybody being able to see them. Hugging her, he reassured her that after the way they had just exited, nobody would be so foolish as to come looking for them. Besides, if they were going to go and make the effort of going looking for them and actually looking inside the tent, well, then they deserved to see whatever they got to. Grinning, they didn't waste another minute. In no time at all, the young pirate discarded his shirt, lost his pants and dropped unto the recliner. Stretching his long legs out in front of him, he leaned back, crossing his arms behind his head. Marina dropped down unto the ground next to him. She put a bottle of water they had grabbed on their way out on the low table beside her, making room for it among the shells and driftwood. Then she dug her knees into the soft sand, making herself as comfortable as possible. She couldn't stop smiling now.

Carlos sighed. Her hands began on top, working on his shoulders before going down to his chest, splayed fingers digging in gently. They danced around each other, swirling circles and patterns, his chest hair soft under her palms, catching on his nipples for a moment before continuing down, sliding along his ribs. He sighed again. Now she was kneading his torso, momentarily distracted by his belly button. Lowering her head she dipped her tongue into it, making him shudder. Rippling his belly, he got her off him so she could continue with what she was doing. He smiled to himself as Marina giggled in the dark. Her hands skipped the important parts and caught his legs. Quickly skimming over his ankles, she caught his calves and massaged them for a moment. Then Marina got down to what she came here for. Slowly, she massaged his thighs. First one, and then the other. Her hands changed their rhythm, going from kneading to skimming again. His legs spread wider to accommodate them, allowing her to caress the inside of his thighs. He sighed again. Her hair brushed his hip as she continued her ministrations. Now her hands went in opposite directions. One followed the path from his navel downward, and the other one went to meet it, gliding up one of his thighs. Finally, she made contact.

Carlos moaned. Softly, under his breath, but moaned nevertheless. She found his sac. Curiously, she explored the soft thin skin, feeling his testicles inside. First one, then the other, and then both at the same time. He felt her toss her hair to one side and swoop down on him. Moving his member gently out of the way, she replaced her busy hand with her mouth. A shuddery breath escaped him. Softly, she took one testicle into her mouth, being as gentle as she could, making sure she didn't hurt him. Then she did the same to the other, sucking softly, cradling it on her tongue. Finally, she opened wide and took them both, rolling them inside her mouth gently, as if they were her favorite candy. Her other hand crept, sweeping curls out of the way. Her mouth released him, and the ocean breeze hit him. Before he could even protest, both her hands met at the top of his member. By now, hard and ready, it was practically clamoring for attention. They skimmed down the sides, brushing to the side all his short hairs. Then he felt the tip of her tongue flick against the tip of his member. He smiled. It was on. Far from timid, her tongue glided down to the bottom of his shaft, along the small bump of his vein, and back up again, stopping at the top. There it swirled around the head, feeling along the ridge, making it slippery and wet. Her lips closed around it, creating a seal. Before she did anything else, however, her tongue danced on the tip, flicking, tickling, until he thought he would explode. And next thing he knew, she was just doing it. His hands caught her head, his fingers slipping in her hair.

Carlos groaned. His whole world was sensorial. Her hair through his fingers felt sexy to him. His ears filled with the sound of the water lapping on the shore, the breeze ruffling the fabrics inside the tent, and the wet noise of her mouth on his skin. Marina was on a mission. She went up, down, all around. She licked, lapped and sucked until he couldn't think anymore. Meanwhile, he got harder, bigger, and longer. He didn't feel like flesh in her mouth anymore. Now it was just this big cylinder she got to handle and make go away again. She was devoted to doing just that and pleasing her man while she was at it. His hands held her head, his fingers gently pushing and pulling. Meanwhile, she held a party in her mouth, rattling, rocking and rolling him inside it, to the tune of music only she could hear. Taking a deep breath, she sealed her lips around him once more and slid her head up and down.

Carlos gasped. He was so close. Now she was even actually humming with him inside her mouth, the vibration making him tighten even more. He felt her smile around him when his toes curled. But now he was closer. His fingers massaged her scalp to the same rhythm her mouth massaged his member. His thighs tightened. "I'm going to come," he whispered hoarsely. Needlessly, as it turned out. Marina was already curling her tongue. In the next instant, she was catching everything under it, as his sperm filled her mouth, cleverly bypassing all the taste buds on top of her tongue. She kept her lips sealed around his shaft as he pumped into her mouth, sucking in rhythm. When she thought she couldn't hold any more, he finished. She swallowed. He didn't have to see her to know she was grinning. But then her lips were engulfing him again. Marina wasn't stopping. The suction of her lips made him cry out, his body tensing like a board, his fingers trying to pry her away from him. Placing both her hands over his, she remained where she was, ignoring his soft protests. He moaned and groaned and shivered as if he had chills, but she just wouldn't let go, making him go back to his original size. Then and only then, did Marina perform one long slow suck on him, finally letting him slip out of her mouth.

Carlos shuddered. The breeze felt cool on his saliva slick skin. He could barely think. But there was one thought. Married sex far exceeded anything he had ever anticipated. All he could do was smile when she smacked her lips. She gently pulled his hands out of her hair, placing them on his own belly. He looked at her through slit eyes as she wiped her mouth with the back of her hand and reached for the bottle of water next to her. He watched her take a sip and swallow. Before she could do it again, he hoisted himself upright and caught her face between her hands, kissing her fiercely. He could barely taste himself, but his tongue insisted on washing all trace of himself off her own tongue.

Knowing what he was doing, Marina smiled to herself. She let herself be kissed for a while. Then she pulled away to look at him. Smiling mischievously, she cocked her head to one side. "I guess you're not tense anymore."

He grinned. "Not at all, by any means." He stole a kiss. "You've gotten good at this." He stole another kiss. "I am keeping you, Aguilar," he warned softly, as they both got to their feet.

Bending down, Marina retrieved his pants and handed them to him. "And a good thing that is," she teased gently, now picking up his shirt, "because I have your papers, mister."

The pirate laughed as he quickly stepped back into his pants. "Is that right?" he teased back. "And whatever does that mean?" Reaching for his shirt he quickly put it on, but left it open, the breeze spreading it away from his broad chest, the white fabric billowing around him.

Marina quickly picked up the bottle of water, taking it with them as he grabbed her hand and dragged her out of the tent behind them. "It means I've got you, babe." She smiled. "You are mine."

Carlos snagged the tiki torch as they walked by it, bringing her hand to his mouth for a deep kiss. "I'm glad." He winked at her, knowing by now that without fail, it always got her panties wet. "That makes you mine."

Marina smiled to herself, feeling a glow growing from the inside out. Now that the blow job was over, she felt shy. Not embarrassed. No one could be that embarrassed after sharing so many body fluids. Just shy. After all, she had a big crush on this guy. Laughing softly, her pirate led her back through the jungle and around Villa Azúl, up the hill side. He had further plans for his girl. They included hot springs in the middle of a cave.

"What else have you got?" Mark Ross was definitely interested. His curiosity had brought him here, besides the invitation to breakfast. It wasn't easy being the mayor of Blue Bay. The seaside town was struggling as it hadn't in decades. Its astounding beauty surpassed its downfalls however, but it still wasn't enough. They needed something. Bad. And here he was, at the Hacienda Aguilar-Banks, looking at something that would not only make Blue Bay a little bit more interesting, but it would also help generate him some of the votes he needed to keep his seat as Mayor and finish what he started. Now he was facing the beautiful Oriental charge of the Aguilar-Banks. "Any other ideas?"

Xaira nodded. All traces of the excellent breakfast they had just shared were long gone and instead, the round table was littered with papers and pictures for the Mayor's inspections. "May I be bold?" At his nod, she dove in. "I want you to close Front Street, right in front of our block. I want you to take advantage of the islands on either end, and make a pedestrian walk instead. In the very center, you can put one of those fountains that spurt right out of the ground. I already priced what it would cost to break the street, connect some pipes to the fire hydrants on the opposite sides of the block, and re-tile, creating a fountain." Leaning over the table, she pushed some papers at him. "You can put flowers on the islands, as well as a nice park bench at each. More benches along the buildings, on either side of the street." She paused to take a deep breath, her almond eyes intent on the papers in front of them. Her straight as glass hair hung over her face like a curtain.

Mark stopped her with a smile. "I am sorry, but refresh my memory. What is exactly at the base of your building, and what have you got across the street?"

Xaira smiled. She looked especially beautiful today. A studded black leather belt circled her waist over a simple white linen sheath. Sleeveless, modest, the round neckline only hinted at a cleavage and the length was down to her knees. On her feet, however, she wore red leather gladiator sandals with strands of red coral draping her pretty feet. Black polish on her toenails and fingernails. Chunky diver's watch on her right wrist while on her left, a beautiful tennis bracelet made of platinum and diamonds which Pablo and Joe had presented her with for her quinceañero. Holding her hair away from her face, a black leather studded headband to match her belt. Large silver hoops at her ears. A little kohl and nude lipstick completed the look. She looked like the model she was. Xaira Chang was stunning. "Facing our building, on the left corner we have *Sea Side Styles*. It's a hair salon run by Marquez Robinson."

The Mayor nodded. "Is he any good?"

Xaira nodded. "He does all our hair," she said, looking up for a moment and waving her hand around to include the Aguilars, the Banks, and the Butlers. "You should go sometime. He would be honored. Marquez is real cool. Smart, he reads a lot, and he has a lot of stories. Kids love him." When he nodded again, she continued. "Next, comes *Rain Dance*. It is Rain's dance studio."

"What does she teach?"

Xaira laughed and shook her head with a shrug. "Anything. Everything. She's got baby ballet, and on up. She teaches line dancing, salsa, merengue, hip-hop, ballroom, you name it. Anything anybody needs to learn to dance, she will teach them. She choreographs for the cheerleaders at the middle school, high school, and junior college."

Now he laughed. "She must be busy."

Xaira agreed. "Yeah. But she doesn't have any children, so that helps," she said softly. "Next comes *Tae Kwon Do*."

Now Mark turned to his hosts. "That's your school, isn't it?"

Joe nodded. "We run it and supervise it, but we have instructors giving the actual classes. Derek teaches boys from ages three to eighteen, and Tyler teaches the adults. Xaira teaches the girls, and Jackson supervises the three of them. Pablo and I just give private lessons to some chosen few, mainly the Abdul Shahids." He laughed, nodding at the unspoken question, as expressed by an upraised eyebrow. "Yes, sir, we do. We like to keep it all in the family."

"Next, comes *Snake's Tattoos*," Xaira continued. "That's run by him. Hands on, he's the master artist in there and he has a beautiful Goth girl named Sage who works for him. They have steady clients, with all his biker and cowboy buddies. Then she attracts the younger crowd. Next to him there's an empty space, and then the entrance to our underground garage. That's the only way, except for the hall running behind all these stores, to get upstairs. Derek and Tyler occupy the first floor, Jackson and Salomé the second, and Marina and I got the top floor. All six of us share the garage and the roof." She shrugged, looking at the Butler guys for support. "We all live together." Back to business, she continued. "All these stores face Front Street. Facing the beach in back, we have storage rooms, all closed up." Pushing some papers towards the Mayor, she showed him a watercolor. "This is what it would cost to get this mural on our building. It will take a couple of days. María Isabel Gaitano has generously offered to take care of getting it done. We can start today. All you have to do is say okay."

Thoughtfully, Mark Ross turned to the pirate's wife. Today she was wearing a dress also, but this one was navy blue, all draped like a Grecian robe. The color did wonderful things to her sea green eyes. Her jewelry consisted of baroque pearls in primitive settings. Mouthwatering, they commanded attention, beautifully displayed at her ears, throat and wrists. "And you say your husband will be back in a couple of days with your sons?"

"That's right, Mayor. Carlos had to go back home for a moment and take care of some urgent personal business. He is due in a couple of days," she nodded. Her black hair fell like a cloud around her shoulders, and her mouth seduced, with the soft wine stain she had applied.

Shaking his head the Mayor dragged his eyes off this stunning, hot married woman whose husband they were talking about. The women around the table exchanged furtive looks and secret smiles. Men were so predictable. Mark Ross turned to the men, which were safer. "You all are part of this."

"Well, we split the cost of the billboard on the building and the electronic ones five ways." Pablo raised his hand and counted them off. "Pablo Aguilar, Joe Banks, Shane Butler, María Isabel Sandoval on behalf of Don Carlos Gaitano and herself, and Xaira Chang. The billboard on our building will have a photo, as will one of the electronic ones, which will shuffle a few at a time, providing a slide show. But the other one, the one you would be facing when you turn on Front Street with our building to your left, will have videos."

The mayor nodded thoughtfully. "So if you're closing that stretch of street on your block…"

"You divert traffic unto Main, behind it. You create parking on both sides of Sand Dune Lane, and Sea Breeze Avenue, flanking our block, all the way down to the beach." Joe tapped a map in front of them.

"Think about it, Mark," Shayla suggested softly. "What will it hurt? We're not getting much traffic down there, the place looks like a dump. If we make it not only beautiful, but unique as well, wouldn't that have a lot to say about your administration?"

The Mayor grinned at her. "Twist my arm, girlfriend." They laughed at each other. He was such a boy. Going back to matters at hand, he continued getting details of this Heaven sent project. "Any parking at all, in front of your building?"

Xaira shook her head. "Not for cars. Our side of the street will be reserved exclusively for Uncle Jesse's biker friends. There are plenty of them," she added mischievously.

"Will you be offering parking out of the basement of your building?" he asked the men.

"No." This time it was Shane who spoke up. "We reserve the right for our stores and our kids. There is a very small parking next to the building for the tenants, storeowners and customers across the street. So ours would be just for us. No one else."

"And those businesses across the street. These would be…?"

This time it was Xaira who counted off on her fingers. "Laundromat, grocery store, drug store, souvenir store, and another empty shop. This building is only three stories tall, so they only have two apartment floors, very nice, front and back, but with no view of the ocean like we have. That's why we want to give them something pretty to look at." She grinned, making everyone smile. "The floors are divided into three apartments each; one on each corner and one in the middle. They have beautiful scrollwork balconies, but," she took a deep breath and looked straight into the Mayor's eyes, "I want to do something Oprah did once."

The mayor bit back a chuckle but couldn't hide a grin. "What did Oprah do?" he asked, genuinely curious.

"She treated her neighbors across the street from her Harpo Studios to a balcony makeover. She went to one of those big stores and got them plants and patio furniture, and wind chimes and stuff like that. Not a lot, but she had a lot of neighbors. We only have half a dozen. Totally doable, and María Isabel offered to take care of that, also, on behalf of Don Carlos and herself."

This time, Mark Ross turned to the pirate's wife with the smile that won him all the female votes of Blue Bay. "Very generous of you, María Isabel. What brings you and Don Carlos to our humble town?"

Pablo stepped in before she could answer. "Carlos and María Isabel come from the islands. Our children met them there while on Spring Break. Marina ended up marrying their son Carlitos after a whirlwind courtship. It is a very good match. Salomé is dating their other son, Indio. Now the Gaitanos want to come to our city and make some investments. The town being in the state it is in at the moment, this is the best time for them to come in."

The Mayor raised his eyebrows. "Investments…" he said thoughtfully.

María Isabel laughed throatily, once again getting all his attention. "The Gaitanos are very old money, Mayor." She smiled at her own private joke. "We are looking for somewhere to put down some roots and make a few investments. Seeing as how our children…" she drifted off for a moment, but then beamed at him, "hooked up, as you say, how could it be anywhere but Blue Bay?"

"Admit it, Mark," Heather told him, sipping from her cup of coffee. She sat with her girlfriends, not as elegant as María Isabel, or as businesslike as Xaira, but very pretty nevertheless, the three of them in beautiful tropical sundresses. "This town needs it. Obviously, it doesn't have the budget at the moment, but if you got something going, baby," she said, with the familiarity that she had earned, from having gone to school with him and maintained a friendship with him along with her husband and the rest of their friends throughout the years. "Something real good, well," she shrugged, tossing her short brown curls, "money attracts money, what can I say…"

"It's going to be great for the town, Mark," Sloane urged. "What do you say?"

Mark Ross had already made up his mind a few minutes ago. But spying the look on his friends' faces, he decided to prolong the suspense for a few minutes longer. "And what is it that you call this project, Xaira?"

Xaira tried not to grin. "Captured by Caribe."

Now the mayor turned to the young man sitting quietly between Derek and Tyler. "That would be you?"

Caribe nodded with a smile. "Yes, sir. That would be me." His thick long dreads were gone after a trip with Xaira to Marquez, and now he had a younger, shorter, much neater version of them sprouting from his head. All the hair he had carried until recently had distracted from the very muscular frame he owned, with broad shoulders and wide chest. He looked like any young man from town. "I capture the images and Xaira is my manager." He waved his hands over the photographs on the table. "We want to present the beauty of Blue Bay and its people in such a way that the locals can't ignore that. Once you capture the attention of your own people, the tourists will come."

"You are right about that, Caribe. And I want to thank you for you and María Isabel and Don Carlos taking an interest in our town." Turning abruptly to his guests, he put his hands on the table and stood up. "The answer is yes. I especially love the idea of the fountain." He smiled, delighted. "You are on. I will set up an emergency meeting with the town assembly for them to take a vote." He couldn't help grinning. "They are going to freak. Say yes in a heartbeat. Then I will go ahead and hook you up with everyone you need to make this possible." He turned to Xaira. "What's your time frame?"

The girl couldn't help but grin, her eyes eagerly searching Caribe's before turning back to the Mayor of Blue Bay. "Well," she glanced at her watch. "It is 9:30. If we get on this right now, we should be done by tomorrow night."

He stared at her, a happy smile spreading on his face. "You're kidding, right?"

She shook her head happily. "Not."

His voice held wonder. "That quick?" He looked around him. Everyone nodded. He spread his hands. "Okay. Give me a couple of hours to do my part and make it official, get you all squared away with the Police Department and the City. Then... Go for it. Meanwhile, I think I'll be calling your Marquez for an appointment. Got his number?" Quickly, Xaira provided him the number out of her cell phone. Saving it in his own, he turned to his hostesses. "Ladies," taking each of their hands in his, he kissed them one by one, "I only hope I am soon as deserving of another breakfast in this fine home as I was today." Finally he took María Isabel's hand and kissed it. Holding it for a moment, his blue eyes met her soft sea green ones. "Welcome to Blue Bay."

Outside, the Mayor of Blue Bay stood around with his friends. The wind ruffled his still blond hair, and his bright blue eyes sparkled happily. He was tall, handsome, and single. A running joke with his friends. Now, he was sorry he had to leave. "Dudes, thanks for having me over. I haven't been here in a while," he said, shaking his head.

"Well, why not, man?" Joe asked. "What does your social life look like, anyway?"

"Boring," Mark laughed.

"Yeah, right," Pablo squinted his eyes at him. "I hear you date a lot."

"Well, that's true," the Mayor admitted. "Just goes to show, that I can't find anyone."

The men laughed. "Well, you should stick with us," Pablo offered. "There are plenty of women in our lives. All you have to do is go down to Sloane's shop." They laughed.

"Who are you hanging with these days?" Mark asked.

"Jamal, Rashawn, Snake, Blue Cat," Pablo shrugged. "The usual."

Mark nodded. "Sounds good. Call me next time you get together for a game of basketball."

"Will do," Joe assured him.

"Thanks for giving Xaira a break, man." Pablo looked at him. "Little girl really deserves it."

"Little girl is extremely talented. You must be proud of her."

"We are," Joe and Pablo said in unison.

"And Caribe is just as talented," Shane reminded them. "After all, it is his vision that we are portraying."

"Together they'll be indestructible, huh?" Mark teased them. "Good job, gentlemen. Thank you for breakfast. It was excellent. See you soon." A round of hand slapping and embraces, and the Mayor of Blue Bay was gone.

Light crept into the cave like a thief. The skylights were beginning to glow and the entrance beckoned. The breeze was already warm. It felt wonderful as it swept over the couple spread on the bed. Somewhere outside a bird called once. And once more. Then, repeatedly, over and over again.

The pirate chuckled, the sound rumbling in his chest. "Indio is coming."

Marina moaned, burying her face into his side. "No, please, we just went to bed."

Carlos laughed. "It must be important." Jumping out of bed, he threw her the panties that were on the cave floor. Marina snatched them from mid-air and thrust them under the covers. Raising her knees, she quickly slipped her feet in the holes. With one swift movement, she flung herself into them in a graceful arc, slipping them over her butt snugly. She fell back on the bed with a soft bounce. Bringing her hands back out, she fitted the sheet over her chest, pinned it under her arms. Her husband raised an eyebrow in approval. "Bravo, *querida*," he murmured.

Marina grinned at him happily. "I've never had to do that. Pretty good, huh?"

A low laugh rumbled from the entrance of the cave. Indio stood silhouetted, grinning. "Was that a mermaid I saw?"

Not shy and still naked, his brother faced him. "What's up, Indio?"

Indio shrugged, gesturing at the small waterfall they called a shower. "You better get ready." Their eyes met.

Carlos looked hard, but Indio wasn't giving anything away as he strode towards the bed. Joining his girl, he made himself comfortable on top of the sheets. The brothers grinned at each other. "Okay." Turning away, Carlos crouched to pick up his own pants from the cave floor and strode purposefully to the cascading water sprouting from the far wall.

Indio turned to smile at his brother's wife. Slipping an arm around her, he kissed her forehead. "Hey, baby…"

Marina sighed happily. "Hey, baby…" Laying her head on his chest, she closed her eyes for a nap as he stroked her hair.

It seemed that Carlos was back in a moment. The fabric of his pants clung to his skin and he shook the water out of his hair like a wet dog. Reaching for a bowl of water on the nearest table, he scrubbed his face and rinsed his mouth with the paste lying next to it. Flicking the water off his face, he turned to his brother with a grin. "Now…"

"We have to go."

"No!" Marina wailed softly, fingernails digging into his chest.

Indio laughed. "This is different. Come on," he urged, leaving her side.

Marina sat up and slit her eyes at him. "This better be good." Keeping the sheet pinned to her chest, she wrapped it around her, flung the end over her arm like a train, and climbed out of bed.

Indio followed. "I have to show you something." Laughing, he led them to the entrance of the cave. Outside, the sun was already completely out of the water. Being higher up on the hillside, they had a great view. Down below, Villa Azúl lay quiet. Nobody up yet, except for the servants milling around quietly. The jungle rustled around them, and the palm trees swayed on the beach. Out over the ocean, a galleon.

Carlos whistled, laughter making him look like a teenager. "How did we get so lucky, Indio?"

Indio grinned back. "God is good. It couldn't have come at a better time."

"This may be the last time," his brother agreed.

"I am so going with you guys," Marina murmured.

They both turned to stare at her between them. Their eyes met over her head, a smile splitting both their faces. "You have earned it," her husband conceded.

"You do the last part. Might as well be there for the whole thing," Indio agreed.

Marina smiled at them. "Thank you, boys." Turning her back on them, she walked back inside, dropping the sheet naughtily, swinging her hips as she went, the white of her panties glowing in the dark. The brothers watched as she reached her own cut-off pants, snatching them from the cave floor along with her flowered top, always keeping her back to them. Continuing farther into the cave, she reached the shower. Giving her privacy, the pirates turned back to the entrance of the cave. They grinned.

Indio raised an eyebrow at his brother. "Marina has become saucy, hasn't she?"

Carlos nodded. "Yes."

"You love it."

"I do."

"She has bruises."

Carlos glanced at him, shooting a look over his shoulder. Marina was happily singing under the cascading water, getting clean. He pondered for a moment, and finally sighed. "Marina likes it rough, papi." The confession was a whisper.

Indio frowned. "All the time?"

Carlos chuckled. "No." He stared thoughtfully off into space before turning back to him. "There are times, though…" He shook his head, letting out a low wolf whistle.

Indio looked deep into his eyes and nodded. "Be careful," he whispered back.

Carlos nodded. "I will."

"You are marking her."

"I know."

"Don't hurt her."

"I don't. Or at least I don't think I do." He shook his head, chuckling to himself. "I don't think she would tell me if I did, though." His eyes searched his brother's.

Indio returned his gaze steadily, looking deep into the twin pools. Something moved in their depths. He took a deep breath. "I am thinking Marina approaches lovemaking, at times as you say, with the same ferocity with which she fights Solomon." His brother pressed his lips together and didn't say anything. Instead, he raised an eyebrow and cocked his head to one side. Indio smiled. "How do you feel about that?"

Carlos grinned. "Blessed." He shrugged. "There's good balance. The rest of the time is Heaven anyway. What can I say?"

"Say what you mean."

"I am so whipped…"

"I have never seen you like this."

"Indio, she blows my mind."

Indio just grunted. Turning back to the view before them, they started calling like birds, down to Villa Azúl. Over and over they called. Marina joined them as the first pirate appeared. It was Don Carlos. Walking out to the middle of his courtyard, he turned to look up at them. Then followed Tío Miguel and Juan. Jackson was next. Storm and Rouge. Giancarlo and Solomon. Salomé. They all turned to peer up at the trio. The brothers gestured at them. Excited, all the pirates ran up the stairs of Villa Azúl, to gather at the balcony facing the ocean. A cheer shattered the still morning air as they spied the galleon. Out came the Council. The Blackmons, Cat and Snake looked puzzled. Indio and Carlos looked at each other and smiled.

"Tío is going to kill us."

Don Miguel Gaitano chuckled. "No, he won't," he reassured Catamaran. "A few weeks ago, it was he who was standing where you are right now, along with Joe."

Catamaran snorted. "But last time, their kids weren't in the middle of pirates taking over a galleon."

The older pirate laughed. "You are right about that, but how do you stop them?"

His brother Juan grinned. "They are grown adults," he reminded them.

"They are," agreed Jesse, turning to stare at Catamaran. "We are not here on a rescue mission, Cat, remember?"

"That's right," Jamal said. "We only came here to see for ourselves what they were up to." He took a deep breath and let out a long sigh.

Rashawn laughed. "Come on, man, admit it, Cat. You're just jealous."

The men laughed. They had left Villa Azúl in a rush an hour ago, after the bird calls from Gaitano's cave. Now they found themselves sitting on the deck of the *Starfish*, glued to their spyglasses. The objects of their affection and their attention were now in the middle of the takeover of the galleon. As with the taking of *La Diosa del Mar*, Carlos Gaitano's fastest ships had gone out and quickly surrounded the galleon. A few cannonballs had been flung back and forth, but then the pirates had all fired at the same time in beautiful synchronization. The galleon had seemed to go into shock as it got splashed from all sides in very near misses. The circumstances overwhelmed the vessel and its sailors, forcing it to surrender. The crew of La Gitana had approached the vessel in the *Tiburón*, leaving the females on it while the men boarded the immense ship. At the Captain's signal, the women joined the men, given the task of watching the captured sailors. It had been bold and brazen on part of the younger Gaitano brothers, to take the girls. But they had. The whole thing had gone down with flawless precision.

"Nah, not jealous," Cat denied. "I didn't come all the way here to play…" He drifted off, shaking his head at what he was about to say.

Jesse laughed. "Pirates?"

Rashawn patted him on the back. "You missed the cave for the Old West, Cat, if you wanted to play cowboys and Indians." He laughed as Catamaran shrugged his hand off with a growl.

Jamal hushed them. "That's enough, boys," he cautioned. They all fell silent. "Miguel, how does this work again?"

Miguel Gaitano sighed, his own spyglass glued to the galleon. "The capture of the galleon is orchestrated by the Quartermaster. That would be Indio. He gets most of the treasure, and the galleon itself."

"Nice," murmured Cat.

"What does Gaitano get?" Jesse wanted to know.

The pirates laughed. "Anything he wants," Juan informed them.

"Does he get more than Indio?" Rashawn was curious.

"Usually. Officially." Don Miguel turned to them. "You need to remember that Carlitos and Indio are brothers. Their relationship goes over and beyond that of Captain and Quartermaster."

"Except for Giancarlo and Solomon, in front of their men they keep up their ranks. In private, although they have their own possessions, they share pretty much alike," Juan explained.

"Everything?" Cat was curious.

The pirates laughed again. "Most things," Don Miguel told them. "Until now. Now they both found what they most wanted, and have been lucky enough to find two. They each get one."

"The galleons?" Jesse asked.

The pirates turned to look at them. They answered at the same time. "The girls." The visitors sighed.

"So how does the treasure get divided?" Jamal asked.

"By rank and in order of direct participation," Miguel answered.

"Participation?" Rashawn wondered.

"*Direct* participation," stressed Juan. "In other words, those who are on the galleon at this moment."

"So they all get a piece of the action." Jesse whistled under his breath.

Rashawn laughed, not being able to look away from the scene before them. "Good thing I'm Jackson's best friend," he teased.

Catamaran snorted. "Salomé doesn't need to do more than just stand there and look beautiful. As usual." He sighed. "She's with Indio. Why does she even have to be there at all?"

The pirates laughed again. "You should know better than anyone the answer to that," Miguel told him. "Other than her fathers and her mothers, the two people she loves most in the whole world are on that ship. And Indio…"

"And Marina?"

More laughter. "Marina is the accountant," Juan reminded them. "She has to deal with the inventory and the division of the treasure. On this occasion, she decided to join them." He shrugged. "The boys agreed that it would be good for her to take part in the process from the beginning." Admiration poured into his voice. "Married to Carlitos, she shares what's his since they got together. She renounced to anything before that. But on this occasion, she gets double her share."

"I get it," Rashawn said, nodding his head. "Marina gets something anyway for being the accountant, but now she gets something for participating in the galleon's takeover." He sighed. "Not bad for having been marooned."

The pirates agreed. "Not bad at all." Don Miguel laughed, the sound rumbling in his chest. "Indio is going to, how do you say?" he wondered, searching for the right expression. "Hook her up?"

Juan nodded in agreement. "Big time," he intoned solemnly.

"Marina is a pirate at heart."

Cat frowned. "How would you know, Don Miguel? You just met her…" He trailed off, as the pirates laughed at him.

"Just wait, Catamaran," the pirate advised. "You will see a side of her you never knew existed." He laughed again. "Her being in the company of pirates has brought it out. A dark side." His laugh was sinister, making chills go down their spines.

Jamal suppressed a shudder. "I have heard about it. In the way she fights Solomon." He sighed. "She's always loved and been good at Tae Kwon Do, but nothing like what I have been told about her here with Solomon," he admitted.

Rashawn agreed. "I noticed that too." He also sighed. "Not only physically. She's thinner and prettier, but," he pulled away from his spyglass to turn and look at the pirates, "she's sharper, too... scarier."

"Scary." Jesse nodded. "I never thought of it like that, but you're right. It's not something you can see…"

"But you can feel it," Jamal finished for him. "She's meaner." He sighed. "Poor baby."

The pirates laughed once more. "No, poor she is not," Juan informed them. "And if Marina loves the way she fights, Carlitos has found his match for life." He chuckled. "They are both savages."

"And then, Jackson's not leaving his sisters," Catamaran murmured.

The pirates turned to look at him. "How would you feel if your girlfriend was the pirate?" Don Miguel asked.

Catamaran sighed. "I would be on that ship, trying to be the pirate this time."

"Exactly."

"What about Don Carlos?" Jesse wanted to know. "I imagine that being older and a pirate for longer he must have treasures beyond our dreams."

Catamaran snickered. "For sure. He's just quiet about his business."

"Do his sons cut him in equally anyway?" Jesse asked.

Miguel nodded. "Absolutely. Carlitos and Indio adore their father."

"Now if you gentlemen are ready, it seems that this takeover has concluded," Juan informed them. Striding to the wheel, he began steering as the men pulled anchor. The Gaitano ships made a convoy back to Encantada, the Spanish galleon in the center.

As it turned out, the galleon was twin to *La Diosa del Mar*, the Goddess of the Sea. This one was called *La Reina del Mar*, the Queen of the Sea. Their inventory was pretty similar to each other. The gold, the slaves, the treasures. On this occasion, the slave driver was smarter than the first one. He survived the pirates. The ship's Captain and immediate crew happened to know the sailors taken from La Diosa. It was a good thing. The transition would be easier. The slaves were quickly escorted to the village where they were integrated with the last group of slaves. Pedro Barbosa had boarded the ship to impart instructions, and had been delighted to discover that there was even a nice sized herd of horses aboard. Indio had waved a hand at him that he could have them, and had then proceeded to hole up in the Gaitano warehouse with Marina. Once their business had concluded, they invited everybody in to join them.

"This looks like a family meeting," Jackson joked.

"It is," Indio agreed. "We need to know what we are going to do. The storm is tomorrow."

"You have to disappear," Miguel told him. "There is no other way."

"We have to say you drowned," Juan said.

"How are you going to do that?" Jamal was curious. Amused, the Council sat back, knowing smiles on their faces.

"The ships go out, with us on them, and crash. The storm is tomorrow," Indio reminded him. "The only thing is, we will be in the cave, catching a time warp." The visitors nodded.

"We need to take off the figureheads." Everyone turned to look at Don Carlos.

Marina gasped softly, her hazel eyes shining with the sunlight streaming in the window. "Bring them, Carlos," she murmured to her husband. "They are worth a fortune in our world."

He frowned at her. "They are large."

She smiled at him. "I have room." He nodded.

"First," Indio reminded them, "we have to take care of what we are leaving here. Jack," he said, turning to the young redhead, "you had something to say."

"Yes," Jack nodded, moving to the center of the group. "Well, first, I wanted to move in to Gaitano's cave, but he won't let me." He grinned as the pirates booed and hissed at him.

"Poor baby," teased Rouge, laughter making her beautiful brown eyes crinkle at the corners. Around her head, her hair tumbled like flames. Next to Giancarlo, she absolutely glowed.

"So now, I need to move into Giancarlo's palace." Turning serious, he continued. "I will handle the Sea Gypsy for Rouge. Keep it in the family. Anything I make off it, I will share with her, thus providing her an income in the visitors' world."

"So you intend to remain in contact with them from here," Rashawn turned his head to look at him, wonder in his voice.

Jack nodded. "We have the timetable Pablo made with Jackson, thanks to Leila. It's about meeting at the cave after a storm."

Catamaran looked at him thoughtfully. "Makes sense, I guess."

Carlos stood up and stepped forward to stand next to Indio. "So, we take the figureheads off the ships, and..." he drifted off, turning to look at his uncles.

"You have four," his Tío Miguel told him. "*La Gitana, Tiburón, Poseidón* and *Starfish.* There will be four left in the Council." He nodded towards them. "Jack, Jai-Ling, Suleiman and Sultan. They each offer to take care of one for you."

Carlos turned towards them, smile lighting up his face, his eyes clear as pools. "I would want a share of whatever profit you make off my ships."

The Council agreed. "Aye."

Carlos looked at his uncle and narrowed his eyes. "Four left. What about you? Why won't you be in the Council anymore?" Tío Miguel waved a hand, dismissing him and looked at his brother.

Indio frowned. "What about my galleons?"

Don Carlos smiled. "I have come to find out, *hijo*, that there are a group of African slaves that will be more than happy to be pirates themselves. The Spaniards, Don Andrés and Don Luis are ecstatic at the thought of commandeering *La Diosa* for them." He chuckled. "They think it is divine justice. Of course, all this under the Council." He turned his head to look at his son. "Indio." He smiled when their eyes met. "Offer them the same deal as Jack and Rouge. Have them put away a share for you periodically, which you may have access to."

Indio nodded. "Aye."

"Same thing with this new one, *La Reina del Mar*. Once again, all this under the Council. You'll be set for life," Miguel raised his eyebrows at his nephew. Indio grunted.

"The Council will also be able to take care of, in the same manner, *La Sirena*, my own ship. We are leaving open the possibility of just selling to them, somewhere down the line," Don Carlos told them.

Carlos nodded thoughtfully. "Now that option I really like." He turned to his brother. "We should see how it goes at first, and check out where we stand. If it's what we want, we can just sell." Indio nodded.

Their father agreed. "The council will be more than happy to buy you out," he chuckled. "They will also be staying at Villa Azúl during our absence." Thoughtfully, he looked at them. "I propose we leave the Spaniards in charge of governing Encantada, for appearance's sakes."

Everyone agreed. "Aye!"

"The island will mourn the passing of Gaitano and his crew, once again, for appearance's sake, while Miguel and Juan quickly establish the new Encantada before they leave." Don Carlos turned thoughtfully towards his brothers. "What happens with this incident with Don Gerardo?"

"I'd rather talk about this in private," Juan told him.

The pirates around them agreed to grant them privacy. "Aye."

Don Carlos nodded at his brothers. "Aye."

Carlos spoke again. "I believe that now we have a lot of work to do."

Indio agreed. "This meeting is over. Thank you all for being here."

"Aye!"

"Gaitano!"

The young pirate looked up at the stage whisper. He raised an eyebrow. "Aguilar?"

"Come here."

He walked over to his girl. She promptly slipped her arms around his neck and stood on tiptoe, pressing her chest against his. He stroked her back. "What's up, baby?"

"I want to do acrobatics with you, Carlos."

Pulling away from her, he looked into her eyes and grinned. His own eyes sparkled with wicked thoughts. "Can't get enough, *divina*?" he murmured.

Shaking her head she embraced him again, her voice was passionate, strumming a chord way deep inside him. "Never!"

"Neither can I," he confessed in her ear.

Pulling back to look at him, she smiled. "You rock, papi."

"Later," he whispered back.

Marina nodded. "Gator." She let him go and stepped back. Without breaking eye contact, they high-fived, then patted each other on the butt as they walked past.

The rest of the afternoon was a blur. Their first stop had been the Klines' store, where the pirates had gotten several chests. First order of business had been to drop the girls off at the village, where they had personal belongings they had accumulated throughout their stay in Encantada. Into their respective sea chests went flowered fabrics, and beautiful dark glass bottles. They gathered their clothes and jewelry, and primitive personal care tools. Marina took down the babies' scribbles from the wall. Salomé carefully folded a couple of select dresses she had concocted while she had worked with Liana at the dress shop in town. She even remembered to grab the toy box filled with accessories from the fashion show that she put on at the Pirates' Convention Expo. Down came the hammocks, and into their chests. Taking one last look around them, they left their hut. Meeting Jackson in front of Caribe's hut with his own hammock over his shoulder, they helped him take down the sketches of themselves and their parents. One last visit to Leila and Don Manuel. These gifted them with trinkets and jewelry made of shells and beads, feathers and seeds. A brief stop at Leilani's home provided them with one last, but not final, squeal and snuggle with everybody's favorite nappy headed twins, Juan and Jaime. Little Ali looked ready to cry as Jackson crooned to her while carrying her. He had to walk her around in a circle, stroking her back as she sobbed. Ali didn't understand every-thing that was going on, but she was emotionally distressed at what her little heart was telling her. Finally, her mother, Reina, took her away so the twins wouldn't start a symphony with their own wailing. Leilani gave them each a hug and a kiss, and turned away with tears in her eyes. Sighing, Jackson and his sisters made their way through the jungle, back into town.

It was understood that the Lair would be kept for Giancarlo by Silas and Jimmy, as if the Italian were still in Encantada. On the way there, the Aguilar-Banks passed the Klines' store, wanting to leave that for their last goodbye the next day. Instead, they popped into the dress shop and said their goodbyes to Liana and the fine Dr. Kyle Richardson, her ardent beau. From there, they avoided Padre Ignacio's church, but begged a conch shell each as a souvenir, from Pedro Barbosa's notorious rock and seashell garden. The law-man shook his head at them, but gave in with a sigh. He presented them with what they wanted, and walked them to the Lair. There, the trio left their chests and Pedro Barbosa, and went out again to Indio's place, where Salomé had personal belongings. They helped her gather her own jewelry and her and Indio's best outfits. Those from El Baile del Luto, and from Marina's wedding. Looking around one last time at the beautiful room with the stained glass over the door, they went back to the Lair.

Pedro Barbosa joined the lawmen sitting together in a corner. In the group were Juan Gaitano, John Hawthorne and his sons, Jamal Blackmon and Rashawn. With them, Don Carlos and Don Miguel.

"Am I late?" the lawman asked them, turning a chair around and straddling it.

"Not at all," Juan assured him.

"Do you have the papers for Jamal?" Don Carlos asked.

Pedro nodded. Shuffling some papers in his hand, he looked at them quickly for a moment. Turning his head, he looked at Jamal. "These are the papers absolving Marina of Xavier's death." He shrugged with a smile. "Well, the copies, at least. We are keeping the originals."

Jamal took them. "Thank you, Barbosa. Pablo and Joe will appreciate this."

Pedro laughed at them. "I know they will."

It was Juan's turn. "I have for you, Carlitos and Marina's marriage certificate. The original. I will keep a copy for my records. Also, an original with the date but without the year for you to fill in when you get home."

Jamal smiled, admiration filling his eyes for the young pirate. "I appreciate your thoughtfulness, Juan. This is very kind of you."

Juan smiled back and turned once again to matters at hand. He looked at his brothers. "You wanted to know about the situation with Don Gerardo, Carlos." He waited for his older brother to nod. Lowering his voice, he leaned closer towards him. "This isn't going away, Carlos." He turned his head to look at his oldest brother. "Miguel. The Spaniards are intent on finding Carlitos and Indio and bringing them to justice." Blood rushed into his knuckles as he clenched and unclenched his fists. "The story of their drowning will be accepted, for a while." Before he could stop himself, his eyes drifted to the Aguilar-Banks trio at the end of the bar. "The girls and their brother are just casualties." He turned back to the men in front of him. "But then, somebody is going to get to thinking and will eventually come after me." He sighed, shaking his head sadly. "It looks like the Gaitanos are done."

Don Carlos looked in shock from one brother to the other. "You too, Miguel?"

Miguel sighed. His energy wrapped around all the men next to him in an embrace. "I will not leave Juan." His hand waved in the air.

"The Hawthorne scoundrels have made me an offer for *La Gaviota*. I will take it, regardless of…" He trailed off, his eyes meeting his brother's. He shook his head. "Not this storm." He shrugged. "Who knows, maybe…"

"But for now," interrupted Juan, "we need to make a plan. "We need to synchronize the crew of La Gitana's disappearance, along with our own," he gestured to Miguel and himself.

John Hawthorne cleared his throat. "I will sail your *Prisión* back to San Juan, if you want. Let the Spaniards deal with that, too." The pirates laughed.

Jamal and Rashawn looked at each other. The older detective frowned. "I imagine that the Spaniards are smart enough to request an investigation of the events." He looked at Juan Gaitano. "Won't they suspect something?"

Juan looked right back at him for a moment, not saying anything. Finally, he shrugged. "For now, Jamal, the most important thing is to get Carlitos and his crew off this island." He shook his head. "The rest doesn't matter."

Deveraux Azure sighed. He had thought about this long and hard. He had almost turned back once he reached the underground garage. But his body had just seemed to hurl itself out of his car, and quickly stride between the silent vehicles, out to the dying daylight. Now he stood in front of Snake's Tattoos. He knew Snake wasn't there. His uncle was with Catamaran and the Blackmons in Encantada with the pirate. But inside was the one person he was hoping to see. Taking a deep breath, he pushed open the door and stepped in. Over his head a small brass bell tinkled, making the accompanying metal dragon and bright red tassel sway, announcing his presence. The door fell shut behind him. Adjusting his eyes, he swept them over the room. Jesse's station was quiet, his chairs empty, his instruments lined up and gleaming softly at his table. Along the back wall, a beautiful poster of a supermodel on her side, naked but for a huge boa, snake, not feather, wrapped around her covering her private parts. The heavy elaborate frame and the pin lights on it made it look like a museum masterpiece. A gallery of ink drawings and flash lined the main wall. Dividing the artists' stations, a large terrarium holding a large python, sat sandwiched between two aquariums of the same size. Beautifully lit, the display provided eye candy, a relaxing contrast to the black and white posters and art in the tattoo parlor. On the radio Pink Floyd soothed with timeless expressions about the dark side of the moon. The smell of incense wafted in the air. Turning his head he looked at the other station right next to him. Sitting in her chair, swiveling in half circles back and forth, sat the object of his attention. She smiled.

"Hey, stranger," she drawled. "Haven't seen you in a while. You lose something?" Bright blue eyes flashed at him before going back to what she was doing, which at the moment was playing with a baby snake in her hands. The beautiful young woman sat framed by the plate glass window which was the store front. Dressed in black from head to toe, as usual, she looked alluring and mysterious. It didn't matter that today she was wearing jeans and T-shirt. It was how she wore them. Her black cat enhanced her look, curled up in its own chair beside her. "You look like one bookend."

Relaxing, he smiled back. "Yeah, yeah, whatever." Crossing over to her, he dropped into the empty chair in front of her. "It smells good in here," he commented.

"I quit smoking." She grinned. "Cigarettes..."

He raised his eyebrows in silent admiration. "Good for you. How's it going?"

"Tough," she admitted. "But I like it so much better now."

"You busy, Sage?"

Raising her hands, she tried to look into the baby snake's eyes. "What do you want, handsome?"

You. Shaking his head, he mentally bit his tongue before the word left his mouth. Instead, he shrugged. "I was thinking about an arm band. Something tribal, maybe."

She nodded, meeting his eyes over the infant reptile. "Full band all around, or do you just want the front?"

His eyes crinkled at the corners. "I don't know. How much time do you have?"

She rolled her eyes and stilled her chair. "For you? All in the world." Standing up abruptly in order to disguise her pounding heart, she reached him, holding out the baby snake. "Do you like him?"

Deveraux found himself peering into the baby snake eyes, stroking the tiny scales with one finger. "Is he yours?"

She frowned thoughtfully. "I don't know yet. We are doing an experiment, Jesse and I." Walking to her table, she uncovered a small plastic terrarium and gently placed it inside. "If I can stand it, I get to keep him." Turning back to him, she grinned. "I haven't made up my mind, yet." Reaching for a large binder, she quickly opened it and passed some pages until she found what she was looking for. Placing the binder in his lap for him to look at, she smiled at him again. "Left or right?"

Teasing, he flexed his muscles for her. "Which do you think?"

Sage laughed, tossing her long black hair. "If you are right handed, get it on your left. It will give you balance." She looked pointedly at the book in his lap. "See anything you like, handsome?" Nodding slowly, he pointed out something that looked like spiky waves. "That one's my favorite," she told him. They smiled at each other, and she got to work. Moving around briskly, she prepared her gun and her ink.

Deveraux signed the paper she gave him and sighed content-edly. "I like it when you call me handsome."

Momentarily distracted, she glanced at him before turning back to what she was doing. "I call it like I see it. You are very handsome."

He couldn't help but grin. "So, do I get to call you beautiful?" He felt his breath catch as her eyes met his. "You are very beautiful."

Sage sighed. "Now you are just playing with me."

He laughed. "Like I have nothing better to do."

Playing along with him, she laughed. "And that is why you are here." She slipped on some latex gloves and pulled out a brand new needle, passing it to him for inspection. While he did that, she slowly prepared the design. He carefully studied the package in his hand, making sure it was completely sealed, guaranteeing the sterility of the needle, before passing it back to her. Cleaning his skin, she laid the design around his left bicep. Satisfied, she readied herself.

Blue kept quiet for a while, letting her work, until the parlor was filled with the sound of the buzzing needle. They smiled at each other and she began. "It looks busy around here."

Smiling, Sage nodded. "Yeah. They've been working on the street all day."

"What are they working on?"

"Not sure. I guess it's kind of a surprise." She leaned closer towards him, concentrating on her task. "I know they're painting the building, and fixing the balconies across the street. They tore up the street today, but I'm not sure why."

Blue frowned. "Are they going to be working all through the night?"

Sage nodded. "Yeah. Whatever it is, someone wants it done already."

"And why haven't you gone home yet?" he asked her. "If Jesse isn't even here, I'm sure he wouldn't mind if you closed if the shop is empty."

"You're right, he wouldn't." She shook her head. "I guess I have nothing to go home to." And as any good female would, she changed the subject. "You look lonely. Missing Cat?"

Deveraux grinned. "Busted." He sighed. "You'd think that now that we are older it would be different." He shrugged. "I guess there's a lot more to being twins than people realize. I know I didn't."

Sage smiled, her eyes never wavering from her buzzing needle. "I guess there is. He's with Snake, though. They'll be fine," she reassured. "They went with the pirate."

He looked at her. "You know Don Carlos?"

She nodded. "Met him. He's real nice. Been here a few times."

"He get a tattoo?"

Smiling, she shook her head, making her hair swish around her shoulders. "Not yet. He's waiting for his sons."

Deveraux nodded and thought for a moment. "Do you believe he's a pirate?"

She was so quiet for a moment that he thought she wasn't going to answer, but then she nodded. "Yes." She explained. "Jesse told me all about your meeting Don Carlos and his wife at the Hacienda. So, yes. I know they are the real thing." And once again, she changed the subject.

So, they hung out while the tattooing took place and chatted. Like they never had before. They had known each other for a while. It was inevitable that they ran to each other. She was Snake's employee. Snake was married to his aunt, and they worked in his tíos' building. They couldn't escape each other. But they had never found themselves as close and all alone as now. Neither noticed how they kept sneaking glances at each other. The minutes flew by, and before they knew it, it was done. She cleaned him up, gave him instructions for the care of his brand new tattoo and took his money with a smile. But still, they sat. Now, having fallen into the comfortable space of people who have just discovered they have a world in common, they continued exploring each other. Music, movies, books, politics, religion, past relationships, pets, cars; the topics were endless. And the more they talked, the more they liked what they were learning. Oblivious to the darkness that had descended outside, amidst the symphony of street renovations, they sat. The aquariums and terrarium glowed next to them, and the only other light was the pin lights on the picture on the back wall and those over her station. But still, they sat. The dragon bell announced a visitor, and they both turned to look.

Rain Coltrane stepped in. Looking from one to the other she hesitated, a soft frown on her face. "Hi. Am I interrupting something?"

Deveraux shook his head and stood up to greet her. Although in fact their relationship was aunt and nephew, the difference in age was so small, barely a few years actually, she was more like a big sister. A hug and a kiss, and he sat back down. "No. We're just hanging. What's up, Rain?" Folding his hands over his belly, he looked up at her.

Rain looked at him and studied his artwork. She nodded. "Nice tat, Blue. New lure for the ladies?"

He grinned and shook his head at her. "Whatever."

Rain grinned back. At the moment she looked like a teenager. A short denim skirt stopped at mid-thigh, and a tight tank top exposed her midriff and announced generous breasts under the soft material. She was built like the dancer she was. Long, strong legs, tight butt and abs, flowing grace. Both her hips and her lips were nice and full. Her eyes were soft brown like Joe's, now laughing at him. Silver hoops hung from her ears, peeking out from the riot of curls and springs that was her hair, framing her exquisitely beautiful face. She turned to the girl. "Sage? Why are you still here, girlfriend? Don't you want to go home?"

Smiling, Sage shook her head. "No, not yet." She gestured at all the activity outside the window. "Nothing ever happens around here.

I want to stay here a little longer and see what they're up to. Deveraux and I are hanging."

"Well, when you step outside, make sure you look up," Rain laughed. "A bucket of paint may fall on your head."

The young woman laughed back. "Can you believe they are finally painting this building?"

Rain rolled her eyes. "About damn time, if you ask me." She turned to her relative. "Blue, when's Jesse coming home?"

Not knowing how much she knew, he pressed his lips together for a moment, thinking. "Didn't he tell you?"

She shook her head. "He wasn't specific. All I know is he's with Cat, and they went to get Jax and the girls." She thought for a moment. "He said something about tomorrow."

Blue nodded, distracting her for a moment, before she got to pondering about the strange situation. "That's all I know, baby. Sometime," he shrugged, "anytime tomorrow."

Rain took a deep breath and sighed. "All right. Well, I guess I'll be going home." She grinned. "I can't wait to have Jesse back. He better bring me something."

Blue smiled. "I am sure he will."

Satisfied, she nodded. "Okay. Catch you guys later." She waved her fingers at them and moved to leave. At the door, she turned back to them, mischief sparkling in her eyes. "You guys make a beautiful couple. Simply adorable..." Laughing, and before they could react, she let the door fall shut behind her.

Their eyes turned to each other, but then they were interrupted again as the dragon bell tinkled once more. This time it was a man. His dog followed him in, making a beeline for the feline in the room. The black cat turned to look at him and stood. Stretching and arching its back, it yawned and then leaned towards the dog. The two animals met, nose to nose for a moment. Satisfied with the greeting, they parted ways once more. The dog to his master's side, the cat curling up again for another snooze.

"Why are you still here, child?" Marquez Robinson stood before them, a frown on his face. His voice was deep and musical in his chest, as if he should be singing the blues.

Amused, Blue waved a hand at the girl in front of him. "I've been trying to go home, but she won't stop talking," he teased.

Marquez scowled deeper. "Wasn't talking to no grown man. Talking to baby girl, here."

Blue laughed. "Relax, old man. I won't keep her much longer."

Sage reached for the man's hand and squeezed it. With the other, she lovingly scratched his dog behind its ear. "Hey, Wolf. You good, boy?" She smiled at the beautifully colored mutt, speaking to him gently, and getting love in its eyes in return. Her voice was soft. "Going home, Marquez?" She turned back to its owner. "Why are you here so late?"

"I got a customer," he growled. "Damn Mayor didn't have any better time to come in, but now." The couple in front of him looked at each other, making him smile.

Sage laughed, the soft sound lifting both men's hearts. "Did you take his picture? That's what the camera I gave you was for. Important customers."

The older man softened towards the girl even more, genuine affection shining in his face. "I sure did, sunshine." Smiling, he sighed. "Building's a little quiet without the savages, isn't it?"

Sage laughed again, this time stronger. "It sure is. Not tonight, though. But you know they will be back before you know it, Marquez."

"Yeah, yeah, I know."

Blue looked at him thoughtfully. "Missing Jesse, Marquez?" It was no secret that Marquez Robinson was as attached to Jesse Coltrane as if he were his own dad. They were as tight as a real father and son team. What nobody could quite figure out was why. But everybody respected their unique and special relationship.

"Yeah." Abruptly, and gruff, he turned away. "Don't let this fool keep you here much longer, sunshine." And he, too, was gone.

The couple looked at each other, alone once more. Sage smiled. "Now," she said, looking into his eyes. "What's on your mind?"

Blue felt himself drown in her gaze. He didn't refute her words, didn't ask how she knew. They'd gone past all games, hours ago. Now he just nodded. "I have a function coming up." Relieved, he saw her sit back, making herself comfortable. "It's just a dinner from my work." He shrugged. "Banquet, a little entertainment, a lot of ass kissing." She nodded, urging him to continue. Turning away, he gestured with a hand. "There's a certain lady in my law firm," he grimaced before he could stop himself, making her laugh silently, "that has taken a great liking to me." Looking at her again, their eyes met once more. "The feeling is not mutual."

"So, what's the problem?"

He couldn't be more direct. "I don't feel like dealing with it."

They looked at each other in silence for a moment. Sage sighed, and smiled slowly. "Deveraux," she said softly. "Did you come here to bitch?" She raised her beautifully arched eyebrows, treading gently, lest he notice her heart pounding out of control. "Or did you come here to ask me out on a date?"

Taking a deep breath, Blue raised his hands and passed them over his cornrows. As he did, the skin on his bicep stretched, tingling and itching from the new ink. Standing up abruptly, he approached her, stealth in his step. "It depends."

Sage looked up at him as he came closer. "On what?"

Without warning, he reached her. Putting his hands on the arm rests of her swivel chair, he swooped and stole a kiss. Startled, they stared at each other. Blue swooped again, this time slower. And kissed her again, this time longer. No open mouth, no tongue. Not yet. Just two pairs of lips, warm and soft, pressing against each other in a deep, fabulous smooch. The most unforgettable first kiss. Drawing away from each other, they dove into each other's eyes again. Now things were different. When Blue finally spoke, his voice was hoarse. "I am asking you out on a date." He felt the need to confess. "Cool as it is, the tattoo was a reason to see you, my co-worker is just an excuse."

Sage gently held his face between her hands, thrilled at the turn of events. Her voice was barely audible, as she gazed into his clear jade eyes. "I know, Deveraux."

He caught one of her hands and kissed it, pressing his lips hard to her palm. "Will you go out with me, Sage?"

Cocking her head to one side, she gazed at him, stroking his face with her free hand. "You trust me to not embarrass you?" She laughed softly. "I am a Goth girl, after all."

He licked his lips and nodded. "Yes. I like your style."

She nodded slowly. "All right then, Deveraux. We have a date."

Grinning, he pulled her out of her chair. "Come on. I'll help you close up."

Together, they put some things away. Went out the back into the corridor that ran along the length of the building, making sure all the doors were locked at the other businesses and at the storerooms. Reaching the parlor again, they turned out all the lights but for the aquariums and terrarium, leaving them on as night lights. Taking one last look around the place, they turned off the radio and opened the door, following the black cat out. Walking together without saying a word, they left the now brightly lit and loud street, ducking into the underground garage. Always the gentleman, he walked her to her vehicle, an older, well kept black Volkswagen Beetle. There, they just looked at each other for a moment. Shyly, she smiled at him. "Thanks for keeping me company, Deveraux." She nodded. "It's been nice."

He smiled back. "Yeah," he agreed. "Real nice. Catch you later, Sage." Taking her face between his hands once more, he pressed his lips against hers again. Then, not wanting to ruin it, they parted ways.

"Who stops them?"

The pirates laughed. They were all gathered at the bamboo grove behind Villa Azúl. In the center, displaying their strength and talent were Marina and Solomon, caught up in one of their epic fights. The pirates had placed tiki torches around the perimeter of the area, the firelight casting flickering shadows in their faces and those of the combatants. They seemed to be surrounded by a ring of fire. The men turned to look at Catamaran.

"Pablo," answered Don Carlos.

Catamaran stared at him, a frown on his face. "Tío isn't here."

Don Carlos shrugged, eyes twinkling with mischief. "Well, I suppose there is no stopping them, then."

Jesse snickered. "Just can't stand it, can you, Cat?" He pressed his lips against the soft dark head of the baby in his arms.

Rashawn agreed. "Marina's not your baby anymore, Cat. Let her go, man."

"That's right." Jesse couldn't stop. "Gaitano's not sharing." The pirates laughed.

"*I'll* stop them," announced Jackson. The pirates and the visitors watched as he strode determinedly towards the fighting pair. He reached them, the fighters on pause, it seemed. Frozen in their fighting stance, fists in the air, they breathed heavily, listening to Jackson. Then, as one, they both turned on him, kicking and punching until he couldn't defend himself any longer. Turning tail, the brother ran. The bamboo grove seemed to explode with laughter.

Jesse patted him on the shoulder. "I guess it's not your job, Jackson."

Shaking his head, Catamaran turned to Gaitano. "You're her husband. Why don't *you* stop them?"

"No, not me, I gave up a long time ago." The young pirate shook his head. "I benefit greatly from my girl and my Boatswain fighting." Turning to the visitors, he raised his eyebrows. "Solomon is practically in our wedding vows." His father and uncles chuckled at the memory. He laughed. "I'm not stopping anything." Catamaran sighed.

Jamal shook his head. "I have never seen her like this." He explained to the pirates. "Marina's never fought with so much violence."

Don Carlos turned to him. "A gift," he teased, "from us to you." Once more, the pirates laughed. The visitors had no choice but to join them. The grove sang with laughter and camaraderie. Except for Marina and Solomon. They just fought.

Pablo Aguilar, Joe Banks, and Shane Butler sat back and smiled. They had camped themselves on some beach chairs across the street from their building on Front Street. Closing the street and diverting the traffic had turned out to be an easy task, since they never got much traffic cruising in front of this block, anyway. In front of them was a bustle of activity, accompanied by bright lights and very loud noise. The activity seemed to be endless. There were at least a dozen people all over their building, scaffolds at different levels, painting with the aid of very bright lights. Directly across from them the aquariums and terrariums glowed inside Snake's tattoo parlor, framed by the front window with its colorful serpents around the border. Rain's studio and Marquez's salon were dark except for night lights of some sort. Above them, Derek and Tyler's floor glowed, while Jackson and Salomé's sat dark over it. The top floor which Xaira shared with Marina also glowed softly, even though nobody was home right now. Behind them, the laundromat, grocery store and drugstore were closed already, dark except for their respective night lights. Above their heads, they knew, their neighbors were busy, excited with their balcony remodeling, thanks to the generous María Isabel Sandoval de Gaitano. The steady rhythm of a jackhammer had stopped a while ago, leaving the noise at a more manageable level. There was whir-ring, pounding, hammering, and the sounds of people. Men and women laughed and called to each other. Somebody had brought out a boom box and hooked it up to some speakers, spread out as far as possible from each other. From it came the likes of Three Dog Night, Steppenwolf, Jefferson Airplane, and others. Good old rock and roll. The atmosphere was charged with excitement and hard work, the mood light and happy. The street was being repaired once more, the pipes for the fountain already in place. On either side, tiles were being put down, laid out in a beautiful design. Park benches sat stacked on one street corner, waiting to be situated. On the opposite ends of the block, people were busy working on the concrete islands. Plants and flowers waited patiently, carefully placed where they wouldn't be damaged while their new homes were repaired, painted and decorated with mosaics. A crane had come during the day and placed the electronic billboards, now dark and silent sentinels, yet to be brought to life. There had been mild curiosity from among the locals. They'd wander by and ask a few questions. Those who knew the answers were evasive, and those who didn't just shrugged and shook their heads with a laugh. But for the most part, people stayed away, annoyed with the noise and inconvenience. The men laughed. They couldn't help it. Their building had been an impulse on their part. What was going on around them was an impulse on Xaira's part. To say they were delighted was an understatement. Now the girl of their hearts was walking right past them.

"Xaira!" Pablo stopped her before she disappeared again.

The girl stopped and turned back towards them with a smile. "Papi!" she exclaimed happily. "Isn't this awesome?" she asked, almost bursting with excitement.

The men nodded. Pablo laughed, his heart swelling with love for the girl. "How're you doing, *mamita*?"

She shrugged, tossing her long hair. "A little tired, but hanging in there." She took a deep breath. "What do you guys think?"

Shane adjusted the glasses on his face with a smile. "I like it."

Joe laughed. "Don't mind Shane. Inside he's like a little boy at Christmas," he told her, making her grin.

"I think," Pablo told her, "that you have done something really good, Xaira." He stood up and pulled her into his arms for a hug. "I am proud of you, baby," he murmured in her ear. Then he sneaked a quick nuzzle, making her squeal, squirm and giggle, just like when she was younger. It reminded him of the shattered young female that entered his home a few years ago, who turned out to be a little girl at heart, besides in age.

Gasping for air, she broke away, her eyes sparkling. "Thanks, Papi." She turned to his companions. "So, you are all good with all this?"

Joe and Shane stood, joining Pablo. Joe hugged her, also. "This was a great idea, baby."

It was Shane's turn to hug her. "You've done very good, sweetheart. We appreciate all your hard work."

Happy, she shrugged again. "It's nothing." She waved a hand at the street. "This crew is going to work through the night, and first thing in the morning there will be a new one to replace them." Stretching, she yawned. "But I'm going home. I'm really tired."

Pablo nodded and reached for his beach chair. "Come on. We'll take you home." His friends folded their own chairs and joined them.

"Sure," she smiled. And caught up in the net of their love, Xaira went home accompanied by the men who saved her life.

They had barely seen each other since the capture of the galleon. Both had been busy, each involved in their own preparations. She, packing, basically collecting everything she wanted to take back home. He, God knew where. But he was here now, with her, in their lighthouse. Marina had already taken down the drawings from the walls and the beautiful perfume bottles from the primitive *coqueta*. She had gathered the collection of kaleidoscopes and spyglasses, the tribal masks from Africa, the leopard skin hammock, the antique- --even by Encantada standards---crucifix over their door, a couple of small stuffed toys, and a few choice throws from the trunk by the bed. Oh. And the globe. There was no way she was leaving her Captain husband's globe, so different from the ones in her own time. The wind whipped around the almost bare walls, a screen for the shadows cast in the almost empty room. The only thing left was the furniture. And if Marina could have taken it with her, God knows she would have. But for now, she was happy that they were using the hell out of it.

Acrobatics. That's what Marina asked for. That's what Carlos gave her. Acrobatics. All over the bed. It seemed to them that the harder, the tighter, the deeper, the fiercer, the better. There would be hell to pay in the morning, but they didn't care. There was only one thing on their mind, and that was that it was their last night in Encantada. For a while. But they couldn't think about that.

Now was the only thing that mattered. And the only thing that mattered was them. Scratching, biting, gasping, coming. At the end, when everything was sore as it cooled in the night breeze, it was all about them. Cuddling, sighing, kissing, sleeping. Not even caring that the sun was already rising on their last day in Encantada. It was all about them. The pirate, Captain Carlos Gaitano y Sandoval, and his accountant, Marina Aguilar de Gaitano, his wife.

"You're scaring me."

"Good." Blue smiled at the beautiful girl in front of him. "It will give us an edge."

Sage smiled back. His use of the word *us* gave her a secret thrill. Today her hair was gathered away from her face with a black bandana printed with skulls and crossbones. Silver hoops cascaded along her earlobes, ranging in size from small to large. She was wearing faded jeans with a black gauze peasant top, which only hinted at the bounty underneath. An armful of thick black rubber bangles, black Teva surfer flip flops, and black nail polish on her fingers and toes completed the look. "What are you up to, Deveraux?" She watched him as he pulled his cell phone out of his jean pocket and flipped it open, pointing the camera at her.

Taking her picture, he grinned. "I needed a picture." He inspected the screen and sighed. She came out very pretty. "To go with a number," he explained, "for the girl who is to accompany me tonight."

Raising her eyebrows, she laughed softly. "Aaah, so it's tonight," she teased.

He laughed back as she drew out her own cell phone out of her jean pocket and took his picture. They exchanged numbers and put their cell phones away. "I apologize for that. I was a little distracted," he confessed, his eyes sweeping over her appreciatively. "You'll still go out with me, won't you?" he asked suddenly. "I mean, you have something to wear, don't you?"

Sage fought to not burst out laughing. "Chill, Deveraux," she crooned, reaching out to stroke his face.

Blue caught her hand and kissed it. "Have you had breakfast yet?"

She shook her head. "Not yet. Marquez, Rain, Jesse and I usually have breakfast together. We take turns cooking in the back."

"Okay, then. I'll cook you all breakfast today. It's my day off and I would love to hang out for a while, but I have to go to the office first and take some papers." He walked towards the door and paused. "And to show the guys I work with the girl I'm bringing tonight." Laughing, he left her alone shaking her head.

"Get out."

Jackson looked around at the pirate. "You're kidding, right?" They were standing next to the lagoon which they had come to know as Marina and Carlos' pool. It was their final destination after one last run through the jungle. They had already gone swimming and he was ready to go back, Salomé next to him. Only Marina remained in the water, swimming laps. He had been ready to call her out when the pirate appeared out of nowhere.

Carlos glanced at him briefly, barely able to take his eyes off Marina. Throwing his sword on the ground, he reached down to take off his boots. "Does it look like I'm kidding?"

Salomé took her brother's hand. "Come on, Jax," she urged softly. "It'll be their last time here. Let's go."

But Jackson hesitated. Frowning, he looked at his brother-in-law. "Dude, the storm will be earlier today."

Reaching for his pants, Gaitano grinned. "Don't make us late, then."

"Jax!" Tugging on his hand, Salomé dragged her brother away.

"Carlos!" Marina sighed. She had just reached the rocky edge of the pool and taken a breath. Turning around to swim another lap, she had found herself suddenly and unexpectedly caught between the pirate's arms. Her hands went around his neck, and her legs around his waist. He was naked, and as delighted as she was, loving that she was not. Her wet clothes created a barrier. He couldn't resist a challenge.

The pirate smiled. "Marina," he breathed. They were caught in sharp sunlight. He tilted her head back to look at him, noticing that her hazel eyes glowed with an inner fire. Like the kaleidoscopes he collected, the fire sparked with distinct green, gray, and brown lights. And as it always happened whenever he gazed into her eyes, he got tight in all the right places. He squeezed her closer, tilting his head, watching her smile back. What he didn't realize was that she was going through the same thing as she gazed into his eyes. In the bright light, his looked like pools, just like the one they were in. Only, she didn't get tight. She got wet.

Carlos Gaitano kissed his girl. And that's how he would always think of her. His girl. It didn't matter how many hats she wore. She worked for him, and better yet, danced for him. He worked out with her, and made love with her. They could talk and they could fuck. And he had married her. She was his wife. Lover. Best friend. But in his mind, his heart and his groin he felt the same thrill and even more, like when he first got to know her. So she was his girlfriend. His girl. Reaching down between them underwater, he gently peeled off her pants and placed them on the ledge behind her. He laughed softly as she purred. Her panties he just moved to the side. Exploring, he made sure she was ready for him. And then, he just entered her. Marina warbled softly in his ear at first, adjusting herself on him, squeezing him deep inside. And then she sighed. He kissed her again. Wrapping his arms around her so she wouldn't scratch her back on the rock, he plunged deep inside her. Now she moaned softly. He chuckled inside, but in fact he couldn't stop kissing her. It was something that whispered in the back of his mind. *Obsession.* The word just wouldn't go away. But somehow, he always managed to shut it out. He loved Marina with his whole being. He didn't want to think he was obsessed with her. But he couldn't stop kissing her. Marina gasped, dragging her mouth away. "Carlos!" Her eyes smoldered into his, caught up in his passion.

"I don't want to hurt you," he said, his voice hoarse.

Marina frowned. "You don't hurt me." She searched his eyes. "Not really."

"I don't believe you," he told her, looking back into her eyes. The exchange of words with Indio was still fresh on his mind. Sliding his hands to her hips, creating small waves between them, he moved them to her backside. Her breasts floated invitingly between them, brushing against his chest. "And what's worse, I don't believe you would tell me if I was." To prove his point, he grasped her butt cheeks, his fingers digging in painfully, and rammed into her, the water taking away some of the force, but none of the intensity.

Marina gasped. Indeed, he was hurting her. But he was also right. She would never tell him he was. Her threshold for pain seemed to be expanding. Marina knew she was pressing her limits. But she didn't care. "Oh, please, Carlos," she moaned under her breath, her mouth pressed against his ear. Tears came to her eyes as she confessed. "It hurts so good." And to distract him, she kissed him. It worked. The pirate gave her what she wanted, setting the rhythm, rocking their pool.

Breakfast turned out to be very pleasant, indeed. True to his word, Blue had gone to his office for a few minutes, and had returned promptly. A quick trip across the street provided him with all the ingredients he needed to treat them. He got eggs and bacon, a warm loaf of freshly baked bread, and a basket of fruit. All the businesses had small kitchenettes in the back, fully equipped with small refrigerator, microwave, electric burners and a sink. He whipped up a quick omelet, light and fluffy, spiked with peppers and onions. He fried the bacon, and then diligently blotted it with thick paper towels. Heated the bread so the butter on it would melt. Made a pot of coffee and poured real orange juice. Then he called Rain and Marquez over. They were delighted. Music played softly on the radio, and the aquariums gurgled contentedly. Once they ate, he quickly cleaned up after them, offering one last cup of coffee, one more glass of juice. They hung around for a while, happy, quietly sitting together.

Marquez Robinson turned to Blue. His legs were stretched comfortably in front of him, faded jeans frayed at the knees, brand new sneakers on his feet. His old T-shirt strained against his chest, hinting at the strong man he was, a mobile billboard announcing his preference for Bob Marley. A coffee cup firmly clasped in one hand, while the other absently scratched his beautiful mutt behind the ears. Looking at Deveraux Azure, he fixed him with his steady gaze. "Breakfast was excellent, Blue." He took a sip of his coffee, smacking his lips with appreciation. "What do you want?"

Blue laughed. "What makes you think I want anything, old man?"

"Now, come on, son," Marquez drawled, his eyes twinkling with mischief. "I have seen more of you in the last twenty-four hours than I have seen of you in the past six months."

Rain snickered, hiding her grin in her own coffee cup. Rolling her eyes, she winked at Sage. "So busted," she sighed, shaking her head. Today she wore a flowing skirt made of thin gauzy material with a tank top, her riot of springs and curls held back by a wide scarf wrapped around her head. Her face was left in stark relief, her soft brown eyes big and wide in her face, at the moment full of mischief.

Blue tried to frown at her, but he failed, grinning instead. "Busted, yeah, I guess so," he agreed with a laugh. "The truth is, Marquez, I needed someone to go with me to a banquet tonight and I asked Sage."

The older man nodded, thoughtfully looking from one to the other. "And did she say yes?"

So happy he couldn't hide it, Blue nodded. "Yes, she did." His eyes sparkled. "I'm stoked," he told him.

Sage nodded when Marquez turned to look at her. "So am I."

Marquez grunted. "We will not be having any hearts broken here," he warned Blue. "We don't stand for that kind of stuff."

Blue smiled at him, humoring him. "What if she breaks mine?" he asked softly.

Marquez just looked at him sternly. "Like I said," he repeated, flashing Sage a look, "we don't stand for that kind of stuff."

"Relax, old man, I promise to be a gentleman…" he drifted off to look at the females.

"Awww," Sage teased. "Don't I even get a chance to fend you off?"

Marquez laughed. "Haven't gone out yet and already you have a handful, Blue." Standing up, he put his worn baseball cap back on his head, and got ready to leave, his dog alert at his side. He turned to wink at the girls before looking back at Blue. "Be nice," he warned softly, and opened the door.

"Marquez!" Sage called him, just as he was getting ready to step outside. The man paused, turning to look at her. She smiled gently at him. "Jesse's on his way back," she said softly. "He'll be by right after the storm," she reassured him.

Rain squealed, excitement seeming to burst from her pores. "He is? Are you sure?"

Marquez frowned, looking up at the sky outside, and then turning back to her. "It's dark, but I didn't think it was going to rain here today." He waved a hand at all the activity out on the street. "At least I hope it doesn't."

"No, it won't rain here," Sage assured him, "but it will over the ocean. When that passes, Jesse will be back."

Smiling, Marquez nodded at her. "I can't wait," he grunted, and he was gone.

"Are you sure?" Rain demanded once again.

Sage nodded. "I am." She stood and faced her friend. "A few hours more."

Impulsively, Rain hugged her and laughed. "I can't wait," she whispered fiercely. Then, she too left.

Laughing, Sage and Blue turned to each other. They smiled. Blue sat in her empty chair and followed her with his eyes as she went to her work station. Lifting the lid off the small plastic reptile container, she lifted out the baby snake gently and coiled it around her hand, peering at it and crooning to it. He chuckled. "Is it winning you over?"

She shrugged with a laugh. "I don't know yet. Too soon to tell. I do feel more comfortable each time, though," she admitted.

"Do you want to fend me off?" he asked suddenly.

Startled, Sage's eyes flew to his. Her heart skipped a beat as she caught the expression in them. She knew she was beautiful, naturally comfortable in her own skin. She wasn't conceited at all, being quite practical instead. Men flocked to her in droves, attracted to her for all kinds of reasons. It was as if her style, her dark Goth style, were a siren's call to them. But never had she felt the intensity of the desire in Blue's eyes. Finally, she could answer. "Occasionally," she admitted.

Blue nodded slowly, licking his lips, his eyes scanning her from head to toe before smiling into hers. "I can arrange that," he said. His voice was hoarse.

Sage just smiled back. "Cool," she told him.

They hung out for the rest of the morning, and for part of the afternoon. Getting to know someone had never been so exciting and breathtaking as it was for them on that day. At one point they got a little cabin fever and took it outside. The crew working out on the street seemed to be in a synchronized frenzy. The park benches were already in place and the street was almost done. They parked themselves across the way where Pablo, Joe and Shane had been the night before. The mural was practically finished after having been worked on all night, and already a picture was in place in the billboard in the middle of the building. Plants had been lovingly arranged in beautiful pots on the islands at each end. Even the trash cans on the corners had been carted away, now replaced by eye-catching containers shaped like frolicking dolphins. The electronic billboards stood like huge sentinels on opposite sides, no longer dark and silent. They were lit by now, patiently waiting for the images and messages they were to share with their small world. So Blue and Sage just sat, no longer talking, just happy to be together. They each pointed out to the other things of interest, laughing at the same things. Not being able to stand it anymore, Blue reached for her hand and locked fingers with hers. Gratefully, Sage squeezed his hand and sighed contentedly. The sky above them remained dark, clouds threatening, but not being able to come through as the wind guided them back over the ocean. Sage had been right. It would storm alright, but not in town. The storm would break out at sea. After a while, Sage stood to leave. Blue protested, but she shook her head at him with a smile.

"Deveraux," she smiled at him, "how nice do you want me to look tonight?"

Blue hesitated, frowning, wondering if she were playing with him. "As nice as possible. Why?"

"Then you better let me go. I don't want to disappoint you."

He grinned, nodding that he understood. "Then I guess you better go." He squeezed her hand. "Banquet's at eight. I'll be by to get you around seven thirty."

She nodded, smiling into his eyes. "I'll be ready."

"I'll call you." Taking her hand, he walked her back to the tattoo parlor. Pressing his lips against hers, he left her at the door, whistling as he walked away.

Good-byes suck. Big time. That's why Marina left the Klines' store until the very end. It wasn't that she was going to be so devastated, heartbroken over not seeing them anymore. First, she had a feeling that she would be back some day, not necessarily soon. Besides, she had only been in Encantada for a short while. John tousled her hair, kissed her cheek, and thanked her for all her help with his son. Already he had approached Joaquin and Reina in hopes of having Leilani, their eldest, pick up where Marina left off. Larissa was a little more expressive, trying as hard as possible not to cry, her eyes flooding with tears nonetheless. Marina hugged her, squeezed her, and reassured her. Taking her away to a corner where they couldn't be overheard she quietly confided in Larissa the real reason behind their sudden departure, leaving out specifics at the moment. Then she held her tight, whispering in her ear that she should be happy because she had gotten her fabulous handsome pirate. The older girl nodded but in the end turned away, seeking comfort from the fabulous handsome pirate himself. But Max… That's when Marina thought she would lose it. She carried him, walking him around in circles, bouncing him on her hip. She made him gurgle, laugh and squeal, and cling to her for dear life as she whipped him around in circles in her arms. She held him tight, and breathed him in deeply, rubbing her face on his soft black baby hair. She peered into his beautiful green eyes. And when he gazed back with all the love in the world for her, his tiny heart in his spectacular eyes, she did lose it. Shuddering, she took a deep breath and pressed her lips against his head, his own mouth seeking her skin. She squeezed her eyes shut tight, but tears began cascading down her face anyway. Carlos saved her. Her husband, her pirate, her hero, came to her rescue. Suddenly, Max wasn't in her arms anymore, and she was wrapping them tightly around her guy instead. He caught a sob against his chest and dropped his head down next to hers, his mouth pressed against her ear. His voice crooned consolingly. "*Divina*, we will have our own. You will see Max again. I promise." And that was that. Next thing she knew, they were walking down the beach, going towards the cave to join the rest of their group. Nothing had been said, there was nothing else to say. So they held hands, fingers locked, each lost in their own thoughts. Next to them, the ocean churned with the approaching storm.

"What do you think?"

Joe turned his head to look at Pablo. They were gathered together on the top floor of their building, the two of them, their lawyer and his sons. Below them, their wives, along with María Isabel, were busy preparing Jackson and Salomé's apartment, making it ready for their return. Everyone had bailed today, not going to work, opting for awaiting the return of their loved ones instead. So now they found themselves in Marina and Xaira's floor, side by side on the terrace looking out over the ocean, praying for rain. "I'm not sure," he answered slowly.

Pablo dragged his fingers through his hair. He absolutely could not wait to see his *nena*. Any of them for that matter, and it showed. Restless, he slammed his hands down on the terrace's wall and tried to shake it. Of course it didn't budge. "I'm not either," he growled. Exasperated, he looked up at the sky. "So many clouds, and not a single drop!"

Shane chuckled. "If you ask me, it couldn't hurt." Next to him, his sons grinned. "Let's figure this thing out. Walk us through the storm again."

Joe shook his head. He also ran his hands over his own hair, rippling over the cornrows. "It's just a storm." He shrugged, and gestured at the ocean. "You're supposed to be in the cave, I think." He turned to Pablo for support.

"That's what I think too," Pablo confirmed, nodding. "The storm comes, and something happens." He waved his hands in the air, in opposing circular motions. "It was dark for us, but something happens with the sky and the ocean. It's as if they run away from each other, and then collide." He clapped his hands together suddenly, and let them drop to express his point.

"I remember wind," Joe added. He nodded, sure of his words. "The water gets sucked into the sky, and then dropped back into the ocean. But then this air comes rushing over the water, blasting into the cave."

Pablo turned to look at him, remembering. "That's right. I recall now thinking that it seemed as if everything rippled for a moment, like when you see stuff through smoke or water. And then everything is back to normal, except that you are either here or in Encantada."

"So it's a physical phenomenon," Derek suggested, the breeze ruffling the curls around his head.

"If it's physical, we can see it," Tyler added. "And if we can see it, that funnel you're talking about between the ocean and the sky, we can stay behind it." He turned to his father. "We can do this, Dad."

"Yeah, Dad," his brother said. "Besides, apart from all the time we are going to save not hanging around waiting for them to call, imagine their surprise…" His voice trailed off, as he laughed, his eyebrows shooting up expressively.

Shane turned to his friends and adjusted his eyeglasses on his face as they looked at his sons thoughtfully. "You know they are right," he finally said. "They could keep behind this water thing and wait for it to pass. They can handle the *Atlántica* as well as any of us can."

Pablo sighed and looked at his brother and best friend. "Joe?"

Joe looked at him, searching his eyes for a moment. Finally, he nodded. "I say yes. The *Jasama* is ready in case of anything."

Pablo let out a sigh, and managed a smile. "I say yes, too. We can back them up if need be." He turned to the boys. "Go for it, *muchachos*."

The young men smiled. Even a year ago they would have been hooting and hollering from excitement. But having matured some since then, they just high-fived quietly and nodded, almost crackling with contained energy. "We'll head to the marina now and get everything ready," Tyler said.

Derek turned to the elders. "Where are you guys going to be?" he asked curiously. "Are you just going to wait here?"

Shane laughed. "Not a chance," he told his son. "They'll end up jumping from this balcony." He turned to his friends and partners. "I suggest we go down to the marina ourselves, guys. Let's hang at the *Cool Change*. We'll be closer."

The men agreed. Turning away from the view, they went back inside. They checked the rooms, scanned the entire floor and locked up behind them, leaving the dogs to guard. Stopping at Jackson's and Salomé's floor they informed the women of their plans. Then with one goal in mind, they left.

"This is a *dujo*," Jackson was saying slowly, pronouncing it *doo-hoe*, when Carlos and Marina finally made it to the cave. The pirates were standing around him in a half circle, allowing the daylight to spill on Jackson. "As you can see, it is nothing but a low bench carved out of stone. The *caciques* would sit on them like this." Straddling it, he lowered his butt on the seat and leaned back on the higher curve. The pirates sighed, expressing that they understood. "What would distinguish the *caciques* from the rest of the *taínos* would be this." Reaching into a burlap bag at his side, he drew out a large round gold disc on a cord. "This is a *guanín*." Slipping it over his head, he centered the disc on his bare chest. "Only *caciques* wore this." Looking up from his dujo, he did indeed look like a young primitive chief.

Storm sighed, expressing what they all thought of his appearance. "Jackson…"

Jackson looked at them steadily. "That's how the Spaniards defeated them. They noticed all the other taínos standing around, and consulting with the guy with the gold disc. So they would kill that guy first, leaving his buddies and village without a leader." He shook his head and took off the gold disc. Standing up, he placed it carefully on the dujo. Then he poured out the contents of the burlap bag. Out tumbled a few *cemís*, a couple of golden arm bands, and assorted trinkets made out of gold, leather, string, shells, feathers and seeds. Fine trinkets. Fit for a king. Or a cacique. Jackson laid it all out for a moment, so they could all look at them. Then he scooped them all up, including the guanín, and put them back in the burlap bag. Tying the bag, he laid it on top of the dujo. Then he turned to his uncle. "It's all there, Jesse. That's all Cacique's legacy."

Jesse nodded, bouncing the baby on his hip. Cacique was thoughtfully sucking his thumb, his beautiful chocolate eyes going from the dujo on the ground, to his new daddy holding him. "You see that, Cacique," Jesse crooned to him. "That's all yours, baby boy. That makes you a chief." The baby just leaned back against his shoulder and continued sucking his thumb. Jesse smiled. "Thank you, guys." His kids just smiled and nodded.

Miguel stepped up, greeting the couple that just arrived. "Marina," he rumbled. The Council, Juan and I came to see you off, but we have to go." He looked meaningfully at the dark sky behind them. "This storm will be here any minute," he mumbled, and turned back to them. He grinned at her. "We bring you gifts as tokens of our appreciation." And before she could react, he thrust something into her hand. Astounded, her family and friends stood to one side, watching with awe at the display of love and gratitude expressed towards her.

The Council paraded before her in a blur, since her eyes were filled with tears. Miguel Gaitano, Captain of *La Gaviota*, had left in her hands a seagull carved from ivory. Jai-Ling, Captain of the *Ocean Wind*, left her the kimono he wore at the infamous *Baile del Luto*, which now seemed to have taken place ages ago, in a cavern in Carey. Made of the finest silk, it was pure black with a majestic sea dragon embroidered on it in gold and silver silk threads. Suleiman, Captain of the *Chymera* gave her one of his wicked curved swords. Rouge, Captain of the *Sea Gypsy* gave her a miniature of the figurehead on her ship, and a beautiful gypsy's outfit, complete with coin belt and gold hoop earrings. Jack, Captain of the *Black Mermaid*, gave her a stunning mermaid carved out of black stone. Sultan, Captain of the *Kalahari*, gave her a lion's claw on a cord. Before she could protest, he reminded her that she did not have just one single fingernail. Laughing, he explained that he had killed the lion himself, and had already lost one claw to Storm, expressed he had more, and it was done. From her own crew of *La Gitana*, she received a gold chain with large diamonds wrapped and caged in gold wire, in the shape of a stunning cross. And finally, her most recent boss, and one of her champions, Don Carlos Gaitano, Captain of *La Sirena*, presented her with a jewelry box the size of a shoe box, completely filled with Spanish gold coins. Salomé had thought of opening Marina's chest to receive all the gifts, and now slammed the lid shut, sitting on it. Their companions laughed. The pirates expressed their love and gratitude one last time and left. Except for Juan and Miguel. In the distance, thunder rumbled.

"Juan!" Jamal Blackmon beckoned to the pirate, gesturing him over with his head. The wind was whipping around the cliff side by now, the foliage rustling with urgency. The men looked at each other and smiled. They had had the opportunity to spend some time together, both being lawmen, sharing experiences and anecdotes of each of their worlds. Being in the same line of work had created a bond between them. Now they stood, heads together, the one smooth, the other dark and messy. The men looked at each other. "This is it, isn't it?" Jamal began, not quite sure of how to express what was on his mind, without offending. "The Gaitanos…" He hesitated, not quite knowing what to say.

Juan smiled in understanding. "The Gaitanos are moving on, Jamal." Taking a deep breath he passed his hands over his hair and sighed, eyes squinting at the approaching storm coming over the ocean. Turning back to his friend, he laughed. "It was a good long run. We have been blessed and very lucky." Growing thoughtful, he glanced at those inside the cave. "My nephews have been very active in these waters since they came to their own. Liked, respected, feared," he shrugged and waved his hand at the ocean. "Does it matter when the results are the same? They were born into a world where they have had the privilege of being educated. That, combined with their name has gained them entrance to a place otherwise reserved for ruthless cutthroats. In it, they achieved their own wealth, to add to that which is theirs by inheritance. Basically, they have had the time of their lives. But as all good things, there comes a moment when it is done and over with." He sighed again. "That the end of the Gaitanos was to come in the shape and form of a smart, beautiful, fierce young woman named Marina Aguilar, well," he drifted off again, and looked into the visitor's eyes, "that's just fate showing her hand." He glanced over his shoulder again, for a moment, and looked back over the ocean. "Our time has come. Carlos has gone exploring in your world, and seems to like it just fine. Now he is taking his sons. They are taking their crew." He shrugged again, their eyes meeting once more. "Miguel and I are left to face the music."

"You mean the Spaniards," Jamal said, not being fooled by the pirate's casual shrug. "They are going to pursue this thing with Don Gerardo." He shook his head. It was his turn to sigh deeply as the pirate just looked back at him. "We just saw proof of their story. There is a baby, which means there was a mother. They have the cacique's belongings. But none of that matters, does it? They're just out for Gaitano blood. Even when John Hawthorne sails *La Prisión* back to San Juan, there will still be an investigation, won't there? They will be coming to Encantada to check out the Gaitano brothers, and then they will discover your secure, safe pirates' haven." His friend's silence spoke volumes. Jamal held his gaze. "Come with us, Juan. You and Miguel, both. Why don't you just come?" Just then a flash of lightning split the sky, followed by a low growl from the sky.

Juan scowled. "We have to clean up the mess the boys are leaving behind."

"What mess?" Jamal demanded. "The one Don Gerardo himself caused? It is my experience Juan, that someone like him is a repeat offender. I am sure that if you interviewed a few people you will find the wickedness and ruthlessness evident that our kids were witness to."

Juan nodded. "Be that as it may, it is still a mess of major proportions."

"Agreed," Jamal said. Another flash followed by another growl caught their attention for an instant. "So, call me."

The pirate looked at him as if the detective had gone mad. "Call you? How the hell am I going to do that?" he asked, puzzled.

"Take care of your business. Go to San Juan, or send the Hawthornes while you plan the demise of your family. Get together with Jack. He has the timetable on these storms. If I am not mistaken, the next one will be in a couple of weeks. Call me. Stand right here, or down on the beach when you are ready, and call me by name. *Jamal Blackmon.*"

Now Juan was immensely amused, his brown eyes crinkling at the corners, his laugh snatched by the wind. "And do you think you will hear me?"

Jamal shrugged. "Have Miguel call me, then." The men laughed. Their eyes met. "I will hear you."

Juan nodded. "We will see." He glanced at the sky once more, and grinned. "We have to go. Have a safe trip, Jamal." The men embraced and patted each other on the back. Impulsively they pressed their foreheads together, closing their eyes in communion.

"Call me, Juan," urged Jamal one last time. The pirate nodded and turned away to say good-bye to his new found friends and his family. Miguel Gaitano followed his example, and they were gone.

"This is nice," Marina sighed, finally taking a good look around the cave. All four figureheads from Gaitano's ships stood leaning quietly against each other along the far wall. To one side were the pirates' belongings in assorted bags. There were seven of them in all. In the middle of the cave was the *dujo* with Cacique's treasure, right where Jackson had left it, and behind that, whatever the visitors had found of interest. Against the other wall were three chests. These belonged to Jackson, Salomé and Marina.

Salomé frowned and looked around her. "If I didn't know better, I'd say there were things missing, if we're all leaving."

Jackson nodded. "You're right."

"You are," agreed Marina. "Gaitano!"

The pirate turned to look at her. He lifted an eyebrow. "Aguilar?"

She smiled at him. "Where were you all day yesterday?"

He smiled back at her. Next to him, Indio chuckled. "Working," he shrugged. "What's really on your mind?" he challenged gently. She didn't let him down.

"Where's your treasure?"

Now his whole crew laughed. Grinning himself, Gaitano could only shake his head. "What do the people in your days say we do with our treasure?"

Salomé couldn't resist. "That you bury it." The pirates' amused silence was answer enough.

Jackson shook his head. "Dude…" And then they were interrupted.

A big flash of lightning slashed the darkening sky. The growl that followed was louder and longer than any they had heard so far. As a pack, the Aguilar-Banks looked towards the entrance of the cave. Without saying a word, they moved towards it and stepped outside. Used to them by now, Storm just followed them without saying anything herself. The rest of the pirates sighed deeply. From their vantage point they could see as the wind began tearing at their clothes. The girls' hair whipped around their faces, and Jackson's shirt billowed around him like a sail. The pirates and the visitors went to join them. Before them the ocean began churning, the sky doing its part in the opposite direction. Everyone smiled. Jackson, Salomé and Marina, well, they began to howl.

Derek and Tyler looked away from their binoculars and turned towards each other. They grinned. They had made good time in the *Atlántica* and had held back, a few nautical miles behind the storm. They didn't want to risk getting caught up in its aftermath. But as it turned out, they had arrived in time to catch it in all its splendor. Pablo and Joe had given a good description of what they were to look out for. And here it was. They looked through their respective binoculars once again.

The ocean and sky provided a monochrome landscape, each being a different shade of dark gray. They could tell they were moving, because the water was churning whitecaps as it sought escape from the whirlpool it was creating. The tempo picked up, everything moving a little bit faster. As they watched, a small silver spot appeared. And then, another one. Their eyes glued to their binoculars, they saw them grow larger. Then they realized that they weren't spots at all. Instead, it was the sky opening up a space in the clouds. The ocean was reflecting the lighter color, the water becoming a mirror. And as they continued watching in disbelief, a thread of water broke the law of gravity and reached heavenward. Trembling and unsteady at first, it grew stronger as the funnel it created grew larger. The clouds above and the waves below danced in a frenzy faster and faster, creating a liquid battleground. Around the natural phenomenon, thunder and lightning clamored for attention. The brothers paid no mind, however. Riveted, they couldn't take their eyes away. And when finally, as they watched, the water rushed into the sky, they could only gasp.

"Whoa…"

"Dude…"

Don Carlos raised an eyebrow at Jamal. "What are they doing now?"

"They're howling."

Next to them, Catamaran snickered. "They've been doing that since they were cubs."

"Cubs?"

Jamal grinned. "When they were little, they protested against the story of the three little pigs. They decided to become the three little wolves, instead. They were restricted by their moms in their times to howl, however, limiting them to storms and the full moon." He waved a hand at the trio. "It's storming." Laughing, he went to join them. "They're howling." And to the astonishment of Don Carlos and company, Detective Jamal Blackmon began howling with them. In a moment, he was joined by his nephew, Catamaran, Jesse and his son, Cacique. The hillside rang with the baying of the pack of visitors, and the squeals of laughter of a *taíno* baby boy. The pirates looked at each other and grinned. A moment later, they too were howling.

The cliff seemed to vibrate. The cacophony of sounds made by the wind, thunder, lightning, sky and ocean, reverberated in the air. Their jungle world intensified with the display of energy and light and power. Since it was daylight on this occasion, they could see everything. The funnel over the air in front of them spread wider, and a coil of water flew up into it, disappearing into the sky. The howling subsided as man and nature held its breath. Their hearts beat. The sky opened wider. A ripple of energy rushed towards them from across the ocean, its force blowing their hair back for a moment with its own wind. Time shifted. The water fell back into the ocean in cascades. The clouds seemed to slow to a stop, and the ocean waves were suddenly tamed. Once everything settled, it rained.

Laughing, Jackson, Salomé and Marina looked at each other, and then turned to the pirates.

"That was it!" Jackson grinned at them. "Now you are in *our* world."

"We will make your stay as pleasant as possible," Salomé said happily.

Indio smiled back. He couldn't resist teasing her. "What, no adventure?"

Salomé opened her eyes at him in mock shock. "Be careful what you wish for…" she warned.

"Jackson," Giancarlo said, "tell me about your world." And as Jackson eagerly began telling him, enthralling the Sailing Master as well as the Boatswain and the female pyrates, Marina slipped away.

Quietly, she stepped back into the cave. Last time she had gone through the storm, she hadn't been conscious of what was going on. All she and Salomé had done was seek shelter from the elements. And look what happened. But now, she was anxious to actually see what happened.

Against the far wall of the cave, Gaitano's figureheads still kept silent, leaning on one another. The pirates' assorted bags were still there to one side, as was Cacique's dujo and belongings in the middle of the cave. The treasure chests belonging to her brother, her sister and herself were there, too. Looking closely, she scanned her eyes over the area. Then her heart skipped a beat. On the ground next to the figureheads, was her backpack. Biting her lip to stifle a cry, she rushed to it. Diving inside, she stirred things around. There was a change of clothing, her wallet, and an empty bottle of wine wrapped up in a beach towel. Brushing back her tears, she sighed shakily.

"Marina…"

Startled, she jumped at the sound of her husband's voice. Wiping her face hastily, she smiled shakily at him. "Carlos."

He stood silhouetted against the cave entrance, his features dark. But there was nothing dark about his voice. On the contrary, it held nothing but the deepest affection for her. "*Divina,*" he crooned, stepping closer.

"I'm all right, baby," she reassured him. Laughing, she waved her hands around her. "Look at all these things in here. This," she told him, clutching her backpack, "is mine." She pointed out a group of backpacks nearby. "These are ours. We use them to carry our stuff around. They are quite indispensable in our world." And then they weren't alone anymore.

"Are we back yet?" Catamaran demanded.

Marina smiled at him and waved a hand at the pile of backpacks. "See for yourself."

He grinned back at her. "Man, I can't wait to go home." Striding to the pile he pulled out his own with one swift movement. The young pirate kept silent as his wife's godfather dove into his backpack and pulled out an interesting contraption. Catamaran flipped it open, seemed to caress it with his thumb, then put it to his ear. Suddenly, his face lit up. "Blue! Yo, man! We're back!" Smiling, he turned to face Marina. "Yeah, we got the kids. Bro, it was like all those sketches of Caribe's coming to life. Totally unreal. Wish you were here," he laughed. "We're just waiting to get picked up, man. Where's Tío? Well, he better hurry. Hopefully we'll see you real soon. I got a favor to ask you, though. I need you to go around town and pick up a few blue cats for us, you know, stuffed toys. Large, small, I don't care. Just grab a few and have them delivered to Rain with a nice flower arrangement, a balloon, the works. The occasion?" Cat laughed. "You'll find out when she does." He frowned, listening for a moment. "The banquet's tonight? Damn! I forgot all about it, I've been a little busy," he laughed again. "Well, you know I wouldn't miss it for the world. We'll see you in a while. Love you, bro." Hanging up, he turned to Marina with a grin. "There's a lady lawyer he wants off his back. I'm supposed to go and show support." He shook his head.

Marina grinned back. "Blue can take care of himself."

"Yeah, I know." Catamaran looked at her thoughtfully. "Personally, I'm just curious about this woman. He's been bitching about her for a while." He sighed.

"Marina!" Startled, they turned to the cave entrance. Salomé was beckoning wildly. "Come here!" she urged, waving at them to go outside. "Look!" Joining her, they saw what she was pointing at. Flying over the water, heading their way, was a boat. Salomé grinned. "Someone's coming," she sighed happily. "I'm going to get my stuff." Turning hastily, she went inside the cave, her brother and family behind her. Don Carlos turned to join them. The rest of the pirates all stood by Marina's side, watching the approaching vessel in awed silence.

Carlos moved closer to her, always her protector. His voice was soft and steady. "Who's coming, Marina?"

Marina glanced at him and it was then that she realized that his hand was on his sword. Looking at their companions, she saw that they were also reaching for theirs. She shook her head. "I can't tell yet."

They were rejoined by the others. Salomé and Jackson came out with their packs on their backs and their chests in their arms. The rest put their own backpacks on the ground next to them. Jesse bounced Cacique in his arms. Silently, they waited. The boat kept coming closer, leaving a fierce white trail in the dark ocean. Thunder rumbled again overhead, this time softer as the storm moved away slowly. Lightning flashed in protest, reflecting off the rolling clouds. And as the visitors and the pirates watched, the trail of water suddenly disappeared. The boat stopped. A few moments later, from inside a backpack, a cell phone rang.

Happily, Jackson's hand dove into his bag and pulled it out. Flipping it open, he pressed it to his ear. "Yo! Derek! Hey, what's up, man? Nice to hear you. Is that you guys out there? So, what's going on? You coming or not?" He chuckled. "Yeah, man, you're right. Okay, man. Later." He hung up.

Marina turned to him. "So, what's going on, Jax? Why'd they stop?" At Jackson's amused shrug, she snatched the cell phone from him. "Give me that," she muttered, flipping it open and hitting Send twice. "Hey! What's up, guy? Why aren't you coming closer?"

"Hey, Marina! I've missed you, baby," Derek smiled into the phone.

"Missed you too. So, what's going on? Why aren't you coming closer?""

"I'm not sure about this…"

"Come get us, dude."

"Well, that's why we are here, but…"

"No buts. If that's what you're here for, come get us."

"It's not that easy, baby."

"Why not?"

"We're not exactly equipped."

Exasperated, Marina brushed the hair out of her face. "What do you need to be equipped for? We are here, you are there. We are stranded and you got the boat. Come get us."

"We can't."

Stubbornly, Marina shook her head. "Yes, you can. Come get us, Derek. Now."

Derek frowned. "Not happening, Marina."

She decided to change tactics. "Please, Derek, we've been away for so long, I'm dying to go home. We're tired, and hungry, and it's no fun up here. Please…"

"No."

"Come on, Derek…"

"No."

"Derek Butler!" She stamped her foot. "If you don't come get us right now, I swear I will slash your tires and laugh while I'm doing it!"

Derek's anger matched hers. "You're going to have to wait, Marina! It's not happening right now."

Marina narrowed her eyes, fighting the tears that suddenly stung them. "Dude, my boyfriend is so going to beat you up!"

Disgusted now, Derek had enough. "Let me speak to a grown adult!"

"I *am* a grown adult!" she yelled at him.

Stepping in before she threw it down the cliff, Jamal caught her in his arms, gently hushing her as he took the cell phone from her. "I got this," he reassured the pirates. "Hey, Derek. What's going on, baby?"

"We have to regroup, Jamal," Derek answered, still angry with Marina. "There are too many of you. The *Atlántica* can't handle all of you and all of your stuff, I'm sure. I'm going to call Tío and let him know what's going on. *Jasama* is better for this," he explained, referring to the Aguilar-Banks' own boat.

Jamal sighed, keeping Marina quiet in the cradle of his arm. "You are right, of course, it makes sense." He smiled. "I suggest you come over and make nice, however, while we wait."

"Just tie Marina up."

At this, the detective had to laugh out loud. "Don't worry. I got her. And she will not be slashing any tires," he reassured him. "But if she does by any chance, I'll try and make sure she's not laughing while she's doing it," he teased.

"He has to sleep sometime," Marina muttered.

Over her head, Jamal raised his eyebrows at the pirates. "Her boyfriend will not be beating you up, either," he chuckled. "Actually, he's more civilized than she is," he added, making the pirates laugh. "We'll see you in a bit." Flipping the cell phone shut, he handed it back to Jackson. "We have to wait a little while," he explained to his companions. "There are too many of us, and we don't all fit on the boat, especially not with all our stuff." Sighing, he pulled Marina closer and murmured in her ear.

"Jesse!"

"Change!"

"You're back, man! Missed you. What's up? Where you at?"

Jesse smiled affectionately as his younger brother's voice filled his head like music to his ears. "I'm back, but can't get out. Need you to pick me up."

"I'll be right there. Tell me where you are."

"I need you to do me a favor and get me a few things first, so you can bring them with you."

"Sure. Anything."

"I need some big ice chests. You know, like those used in the fishing boats, about six of them. They don't have to be brand new, just clean and empty. Get a box of large hefty trash bags. And some diapers."

"Diapers?" Change laughed on the other end of the line. Then he lowered his voice. "You got a pirate baby with you?"

Jesse smiled. "You could say that."

Now his brother sighed. "How old?"

"About eight, nine months old."

"All right. As soon as I get everything together for you, I will be right there."

"Cool."

"Nah, he can't make it. It'll be just me." They laughed.

Pablo frowned as his cell phone chimed. He had just received a message. Flipping it open, he saw he had been sent a picture. Frowning, he peered at it for a few moments, Joe and Shane looking on. As his brain confirmed what his eyes were seeing. He took a deep breath and sighed shakily. It was a picture of a beach with a group of people. A larger than expected group of people. Then the phone rang.

"Houston!"

"Derek?"

"We need help, man. We can't fit them all on the *Atlántica*. Marina's having a heart attack over it, but there are just too many of them."

Pablo nodded, rubbing his eyes. "Chill, baby. We'll be right there."

"Thanks, Tío."

"No problem. See you in a bit." Ending the call, he turned the cell phone towards his companions. They looked, saw, and turned to him in shock. He sighed again. "Good thing the *Jasama* is always ready. Let's go." Standing up, they prepared to leave Jesse's brother's business. Outside the big plate glass windows next to the table they had been sitting at, the marina beckoned, its boats bobbing gently in their respective slips.

Just then Change himself came up to them. The young man was the antithesis of his older brother. Where the other one was dark, this one was blond. While Jesse's face was scarred, his was as smooth as a Greek statue's. Jesse's eyes were the shade of the deep blue ocean. Change's eyes were the color of a cloudless sky. One was tanned like a cowboy, the other like a surfer. But in spite of all their differences, the similarities were there. Although one's smile was slow and the other one's was quick, they were the same. "You know they are back," he said quietly. The men nodded. "Jesse just called me. I need to get some things together for him and go pick him up."

Joe sighed. "We'll wait for you. We have to take the *Jasama* out there ourselves."

Shane smiled. "We'll all go together. So, what do you need?"

"Half a dozen coolers and some diapers."

"*Diapers?*" They all asked at the same time.

Change shrugged and grinned. "You know Jesse. It could be anything."

Laughing, they all left together.

"Rashawn!"

Rashawn smiled into his own cell phone. The voice came over the line in a mixture of delight and relief. "Hey, Summer. How ya doing, baby girl? Miss me?"

His girlfriend growled in his ear. "Wait till you see me, and I'll show you." There was a pause, and she spoke again in a whisper. "Did you get them?"

"I sure did, baby."

Now she screamed. "*You did?* Oh, God, Rashawn…" Her voice broke, and he could hear her crying quietly.

"Summer," he crooned gently, his deep voice rumbling over the line, comforting her. "It's all good. Get yourself together, and we'll see each other in a little while."

"Oh, God, Rashawn…" she whimpered.

Passing his hand over his cornrows, he sighed. "I know, baby, I know…"

The young pirate smiled. "So you are the one I am supposed to beat up."

Derek smiled back. "That would be me," he confirmed. "I'm Derek. This is my brother Tyler," he introduced hastily, reaching out to shake hands with the pirate. "We live with these people."

Carlos nodded. "Nice to meet you." He turned to his crew and introduced them.

The Butler boys looked over their shoulders, making sure the dads and Change were right behind them. Tyler shook hands with Gaitano now. "We're sorry we took so long," he smiled. "We weren't expecting so many of you."

"We had to do it this way."

"We understand," Derek laughed. "Actually," he confessed, "we're stoked."

The pirate grinned, his eyes crinkling at the corners. "So are we," he admitted.

"Not more than we are," Tyler laughed. "We are so relieved, dude, you have no idea. It's about time someone else dealt with Marina."

Solomon snickered. "It seems like only my Captain can handle her, by the look of it."

"Barely," Indio chuckled.

"Captain!" Giancarlo called out. "We have company!"

Turning away from the young men before him, Gaitano looked back out over the ocean. Absently, his hand went back to his sword. "It seems like we do," he agreed.

"At ease, men," Jamal cautioned. "It's just the Aguilar-Banks with the *Jasama*, and Jesse's brother with the *Cool Change*."

Jesse smiled to himself. Change couldn't take his eyes off him. His little brother had acted like a trooper throughout his whole encounter with the pirates. Had barely batted an eye when the pirates had filled the large coolers he had asked for with treasure. Hadn't even reacted when a beautiful figurehead had been loaded onto the Cool Change. But the sight of Cacique... Jesse sighed. Now Change was gazing at him like he used to when he was sixteen and Jesse was eighteen and his hero. "Say it," he finally said.

"Rain is going to kill you," sang Change in a tone of *Oooooo, you're in trouble...*

Jesse laughed. "Not! You just wait till she sets eyes on this precious bundle," he murmured at the baby in his arms. Cacique snuggled contentedly, his little back solid against Jesse's chest, entranced by the wind in his face.

"What's his name, and how'd you get him?" Change asked, reaching out with a finger to stroke the baby's dark cheek.

Jesse kissed the top of the baby's head. "Cacique. Marina." And he said no more.

Change nodded, chuckling to himself. Actually, he was practically chortling with glee. Reaching into his pocket, he drew out his cell phone. The wind whipped his curly blond hair around him, making him look like an angel, his blue eyes sparkling. A moment later he was laughing when whoever called picked up. "Jill! Hi, darling! I need you to do me a favor. Go ahead and close the shop for me. No, don't worry, I'll talk to Cool. Just close down for the day, have Rain come over so she can meet us there, and wait for me." He laughed again. "Jesse has a surprise for Rain. You're gonna die," he reassured her happily. "I'll see you in a little while, darling." And after kisses blown, Change hung up with his wife. Smug, he turned back to his older brother. "Rain is going to kill you," he told him. Then he turned back to sailing his boat, the *Cool Change*, back into the harbor.

The pirates were elated. A little scared, yes, but thrilled nevertheless, to the core of their being. They had all boarded the *Jasama*, along with Don Carlos, leaving the Butler brothers to transport the Blackmons, Jackson and Storm, Salomé and Marina. Jesse and Cacique were riding back with Change. What absolutely thrilled them the most so far was the speed of the boat. The pirates laughed happily at the feel of sheer power under their feet as the fiberglass slapped against the waves. The intensity with which the wind blew their hair back and the force with which it pressed against their chests, so different than how it felt on their own ships, was exhilarating to them. And now they had arrived. Having been sternly lectured by Don Carlos, they knew that they had to be careful with their reactions to everything they saw and heard until they reached their destination. Finally they arrived at a small marina where other boats of all styles and sizes bobbed gently under the cloudy sky. They were the first ones to arrive and were now standing in front of the *Cool Change*, the establishment. The others soon joined them. As the brothers Coltrane approached, Jesse handed Cacique to Change in order to free his arms. As if on cue, a female voice shrieked from inside the shop.

Sage smiled to herself. Deveraux looked at her and raised an eyebrow. "They're here," she laughed softly.

Deveraux nodded and cocked his head to one side, studying her closely. He was falling deeper in like with her. "How do you know?" He hadn't told her about Catamaran's phone call, and she hadn't been around when he received it.

Sage just looked at him as if he should know better. "Jesse and I are connected," she explained. "I can feel him."

Blue just nodded. Then he reached for her hand. "Were I to be so connected to you."

"You will, Deveraux." She smiled at him as he raised her hand to his lips to kiss it.

Just then Marquez decided to burst in. "Are they back yet?" he demanded of Sage, his lightning frown in Deveraux's direction the only indication that he had seen the exchange between them. Blue just laughed, of course, and with a squeeze of Sage's hand, locked his fingers with hers.

"They are back, Marquez," she told him gently.

Marquez's eyes crinkled, accompanying the huge smile that spread over his face. "My boy is back," he breathed a sigh of relief. Quickly, he blinked back tears.

"Marquez," Sage called softly, letting go of Blue and taking one of the older man's hands between both of hers, stroking it gently. "Jesse's been away before. What is it about this time that has you so emotional?"

Marquez fell silent for a moment. Then he looked at each of them, his eyes lost. "I don't know where Jesse went to get them upstairs kids, and I don't want to know. This time was different. Risky. Scary." He shook his head. "I don't want to know and I don't want him to do it again." And then he was gone.

"Jesse!" Rain flew through the air and landed in his arms, raining kisses on his face.

Laughing, Jesse walked her backwards into his brother's establishment. "Hey, baby! Missed me?" He hugged her tightly, kissing her face.

"With all my heart!" Rain took his face between her hands and gazed into his eyes. She was completely oblivious to all the people surrounding them. "Did you bring me something?" she asked, her voice soft and teasing.

Jesse laughed again. "I sure did." Then he just looked at her.

Rain's heart skipped a beat. Something flickered deep in Jesse's eyes. "What?"

Jesse shook his head and laughed at himself. Taking a deep breath he braced himself. Then he pulled Change to stand next to him. "I brought you a baby," he said softly.

Rain could only look at him, not comprehending. "A baby?"

Jesse nodded. "Yeah. A baby," he said, tenderly smoothing his hand over Cacique's head.

"Whose baby, Jesse?" Rain choked out, her eyes riveted now on the baby's raven head.

"Mine."

"Your baby?" She pulled away from him, walking a few steps backwards. Her voice rose. "*Your* baby, Jesse?" She whirled around and stamped her foot, her hands going to the top of her head. Turning back to him, she crossed her arms, glowering through the tears in her eyes. "You come in here with a black-haired baby and claim it is yours," she gasped. "Do I know the hoe who's the baby's mama?" she demanded.

"*Rain!*" Joe's voice lashed out at her, freezing her where she stood. It would have done Don Miguel proud.

Jesse just shook his head in disbelief. "You know me better than that!" he accused. "I would never cheat on you, much less have a baby with someone else, Rain!"

"Then explain the baby!" she cried out, eyes blazing.

"*Marina!*"

Marina jumped, startled out of her skin. "Jesse!" she gasped. He had never thundered at her before.

Salomé stepped in, throwing her arm around Marina in sisterly support. "Now, Rain, calm down..."

"Why do I have to calm down?" she turned on Salomé, teeth gritted, eyes narrowed.

"Because," Salomé responded insolently, intent on defending her sister and her choices at all cost. "Marina has a story to tell, so you better listen, girlfriend!" she said, pointing a finger at her aunt. "This is all about you."

Rain slowly dragged her eyes off her older niece and laid them on the younger one. She nodded. "Speak."

Marina swallowed. "Well, Rain, you know..." she trailed off, swallowing again. She shook her head slowly. Gaitano looked carefully from one female to the other. He hadn't believed Marina was afraid of anybody. Maybe he had been wrong.

Jackson stepped closer, moving to stand by Marina's side. "You know how much we love you," he said.

Rain turned narrowed eyes on him. "What do *you* want?"

For you to shut up, for one, Jackson thought with a laugh. But he kept the words inside his head. Instead, he appeased her. "Just listen, boo."

Rain nodded again. "Marina?"

Marina's eyes met hers. She took a deep breath. "We were minding our own business," she began steadily. "Jackson, Salomé and I were having a picnic with the pirates," she continued, not knowing nor caring how much Rain knew. "Along comes this beautiful native girl with this gorgeous baby. She's running from someone who wants to take this baby." She motioned at the baby in Change's arms, drawing all eyes to him. "This man followed her. We hid with the baby. He demanded to know where the baby was. When she wouldn't tell him, he killed her. Right before our eyes. We killed him. So we took the baby," she said softly, ignoring the shock in Rain's face. "I saved him for Jesse, Rain." Marina sighed, looking deep into her eyes. "Because even though I know that the two of you have made a childless life for yourselves, completely consumed by your jobs and by each other," she rushed on, "I know Jesse's heart and I know for a fact that not having a baby with you is his deepest, secret sorrow---"

"*Marina!*" Jesse growled at her.

Marina ignored him. "So I got him for both of you because I believe this baby's life will be richer and his destiny will be fulfilled by having you as parents. But if you don't want him..."

"I already told Jesse that I can be Papi," Catamaran chuckled.

"*Shut up!*" Rain snapped at him. Everyone else just stared, speechless, fascinated. She turned back to her husband. "So, we're keeping him?" she demanded. "Because you and I dividing over anything is not an option, Jesse. You hear me? Not when we've come this far!"

Jesse nodded. Taking his son out of his brother's arms, he bounced him gently. Closing his yes, he pressed his lips against the baby's head. Then he looked steadily at his wife. "We are keeping this baby."

Rain's hands went to wipe the moisture off her face. Drying them nervously on her skirt, she then patted her hair down and straightened her top. "What's his name?"

"Cacique."

"Cacique," she repeated slowly, savoring the name.

Change's wife stroked her arm reassuringly. "It's okay, baby, we'll help you. Now I get to be Aunt Jill instead of Mommy, for once."

Rain smiled through her tears and looked at her husband. Her lower lip trembled. "I guess we have a baby."

Jesse nodded, his lips pressed against Cacique's silky black hair. Letting go reluctantly, he beckoned Rain to come over. When she did, he threw his arm around her, kissing her hard on the lips. "We have a baby, baby," he whispered. Then he turned to a very curious baby. "I am Papi," he crooned, smiling until the baby's eyes lit up, "and this is Mami." Cacique looked from one to the other. Having learned from Marina, Jesse pulled Rain closer and kissed her deeply on the temple. Jesse smiled at the baby again. "Mami," he repeated dreamily. Cacique just looked at her for a moment, glancing at Jesse to make sure it was okay. Then he reached over. Taking Rain's face between his baby hands, he pressed his little mouth against hers.

The pirates looked up. They had never seen anything like it. They had been warned about the advances in the modern world, but they hadn't expected their introduction into it to be quite so sudden. Before them was a contraption. A very tall contraption. Stories tall. It seemed to consist of a thick long black tubular structure holding up a large rectangle on the top. In the rectangle, waves of color filled it with flickering images. So they stared. Up above them, on the biggest screen imaginable was a picture. Words faded in, flowing in a beautiful script. They read **The Pirate's Wife.** The words faded out again, and the camera focused on a figure. It zoomed in little by little, capturing more and more details. They could see the back of a woman. She was draped over a table, head down, face hidden in her arms. Her shoulders were shaking beneath the sleek black cape of her long hair. Clasped in her hands were a large wooden rosary and a picture. The camera zoomed in tighter. The picture was a beautiful black and white hand sketched portrait of a pirate. It was Don Carlos Gaitano y Mendoza. The exquisite detail could have been so lovingly captured by one person only. Caribe. The camera zoomed out quickly as the woman looked suddenly into the mirror in front of her. It was María Isabel Sandoval. Thrusting one hand through the rosary, she clasped Don Carlos' picture to her chest. With the other one she brushed at the stream of tears pouring down her face. They all watched her lips tremble as she mouthed the word *Carlos,* her eyes swimming in the pools of her tears. Taking the picture in both hands, she pressed her lips against it, before putting it down, leaning it against the mirror. Gently, she placed the rosary down next to it. María Isabel then reached down for something next to her. There was a black flash as something whipped up, settling down in a gentle wave. The camera followed her as she strode away from it, focussing on the black fabric draped around her shoulders. It was a skull and crossbones flag. María Isabel stopped at a balcony. The camera went around her, catching a glimpse of her stunning profile. Words faded in again, but this time they read **Captured by Caribe.** And everything faded to black. Words appeared magically again, this time reading **The Pirate's Return.** The screen quickly lightened, and in a corner were small words indicating it was a LIVE FEED. The musical soundtrack was appropriate. It played Vangelis with one of his ocean themed symphonies. The haunting notes captured the senses of the fascinated onlookers as they watched in breathless anticipation. The camera sought María Isabel out, standing on the balcony again. She still had the pirate flag around her shoulders, but on this occasion her outfit was different. She was wearing a beautiful dress in deep black. Multicolored jewels sparkled on her chest and in her ears. She clasped her hands in silent prayer for a moment, and cascades of chunky jeweled bracelets slipped down her arm. She looked like an ad for a very expensive jeweler. Then they saw her perk up, turning quickly toward some sound. The camera whirled and caught the pirate striding straight towards it. It seemed to scoot out of the way as María Isabel flew right by it. Imposing in his full pirate attire, you could almost hear the jangle of the sword at his hip and the stomp of his boots as he crossed the floor. His shirt was open, baring his chest, the bandana on his head hiding the stray silver threads in his hair, his gray eyes bright against his tanned face. His earrings sparkled as he passed under the skylight. The pirate and his wife seemed to fuse more than collide when they made contact. Don Carlos picked María Isabel up, whirling her around in a circle. She flung her arms around his neck and threw her head back in abandon, the tears flying out of her eyes even as she laughed with joy. He set her down, catching her face between his hands, pure love shining out of his eyes, rubbing the tears that fell out of her own. The camera zoomed in. The pirate kissed his wife.

The Aguilar-Banks grinned. The pirates' reaction and expressions were much the same as Caribe's had been when he first rode up on the service elevator in their building. Eyes wide, shock in their faces. They didn't tease them but didn't soothe them either. Instead they kept silent, and literally waited for them to ride it out. They had all agreed to go to Marina and Xaira's place first, just so that they could get their bearings before continuing. Reaching the top floor of the building, the elevator came to a halt. The doors opened and everyone stepped out, leaving the pirates behind. These looked at each other and sighed, following their hosts. All of a sudden there was a noise as claws raced across tiles to reach them.

"Hey! Samson! Dalilah!" Tyler cried out, concern in his voice.

"Don't move, guys!" Derek warned. Needlessly, it turned out for the pirates had frozen in place. Everyone stopped in their tracks.

"These are our guards," Jackson told them. "You're with us, so you'll be okay. Just don't make any sudden moves."

The pirates did as they were told as the rottweilers circled them. They were wary, never having seen anything like them before. The dogs went up to them, sniffing them one by one, butting their heads against their hips and thighs. Once done, they sat down in unison and stared at them for a moment. Then as if by mutual agreement, they trotted to Indio. Standing on their hind legs, they both reached up to him nuzzling him and licking him. The pirates laughed. Their friends stared. Then the pair sat down on their haunches in front of the Quartermaster as if waiting instructions. Everyone smiled.

Salomé looked at her man in wonder and with pride. "Dude," she breathed, "you're the Beast-master..."

Indio thought about that for a moment. Then he nodded, a smile breaking out on his face. "That, I am."

Jackson shook his head. "Well, you should work with animals, that's for sure." Then he turned to his sisters with a laugh. "That's one down!"

"Marina!"

Marina braced herself as the oriental girl came flying through the air at her. "Xaira!" She caught her in a tight embrace. Xaira burst into tears. Startled, Marina pulled back to look at her. "Xaira! What's wrong, mami?"

Xaira sobbed, tears streaming down her face, oblivious of the pirates frozen in place. "I was so scared!" she howled. "I thought you were never coming back!"

Marina held her in her arms, her hands rubbing the other girl's back. "I'm so sorry, baby," she crooned, tears stinging her own eyes. "I never meant to be gone at all."

"I looked for you, and looked for you, and I couldn't find you!" Xaira sobbed. "I thought you were going to miss our graduation!"

Marina stopped. "Your graduation?" she repeated. "Oh, my God! Your graduation!" she whispered in shock, remembering. She squeezed Xaira, rubbing her head against the younger girl's. "When is it, mami?"

"Next Wednesday," Xaira whimpered, getting ready to howl again. Suddenly she noticed the pirate standing to one side. *"You took her!"* she accused, with a fresh wave of tears. *"You kept her!"* she screamed at him.

Gaitano pressed his lips together. He had never before witnessed such intense female drama. Now he could only nod. Obviously, the younger girl was in deep emotional distress, on the verge of a breakdown. He sighed. Holding a hand out, he appeased her. "I am so sorry, Xaira. I brought her back because I know you needed her. Marina was dying without you, also."

Xaira hiccuped, glaring at the pirate through her tears. "I do need her! It's my turn now! You can wait!"

Marina laughed softly, glad for the save. "It is your turn, baby." Holding Xaira away from her, she wiped the tears from the girl's face with both hands. "Carlos is going to wait while you and I catch up. You can meet him and his men later." She began walking her away. "Now you can tell me all about what's been going on with you while I was gone."

Gaitano sighed, staring after them. Shaking his head, he turned to look at Salomé. "Is she always this emotional?"

"Xaira?" Salomé squealed in surprise. She giggled. "Xaira Chang is one of the most mature, calm, cool..." she drifted off. Then she shook her head. "Cold, actually, young ladies you will ever have the chance to meet. But when it comes to Marina..." She shook her head again.

"Marina is her mommy," Jackson laughed. He clapped his brother-in-law on the shoulder. "Come on, man, let me show you around. You need to see how some basic things work." And turning the pirate around, he wandered off, the rest of the crew of La Gitana behind them.

Soon, they found themselves back on the ground floor of the building again. They walked along the hallway that divided the floor in half. On the side facing the street were four businesses. Sea Side Styles, Rain Dance, Snake's Tattoos, and an empty locale which hadn't been rented out yet. On the side that faced the ocean, were a couple of rooms used for storage and two apartments, empty and abandoned.

Giancarlo swooped down on Jackson. "Tell me about these two places. Why are they vacant? Why is not anybody living in them?"

Jackson laughed. "Well, we all lived in them, while work was being done in each of our floors. First Marina and Xaira, then Salomé and me, and ending up with Derek and Tyler. Once the work was done, we would move back and the next pair of roommates would use them. When the work was done for Derek and Tyler, they moved back home and these have been empty ever since."

"So what are you doing with them now?" Giancarlo insisted.

Jackson laughed again. "Why are you so interested, Gian?"

"Storm is going to go live with you, right?" the Sailing Master asked him.

Jackson rolled his eyes teasingly. "Of course."

"Indio's going with Salomé, and the Captain lives with Marina," Solomon told him.

"Right."

"So where are we going to go?" Solomon asked.

Jackson looked from one to the other. "You are worried about this?" He smiled when the pirates nodded. These were his friends and it was up to him to calm them. "We'll give you a place."

"Give us these. There's two of them. One for Rouge and myself, and one for Solomon," Giancarlo requested.

"We will pay, of course, as you pay to the owners of the building."

Jackson just had to grin at that. He called over his shoulder. "Yo! Owners of the building!"

"Yo! Tenant!" Joe laughed back.

"Owner of the building present," teased Pablo as he joined them, his eyes sparkling.

"And one more makes three," laughed Shane.

"Sailing Master and Boatswain need a place to stay," Jackson explained. "They are looking at two empty apartments and are making an offer."

"Apartments need some work, men," Shane told them.

"They haven't been used in months," Joe explained, "and nobody but these kids have ever stayed in them, so they're in very good shape. But as you can tell, we've been using them for storage lately. They will clean up real good, you'll see. Just need a little makeover."

"If you can fix them up, get them going, fill them up, they're yours," Pablo offered. "We will talk about rent later. For now, they are just sitting there. We'll give you the time you need to get them ready."

Solomon and Giancarlo and Rouge grinned. "Aye!"

That settled, they moved on. Finally, they went in the back of Snake's Tattoos, where Sage and Deveraux were hanging. The Aguilar-

Banks dads made the introductions and the pirates settled themselves across the shop. They could only stare at Blue for a moment, silent, thoughts raging.

Deveraux smiled. "You can relax, men," he finally said to them, "I am not like my twin. Cat gave you a hard time, huh?" At their nods he laughed. "That's the way he is." He shrugged. "Just don't kill him, okay? I'm kind of attached to him."

"I have come close," Gaitano admitted.

Blue turned to look at him. "I'm sure they explained how Catamaran is Marina's godfather."

The pirate nodded. "They did. We just couldn't figure out if he was a pest for real, or just trying to be one."

Blue laughed again. "Oh, for real!" he assured him.

Sage stepped in, smile bright and distracting. "Well, seeing as how you've been with Catamaran this whole time, now you will get a nice break from him. I am Sage," she introduced herself shyly. "I work for Jesse."

"Now Blue's girlfriend," Deveraux smiled, accepting the soft congratulations.

"Are you into snakes also?" Giancarlo asked curiously, peering at her baby snake in his pen.

"Not really. We are making an experiment, Jesse and I. If I can stand it, I get to keep him," Sage explained.

"Do you have more baby snakes?" Giancarlo asked.

Sage nodded. "Would you like one?" At his nod she turned to look at all of them. "Each of you?"

The pirates laughed. "Sure!" Solomon grinned.

"I would like one too," Rouge smiled. "It will be a pirate thing."

"That means I get one too," Storm laughed. "I hope Jackson isn't afraid---" she ended in a squeal as he rushed her, murmuring in her ear about bigger snakes she should be afraid of.

Sage laughed. Everyone seemed happy and relaxed. The pirates drifted around the shop, taking in all the flash on the walls, and the albums at the stations. They were fascinated, as children usually are when they find themselves at a new place. Especially the Captain.

Now he was crouched down staring at her pet. "Do you like cats, Captain?"

He nodded. "Very much. Especially black ones." He reached over slowly, and stroked the big tomcat between the ears. It seemed as if he started a motor. The purring was audible. "May I get a baby one?" he inquired curiously. "Could you do this for me?"

Sage's eyes met his. They connected. And they each smiled at the other. "Aye."

Gaitano sighed. He rubbed his eyes and passed his hand over his hair, lacing his fingers behind his head. The mattress felt wonderful under his back. He had never experienced anything like it. There was a lot to be said about modern conveniences, that was for sure. Crossing his ankles, he made himself more comfortable on Marina's bed and stared up at the skylight. There was nothing much to see, the late afternoon sky was the color of lead. But just the thought that he could actually look up at the sky through the roof... Chuckling, he smiled to himself. Reminded him of the Bat Cave he left back home in Encantada. No wonder Marina had been so drawn to it. It must have reminded her of her own home, her own space. He turned his head at the sound of a soft knock. He rumbled softly and it was followed by a click as the door opened.

Salomé came in with a smile, leaving the door open behind her. Her smile widened into a grin. "How's it going?"

The pirate grinned back. "Fine, just fine."

Crossing her arms, she leaned against the doorway. "How are you liking it so far?"

He shrugged his shoulders. "So far, so good, I guess. Jackson showed us some things in order for us not to embarrass ourselves."

Salomé strode over to the bed and motioned him to move. Scooting over to the edge, he made room for her. Salomé sat on the side and laid down, perpendicular to him, resting her head on his stomach, propping her feet on the wall. "Well, that's good, at least. It will take a little time," she warned him, also staring up at the ceiling.

The pirate grinned. "Time, we've got."

"You do," she agreed. "So you better make good use of it."

He laughed softly, making her head bounce. "I think the viejos have plans for us. Something about keeping us away from the rest of society until they are sure we can be let loose."

This time it was Salomé's turn to laugh softly. "Society has no idea what they are in for."

"May I join you?" Marina asked from the doorway.

Salomé giggled. "Please do," she waved a hand over the space on the bed next to her. "The Captain and I are just discussing what society is in for once the pirates are let loose."

Marina laughed, lying next to her, her own head on her husband's thigh. "They have no idea. Of course, these pirates should be able to contribute to this clueless society."

The pirate laughed again, reaching down to stroke her hair. "You can laugh all you want. These pirates will not only take society by storm, but it will also be the best thing that ever happened to them."

"Aye," the girls chorused softly.

"Shouldn't take too long," he continued. "We are smart, educated men."

"Aye," the sisters agreed once more.

"Respectable, handsome..."

"Nay," Salomé laughed. "Breathtakingly gorgeous!"

"Aye," Marina giggled.

"That too," murmured her husband. "Talented, generous..."

"Not very modest, though," Salomé pointed out.

"No," he agreed. "Modesty has no place in the face of truth." Smiling, they all sighed, getting lost in thought for a moment.

Salomé turned her head on her improvised pillow to look at her sister. "How's Xaira doing?"

Marina looked at her. "Okay, now. I guess she really went through it." Tears stung her eyes. "Strong as she is, Salomé, I think this messed her up a little bit."

Salomé reached over and stroked her face. "It's okay," she whispered. "We'll fix her up. Xaira is the strongest person I know."

"She blames me," the pirate rumbled under their heads.

"No," Marina told him without breaking eye contact with her sister. "Xaira is smart. She knows there was no way to avoid the inevitable. She's just a little upset because of the way things turned out. But she will grow to love you, Carlos," she reassured him. "She won't be able to help herself."

"Yes," Salomé agreed. "The pirate charm will win her over." She reached over and squeezed her sister's hand. "Good thing we made it back in time for graduation."

"Very good thing," agreed Marina. "I can't imagine what it would have done to her otherwise."

"Is the little girl okay?" a voice rumbled from the doorway. They all turned their heads to look at Indio.

"Okay, I guess. Hanging in there," Marina told him. "Caribe has been crucial..."

The brave nodded. "I understand." He sighed. "You are going to have to fix this, Carlitos," he grinned at his brother.

Gaitano sighed. "I will."

Indio laughed. "Jackson went downstairs with Storm. If I didn't know any better, I would say she's scared out of her mind right about now." He held a hand out to his girlfriend. "Come, Salomé," he rumbled, "show me where you live."

Sighing, Salomé leaned forward and took her sister's face between her hands to kiss her on the cheek. The girls embraced where they lay, on the captain, and sat up slowly. "See you later, mami," she whispered.

"Later," Marina whispered back. "Have fun, Indio," she called to him as Salomé joined him.

"Oh, I intend to," he reassured her. Slipping his arm over Salomé as she joined him, they turned away.

Marina laid back down, this time next to her husband, snuggling against him. "Carlos," she sighed, tears stinging her eyes. "Xaira has been so scared..." Her voice broke.

Gaitano slipped his arm around her and held her close against him. He stared back up through the skylight. "I'll fix it," he reassured his wife.

Indio and Storm looked at each other. They smiled. Jackson and Salomé's place was really nice. One floor below Marina and Xaira's, it still had the high ceilings of a warehouse as did Derek and Tyler's floor down below. Where upstairs there were skylights, down here were assorted chandeliers, ranging from the simpler ones to the more elaborate. The more formal eating area boasted a traditional one with crystal drops. The dining room set was made of heavy wood with comfortably cushioned high-backed chairs. They were covered in lush tropical fabrics with a beautiful exotic print of bright birds of paradise flowers on a tan background. On the oval table the focal point was a lead crystal vase with real birds of paradise in water, its sloping sides reflecting the light from the chandelier overhead. The table was set with plain bamboo place mats. On them were bright orange plates, dishes, bowls and cups both solid and in gorgeous designs and patterns. They matched the birds of paradise. The real ones as well as the ones stamped in luscious fabric. The silverware was modern yet rustic. The forks, knives, and spoons were beautiful in their simple design, everything rounded and shiny, yet with real bamboo handles. The contrast and beauty of it all turned the setting into a work of art. A large cupboard stood to one side with glass doors, displaying beautiful fine old china in a yellow rosebud pattern, and crystal glassware. On the other side of a brick wall with an arch, the kitchen was very modern with all the latest appliances and gadgets. It consisted of a lot of glass and stainless steel, black marble countertops and a nice matching counter with sturdy chrome and black cushioned stools overlooking the city. Hanging from the bricks were wonderful oil paintings done lovingly by Jamaican artists. The vibrant colors contrasted beautifully with the colder look of the kitchen, automatically making it seem warmer and cozier. Here, the overhead lights were industrial type, plain aluminum domes suspended from long tubes attached to the ceiling. Their family space boasted a chandelier made of deer antlers and had more of a Southwest feel to it. It held paintings and bronze sculptures of cowboys and Indians on the Trail of Tears. Everything was rustic, although they had the same jean and Navaho blanket covered furniture as Marina and Xaira did upstairs. The difference was the whole feel of the space. Bookshelves made out of logs displayed the museum quality pieces with discreet lighting, as well as the siblings' personal collections of books. Here were peace pipes and dreamcatchers, rain sticks and prints of old sepia toned photographs of different tribes and their members. Another place they also had was reserved purely for exercise, with enough room to put in an indoor basket for Jackson to practice shooting hoops and a corner with mirrored walls for Salomé to dance and work out. Where upstairs fish tanks dominated the décor, here, although they had a couple, the tenants had opted for beautiful standing bird cages with lovebirds, parrots and cockatoos. The cages themselves were pieces of art, ranging from home made ones made out of sturdy bamboo scattered all throughout the apartment, to gorgeous metals one with fine scrolls decorating them like the ones in the kitchen. Plants were also abundant here as they were upstairs. To the street side of the building the windows were panoramic, looking out on the building across the street and the city beyond it. To the front of the apartment, facing the ocean, they had ceiling to floor glass panels, as all the apartments did. A balcony overlooking the beach with sliding glass doors took over their living room decorated with light rattan furniture and an overhead paddle fan. Smaller balconies with the same sliding glass doors came out of the Southwest room and each of their bedrooms on opposite sides of the building. Heavy wooden double doors inlaid with panels of etched frosted glass led to each bedroom, the same as on each floor.

Storm sighed happily and looked up at Jackson. "I can get used to this," she said huskily.

Jackson grinned. "You better."

Indio just looked at Salomé. "This is very nice." He smiled slowly, his eyes locking with hers. "Now show me your room."

Jackson rolled his eyes and hauled Storm behind him. "Come on, baby," he mumbled, "I'll show you mine." Laughing, his girlfriend stumbled after him.

Salomé stood back with a smile. They were in her bedroom. Inside she was thrilled to pieces. Here was Indio Gaitano, with her, in her place, looking around him as if it would do just fine. She kept quiet as he looked, walked around, stopped to study a few pieces. A picture of her with Marina and Rashawn, and another of her cheerleading team in high school. He couldn't resist a spinning rack with necklaces and bracelets and set it in motion. He picked up the book on her bedside table and read the back silently. He looked at her and nodded without saying anything. He gazed at himself for a moment in the full length mirror that was the door to her large walk-in closet. He stood at her small balcony for a moment and surveyed the almost empty beach in front of him. Coming back inside, he took her in his arms and kissed her passionately. Then without a word he sat on the edge of her bed and began pulling his boots off.

Dazed, Salomé could only look at him for a moment. "What are you doing, baby?"

Indio smiled. "First one to get their clothes off gets to be on the bottom." In an instant their clothes went flying through the air. A moment later Salomé sighed happily. Finally, he was here. Indio Gaitano, in her room, in her bed, deep inside her... Wrapping her arms and legs around him she pressed her mouth against his and held on as he pounded her into her mattress. Salomé was exactly where she wanted to be.

"You've got her back," Caribe laughed. They were up on the roof terrace. The wind blew through their hair, snatching at their clothes, dispersing the lower clouds, leaving the darker bank above.

Xaira glowered, her hair whipping around her face. "Marina brought him with her."

"You mean, Gaitano came with his wife," he chuckled.

"Whatever! She should have left him behind!"

"Xaira..." He shook his head at her and grabbed her by one wrist, pulling her into the circle of his arms. "The pirate is never going to leave her, he married her. She saved his fortune, his island, his reputation, his name..."

"I know, I know," she interrupted impatiently. "But *I* need her, Caribe!" she exclaimed.

"It could have been worse, mami, he could have kept her, stayed in Encantada…" he let his voice trail off, waiting for his words to sink in.

But his new girlfriend would not be appeased so easily. "I'm not ready to be without her yet!"

"So I guess he'll share, Xaira, he won't leave you without her."

"Promise?"

Caribe laughed again. "Promise." He breathed a big sigh of relief as the girl finally quieted down in his arms.

Carlos Gaitano turned to look at his wife. They had just said good-bye to Caribe and Xaira, who would be staying at the Hacienda until some more permanent living arrangements were made for everyone. Xaira had been adamant about giving Marina her newly-wed bride privacy. Although the truth was she was still a little wary of the pirate.

The pirate had picked up on this and couldn't resist teasing her a little bit in a genuine effort to break the ice with her. "I really like your place," he had told her, looking around him with appreciation.

Xaira had just looked at him steadily. Finally, she had tossed her head. "I'll tell you what," she offered slowly, encouraged by his raised eyebrow. She had caught his attention. "If you find me a nice place of my own, you can keep my part of the apartment."

The pirate had smiled, absurdly pleased with himself and what he thought of as a breakthrough. "I will find you a place so excellent you will thank me," he replied, bowing over her hand and kissing it. Straightening up he winked at her. At least her eyes smiled. Tossing her head again, she turned and left. Caribe went with her so she wouldn't be alone. Now they had the apartment all to themselves.

The pirate raised an eyebrow at his girl and leered playfully. Marina smiled back. Like his brother downstairs, Carlos went around the bedroom surveying different things. There was a dry erase board on one wall a couple of months behind. The writing in it was neat and tidy in some places, like for work and school. Playtime was filled in bright blue, big slanted print. Below that was a small desk with a nice modern slim desktop computer. There were jars with assorted shells and other beach related finds. There was a bulletin board filled with pictures of friends and family. The pirate noted that there wasn't a large assortment, and for the most part he already knew most of them. One photograph caught his attention, however. It was black and white, and Marina looked younger, as did her companion.

Carlos raised an eyebrow at her. "Sheik?"

Marina nodded slowly. Her eyes went from the photograph in his hand to his eyes. She didn't say anything. Carlos smiled and put it back. There was a nice *coqueta* that caught his eye. The vanity table was obviously used constantly, its seat cushioned and worn. The mirror was draped with shell necklaces, puka beads, and sharks' teeth on weathered leather cords. The jewelry boxes on the table top were mostly clear glass sugar bowls with bracelets and rings inside them. He studied these closely, intent on getting a feel for her taste in jewelry and baubles. There were beautiful batik fabrics covering the street side windows in rich ocean hues. It gave her privacy from the building across the street. Also, when the sun set, it filtered through the fabric, filling her bedroom with a beautiful blue glow. Already painted aqua, it made the space seem to be underwater. The closet doors and the door that led to her own bathroom were all covered in mirrors, reflecting the beautiful watery light. The effect was instantly soothing. A nice sized flat screen TV graced one corner, with a deep comfortable love seat in a deep blue facing it. On the wall next to that was a poster. Of a pirate. Gaitano stepped closer. This swash-buckler looked like no one he knew, yet seemed familiar. He studied him closely. It could only be one person. He raised an eyebrow at Marina, smiling slowly. "Captain Jack Sparrow?"

Marina smiled back with a nod. "Johnny Depp at his best," she murmured.

Carlos laughed. Next to the poster hung a skull and crossbones flag. Under it he noticed a shelf full of skull and crossbones jewelry. "You were a pirate before I met you," he accused softly. Glancing at her he caught her nod. Turning back to the wall in front of him, he gazed at the last picture. It was a copy of a print of a black-haired pirate wooing a stunning bombshell of a red-haired mermaid on some rocks. The mermaid, for all her beauty and sexiness managed to be portrayed as regal instead, as her suitor offered her a piece of jewelry. It was very beautiful and it struck a chord deep inside the pirate. He turned to Marina again. Looking into her eyes he couldn't speak for a moment. "You have been waiting for me," he finally said, his voice husky with emotion.

Tears stung Marina's eyes. She swallowed and nodded once more. "A very long time."

Carlos smiled gently at her. "I am your dream come true..."

Marina smiled back, her hazel eyes sparkling like kaleidoscopes. "Yes, you are," she replied, her voice husky with tears.

The pirate reached for her hand and without breaking eye contact, brought it to his mouth for a kiss. "I will do everything I can not to disappoint you."

Marina choked on a laugh. "Baby, you couldn't disappoint me if you tried."

Smiling, he rubbed the shadow on his face against the back of her hand. Then he turned to the bedroom's center of attraction. It was a bed like nothing he had ever seen before. And almost anybody else, for that matter. Although he had just been laying on it with both Marina and Salomé, he took the time now to study it carefully. It was a large sleigh bed made of thick clear lucite, the base long enough to accommodate tall people comfortably. The bed itself was of deep foam, and dressed in fish prints on a background of shades of aqua, adorned with an assortment of pillows in solid tones of bright blue scattered among the fish. Both at the head and at the foot of the bed, the frame was contained with chest high walls made of glass blocks. These held magnificent gurgling fish tanks, secured on both sides to matching clear lucite stands. From the skylight right over the bed, yards of luscious sheer fabrics in all kinds of shades of blue cascaded downward, draping over the bed and wrapping it in privacy. The effect was magical. "I want to make love to you," he said suddenly.

Marina's heart skipped a beat. Her clit throbbed a beat. "Now?" she breathed.

The pirate whipped his shirt over his head. In an instant his pants were on the floor next to it, his boots kicked across the room.

Reaching for his girl, he gazed at her, his eyes smoldering with desire as he rubbed his hardening front against her. He walked her backwards until they reached the bed. Laying her down, he gazed at her for a moment. His thoughts raged inside, but he controlled himself. After all, he didn't want to scare her with the full force of his passion. The thought made him smile. Sometimes she scared him with her own passion for him, not that he would ever admit it to her. But it only scared him because it absolutely matched his own. It didn't matter, though. He was crazy about her. He kissed her. Hard, tasting her mouth, savoring it. Wordlessly he made her clothes disappear. His hands toured her body, making her squirm, his talented fingers readying her for him. Marina stretched, responding to his caresses until she was warm and pliant, open and wet. "Yes. Now," he finally whispered in her ear, lowering his weight on her. "In your bed." Letting himself in, he moaned softly. Gaitano was exactly where he wanted to be. Horizontal and inside Marina.

Marina sighed. She couldn't remember anything but the feel of her man inside her and the smell of him on her. "Okay," she breathed, squeezing him hard with the muscles deep inside her. He groaned in her ear, welcoming her nails on his back. The pirate loved his girl. Absolutely adored her. And he would do anything at all to keep her. Especially now that they were in her world. Carlos stroked deep inside her, groaning with satisfaction when she moaned in his ear in reply. He stroked her again and felt her nails digging deeper before beginning to scratch. He would have trails in the morning. The pirate laughed. He didn't care. Her nipples pressed against his chest, a combination of intense arousal and the air conditioning he was so blessed to experience. Especially under these circumstances. Quickening his pace, he slipped his tongue into her mouth. She welcomed it hungrily, sucking on it until he moaned. Laughing softly her hips swung up to smack into his and she licked his lips. The pirate laughed. He stroked her again, this time kissing her deeply. He smiled against her mouth. Clenching him deep inside her, Marina drenched him, pulsating rhythmically.

Sage sighed quietly. She was sitting between the two most handsome men in the whole room, the St. Jacques twins, better known as the Blue Cat to family, coworkers and friends. They looked splendid in their tuxedos, their green eyes luminous in their beautiful dark faces. Deveraux's cornrows were neat, having been redone and conditioned by Marquez earlier that afternoon. A real diamond winked from one ear. Catamaran's dreadlocks were tied back, leaving his handsome face in stark relief. Gold hoops hung at his ears, a habit he had picked up from the pirates. The twins were both so attentive towards her you would think they were both her dates. The truth of the matter was she looked stunning. Her hair was also pulled back from her face, held away with a soft black velvet hair band. Her makeup was minimal, her blue eyes bright in her face with only a coat of mascara on her lashes, and nude gloss on her lips. The only indication of her particular style was the cascade of silver hoops at her ears. Her black dress was simple, enhancing instead of taking away from her own beauty. Made of a shiny slinky material it hugged her curves, falling to her knees. Over it she wore a short black jacket, the hemline reaching her waist, the sleeves completely covering her arms. The material was different than that of the dress, rougher like black denim, stamped with tiny rosebuds embroidered in black silk thread. Sexy black stockings hugged her legs, her feet in stunning black stilettos. Sage felt beautiful, because she looked beautiful. But that wasn't the problem. It was the woman sitting across the table from them. Deveraux's coworker was beautiful herself. Her name was Maureen Brown, and she was a vicious defense lawyer, someone to be reckoned with in court. A stunning black woman with a face fit for a magazine, and curves that wouldn't quit. Her dress was cut low, but tasteful, exposing only a little of her generous cleavage. She sparkled like a Christmas tree however, her jewelry more bling than style. She looked like she had spent hours at a salon before getting there, every single hair perfectly in place. She wore it loose, obviously treated with keratin, expertly blow dried and hot ironed, professionally styled. It was dyed an attractive light brown streaked with honey highlights, hanging to her shoulders, framing the face of an older model. Her mouth pouted with shiny red lipstick. Maureen Brown's one feature that was quite nondescript however, forcing her to make them up for them to be noticeable, was her eyes. They were brown and mean, like those of a grizzly bear. And right now they were shooting daggers at her.

Catamaran chuckled next to Sage, taking one of her delicate hands in his own big one and bringing it to his lips for a kiss. Leaning over he whispered in her ear. "Don't let her get to you, baby. You are Blue's date, not her."

Sage smiled at him. "Thanks, Cat."

"You're welcome, mami."

Feeling better, she leaned back against Deveraux's arm across the back of her chair. She was aware of his fingers playfully tangling in her hair. His boss smiled at her. He was an older man, still strong and handsome, his presence commanding in his tuxedo. He had what was known as salt-and-pepper hair, and his brown eyes danced. "So, Sage," he laughed, "I understand that you work at a tattoo parlor."

"I do, Mr. Wilkerson. Snake's Tattoos, over at Front Street. Been working there since I was in high school."

"You look like you are still in high school, darling," his wife waved a hand at her, her own diamonds flashing in the candlelight on the table. She was dressed in a beautiful gown in a soft dark gray fabric. Her blond hair was just beginning to gray, the lines just beginning to show at the corners of her sparkling blue eyes.

"I have seen the place," the owner of Blue's law firm continued. "The whole building just got a makeover, didn't it? I hear they closed the street in front of it and put in a fountain and everything."

"Yes, sir, it just did. We have beautiful dolphin trash cans, and park benches." She smiled shyly at him. "Now we have a mural on the building."

He frowned, thinking. "Who does it belong to?"

"The Aguilar-Banks."

"Ah, yes, the Aguilar-Banks. They raised Deveraux and Catamaran, didn't they? Very enterprising of them, I must say. They are friends of Shane Butler, aren't they?"

"Shane is their lawyer, yes. He is also part owner of the building."

"That explains it," Mr. Wilkerson smiled at her, eyes twinkling.

"So that's how you came to be acquainted with the Blue Cat?" his wife asked.

Sage turned her smile on her. "Yes, ma'am. Working in the building, you can't get away from them."

"Well, you look pretty chummy," Maureen said cutting in smoothly. "Actually, you look as if you do *everything* together," she purred. "Must make for some quite interesting adventures."

Sage couldn't believe it. The implication wasn't lost on her or on anybody else at the table. Everyone turned to look at Ms. Brown. Sage could only stare at her, feeling the color rush to her face. The woman had been nothing but just short of violent towards her since they had arrived. She could feel the men tensing on either side of her. Raising an eyebrow, she stared at the woman. "Meow..." And without saying another word she pushed her chair back from the table. The twins jumped to their feet, helping her out. Sitting back down, they stared at the other woman.

Catamaran drummed his fingers on the table. If looks could kill, he would be making funeral arrangements for the female lawyer. "Green doesn't become you, sweetheart."

Deveraux stared at her with loathing for a moment, shaking his head before excusing himself. "I have something to take care of," he mumbled, and he was gone.

"Ms. Brown," the boss man growled at her in warning, "I ignore your catty behavior at the office because it is a tank full of piranhas. But your conduct here is inexcusable. These are my guests."

A thrill of trepidation coursed through Maureen's body for a moment, chilling her skin. She was so jealous she could tear the younger girl's hair out, but she wasn't about to lose her hard-earned job over her. "I am sorry, Mr. Wilkerson, I didn't mean anything, really, I'll go apologize right now." Standing up hastily, she left the table.

Mrs. Wilkerson looked at her husband, her eyebrows raised. "Is she always so catty?"

Sighing deeply he nodded. "All the time," he admitted. "Makes for a very scary successful lawyer."

His wife shook his head. "What a witch," she murmured.

Catamaran laughed. "I was thinking of another word, but it rhymes." His companions laughed with him and raised their glasses in a silent toast.

Ms. Brown rolled her eyes the instant she turned her back to the table. Great. Now she had to go console the little tramp Deveraux had brought to the banquet. Maneuvering through the room hastily, she made it to the ladies' rest room. Once inside, she crossed the carpet quickly, one thing on her mind. When she got to the small waiting area she froze in her tracks. Sitting at the vanity table was the little tramp. Sitting next to her was Deveraux. Her mouth dropped, and she could only stare. "What are you doing here?" she demanded, jealousy finally transforming her features, showing her true ugliness.

Around them women drifted, some entering, some exiting, some washing their hands in the row of sinks in front of the stalls, some retouching their makeup at the mirror, all of them interested. Standing from his place on the padded bench next to Sage, Deveraux turned to her, not being able to hide his fury. "Who the hell do you think you are, ragging on my girlfriend?" He wasn't the smooth debonair young lawyer anymore. Now he was Blue. Half of the Blue Cat. One of the reckless twins who had grown up at the Hacienda using the back streets and projects of Blue Bay as their playground. His eyes blazed with the intensity of his anger. "Bitch! Get the fuck out of here!" Some of the women present gasped, the others nodded with satisfaction. Maureen Brown had a reputation for being a difficult woman, someone to be careful of.

"I... I didn't know she was your girlfriend," she stammered.

"Regardless, Sage is a woman just like you, bitch! Fucking do unto others as you would have them fucking do to you." Deveraux was furious, cruel in his rampage. "Sage is my chosen date and she deserves your respect!"

Sage laughed, making all eyes turn towards her. "It's okay, Blue," she said softly, her eyes glittering like blue ice. "I'm just wishing a mother fucker would." Her mouth twisted at the corner as she saw Maureen's own mouth hang open in shock.

Blue shook his head and chuckled for a moment, his eyes filled with pride for his girl. Then he remembered Maureen Brown. He started towards her. "Get out!" he growled. He took another step towards her. "Get the fuck out!" he repeated, shaking with anger. He advanced on her.

Backing away hastily, the woman retreated. She really believed he was capable of hurting her. A moment later she was back at the table, visibly shaken. Maureen had always had a thing for Deveraux and had pursued him relentlessly. Now she was more excited than ever at the unspoken challenge she felt he had presented her with. But she was also fueled by fury and indignation. Sitting down, she gasped with outrage. "Your lawyer," she informed the boss, not being able to disguise her anger, "Deveraux St. Jacques is in the ladies' room consoling his date!"

On a hunch, Catamaran grinned. "You mean his girlfriend."

"Whatever!" she snapped at him.

"Oh, for crying out loud!" exclaimed Mrs. Wilkerson. "I will go see what's going on."

Her husband jumped to his feet to pull back her chair for her. "Thank you, darling, why don't you go and do that for us." Sitting back down, he began an earnest conversation with Catamaran, ignoring Maureen Brown, adding to her temper.

Mrs. Wilkerson entered the rest room and immediately found the couple. "Don't mind me," she assured them. "I just came over because that witch said you were here, Deveraux," she told him.

"I just kicked that bitch out of here, Mrs. Wilkerson," he smiled apologetically. "She has no business being rude and mean to Sage."

"I agree." The older woman sat in an arm chair next to them, crossing her legs and making herself comfortable. "Maureen Brown has been pursuing you for a while, I understand. Borderline sexual harassment."

"That is *her* problem, ma'am," he answered. Then he turned back to his girl. "Sage, I'm really sorry about this, baby. I knew she was a bitch, but I never dreamed she would turn on you like that."

Sage's blue eyes sparkled like diamonds from her unshed tears. "I can take care of myself, Blue. It's just that this isn't my scene, and she is so vicious!"

"It's not my scene either," he chuckled, cradling her face in his hands gently. "I couldn't do this without you. We can leave if you want," he offered.

Sage stared at him aghast. "And leave Cat alone with that woman? You are kidding!"

Blue grinned. "It's what she deserves."

She giggled at the thought. Catamaran would shred the woman with no one around to censor him. She sighed. "I just feel out of place. Like I'm not me."

Deveraux nodded thoughtfully. "Well, you don't look like you," he conceded. "Quite different, in fact. What happened to the girl I know?" he crooned.

"I didn't want to embarrass you," she admitted, a tear escaping down her face. "I didn't want to shock your boss or your associates."

Mrs. Wilkerson waved a hand in the air dismissing the thought. "Oh, darling, nothing shocks Mr. Wilkerson, trust me, I am married to the man." She laughed softly at the preposterous idea.

"Well, my associates aren't shocked, but they are a little bit disappointed," Deveraux admitted. "You look nothing like the picture I showed them on my cell phone."

"Like I said," Sage muttered, brushing away at another tear as it rolled down her face.

"But they liked the picture!" he exclaimed.

"Let me see," Mrs. Wilkerson motioned at him to hand over his cell phone. Taking it from him she stared at the picture for a moment. "Why there's nothing wrong with you, Sage, you are just a

Goth girl." She smiled, flipping the phone shut and handing it back. "No wonder the boys are disappointed, if they've seen this picture. I would love to see the real you, darling."

"Me too," Deveraux agreed. "Now, let's see what you have here in this purse," he said. He looked pointedly at the clutch in her hands with the handcuffs attached. Taking it from her gently he opened it and emptied its contents on the vanity table. Dispersing the articles, he quickly got to work. "Look at me," he commanded. Reaching for a wand of mascara he opened it and swiftly and expertly began applying an extra coat on her lashes. Amused, he smiled at the raised eyebrows around him. "My aunt, who's more like my sister, runs a dance studio," he explained to Mrs. Wilkerson, answering her unspoken question. "Her name is Rain."

The woman instantly perked up with interest. "Rain Dance is your relative's?"

"Yes, ma'am," he drawled, reaching for some black eyeliner. "When Cat and I were in high school she had us work at the studio, making up the dancers for her presentations. We always got a kick out of it. It's incredible to be able to see the change in someone as they morph into a different person. Not only do their faces change, but their posture and their whole attitude. It's as if you create a whole new being." In a moment he had transformed Sage's eyes. Frowning he stared at the lip gloss Sage had brought. Then he smiled, reaching into the inner pocket of his tuxedo. "I bought this for you," he admitted, producing a brand new tube of lipstick. "I wanted to try it out."

Sage was just as surprised as the older woman accompanying them. Her eyes twinkled now with amusement. "Lipstick, Blue?"

He shrugged, shameless. "Sure. It's supposed to be non-transferable." Taking her chin in his hand he wiped off the gloss with a tissue from the ornamental box sitting on the table. Then he lifted her face, parting her lips as he expertly applied the new product. The new shade was rich and dark, more her style. He nodded, pleased with himself. "For the finishing touch..." Without any warning, he slipped off her headband, allowing her hair to fall over her face. Slipping his fingers inside it he mussed it up a bit, as a professional hairstylist would, until he liked the effect. Then he took off her jacket, exposing the bright colors on her arm. Grabbing a handful of black rubber bracelets from the pile in front of him he slipped them on her arm. Reaching into his pocket again, he came out with a black leather wrist band adorned with three rows of pyramid shaped studs. "I got you this too," he admitted, putting it on. "It turns me on," he confessed in a whisper, winking at her. Pleased with the end result, he turned her shoulders so she could look at her reflection in the mirror. "There's my girl," he announced. "This is the lady I asked to come with me."

Mrs. Wilkerson stared at the transformation. "Why, Sage, you look stunning, darling."

Sage smiled at the older woman. "Thank you," she said shyly.

"Now let's try out that lipstick," Blue announced. Without warning he took her face between his hands and pressed his lips against hers.

Sage's heart beat faster, responding to his kiss. Reluctantly they parted, staring at their reflections in the mirror. The color remained on her, but none had passed to him. "Non-transferable," she murmured.

"It's true," he agreed, his green eyes laughing.

"My turn," Mrs. Wilkerson announced softly. Standing up she waved at Sage to trade places with her. Sage laughed at Blue in the mirror and obeyed. The woman pulled out her own wand of mascara and eyeliner from her own purse and sat quietly as he applied it for her. She was adamant on trying the new color however. So she produced some wipes for hygiene, and swabbed at the lipstick before he applied it, and again after he did. Smiling gratefully, she handed the tube back to Sage who made it disappear. "My hair, please, Blue," she urged. Marveling at her reflection in the mirror, she watched as he expertly took it down. Asking her permission, he took off a jeweled broach from her dress and put it in her hair. The effect was breathtaking. With the change in makeup, the darker lipstick and the jewels in the tresses that fell softly around her face, the woman looked years younger. "Now, that is something," she breathed, amazed at the vision in the mirror. Then a naughty look crossed her face. "Non-transferable, huh?" She raised an eyebrow at Sage in the mirror. "May I?" she murmured. She sighed happily as the girl waved a hand at her.

Blue shook his head. "Ladies, you are killing me." Taking the older woman's face between his hands, he gazed at her with a smile. Then he pressed his lips against hers.

In the background they heard Sage giggle as the woman closed her eyes and responded to the handsome young black man. "Mrs. Wilkerson," she called out softly, "now you're just making out with my date."

Pulling back, the woman smiled gratefully at the couple. "I am, I know. That's quite alright, darling, when we get to the table you can make out with mine." Laughing, the trio left the bathroom.

The women reached the table arm in arm, giggling like school-girls. They had just become each other's brand new best friend. They smiled, basking in the men's admiration and Maureen Brown's consternation. "We're back," Deveraux announced unnecessarily, rolling his eyes with amusement behind the females' backs.

Cat laughed happily. "There you are, Sage, I wondered what had happened to you!" Turning to the older woman he let out a low wolf whistle. "And look at you..."

Mr. Wilkerson stared at his wife. His eyes roved over her hungrily. "You've been busy," he murmured, his mind racing with thoughts of how soon he could get her home. Something moved way deep inside him. She looked hot. Sexy like he hadn't thought of her in longer than he cared to remember. He licked his lips, at a loss for something to say. "New color?" he finally asked.

His wife sat down next to him and nodded, looking deep into his eyes. "You should try it out."

"Try it out?" he repeated, not sure of what she was saying.

Mrs. Wilkerson nodded again. "Show him, Sage, darling."

"I would love to," Sage murmured. Leaning down, she turned the older man's face towards her. That he was confused was an understatement. Smiling, she looked deep into his eyes, willing him to relax. Then she pressed her lips against his.

Mr. Wilkerson quickly went from shock to responsive, kissing her back. When she finally pulled back, he turned to his wife, deep emotion in his eyes. "Why, thank you, darlings," he expressed from the heart. "Both of you."

"You're welcome, sir," Sage smiled at him.

"Don't I get a kiss?" Catamaran protested.

"Not a chance," his twin growled at him.

"The lipstick is non-transferable," Mrs. Wilkerson answered her husband's unspoken question.

"Really?" he exclaimed playfully. "Let's try it again, then." And he kissed his wife. Coming up for air, he grinned. "Let me see your mirror." Playing along, his wife produced it for him. "Why, it is!" Giving it back to her, he straightened himself and stood up, pulling her with him. "If you will excuse me, boys," he laughed, "Sage," he nodded at her, purposefully ignoring Maureen Brown. "I need to go home and see for myself where else that lipstick is non-transferable," he explained, eyes twinkling with amusement. "I have a sudden urge to make love to my wife," he announced shamelessly, with the exuberance of a sexy teenager with a beautiful girl, on a mission

Mrs. Wilkerson laughed happily. Reaching into her purse she pulled out a pen and an expensive card with just her name in a beautiful script in raised shiny letters. She scribbled on the back and handed it over to the Goth girl. "Call me, girlfriend," she smiled, winking at her.

"I will," Sage laughed.

"Have a good night, darling," the older woman said, pulling her into her arms for a hug and a kiss. Then she blew a kiss at the twins. "Good-night, boys, enjoy yourselves." And the Wilkersons were gone.

The twins looked at each other. Something passed in their eyes. Deveraux grinned. "Out of here!" he exclaimed softly.

Catamaran laughed. "Done!" Scraping their chairs back, they jumped to their feet, helping Sage up between them.

Maureen Brown flew to hers, swiftly grabbing her purse off the table. "I'll walk with you out to the parking lot. I think it's kind of dark where my car is parked." Pretending not to see the grimaces of disgust on the twins' faces, she joined them as they left. Outside, she waited impatiently as the men embraced and parted ways. Deveraux threw his arm around Sage's shoulders and disappeared into the shadows, reappearing again in the pool of a streetlight. She turned to Catamaran. "Would you please walk me to my car?"

Catamaran grinned. She had no idea who she was messing with. "Why, of course." Ever the gentleman, he escorted to her vehicle, taking her keys and opening it for her. He let his eyes slide all over her legs and curves as she seated herself and sighed to himself. What a waste. Such a pretty package, and such deadly poison inside. He let himself be caught appraising her, looking at her as if he were actually interested, and smiled when her eyes met his. The bitch was actually smirking. He had to bite back a laugh. She took her time putting her legs inside her car, making a show of rearranging her dress, letting her fingers linger on her thighs. Meeting his eyes, she licked her lips. Catamaran laughed to himself. Slowly, he bent over until they were eye level. Licking his own lips, he noticed hers part, breathless. He brought his face closer until their breaths mingled. Her eyes closed. "Sorry, darling," he informed her, his voice low and sexy. "I would kiss you, but I don't know where your filthy mouth has been, or what it's been doing." With a smirk of his own he slammed the door on her face and turned his back, walking away. Behind him he heard her screech, the muffled sounds of her banging her fists on the steering wheel filling the silence. Catamaran laughed.

I am in awe of the chain of events that have led me to visit the pirate haven --- oops, sorry --- I mean island, of Encantada. The Gaitanos are a very powerful family of two generations of pirates. The older brothers paved the way and are leaving a legacy. The younger generation learned the trade and made a name and a living for themselves in their local waters and a little beyond. They are amazing honorable men with good hearts and a lot of power. Carlitos actually owns Encantada!

It's been crazy, man, and quite overwhelming. My mind is racing a thousand miles a minute right now and I can't even think about it anymore. I'll tell you all about it in person, okay?

Rashawn

I have never dreamed of anything like this. Dude, you should come. Encantada is the real thing. I don't even know where to begin. The place is beautiful, the people are real, the pirates are amazing. And I made a friend. Juan Gaitano. He had to stay in Encantada and take care of some business first, but I sure hope he makes it to Blue Bay on the next storm. Wait till you meet this guy, Shane, you're really going to like him.

Jamal

I still can't fucking believe this! Carlitos may be Marina's husband, but the guy's a brat! Can't wait to get him on my turf!

Cat

I got a baby! His name is Cacique! God has been good to me!

Jesse

I have never had a more interesting task than that of being the bridge between Encantada and Blue Bay. The encounter between Carlitos and Gato is neverending, to say the least. They are as stubborn as young bulls. Snake got himself a baby. Marina adores him, they are very close. Jamal and my younger brother hit it off as if they had known each other their whole lives. I expect that friendship will continue and grow. Rashawn was an amazing force at stabilizing the situation between his friends and my sons and their crew. His unconditional acceptance of the situation and my boys has earned him the trust of the pirates. The visitors were a thing of beauty to observe. But the truth is that it has been a wonderful experience to see my world through their eyes. Even better than that is the satisfaction of achieving the mission commended me by my friends, Pablo Aguilar and Joe Banks. I brought their children back to them, and that makes me feel really good.

Carlos Gaitano y Mendoza, Pirata

Shane Butler sighed. He had asked his friends for an account of their thoughts and impressions and this is what he got. Pushing his glasses back on his nose he quickly scanned the paper that Jamal put in his hands when they got back. Obviously they had been overwhelmed so that they couldn't even express themselves. Now they were all going to want to tell him in person. A smile dawned on his face. Encantada must be a hell of a place. Sighing again he shook his head. He would have to go next time.

"Marina!"

"Sage!"

"Is your pirate there with you?"

"Yeah, he sure is."

"Are you naked?"

"No, we're dressed."

"Okay," she called out, imitating perfectly the sing-song tone of a disappointed child. She grinned when Marina giggled. Then her voice came clear, low and wicked. "May I come up?"

"Absolutely. Let me call the dogs." Marina let go of the intercom switched and sent Sage the elevator. She called for the pirate and then called the rottweilers. By the time the elevator was back with Sage on board the four of them, Marina, Gaitano, Samson and Dalilah, were expectantly waiting for her.

Sage laughed, stepping out, her arms full. She freed a hand to approach the rottweilers and greet them first. "Hello, Samson. Hey, Dalilah," she crooned to them, petting them one at a time. The dogs were as familiar with those who worked in the building as they were with the people who lived in it. Relishing her attention, they rolled their heads against the palm of her hand, nuzzling her, letting themselves be scratched behind the ears. "How are you guys doing?"

Marina laughed at her friend. "Hey, Sage, what you got there, mami?"

Sage laughed back. "I brought gifts for the pirate."

It was Gaitano's turn to laugh. "Gifts for the pirate, huh?" He approached her, burning with curiosity. "Let us see these gifts." Taking the bags she held out to him, he set them to one side wondering at what she kept.

Sage drew out the suspense for a moment, waving her hand over a box in her arms. The box seemed to be getting scratched from the inside, as if a live thing were stumbling around in the dark. And then they heard it. A pitiful mew. Sage giggled. "Your baby cat, Captain." Reaching inside the box, she drew out what seemed to be a ball of black fur.

"A baby cat," Marina murmured with a smile, wishing she had a camera. Her husband's face was priceless. His face had transformed into the most angelic smile as he reached for the black ball of fluff now facing him. It had a pair of glowing green eyes, much like the twins'.

The pirate echoed her sentiment. "A baby cat," he breathed, cradling the kitten against his chest. He turned to Sage. "Boy or girl?"

"Boy."

He nodded. "Good. We'll make him a pirate cat."

Sage smiled. "I brought you everything you need to get started. Cat litter and its box, food, a couple of toys, collar and flea collar, and a couple of books on cats and kittens. Shots have been taken care of. All you have to do is get him fixed when he's a little older." She waved a hand at the bag and backed away, her face reflecting the happiness she felt at having surprised and pleased him.

"Good deal, Sage," Marina thanked her. "This is going to be awesome with a kitten around, as long as he doesn't end up fishing," she giggled herself, just thinking of the number of fish tanks around her home.

The Goth girl shrugged. "Just teach him not to." She motioned at the bags again. "There's a spray bottle in there..."

Marina laughed. "You thought of everything!"

"Think of it as a starter kit."

"We appreciate it, Sage. I thank you for my animal," the pirate barely glanced at her, enraptured with the kitten in his hands.

"Thanks again," Marina assured her.

"You are welcome, guys. By the way, his parents are big, so..." And laughing, she was gone.

"Jackson!"

"Hey, Dad! How's it going?" Jackson stopped in his tracks. Doubling back he dragged Storm along with him, his arm hooked around her neck. He was aware of being a little overprotective of her, but he had another reason beyond the obvious. Storm was hot. She turned heads. Especially, those of his friends. So he wasn't letting go. They were strolling by in front of their building, catching the fresh evening breeze. The day had been warm, a harbinger of the heat to come. The kind of day where you are torn between hitting the beach or staying inside and cranking up the air conditioner, power bill be damned. They had done a little of both after the pirates' daily lessons with the Butler boys at the Hacienda. Now it was their turn to hang, but it looked as if the *viejos* wanted a word with them first. Frowning he took in the expression on his father's face. Joe looked worried. "What's up?"

Joe forced a smile. "You got a minute, son?"

"All the time in the world for you, Dad. What's up?" he asked again. He looked suspiciously from his dad to Pablo.

Pablo sighed. "There's something we need to talk to you about." He frowned for a moment, looking beyond Jackson to the big screen looming behind him. "Something we've been meaning to discuss with you."

Jackson nodded. "It sounds serious."

Both men nodded. "It is."

Impatiently Jackson turned to the older pirate accompanying his dads. "You know anything about this?"

Don Carlos nodded. "I do."

Jackson felt his patience coming to an end. "Anybody going to go ahead and tell me what it is?"

"How about if we just show you, boo?" Putting his hands on Jackson's shoulders, Joe gently turned his son around and his girlfriend with him.

Above and in front of them, images flickered on the big screen with a new slide show. Jackson stared. They were dark, but the flash of the camera had caught its subject quite clearly. Words faded in, identifying the subject as ***"Peeping Tom"***. He recognized the rooftop of his building immediately, the skylights unmistakable. They all used the hell out of the roof. The subject had been photographed frozen like a deer caught in headlights. Then there seemed to be a flurry of activity captured in freeze frames, as if the camera were trying to keep up. Startled, the young man caught seemed to go pale as if he had just heard the sound of his name. Shadowy figures in the background, their faces unrecognizable, seemed to surround him. And then there were the resident rottweilers. The young man's expression filled with panic, and suddenly only his back could be seen as he bolted. The camera caught him executing a practiced escape over the railing of the fire escape and followed him in his headlong flight down the stairs. Finally, a frantic dive into the dumpster, with only the bottom of his sneakers visible. The last pictures were of him crawling out and limping away down the street. It had all been captured by Caribe.

A muscle twitched next to Jackson's clenched jaw. "When did this happen?" he asked, voice low with suppressed anger.

"While you were away, obviously." Joe sighed. "We are not sure how long he'd been going up to the rooftop."

"*La nena*," Pablo explained slowly, referring to Xaira, "expressed to Caribe that she felt she was being watched."

"Todd's been stalking her?" Jackson asked, startled.

"Probably not her specifically," Joe soothed him, "but certainly the apartment." His eyes narrowed at the thought. "We found evidence of him having been at all the skylights. The one over the living room and the ones at each bedroom."

Jackson swore under his breath, making Storm rub his back automatically in an attempt to soothe him. "I am going to kill him," he announced softly.

"There won't be any need," Joe told him. "He is going to die when he finds out about this creative slide-show"

"I suppose he hasn't been back."

"Of course not," Pablo laughed. "But it doesn't matter. We have evidence that he's been there." He gestured at the big screen shuffling through the images again. "Obviously."

"Jackson," Don Carlos rumbled softly. "Do not get in trouble because of this person."

Jackson just shook his head. "I'll have to see him sometime," he muttered. And dragging Storm behind him once more he stalked off, his mind black with his thoughts.

"Baby!"

Startled, the bouncer called Baby turned around at the sound of his name. Delighted, he opened his arms to embrace the girl that had called it. "Hey, Salomé, how you doing, baby?" He squeezed her tight for a moment, kissing her on the cheek. "You've been gone," he told her.

Salomé glanced over his shoulder and grinned. "Incoming!"

"Marina?"

She laughed. "Yeah!"

Baby closed his eyes tight and took a deep breath bracing himself. "Let her come---"

"Baby!" Marina flew through the air and jumped on his back.

Stepping back from Salomé, the bouncer hooked his beefy arms over the legs wrapped around his torso. Then he began spinning in place like a dust devil, to the delight of the people around them and the girl on his back. *"Who is this attacking me?"* he roared. *"Let me go, fiend!"*

Marina squealed, hanging on tighter lest she fall. "It is I, Marina, of the long curly hair," she gasped, her eyes sparkling with tears of laughter.

Slowing down, Baby finally came to a stop. Letting her slide off him, he turned around to face her. As always, Marina dissolved into giggles, falling into his arms helpless with laughter. He hugged her tight and kissed her face. Then he pretended to ravage her, making her squeal once more. Finally he set her away from him, the look in his eyes one of tenderness and respect. "Missed you, baby, where've you been?" he asked her.

Marina wiped at the tears of laughter from her face and smiled back with the same expression on her face. "Been away, Baby, to foreign lands. Sailed the high seas in search of adventure and found myself a pirate." Reaching behind her, she took Gaitano by the hand and made him step forward. "He kidnapped me and kept me prisoner for a while, and then I made him marry me to keep my honor." She gasped with laughter once again.

"A *pirate*?" Baby murmured, raising his eyebrows with interest. He turned to look. The men measured each other. Opposite as day and night, they were both large in their own distinctive way. Both were tall, but their mass was different. The pirate was lean but strong, his shoulders broad and his thighs muscular. Dressed in modern clothes he looked like a male model. Jeans, white sneakers and a black polo shirt which made his features stand out. His bright blue eyes gleamed in his tanned face, his curly hair black and hanging over his neck, he was very handsome. Baby on the other hand, was built like a tank. He was black, his hair cut close to his head like a helmet. His eyes were twinkling at the moment, but they had the capacity of chilling one to the bone if he so desired. People mistook his girth for fat, not realizing he was all muscle in spite of his size, solid like a rock. He was one of the bouncers, much loved and respected by the happy patrons at the *Blue Cat*, Catamaran's nightclub. Tame as a pussy cat, he was still a force to reckon with. Studying Gaitano closely, he held out his hand slowly. Catamaran had filled him in with who the pirate was in terms of the Aguilar-Banks, leaving out the obvious time travel part of it. He knew that this particular pirate was the leader of his crew, and that they were new in town, sailors and historians relocating to a new place. Marina had met him on Spring Break and they had gone headfirst into a whirlwind courtship, falling in love desperately, and ending up marrying. He glanced at Marina. She looked relaxed and beautiful. They made an awesome couple. There were going to be some gorgeous babies in this family, that was for sure. Finally he pretended to bat his eyelashes at the pirate. "My, my, aren't you a big handsome fellow?" he drawled.

The crew of La Gitana snickered, amused at this new character. They knew about Baby also, how he loved to play and make people laugh, having learned about him in one of the lessons from the Butler boys over the people that would be prominent in their new lives. This was the first time they were at the *Blue Cat*, and they were impressed, although they kept still. It was Friday night and the line in front seemed to want to wrap around the block. The people standing patiently were cheerful and hopeful, dressed to kill, out on the prowl. The mood was light and happy and expectant, since obviously they were not all going to be allowed in. The club front was dark, the huge plate glass windows tinted with mirrored paper, so all that was visible was their reflections. On the inside however, you could look out on the street in anonymity. The sign was done in tones of turquoises and blues, the logo consisting of the head of a tiger, its mouth open in a silent growl, its stripes glowing with the beautiful neon light. Up above it was the name, *The Blue Cat*, in a flowing script in matching blue neon. Leading to the front door was not a red carpet, but one in the deepest indigo imaginable, adding to the style of the establishment. Now Marina, Salomé and Jackson stood with the pirates, waiting to get in. Gaitano smiled at the bouncer, having heard all about him already. He held out his hand. "Carlos Gaitano, at your service."

"At my service!" Baby crowed, shaking his hand, his eyes all but dancing now, including the pirate in the game. He turned to Marina. "You've taught your man well, child." He looked back at Gaitano. "At my service," he clucked his tongue in apparent delight. Taking the navy blue velvet rope off its hook, he ushered them in, quickly being introduced to the rest of the crew and the lady pyrates accompanying them. As Gaitano moved past, he winked at him and held his hand next to his face, thumb and pinky extended in the universal gesture of a phone. "Call me," he mouthed at the pirate, to the delight of his companions. The pirates snickered once more and made their way inside.

As nightclubs go, this one was really nice. The best part was that it was divided into different areas, the better to cater to the different tastes of their customers. Right inside was a bank of public phones, not a common sight in these cellular times, but much respected and appreciated nevertheless. Especially by the parents of the younger crowd, since these gave their children no excuse to not call home and check in, or ask to be picked up if they couldn't drive for whatever reason. There was a small dining area with a very selective menu, where people frequented, mostly young professionals from all areas. A dance hall to one side specialized in music that made people hot and feel sexy, providing them with a place where they could dance until they had lost a few pounds and some inhibitions. It was very popular with everyone. Then a few steps led down to the heart of things. *Trópico*. The bar was large and prominent in the place, all but invisible for all the people sitting at it, and the others standing around it, two and three deep. It was mostly made of glass blocks, the stools modern in chrome and black leather, swivel with arm rests. Coveted by the patrons, they were all full now. Behind the bar was a huge mirror on the wall which made the whole place seem even grander than it was. Attached to it were floating glass shelves displaying liquor bottles of what they had available, and an assortment of beers, domestic and imported. These were highlighted by pin lights from the high ceiling, making it all eye candy. Over the center of the mirror hung a Puerto Rican flag, glowing from back light. The bar itself was spotlighted subtly, making the different stations stand out. There were three of them, one on each side and one in the middle, with their own computer and sink. One of them was a major service bar, used specifically by the waiters and runners. To one side was a large area used by the bussers with its own cart for the tubs and its own sink. At the moment however, there were only two bartenders, one of the terminals lit but silent. To the sides were small clusters of tables, also full, which they navigated through to get to the bar.

The male bartender looked up, his face showing relief as he spied them. "Marina!" Quickly serving the people right in front of him, he gestured her over.

"Hey, Brian! What's up, man? Looks like a full house tonight," she smiled at him. He was her employee. As General Manager and Head Bartender of Trópico, she made sure to know well everyone working for her, and Brian was by far her favorite. Responsible and hard working, he had never let her down yet. The young man was looking a little frazzled at the moment, though, his blond hair a little messy, his blue eyes clouded with worry, even as they raked the bar, sharp as an eagle's.

"It is, and Ty's out sick," he informed her, referring to the missing bartender.

"Oh, no," Marina moaned. "Is he okay?"

"Running a fever, he couldn't make it. I took the liberty and told him to stay home so he could make it in tomorrow, but look at this place!" He waved a hand, indicating the crowd. "We haven't been this packed on a Friday in a really long time."

Marina nodded, looking around her. "School's almost over. Summer's here. This is what it's going to be like from now on."

"Well, I wasn't ready," he confessed, "I'm really sorry. I need help, Marina! Please come in."

"Awww," she groaned, "I just came in to relax with my crew!" She hurriedly introduced him to her people. "This is Brian. He works for me. Best bartender in the house."

"After you," he grinned, relaxing as he shook hands with the pirates.

"Aye," she agreed softly. Then she turned to her husband apologetically. "He needs my help, Gaitano," she said, making him lean over so he could hear her better over the music that seemed to throb throughout the place.

The pirate grinned. "Then you have to. I'll go sit down somewhere and sight-see."

Marina grinned back. "Behave, pirate, or I'll make you walk the plank!"

Smiling, he stole a kiss and nodded towards the bar. "I'll be around," he reassured her teasingly.

"You better!" she shot back. Sighing, she went around the bar and took her place. Reaching under her station Marina pulled out a black apron she quickly tied around her waist, covering a nice short skirt. Next she took a headset and slipped it on. It connected her to a hidden room where the security cameras that monitored the establishment were. In that room were Catamaran and Raj, Khan's brother who happened to be the main bouncer. Turning on the headset, she took a deep breath and smiled. "Honey, I'm ho-ome." In her head, she could see the grins to match the voices.

"Welcome back, Marina," Catamaran rumbled gently.

"Missed you, baby!" Raj called out.

"Missed *you*, baby!" Marina replied. "Love you both," she told them, the truth evident in her soft musical voice. "Cat, Raj," she blew them each a kiss and got one from each of them back. Taking a deep breath and smiling, she got to work.

It was like riding a bicycle. You never forget. It all came back to her in waves. Marina eased herself into the familiar rhythms of bartending. Serve. Talk. Charge. Give change. Talk some more. Smile. Serve someone else. Laugh. Wipe. Accept tip. Smile wider. Talk to someone else. Laugh harder. Wipe again. Serve still someone else. Make a joke. Wink in conspiracy. Flatter someone. Laugh again. Todd Lowell. She froze. Her senses shut down with an echoing slam. Her body went cold and her heart squeezed in her chest as she took a deep breath, controlling it with sheer will. Marina felt herself invaded by her own darkness. Todd. Todd *Hijo de Puta* Lowell.

Todd smirked. Coming to the *Blue Cat* had been a whim on his part. Strolling into *Trópico* would have been an act of pure genius, had it not been a stroke of sheer luck. It had taken him forever to reach the bar, having been hailed left and right by friends and strangers alike. Few called him by his name, however. For the most part it had been Tom or Peep. It took him the whole way to the bar to finally get the whole story. He had been featured in a Captured by Caribe slide-show on the big screen at Front Street in front of the Aguilar-Banks' building. Of course it was all his fault, he had gotten too cocky and never thought he'd get caught. But the beauty of it was that nobody, at least none of the people that approached him, realized that it had happened for real. That he had actually been busted on that rooftop by the fathers of the Aguilar-Banks and the Butler men. Instead they believed that he had been contracted as a model to pose for that ridiculous story, even laughing to his face about the picture of him fleeing from the loosened rottweilers. This of course was to his advantage, because it would be a while before the truth came out. For the moment, he would just laugh along with everybody else.

Except Marina. She wasn't laughing now. He was. "Hey, sweetheart, long time no see. So glad you made it back safely."

Marina stared. Her body started humming, and a buzz began in her head. Surely her eyes were deceiving her. No way Todd Fucking Lowell was sitting in front of her, smirking and disrespecting her to her own face. Reaching deep inside her Marina found her happy place and caught herself. She inhaled through her nose quietly and blew it out softly. He was. Todd Rest In Peace Lowell. Marina was going to kill him. She glared at him. "Fuck you," she managed to get out.

"Happy to oblige you," he answered. "What time do you get off?" He laughed at his own joke. "Of course that will be later. I meant what time do you get out?"

Outraged, Marina scowled harder. She thought she was going to choke with her own fury. Her voice dripped icicles. "Fuck you," she repeated.

"I would love to," he drawled winking at her. Reaching over the bar he took her hand in his. "Now tell me, Marina, what was it like on that island overnight?"

"Get out," she told him steadily, snatching her hand back and wiping it on her apron.

Todd only shook his head with a laugh. "Sorry, sweetheart, this is a free country. I'm not going anywhere," he informed her, quickly sitting down on the bar stool next to him as the customer occupying it stood up to leave.

"Get... out...," Marina told him slowly, struggling to contain her anger, "of *my* bar..."

"*Your* bar!" he exclaimed, his eyebrows shooting up in delight, his brown eyes just about dancing. Throwing his head back he laughed as if she had just told a clever joke. "I'm a paying customer," he insisted. "Besides, I just want to get together with you after your shift."

"*Cat!*" Marina exclaimed suddenly.

In the control room Catamaran jumped, zooming in on her immediately. She had both hands on the bar as if bracing herself, every bar stool in front of her occupied. "Marina," he called out, his voice husky in her head, for her ears only. "What's wrong, baby?"

"Get him out of my face or I'm jumping over this bar," she growled, not caring what Todd thought about her bizarre behavior.

"On my way, Marina," Raj called out to her, hurrying out of the room and slamming the door behind him in his haste.

"Who is he, Marina?" Cat asked, buying his bouncer some time.

"Todd."

"Yes, sweetheart?" Todd smirked at her.

"Fuck you," she said once again.

Cat's voice soothed in her ear. "Easy, baby, Raj is almost there."

"I will," Todd reassured her, "as soon as you finish in here. I've been waiting a long time."

"You wish," she sneered. "Keep waiting!" Marina clenched her fists. "Get out!"

"Nah," Todd laughed. "I think I'll stay right here and have some fun."

Across the floor the pirates watched with interest from the distance. Their accountant seemed to be getting upset. Solomon became restless. "Who is that?" he demanded.

Jackson turned away from Storm and looked at him. "Who's who?"

"That guy," Indio answered.

Jackson turned to look from one pirate to the other. "What guy?"

"The one at the bar," Giancarlo told him.

Jackson frowned. "The bar is full of guys."

"Who is the one in front of Marina?" Gaitano insisted, getting to his feet. His crew followed.

Jackson joined them and finally saw what they saw. "That's Todd."

The pirates were shocked, having heard the name many times before. "The one who marooned her?" Indio asked. But his brother was already striding across the floor, Jackson hot on his heels.

"Get out!" Marina hissed at him, so focused that she didn't see the cavalry until they were all over him.

"Todd!" Stepping in front of Carlos, Jackson slammed his hands down on his shoulders and yanked him off the bar stool by his shirt. "I've been looking for you, man!" He laughed, spinning him round to face him. "Imagine meeting you here."

Todd's eyes widened for a split second, fear flashing in their depths before he slit them, masking the sudden emotion. "Jackson!" He also laughed, buying time, the taller boy's hands digging painfully into his shoulders. "You've been away, man!"

"Fuck you," Jackson sneered at him.

"What seems to be the problem, boys?" Raj asked. As his name implied, he was of Mediterranean descent. Born and raised in Blue Bay however, it had been hard for his brothers and himself to come to terms with the stigma of their race, especially after 9/11. His parents had come over from the Middle East as students in their youth. They had met and married, eventually becoming parents of four brothers. The Abdul Shahids' link to the Aguilar-Banks as well as the Blue Cat and Rashawn came from school. Their younger brother Sheik had been Jackson's best friend and Marina's boyfriend in high school. Sheik had lost his life however due to some bad decisions on his part. They still mourned his loss. Khan, now the youngest, dabbled in the underworld and a few illicit activities, but was very smart and cunning about his business. At the moment he was busy moving the pirates' treasures. Officially, however, he was the promoter for the *Blue Cat*. A very successful promoter at that, to the delight of the twins and his own family. Omar, the oldest brother, was the Blue Cat's accountant. He was a whiz at investing, maintaining the twins in a lifestyle most people would die and/or kill for. He was happy in keeping himself anonymous however, just doing his job and staying out of the limelight. Raj, on the other hand, was content working for the Blue Cat in a much more visible capacity. His looks brought in the ladies like moths to a flame. The twins were excellent employers and he was making mad money as head bouncer. He was good at what he did, and he was always busy. Both young men turned to look at him. He realized he looked as menacing as one of the forty thieves. His frame was massive, although not quite as Baby's. His color was a rich caramel, very attractive and not out of place in this beach town.

His hair was black, tight rings curling around his head. His teeth flashed brilliantly white under dark eagle eyes. Extremely handsome, he drew a lot of business. But mostly it was his job to keep the business good, weeding the bad guys out. "Let's take this outside," he suggested, his voice rumbling in his chest.

"Yeah!" Jackson agreed happily. "Let's take this outside." Alternately dragging Todd behind him and pushing him in front of him he made his way through the crowded floor.

People turned and stared as the bouncer and Marina's brother half carried, half shoved the young man between them, the pirates right on their heels. Instead of going out the front however, they detoured down a hallway. At the end there was a big door with one of those signs that spelled EXIT in lit red letters. Outside, they all found themselves in the alley that ran behind the Blue Cat. Gaitano and his crew stood to one side and watched with interest as Jackson slammed the shorter young man into the brick wall.

"Hey!" Todd protested. "Easy, man, what's your problem?"

"What's *my* problem?" Jackson raged at him, grabbing him by the front of his shirt and shaking him. "You miserable son of a bitch! You climb unto my rooftop to look down at my girls and you ask me what *my* problem is?" Letting go of his fury he drew back his fist and punched him in the face. Cocking his fist back once more he did it again. When he raised his hand a third time he was allowed a third punch before he was finally stopped.

Raj stepped between them, Jackson's fist in the palm of his hand, thinking the young man wouldn't be able to stand on his own if he got hit again. "Whoa, Jackson, dude! Take it easy man! What seems to be the trouble here? What did this guy do to you?"

Jackson laughed, short and hard. "You want to know? You really want to know?" he demanded. "This animal stranded my sisters on a deserted island on Spring Break!" He glared at him, fists clenched, breathing heavily.

Raj's eyebrows shot up, not being able to hide his surprise. "So this is the one?" he asked. Being close to Catamaran he was of his confidence. The story of what happened to Marina and Salomé was known to him and his family, although they didn't know as many details as Khan did.

Gaitano and his crew stepped closer. "So you are the one who marooned the girls," he said steadily.

Todd's eyes flew to his for a moment, a laugh escaping him unexpectedly. "*Marooned?* What are you, some kind of pirate?"

The pirates laughed. "Some kind," agreed Gaitano inclining his head.

"Not only did he maroon my sisters, leaving them to their fate, but he has also been stalking them, climbing up on our rooftop and looking down at them through the skylights."

Raj frowned menacingly. "You have been doing that?"

Jackson nodded. "My dads, the Butlers and Caribe busted him. It's all in that slide show in front of our building.

Raj nodded. "I heard about it but haven't seen it yet."

"Todd here got caught." Jackson laughed. "Heard you could smell him even after he was out of sight, once they let the dogs loose." The pirates snickered.

"Scared by the puppies," Indio chuckled.

Todd thought he was going to choke at the memory. "*Puppies?*"

"Who were you stalking, Todd?" Jackson demanded. "Marina? She wasn't home while you were there. Xaira? That's what's gonna get you in jail, asshole, she's a minor!" And he punched him again, this time in the stomach.

Todd doubled over, all the air gone out of him in a whoosh. He turned green and gasped for breath. "Jackson, please..."

"Fuck that!" He stood with his fists clenched, breathing heavily for a moment. "And what the fuck were you thinking of, harassing Marina just now?" he demanded. "She's married!"

"Married?" croaked Todd.

Gaitano laughed. "Yes. To me. The pirate." He lowered his voice and slit his eyes, hiding his own fury. "I trust you will never go near my wife again," he said, laughing once again as Todd managed to shake his head.

"It doesn't matter," Jackson said in disgust. "Fuck this guy. Call Jamal," he told Raj. And there they remained, the pirates, the bouncer and the brother, waiting for the police to come.

"Salomé…"

Salomé turned her head to look at her friend. Storm looked fabulous. Her sun streaked hair hung long and loose in soft beach waves to the middle of her back. Silver hoops hung from her ears and her lioness eyes were bright and alert. Her outfit made her blend in with all the other women in the club. A short purple dress fell to above her knees, the rich color bringing out the warmth of her skin tone. Strappy sandals on her feet felt comfortable, her toenails painted a dark wine color. The rest of her accessories were primitive and tribal. Sultan's lion's claw was centered on her chest, suspended from a leather cord around her neck, and her bracelets consisted of beads, seeds and shells, and leather cords. A coat of mascara on her lashes and a light slick of gloss on her lips completed her look. Salomé smiled, pleased and proud of her brother's girl. "What's up, baby?"

"Where are the boys?"

"They went out back with Todd. I'm sure they've had enough fun with him by now." She looked at Storm carefully. "What's wrong, mami? Is something bothering you?"

Storm shook her head quickly then turned to look at her, the amusement in her eyes creeping into her voice. "Not really. But there's someone here who can't take their eyes off me."

Salomé laughed. "I'm sure a lot of people can't take their eyes off you. You look beautiful!"

Storm laughed with her, pleased because she knew it was true. "Well, this one person seems to be having a problem somehow."

Salomé's eyes widened. "Who?"

Just then the pirates came back in from wherever they had been, Jackson and Raj leading them. At the corner of the bar Raj turned to say something, slapped hands with all of them and went around the bar. Taking Marina in his arms, he held her in a warm hug and whispered in her ear.

"You okay?"

Marina nodded, giggling as he was tickling her as he sneaked a snuggle. I'm okay."

"Okay." Raj gave her a last squeeze, kissed her and disappeared.

Jackson's eyes sought Storm out over the distance until he found her. Their eyes met and held for a moment, their smiles solely meant for one another. As Jackson moved to head towards her he was stopped. Storm clenched her fists and turned to Salomé, who had been watching the whole thing. "Her."

Salomé nodded. The *her* they were talking about was all over her brother, arms thrown around his neck, her body plastered to the front of his. She kept Jackson's back to them at the same time she kept an eye on them. She was a beautiful young black woman around their age. Her hair was tastefully done with extensions that hung below her shoulders. Her face was very pretty in a cold distant way, her makeup perfect, accentuating dark eyes and a full mouth. She was wearing a bright red dress that glowed in the club lights like expensive lipstick. It hugged her fabulous curves, making her stand out among her companions. "That's Stacey. Jackson was going out with her when we ended up in Encantada." She laughed wickedly. "She thinks she's Jackson's girlfriend."

Storm grinned. "I guess she's in for a surprise, huh?"

Salomé shook her head and took her hand, leading her away. "Come on," she said in her ear, struggling to be heard over the music, "let's go to the ladies' room. Give Jackson time to get rid of her." Laughing, they made their way through the crowded floor.

At the corner of the bar Jackson wrapped his hands around the arms around his neck and freed himself. His jaw set and his eyes narrowed. "What are you doing?" he demanded.

"Jackson!" Stacey pouted beautifully, knowing full well the impact it had on the male of the species. To her dismay it wasn't working this time when she needed it the most. Laughing now, she threw her arms around his neck and pressed herself against him once again, her dress sliding over the material of his clothes. "I missed you, baby..."

Jackson reached up again and trapped her wrists in his hands, but this time he waited. He didn't have time to play games with her. "Did you now? You could've fooled me."

Puzzled, Stacey frowned before she caught herself. She had no idea what he was talking about. "What are you talking about baby? I waited for you and you just disappeared."

Jackson licked his lips and nodded, his tiger eyes beginning to sparkle with fury. Stacey's heart skipped a beat. She had seen that look before. "You mean back at the hotel. During Spring Break."

This time she couldn't hide her frown. "Of course I mean during Spring Break. That's the last time I saw you."

Jackson laughed, and breathed deeply, reigning in his impulse. His hands began to squeeze slowly. "You see, last time you saw me and last time I saw you were two separate occasions."

Now she narrowed her eyes at him, her own anger making her eyes glitter to match his. "Last time I saw you, we were going on a picnic."

"Exactly," he said, squeezing until he saw the pain in her eyes. "But the last time I saw you, you were *having* a picnic." Then he squeezed harder, slowly unwrapping her arms from around his neck.

"Jackson," she gasped, stumbling against him as her knees buckled. A wave of nausea swept over her, the pain was so intense.

Thoroughly disgusted now, Jackson squeezed as hard as he dared, just short of shattering the bones of her wrist in his hands, and let go. He watched without any emotion as she gasped again and went to rub her bruised wrists, tears welling in her eyes. Reaching into his back pocket he drew out his cell phone. Pressing a few buttons, his eyes lit up when he found what he was looking for. He looked up and glared at the woman in front of him. "Last time I saw you, you were busy." He licked his lips again and glanced at the screen of the cell phone in his hand. A laugh escaped him and he shrugged. Behind him the pirates laughed with him. "Good thing I went looking for you, otherwise I would've never known." Turning the cell phone around so she could see it, he showed it to her. Her friends crowded around her. Jackson began chuckling as enlightenment filled their faces. There were gasps and laughs. Some covered their mouths, other covered their eyes. Except for Stacey. She couldn't move. And Jackson knew why. On the screen of his cell phone was a picture of Stacey. In bed. With his former buddy. Both had been so enraptured with each other and what they were doing that neither had seen Jackson when he came upon them and got as close as he did, neither heard the sound of the cell phone as its camera clicked the moment into captivity. The man's back was what mostly visible, although his turned face made him identifiable. Stacey had one leg over his shoulder and one wrapped around his waist, her nails digging into his back and her mouth open with her moans. Finally, her eyes met his. Jackson grinned, sliding the cell phone shut and making it disappear again. "I always thought you looked good coming," he told her, glancing at her friends as they giggled. Then he turned back to her, his whole demeanor changing. Satisfied, he saw fear in Stacey's eyes. "I thank you for showing someone else. I am with my soulmate now." Turning away from her in disgust he walked away, the pirates at his heels.

"Hey, Stacey!" Storm's head whipped around at Salomé's words. They were standing at the row of sinks in the ladies' room. The young woman who used to go out with Jackson had just come in and was surveying them in shock. "Haven't seen you in a while, girl, not since Spring Break," she rambled on. "Marina and I kind of got lost and Jackson had to come and rescue us, but this is Storm, Jackson's girlfriend, he met her when he came and got us, it was love at first sight, you know how it is..."

Stacey had stopped listening however, and she couldn't take her eyes off Storm. "So you're the soulmate."

Storm turned to face her taking a step forward. Stacey immediately retreated. The pyrate grinned, even as her eyes glittered with a whole different emotion. "Is that what Jackson called me? That's awesome!" she laughed. "Thanks for telling me." Dismissing her with a nod, she headed towards the door.

Salomé followed, shrugging with a laugh. "They're crazy about each other," she told the other girl as she walked by. Stacey couldn't move. She just stayed staring at the closed door.

Outside, Storm reached Jackson with a smile. "So I hear I'm your soulmate," she told him.

Throwing his arm around her, Jackson laughed. "Now where'd you hear that?" he teased, gazing into her eyes.

"Some girl you were going out with."

"Yeah." He hesitated, searching for the right words. "She messed up. Big time. I got over her. And then I met you." He grinned. "Nice timing, by the way. Wouldn't have come out so well had you planned it."

"Why, thank you." Storm laughed. "Any more former girl-friends I need to worry about?"

Jackson quickly shook his head. "Not one."

Storm searched his eyes and nodded. "Good." Reaching up she pressed her lips against his.

Jackson responded to her kiss. Hugging her briefly he pulled her behind him to the dance floor. "Come on. We're here till Marina finishes her shift." Stars in her eyes, his girlfriend followed.

"Damn you, Marina Aguilar!" Todd raged. He was on a wild rampage, already having trashed half his apartment. *"You fucking bitch!"* Stopping in front of his hallway mirror he looked at himself, breathing heavily. His dark blond hair was standing up on end and his brown eyes were blazing, giving him the appearance of a madman. He had a black eye which hurt like hell, a souvenir from Jackson. So was the bill the bondsman was charging him with for bailing him out. Good thing he had some mad money, thanks to the inheritance he'd received from a spinster aunt last summer. Otherwise he'd be keeping company with an assortment of hookers and winos down at the Blue Bay Police Department's cell right now. He clenched and unclenched his fists rapidly, willing his breathing to slow down. Pressing his lips together he roared inside his head, watching the emotion flash in his eyes. Good. He could control it. He was going to need that con-trol. It had been a harrowing experience in that alley, waiting for the police. Jackson and the men with him acted as if he'd just made their night. He probably had. It turned out to be one big happy party. At his expense. Raj had kept him pinned to the brick wall of the alley

while they had joked and laughed until the cops got there. And then, of all people, the Blackmon men. He knew Rashawn from college. Not him personally, but as Summer's boyfriend. Obviously, Rashawn knew all about him. Or thought he did. Because none of them knew, not really, just what he was capable of. And he was capable of a lot. But right now, he would wait. School was almost over, just a few days away from summer vacation. Then he would have plenty of time. All the time in the world, actually. All the time he needed to get even with that bitch. Marina Aguilar would pay. He would make sure of that.

"Jack."

Jamal frowned. "Jack?" He was aware in a detached sort of way that he was dreaming. He could feel the pillow beneath his head and the light blanket covering him, providing a sense of protection between him and the fan. He could even feel the darkness enveloping him. But he sure as hell heard that. In his mind he was on a stretch of beach. Definitely Encantada. He was alone, walking towards town. The ocean was high, next to him, angry with whitecaps. Driftwood and assorted debris lay scattered along the foamy shoreline. Seagulls stood out starkly against the glowering sky as they called to each other overhead. The salty wind tugged at his clothes. But he wasn't alone. He stopped and turned around slowly, his weight shifting, making him sink a little in the moist sand.

The pirate now in front of him nodded. The wind also whipped at his clothes, wrapping around muscles. The rolled down boots were sandy. His eyes were troubled and there was a few days' growth of beard on his face. The cross on his chest glinted faintly with the opaque sun. "Jack. Five days." And he turned around and walked away.

Jamal took a step towards him, but he couldn't follow. *"Juan!"* He was waking up but he fought it, determined to catch whatever remnants of his dream he could. But all he could see was the back of Juan Gaitano as he walked away. Jamal knew what it was about, he realized what was going on. When he left Encantada he had implored with the pirate to call him if he were in trouble. Well, obviously Juan was in trouble. Which meant Don Miguel was too. Jamal sighed, finally opening his eyes, and looked up at the dark ceiling for a moment. He knew exactly what Juan meant, too. Jack was the person the pirates had left in charge of the time table for the storms that created the time warp. They had come to Blue Bay mostly because they had the freedom to go back to Encantada when they needed to and return to Blue Bay. Rouge's cousin Jack had offered to be the person assigned to the task of facilitator on Encantada's end, trusted with their secret. And five days sounded about right, too. That was when the next storm would be. Early next week. Jamal felt a familiar surge of excitement. He had to go back to Encantada. He smiled in the dark, turning over to sleep a little bit longer. Soon.

The pirates smiled. They loved this new adventure because they were continuously exposed to new things. People, places, experiences, tastes, smells, sights, sensations. It was never ending. And the trip was just awesome. As was this. They found themselves at *Hideaway*, the home of Jesse and Rain Coltrane. The occasion was the new baby, Cacique Coltrane. Just getting there had been exciting itself. The couple lived on the outskirts of town. Right outside Blue Bay the scenery had changed from palm trees and cactuses to forests of pine groves. But closer to the Coltranes' it was just bayou. There were swamps to either side of the small one lane road, winding up the countryside a little way through a tunnel of very old majestic trees. This led to a driveway with another shorter tunnel of trees. At the end of that there was a gate, and you couldn't go any further. There was a beautiful stone wall. Inlaid, were night lights that were just beginning to come on. In the middle of it was a heavy wooden drawbridge suspended from huge thick chains. It was a kind of *expect the unexpected* scenario. On the other side of the wall could be found the only thing that should be there. A moat. A real one. With fish and turtles, and a couple of alligators with their accompanying birds. It was fed by a nearby stream, the water running deep and blue-green before continuing its journey through the forest. The electronic gate a few yards back was there to keep distracted visitors from driving on through when the drawbridge was up. The real one. So on Saturday night there was a caravan of vehicles and assorted motorcycles being driven and ridden by family and friends, waiting for the drawbridge to be lowered so they could cross Hideaway's moat and celebrate the arrival of a baby.

The Hideaway was actually a very nice home. Once you passed the moat you found yourself on what seemed to be a small island in the middle of nowhere. It was like a small forest, the trees almost as old as the bayou they had just gone through to get there. The grounds immediately surrounding the house were lush and green with assorted patches. There were rock gardens with various cacti, right next to flower gardens exploding with color. There was even a patch protected by a ring of boulders with half a dozen fir trees. They had been shaped into snakes. The Coltranes had a fish pond with koi and a lily pond with frogs. A small greenhouse reflected the setting sun's rays sparkling on clear glass. The landscaping was spectacular, and all the more so with the lighting that was softly appearing as daylight faded. It was a gorgeous fortress surrounded by a stone wall that held a moat.

The house itself was mostly made of wood, stone, and glass. Modern with towering ceilings it was simple yet sophisticated. The kitchen was huge as was the living room, facing the front of the house. The one had all the modern appliances a family could want. A beautiful six burner range with ceramic top, and a double oven, perfect for entertaining. Kitchen cabinets framed in stainless steel and inlaid with frosted glass, lit on the inside, displaying their contents as colorful hazy shapes. Black marble countertops like Salomé and Jackson had. Deep double sinks bordered by a ceramic mosaic backsplash with a snake theme. Over that, a window looked over the front lawn with the snake fir trees to the side. There was a modern double door refrigerator and freezer with a bottom drawer for bigger items such as party trays. Like the ones being laid out today with all kinds of food. There was another freezer, this one a chest. There was a dishwasher, a microwave oven, a blender, a toaster, and an old fashioned clock radio. Everything gleamed and sparkled and reflected because it was all made out of stainless steel. An island in the middle sported the same black marble as the kitchen countertops. It had its own smaller sink, and a full preparing station with a sophisticated system of drawers also made of stainless steel. A stunning fifty-gallon fish tank sat at one end, the display breathtaking. A few barstools surrounding it completed the outfit. Up above it, pots and pans hung suspended from the high ceiling on iron bars, subtly lighted. To one side, overlooking a tall sunflower patch through a ceiling to floor plate glass window was an old picnic table with its original benches. It was weathered and worn, faded to a dirty gray color where the knots and whorls in the wood felt like ribs. There was graffiti on the table, along with carvings of initials, names, places, phone numbers, and a couple of choice phrases with some nasty words. The benches held more of the same. Suspended over this was a gorgeous crystal chandelier the couple had bought at an estate sale in the next village over which was just like Blue Bay, only a little bit richer, for now. The floor was made of old weathered stone, as were the walls. Bright red accents turned out to be fire extinguishers, although the modern fortress was equipped with a very modern and sophisticated sprinkler system in case of fire. The couple was not going to let the whole house burn down were there ever to be an accident. The room was wide and spacious, decorated with beautiful plants and dotted with assorted seats where guests could sit and hang out. The contrast of rustic with classic blended with modern was warm and cozy. Behind these rooms was a study where Jesse worked out of. Although his job was that of a tattoo artist, his passion was the recovery of lost or wayward children. It wasn't something that he had to do very often, thank God, but on occasion he got a frantic phone call with a con- tract attached. It held a rustic desk made out of a fallen log. His walls were full of maps and pictures. There was a computer with a gurgling aquarium serving as screen saver. Next to that was a fifty-gallon tank with a boa. The room held files, very advanced electronic equipment and a surveillance system of his home and property. A plasma TV, a stereo, and assorted games occupied a place next to the study, the two areas divided by a brick wall like those in the kitchen. It was a guy's room. What is known as a man cave. Adjoining that room was another one where Rain practiced and prepared for her classes. It was also where they danced as a couple for pleasure. It had a wall of huge picture windows facing a small cascade that fell from the roof, and a view of the forest beyond. The other three walls including the door were all mirrored. They had a lot of fun in that room. It was going to be excellent for the baby. Behind the rooms was a large garage, with capacity for six vehicles. They owned only a couple, however, a shiny black Jeep Renegade they shared to get around, and a black and chrome Harley Davidson that Jesse rode into town. The rest of the garage was filled with tools, a smaller enclosed area with more tanks full of snakes, a couple of jet skis with their trailers, a couple of bicycles, an ATV and surfboards. Their driveway was empty outside, vehicles lined against the inner walls of the moat. The reason was, it boasted a basket. Basketball games at the Hideaway were as notorious as those at the Hacienda. Besides, Jesse and Rain played plenty of one-on-one. It was one of the reasons they got along so well. They had played together since they were going out in high school. It was a habit they couldn't break.

Everyone was spread out on the bottom floor of the house, respectfully keeping out of the upstairs where the bedrooms were found. At the moment the pirates found themselves in the kitchen, completely entranced by the youngest modern age people they had met so far.

The Coltrane gang was impressive to say the least. Change's wife Jill was a beautiful tall redhead, tanned and freckled with laughing green eyes. She was slender but curvy with generous breasts and hips, and at the moment very pregnant. She was wearing black leggings under a comfortable heather gray tunic with a tiny flouncy hem at the end. Beautiful crystal chandelier earrings cascaded from her ears and her long hair fell in loose beach waves around her face. The children all seemed to be marine themed. Their oldest was a son named Ocean. Seventeen, tall and lanky, he had the raven black hair of his Uncle Jesse, and his mother's breathtaking beauty. The next child, Reef, was also a son, this one Change's spitting image in coloring and personality. Fifteen, he was the typical teenage surfer. Thirteen year-old identical twins followed, daughters now. Beautiful redheads, just like their mother, but something in their faces spoke about who their daddy was. They weren't dressed identical, however, their clothes expressing their individuality. They turned to one first, dressed in jeans and a snug black top where graffiti seemed to be spray painted on the fabric in silver and metallic blues. She wore hi-tops and an army of black rubber bracelets on one arm. Her hair was tied back in a loose braid that fell down the middle of her back, drawing attention to the beauty of her face. Silver hoops hung from her ears, sparkling as she moved her head, studying the pirates. This one's name was Seashell. The other twin was completely girly in comparison. This other one also had silver hoops and the rubber bangles, but her hair fell loose around her beautiful face. Instead of jeans and top, she sported a short flowery dress. On her feet, strappy flat sandals instead of hi-tops. Her name was Ariel.

The pirate turned to look at his wife. "I can't make the connection," he admitted softly. He didn't want to seem ignorant, but he couldn't figure out what in the world Ariel had to do with the more marine names of Ocean, Reef, and Seashell.

Marina smiled. "The Little Mermaid."

"The Little Mermaid?" he repeated, puzzled. "From the Hans Christian Anderson story? The statue in Copenhagen?"

Marina shook her head with a soft laugh. "Actually, the Walt Disney movie."

"Aaah, Walt Disney." Enlightened, the pirate looked at the twins. It wasn't hard to get their attention. They couldn't take their eyes off him.

Teasingly, Marina turned to the twins in an effort to distract. "Disney movie marathon at the Hacienda tomorrow morning. Pancake brunch." She leaned towards the twins, lowering her voice as if in conspiracy. "The pirates know nothing about the princesses. What do you say?"

Seashell laughed, her daddy's blue eyes dancing with humor. "I'm in!"

"So am I," Ariel giggled. She had the same eyes.

"I understand that in your family, each child gets to name the following baby. So did Reef name you both, or..." Carlos trailed off as they shook their heads.

"I named Seashell," Ocean told them, standing tall in front of the pirates. He didn't want them to see how in awe he was of them, but wanted to represent himself in the best way possible.

Reef stepped up to stand next to his brother. He hadn't made a sound, the surfer's sandals on his feet contributing to his stealth. The boy was already deeply tanned, even though school wasn't over yet. He hooked his thumbs in the front pockets of his faded jeans. His blue eyes were bright and curious, glowing in his happy face, his smile shy. The bright colors on his Hawaiian shirt were spectacular on him. "I named Ariel. I thought you can't beat a princess mermaid."

"Oh, you can't," agreed Carlos, smiling back at the interesting second son. "A mermaid is special all by herself, but to have her also be a princess," he laughed, making the Coltrane crew grin, "why just imagine the beauty, the wealth, the power..." The pirate let his voice trail off as he watched the children, their imaginations already captured.

Ariel giggled. "Thank you. I feel super special now."

"Not to say," Indio rumbled quietly, "that Seashell isn't special. Think about what that means. The symbol of the ocean..."

"A reef," added Solomon, making all heads turn towards him, "is one of the world's most important ecosystems." He smiled, pleased with himself. He had had many conversations with Marina about issues that were important to her. His had paled in comparison.

"The ocean," sighed Giancarlo, "is the most amazing thing. We come from it. It gives us life. It is mysterious and ever-changing. It comforts us." He smiled as the twin girls silently took hold of their oldest brother's hands.

The pirates all turned to the smallest and youngest Coltrane. This one was also black-haired like Ocean, but looked more like Jesse. He was wearing surf baggies in tones of blue, and a navy blue T-shirt with a cartoon dolphin in front. His feet were also in surfer's sandals. He was five. He grinned. "Hi!"

The pirates smiled. "Hi!" they rumbled back.

"That's our baby till the baby is born," Reef smirked.

"Yeah! And I get to be the baby and you don't," the small one shot back.

"That's S. Kai," Ocean laughed. "The twins named him."

"Sky?" Gaitano asked, frowning. The twins giggled.

"Not Sky," gasped Ariel dissolving into even more giggles.

"S. Kai," offered Seashell, her blue eyes dancing with mischief. "It's Sailor Kai. I named him Sailor," she nodded at her sister, biting back a laugh.

"And I named him Kai," sighed Ariel. "It's Hawaiian for Ocean, and I was in love with Cool at the time."

Still frowning, the pirate turned to her. "Who is Cool?"

"*We are!*" they squealed at the same time, dissolving in giggles once more. It was contagious. The pirates laughed at their Captain.

"Cool is my dad's partner since forever," Ocean explained quickly. "They do everything together. That's why the business and the boat are called the Cool Change. For Dad and his friend. He's Hawaiian." He shrugged.

"Aaah," Gaitano nodded, finally understanding. "So they call you S. Kai?" he asked the little boy.

"Yeah," he nodded. "I like Sailor Kai better, though."

Gaitano nodded solemnly, thinking on the child's words for a moment. "May I call you Sailor Kai?" he finally asked.

Beaming, the little boy nodded. "Please."

"That's what we call him," Marina told her husband softly.

He hardly glanced at her, so caught up with the little boy he could barely look away. "And what have you got there?" he asked, pointing at a small zip-loc bag he held in his hand.

"Bubble gum!" Sailor Kai announced proudly. The boy just looked at him for a moment. He had been listening to the grownups' conversations lately. "You are pirates, right?"

"Right," the pirate answered slowly, not sure of what to expect.

"Have you ever had bubble gum?"

"Never," Gaitano admitted.

"Would you like to try?"

"I would love to. My crew also?"

"Of course." Crossing the floor, Sailor Kai made his way to the picnic table. Climbing on top of it, he sat crossed-legged right under the gorgeous chandelier. Quickly, the pirates followed him, making themselves comfortable on the benches. In a moment Sailor Kai was teaching the crew of La Gitana the joys of bubble gum.

Marina and Salomé looked at each other. Leaving the pirates in a world of bubble gum flavors introduced to them by Sailor Kai, they drifted off. In the kitchen where they found themselves at the moment the females mingled, delighted with the occasion. Salomé joined in, instantly getting lost in them as if she had been there all along. Marina made herself comfortable in her favorite rocking chair in the room and sat watching everything unfold. A moment later the kitchen was empty, but for Rain and María Isabel. She watched quietly as Rain paced quickly back and forth for a moment, her energy enveloping her like a cloak. María Isabel busied herself tossing the plastic cups the women who left had just been using.

Rain smoothed her hands over her wild hair, bringing them down to cover her beautiful face for a moment. When she took them away tears shone in her eyes. "How do you do it, Marisabel?" she demanded quietly. "How do you take this child, that is not your blood, in fact he's nothing of yours, and make him love you? Make it so you are the center of his universe?"

María Isabel threw back her head and laughed, no longer pretending to keep herself occupied, the sound filling the kitchen softy. "Why, Rain, *mi amor*, he has no choice in the matter." She waved a hand as if the whole idea were preposterous. "When Carlos and I ended up with Indio, it took our breaths away. We knew him all his life and had taken care of him before, but all of a sudden he was ours!" She shook her head at the memory. "Let me tell you that when Indio realized what was going on, he was not happy about it." She looked Rain straight in the eye. "And he let us know." She smiled at the memory. "Our saving grace was Carlitos," she shrugged with a twinkle in her eye. "Indio was crazy about him, and we were a package deal so to speak." Stepping forward she took the younger woman's face between her hands. "Rain, Cacique has been Jesse's since before he met you. It will be fine."

"I am loving this child so much already!" Rain muttered fiercely, unconsciously clenching her fists.

"And so this child shall love you," María Isabel assured her, crooning to her as a mother to her child.

Rain relaxed visibly, her tears drying, her back straightening, her chin rising. "I will make him love me."

María Isabel slowly let go of her face with a final caress. She rolled her eyes with a laugh. "You will not have to *make* him love you, *querida*. He will want to, and the truth is he already does." Breathing a deep sigh, the gypsy woman pyrate looked into the young dancer's eyes. "Rain, Cacique is crazy about you, *corazón*, just let him express it in his own way." She nodded as if satisfied in what she saw in the other woman's eyes. "Trust me." She winked at her. "Look at Indio."

Rain snatched a paper towel off the roll next to her and hastily blotted her damp face. She sniffed once and wiped her nose, tossed the paper in the trash and rearranged her clothes. "Cacique is my son," she said softly but clearly, as if gathering strength from the words. "Cacique loves me..." Smiling at the women in her kitchen she turned away and left the room.

María Isabel grinned at Marina. "Rain is in for a mayor blessing, *hija*."

Marina grinned back. "I know." Leaving the comfort of her rocking chair, she went over and hooked her arm through her mother-in-law's, gently guiding her after her aunt. "That is why we are here."

The parents were all in the living room, mingling with some of Jesse's more exotic friends. They were an assorted bunch consisting of a few bikers, a couple of cowboys, a former professor, and an old high school buddy who was now a bounty hunter. This particular man was well over six feet tall, muscled and tanned like a surfer, his bright blue eyes sparkling, his sun streaked hair slicked back in a perfect haircut. His name was Corey James and had been part of the Coltrane brothers' lives for many years now and a constant figure in family affairs. The Coltrane children as well as the Aguilar-Banks had grown up with Corey in their lives.

Outside, a black SUV cruised to a stop. The moat had been raised when the previous caravan of vehicles had arrived. Now the driver of this one was facing an intercom.

"A drawbridge?" the girl next to him squealed.

Rashawn laughed at his girlfriend's expression. He had never brought her here, in fact had never even mentioned the Hideaway to her. And here she was, sitting next to him, waiting to get in. Her silky blond hair glowed with the dashboard lights. She was wearing a short dress in a bold Hawaiian print. The surfer girl personified. She was beautiful. They looked good together, he admitted quietly to himself. "Of course a drawbridge, baby," he teased. "How else do you expect to get to a place called the Hideaway?"

"Who goes there?" a voice demanded from the intercom.

Rashawn turned his head to look at Jesse on the monitor, knowing Jesse could see him just as clearly. "Rashawn and Summer. Let us in, baby, before I blast through that rickety gate of yours!"

Jesse laughed. "Go ahead, make my day!" he challenged. "It's feeding time. There's two of you. Each of my gators gets one!" he laughed.

"Gators?" Summer squealed again.

Rashawn flexed his muscle instinctively, the black material of his T-shirt clinging to him just like his girlfriend was. "It's okay, Summer," he reassured her, looking into her blue eyes and stealing a kiss. "They're just a couple of lizards." Then he grinned. "They've been fed already." The drawbridge was down, so they drove through crossing the moat, his uncle Jamal and his wife Maya right behind them.

Inside, Summer found herself surrounded by the Aguilar-Banks. They had spoken on the phone, but hadn't seen each other yet. Facing Jackson, the tall blonde young woman took a fistful of his T-shirt with both hands. Her face crumpled. Pulling him towards her before throwing herself against him, arms wrapped around his neck, she choked on a sob. Then she began crying softly. Jackson wrapped his arms around her and buried his face in her hair, petting her gently. Storm stepped back and watched quietly from the side. She knew exactly what was going on and her heart went out to Rashawn's girlfriend. Salomé and Marina came around each side of her, stroking her, embracing their brother with their free arms. Summer's voice came out muffled from against Jackson's chest. "I was so scared, Jax!" she wailed. "You were nowhere!"

"Aw, Summer, I'm sorry, baby, we're here now," he reassured her.

"How can we make this up to you?" Salomé asked softly, stroking her best friend's hair.

Summer didn't hesitate. "Come to my office on Monday."

"We'll be there," Marina confirmed. The group stayed silent in their quiet embrace for a few moments longer. Then shaking themselves out of their reverie they stepped back and smiled. Everything was all right again.

Summer turned to look at the lady pyrates. She looked from one to the other before staring openly at the redhead. This one was dressed in a short skirt and sleeveless top. Her hair was loose about her shoulders, making her look even younger. A stunning gold and pearl cross graced her neck and golden hoops with large pearl drops hung from her ears. Her eyes were bright and full of intelligence, at the same time disguising her true nature. As kind and as gentle as she was, she was still a pyrate. "You must be Rouge." She smiled as the other young woman nodded slightly, hiding her surprise. "You have a very commanding presence, I can tell you are a Captain. Besides, Rashawn spoke to me about you. About all of you," she admitted. Then she sighed. "You are very beautiful." She smiled again as she saw Rouge relax. Then she turned to the other young woman. This one was dressed in jeans and tank top. She looked more primitive, not as sophisticated as the other one. Her hair hung in braids around her head. She wore shell earrings and the usual lion's claw around her neck, braided leather cords on her wrists. Her lioness eyes were bright and curious, their almond shape making her look exotic. "You are Storm!" Summer exclaimed happily, embracing the girl impulsively. She smiled into her eyes. "Jackson and Rashawn are inseparable, so that makes you my new best friend forever. I want to know everything about you, so maybe we can get together sometime this week and catch up." Hooking her arm through the other girl's she gave it a squeeze. Then she turned to the Aguilar-Banks. "I am ready to meet the rest of the pirates," she said softly. They grinned.

"Are you sure?" Jackson teased.

"We lost them," Marina informed her happily.

"They are somewhere with Sailor Kai," Salomé explained. She rolled her eyes with a smile. "Bubble gum..."

"Oh..." Summer nodded, indicating she understood.

"I'll go get them," Rashawn offered and he was gone.

Finally, they all converged in the big living room that was the center of the house. Marina looked around her with satisfaction, observing the people in attendance. Jesse and Change's mom Savannah was there, having arrived with Marquez and her sister Scarlet. The Coltrane children had surrounded their grandmother and grandaunt, chattering incessantly, their love for the women shining in their faces. After a little whispering they pushed Reef out in front of them, clearly their spokesperson.

Reef shrugged and faced Marquez dead on. "Marquez, when are you marrying Nana?"

Marquez laughed, gently teasing the children. "As soon as she's free."

Scarlet laughed, pride for her grand nephews and nieces in her eyes. "Well, they know what they want!" Shaking her head back, her beautiful long black hair settled around her shoulders like a cape. At first glance, one ended up staring at the sisters. Being identical twins it was mind boggling to look at them, they were so gorgeous. They were both of average height and curvy, their bodies spectacular for their age. Their hair was still black, only the occasional silver streak betraying them. Big blue eyes that could look into your soul were framed by long lashes. The teeth flashed white in the chiseled face. But like Change's own twins, one looked more laid-back and the other looked girly. The children's grandmother was the one wearing the dress.

Savannah nodded, the same pride in her own eyes. "It's the same thing we want!" Reaching out she squeezed Marquez's hand, gazing into his eyes for a moment. Something flickered deep in their depths. Smiling to herself she let go of his hand. Turning away Marquez heaved a deep quiet sigh. All of a sudden Savannah stepped back startled. She found herself surrounded by pirates. Shoulder to shoulder as they were, she couldn't see past the two generations of sailors. And of course all three women, María Isabel, Rouge, and

Storm, stood by their sides. Something was up. Glancing skyward and sighing theatrically, Savannah narrowed her beautiful blue eyes at them. "I know who you are," she advised them in her throaty drawl. "What do you want?"

The pirates cleared their throats and shuffled for a moment. Don Carlos took a step forward. "With all due respect..." And he was at a loss for words in the presence of such a formidable beautiful modern-day older woman. Marquez and the crew of the Sea Gypsy snickered.

María Isabel rolled her eyes and hid a smile at her husband's new found humility. Smiling at Savannah she also stepped forward. "We were just wondering, since we are new to these parts as you well know," she inclined her head towards her, "how do you decide to give your youngest child such a unique name as Change..." She drifted off at the other woman's reaction.

Savannah threw her head back and laughed, her face transforming suddenly, making her look years younger. Scarlet giggled. Marquez chuckled. "I am sorry, it's just that the joke is on me," she tried to explain, giggling to herself. "*I* did no such thing. I would never name a child *Change*. His name is Archangel," she finally explained with a sigh. "When he was born, I let his older brother hold him and I said, 'His name is Archangel, honey, now do you want to call him Archie or Angel?'" Her eyes twinkled with mischief as she finally grinned at them. "And Jesse said, 'I'm going to call him...'"

"'Change'," the pirates breathed. They smiled at her. "Aye," they murmured and they drifted away.

Marquez laughed and went back to her as Savannah breathed a sigh of relief. Reaching for her hand he locked his fingers with hers for an instant, holding it down low between them, just like when they were teenagers. "Did the pirates scare you?" he asked softly with a smile.

Savannah looked into his eyes and melting, smiled back. "A little," she admitted.

Marquez nodded, letting himself get lost for just a moment. "I will protect you!" he exclaimed in a whisper. They laughed softly.

Marquez brought her hand up for a kiss and let it go. They followed the pirates.

Both of Rain's best friends were there with their partners, mingling with Jesse's biker friends. A couple more cowboys from the bar they hung out in on Wednesdays had shown up and were now mingling with the pirates. Jesse made space in the middle of the room and brought out a big chair. This one was made of wicker, with a high rounded back, making it look like a throne. Rain approached the chair and sat on it facing her guests, smoothing the skirt on her lap. Looking up, everyone held their breath. She looked like a queen. Change deposited the baby on her lap, tickling Cacique gently before retreating. Jesse moved to stand beside her, a possessive hand on the back of the chair.

"Everyone is here," Jesse said, smiling at the faces in front of them. "Everyone we care about. Family and friends." He nodded with deep satisfaction. "Rain and I have brought all of you here today to present our new son..." Laughing, he reached over to tousle the baby's head as he craned his little neck to peer at him. "Cacique Coltrane..."

The pirates moved like a pack depositing an old wooden chest at their feet. Rain smiled as Jesse hurriedly whispered a warning in her ear to not open it. Flicking his eyes at Change, Jesse made the chest disappear. Caribe followed with beautifully wrapped rectangles of various sizes. The Aguilar-Banks were next, making a colorful spectacle themselves, along with the lady pyrates. Then Change's family deposited their presents at Rain's feet, starting with Sailor Kai, the smallest, and ending with who would now be Aunt Jill and Uncle Change. Corey James and Rain's girlfriends were next, adding to the pile. The Blackmons, the bikers, the cowboys, all contributed to welcoming the baby taíno. And after they couldn't add another present, they feasted, celebrating the addition to their immediate and extended family. It was all captured by Caribe.

"Summer."

Summer smiled as she spoke into the telephone. "Hey, Andrea, what's up?"

"There are some people here to see you," the company receptionist informed her.

"Really? Who?" Summer asked, frowning slightly. She detected awe in her voice.

"Aguilar-Banks."

"Cool!" Summer exclaimed. "Please send them in." Shuffling the papers on the desk in front of her for a moment, she finally stacked them evenly, matching all the edges and smiled at her boss, sliding a folder towards him. "You have to meet these people, Mr. Jones." And the door opened.

The room suddenly filled with their company. Jackson, Salomé, and Marina filed in, followed by Pablo and Joe. Summer beamed. "Hey, guys! What a surprise!"

Everyone smiled. Jackson kissed her cheek. "Came to take you out to lunch, baby. You down for that?"

"Absolutely!" Standing, she made the introductions.

Mr. Jones shook hands all around with their unexpected company and smiled at the dads. "It is an honor to meet you, gentlemen. My wife has been after me to go catch *The Pirate's Wife* and *The Pirate's Return* over by your building on Front Street. She has been raving about them since they got posted on your billboards."

Pablo laughed. "So do our wives, Mr. Jones."

"You should go," Joe advised, "it's worth the drive down to the beach."

"I will, gentlemen, thank you. It has been nice finally meeting all of you." He turned to Summer with a big smile. "You can go ahead and close that case we were discussing when you come back, Summer. Have fun and enjoy your lunch. Take the rest of the afternoon off to spend with your friends and I will see you tomorrow."

"Thank you, Mr. Jones," Summer flashed him a grin. "I appreciate it, I will do just that. See you tomorrow, sir." Opening her desk drawer she pulled out her purse and dropped the Aguilar-Banks file into the drawer before closing it firmly. Then she turned to her friends, her face lit up with a beautiful smile. "All done," she said softly. "Thanks, you guys. I owe you."

"Are you kidding me?" Joe demanded.

"We owe you, princesa," Pablo smiled at her smoothing his hand over her sleek blond hair. "Let's go. Wherever you want."

"Jamal!"

Jamal frowned. Once again he knew he was dreaming just like the other night. But there was something about this time.

"Jamal!"

Jamal froze. In bed, and in the dream. He was on the beach back in Encantada. This time was different. His sensory perception was sharper, clearer. The storm waves were higher, pounding harder on the shore break. The wind blew fiercer.

"Jamal!"

Jamal sighed. Damn pirate was calling him as if he couldn't find him. Jamal glared at his back. The man was standing right in front of him, was even now turning around to face him, and yet it was as if he didn't see Jamal. *"Juan!"* Jamal called out. But Juan Gaitano couldn't see him. Jamal was invisible to him.

"Jamal!" Juan Gaitano walked up and down a short way along the shore, pacing just this side of where the water slithered up the sand bubbling and foaming, keeping his boots dry. His hair seemed longer as the wind whipped it around his head. The open shirt spread on his chest billowing around him, displaying the cross on the black cord around his neck. Cupping his hands around his mouth he lifted his head and howled in the wind's face. *"Jamal!"*

"Juan!" Jamal shouted, fighting to be heard over the ocean's roar. The salt in the air was thick and unrelenting, already coating his skin and making it slick. Squinting his eyes against the sand flying in the air he took a step towards Juan. And then he stopped and looked down at his feet firmly grounded in the shore. He hadn't moved. Suddenly something out of the corner of his eye caught his attention. Another pirate joined them. In his bed Jamal became restless, mov-

ing without noticing it. On the shore in Encantada he became frustrated. His friend needed him, was calling him just like he had asked him to, but Juan couldn't see he was right there. The other pirate also moved restlessly, his size massive. There was no mistaking that this was Miguel Gaitano, the oldest brother of the older pirate brothers. And when he lifted his hands to cup around his mouth and his head to roar, even the wind and the ocean seemed to stop to listen.

"Jamal Blackmon!!!"

In bed, back in Blue Bay, the Blackmons woke up.

"Oh, no, he didn't! Hell no!" muttered Maya. Blinking the sleep away Jamal could only stare at his wife. Not a hard task for him since she took his breath away no matter what she wore nor how she looked. And right now, pacing angrily at the foot of their bed, caught in moonlit stripes slipping through their vertical blinds, she looked very appealing to him. His old college football jersey fell to her knees covering what he knew was a thong. Her long dark wavy hair was caught back in a sloppy braid down the middle of her back making her look years younger. She was trim and fit like the other wives in their circle of acquaintances. Her carriage was proud and regal like any African queen. Sweeping her hair back with her forearm she raged against the injustice of it all. "I," she informed Jamal with a growl, "am a full grown ass working woman with a j-o-b who needs her sleep. I will *not*," she warned him, "have your pirate friends come into *my* dream, while I am sleeping in *my* bed, in *my* bedroom, shouting for *you* even though you were standing right there..." Drifting off, she stopped suddenly.

Jamal waited quietly while she shook her head trying to clear some cobwebs. As she turned to stare at him with her beautiful now wide brown eyes, he realized he didn't want to lose the moment. "I'm sorry about the pirates, baby, they're nothing but savages, but I guess Juan can't wait anymore," he told her gently, his deep voice rolling over her smoothly.

Maya gazed at him, her head cocked to one side, her braid falling over one shoulder. "How could that ever happen?" she asked in wonder. "Juan's the one who couldn't see you? The young one?"

Jamal nodded automatically. "Yeah. Did you see him? Check out his clothes?"

She nodded. "His shirt was open and he wears a cross. His boots are rolled down and he managed to keep them out of the surf."

"That's right, baby," Jamal encouraged matter-of-factly even as he swallowed his shock. "That's Don Carlos' younger brother. The one who messes with Carlitos all the time," he told her, his voice soothing in the dark light of their bedroom.

Maya frowned. "You told me he sails a prison ship..."

"*La Prisión*," Jamal confirmed.

His wife took a step towards him. "And what about that other huge guy? Is that Don Miguel?"

Jamal laughed softly in the velvet darkness. "That's right. The kids are crazy about him. Did you check out his size?"

Maya nodded and climbed into bed, crawling towards him. "He woke me up." Her husband received her with open arms. "I can see now what you mean about his power. That man could move a mountain," she muttered. Cuddling against him, she laid her head over his heart letting its beat soothe her. "Jamal," she whispered, "I don't know how this happened, how I ended up in your dream, or how I ended up on that beach, and I don't want to know." Taking in a shaky breath she turned her beautiful face to peer at him. Holding her closer he stroked her hair. "You asked Juan to call you and he did, babe. Go get him. And make sure Miguel stays out of my dreams." Falling quiet, she finally fell asleep.

Jamal sighed. He had experienced firsthand how powerful Miguel Gaitano was, but this was extreme. Grinning in the dark he felt a surge of excitement. He couldn't wait to tell him. And to see Juan's face when he finally showed up. Stifling a chuckle he sighed again, making himself more comfortable, ready for the few hours he had left of sleep before he had to get up to begin his day. God, he couldn't wait to ride the storm into Encantada. He just couldn't wait.

Jamal looked around him. Everyone was staring back. He had called an emergency meeting at the Hacienda and was now sitting at the head of the table. "We need to catch the storm this afternoon." He turned apologetically to Xaira. "I realize it's your graduation, sweetheart, and I promise we'll make that, but once the ceremony's over, we've gotta blaze."

Xaira nodded once. "It's okay. I wasn't going to go to the dance anyway."

Now everyone turned and stared at Xaira. "What? Your own graduation dance?" Pablo asked, concern etching lines on his forehead.

"Why not, baby?" Joe asked, rubbing her back.

Xaira looked at both her dads. "There are a few girls that like Caribe a little too much," she told them honestly. "Why would I set myself up?" The men chuckled. "Caribe's taking me dancing. It doesn't have to be tonight. He needs to go see his parents and let them know what's going on. I have to go with him."

"Xaira…" Pablo heaved a deep sigh, running his hands over his hair.

"Encantada is a dangerous place, baby," Joe warned her.

"I know, Dad," she said, grinning suddenly, "how could I not go?" She turned pleading eyes on Pablo. "Papi, you know I'm a great warrior…"

"*Mamita*, it's not about that," Pablo began.

"You are most definitely a great warrior, Xaira," Don Carlos smiled at her. "I will be proud to show you Encantada, if your fathers approve." The pirate turned to his in-laws. "I will take her straight to

Leila and Manuel's place. She can rest there for a while. Larissa will take care of her in town as should the sirens."

"We aren't expecting anyone these days," Carlos added. "That the Medusa was there waiting for us when we got back from San Juan was unfortunate. They should have set sail by now."

"Papi, please, I want to see the village, and see Indio's apartment in town, the shell path to Pedro Barbosa's..." Xaira pleaded.

"Do not deny her, Villa Azúl, *hombre*," Don Carlos murmured.

"The Council's there, by the way, or did you forget?" Xaira jumped at the opportunity. Her dads looked at each other. It took all they had to hide their grins. "I want to see the lighthouse, and the Bat Cave!" Xaira cried out, real tears in her eyes by now. "Marina's tent!" She put one hand on each of their arms and clung to them, flinging her head back, her night black hair floating around her like a curtain. "Ple-ease!" she almost sobbed, "I haven't wanted anything so bad so long, Papi! Dad!"

"*Ya, mamita, tranquila*," hushed Pablo. He patted her hand before taking it in his and bringing it to his mouth for a kiss. He winked at her and let her hand go to tousle her head.

Joe also kissed her hand. "Hush, baby, chill," he crooned. Taking her beautiful face between his hands he caught her tears with his thumbs and kissed her cheeks. The Aguilar-Banks couldn't help but coddle her as a Latino family would. It was cultural with them. Xaira Chang was their little girl. They all spoiled her shamelessly and she was growing up so fast. There was hardly a thing in the world they would ever deny her and to have her get so emotional moved them no end.

"Xaira cannot be safer," Indio pointed out. "Giancarlo and Solomon will be staying with Mamá, Rouge and Storm, but Carlitos and I are going," he added with a grin. "We're going to take advantage of the storm and go ahead and bring some more stuff back."

"I'm going," Don Carlos smiled, raising his hand.

Pablo nodded with satisfaction as both Rashawn and Jamal raised theirs. "You're just going to get Juan," he smiled.

"And Miguel," Joe reminded him.

Everyone turned to look as Change raised his hand slowly. "I need to go. Never going to get another chance to see what Jesse's seen," he admitted with a grin. "Taking Ocean. Have to."

"I'm his sidekick," Ocean grinned.

Now they all turned to look at Reef, the youngest of those present. The young blond surfer shrugged, his daddy's smile shining out of his eyes and face. "Mom won't let me, I've gotta stay and be the oldest. I get to go next time."

"It's all good," Cool laughed. "Reef and I are going to check out the cave and explore a little bit before the storm hits." His laugh was musical and contagious. Hawaiian born and raised, his features were distinctive of his race. Except that an American sailor surfer grandfather contributed to his more chiseled looks, giving him an extremely handsome unique appearance. The pirates understood the Coltrane's twins infatuation with the young sailor and partner of the Cool Change business and diving boat. Not only was he attractive, but Cool also had a magnetic personality.

"We'll also be going on this occasion," Shane said, pointing to himself and his sons. Derek and Tyler beamed on either side of him. "The pirates need muscle…" he shrugged, grinning at his own lame excuse.

"Please! Let me go! Please, oh, please! ¡¡¡Ay, Papi, por favor!!!" Xaira cried out.

"¡Ya, Xairita, por favor, cálmate, mamita!" Pablo exclaimed, taking her in his arms. Over her head he chuckled and shook his head.

"It's okay, baby, you can go," Joe crooned to her rubbing her back.

"Aye!" the pirates exclaimed.

Xaira sighed shakily. She clung to Pablo for a moment, her face buried in his neck in a deep appreciative kiss. Letting go she wrapped her arms around Joe. Joe chuckled deep in his chest as she tried to burrow against him just like when she was a little girl. Bringing his head down to hers she pressed her lips against his cheek before pressing her own against it. She sighed happily. She loved her dads.

The Aguilar-Banks sighed with pleasure. They had waited almost five years for this occasion. Time had been kind and flown by fast. The moment was finally here. They were sitting at Blue Bay's Seaside Park. The graduation was taking place in the open air amphitheater. The small stage where summer concerts were held was all decked out with white and turquoise balloons, the colors of the graduation. The acoustic clam shell gleamed brightly in the sun. Snug inside it was a big screen protected from the day's glare. The audience attending had been treated to a parade of images of the members of the Senior class throughout their activities and sports as individuals and as groups and teams. Now the public was restless. The sun was so sharp it made their skin itch, but the nice breeze blowing in from the ocean took the sting away. Small tarps had been set out stretching over the cement bleachers where the friends and family of the graduates sat proudly. Xaira's people, however, sat all the way in the back in beach chairs in front of the grove of pine trees where it was cooler in the shade. Until that moment everything that was said had become a drone, words running into each other barely making sense. Just blah, blah, blah. But suddenly Marina stood up from her chair. Something had caught her attention.

"Oh, my God," she gasped, her hands going to her heart as if to keep it in.

Startled, her husband jumped to his feet next to her. "What's wrong, Marina? What is the matter?"

Tears came to her eyes and she could only shake her head. "I took that picture," she answered, her voice breaking.

Sinking back down into his chair, the pirate followed her gaze. Around him all eyes were riveted on the screen. Gaitano glanced at his wife in time to catch a tear sliding down her face before staring back at the image. It was of a young girl. A very young oriental girl. The photograph was taken from an alley, the camera angled up. She was framed at a window by a fire escape. Next to her a gauzy curtain billowed in the breeze. Her shoulder length night black hair was tousled around her head, her bangs covering her eyebrows. Beneath them her eyes were as wide as their almond shape allowed in her beautiful pale face. They held a world of hurt. A flimsy white nightgown hid her body, a strap falling off one narrow shoulder, her budding breasts barely noticeable under the light fabric. Leaning out the window she was staring raptly at the photographer, her expression more serious than any child should have.

"This was the day I was reborn." Xaira's musical voice rang loud and clear over the audience, capturing all their attention. "My birth date is of no consequence," she continued. "Neither is where I come from, who I was before this moment, nor what my heritage is." She stopped for a moment and looked out over the crowd, seeking out Marina. Their eyes met and locked. "Because of this day, five years ago, I acquired a family like no other. The Aguilar-Banks. I have Papi, Mami, Mom and Dad. An older brother and two older sisters. Twins included." She stopped for a moment as the crowd began murmuring. Taking a deep breath she continued. "Uncles and aunts, and cousins. I have grandparents in the Southwest, California and Hawaii, the East coast, and the Caribbean." She grinned. "I get to travel." There was a ripple of laughter. "My network includes lawyers, detectives, doctors, teachers, a club owner, and even the Mayor of Blue Bay. Now it has expanded to include the historians known as the pirates. So, yeah, I'm a connected guy," she shrugged happily with a toss of her head. More laughter. "Before I continue, I must say that I need my own partner in crime by my side right now, Ocean Coltrane." She looked desperately around her. "Right. Now. Ocean." A ripple went through the audience as Ocean jumped up on stage and ran towards her, his own toga moving in the breeze. He threw his arms around her in a deep embrace and exchanged kisses with her. Then he stood solidly at her side. She paused as the boys in her class cheered with approval. The pirates, in town for a few days only, had been a daily sight at Blue Bay High School observing Joe Banks at work coaching, and then Ocean was their own basketball star. "I have been living in a world of privilege under an umbrella of unconditional love. I realize my advantages far surpass anybody's wildest dreams, and for this I am eternally grateful to God, for noticing this little girl at a window on this particular day." The picture behind her faded and was replaced with a candid photograph of her at home out on the terrace. With the ocean as a background, the result was a stunning portrait. Her voice broke as she hastily swiped at her tears. "It is because of this that I dedicate my achievements today to my older sister and best friend." She took in a deep breath. "My *life*, Marina Aguilar Gaitano.

The crowd cheered, getting to its feet to crane their necks, peering back at Marina above them. They couldn't see her however, for the pirates had quickly surrounded her, creating a barrier as their accountant quietly sobbed against their captain's chest before composing herself. Saving the day, the principal's gentle voice came over them loud and clear. "Xaira is not only the president of the graduating class, but she is also the student with the most awards. Coincidence?"

"I think not!" chorused the students, eliciting smiles and laughter from the crowd.

Pleased, the principal nodded and chuckled, his eyes twinkling with undisguised pride. He patted Xaira's back gently and turned to the audience behind the graduates. "Chang family, please come forward." The Aguilar-Banks cheered, all jumping to their feet as everyone else laughed and giggled. Moving as a pack, they all climbed down the open-air amphitheater steps and up the ones that led to the stage, striding it, surrounding Xaira in an instant. The effect was breathtaking, their presence commanding. Not only were they powerful as a whole, but individually each and every one of them was very beautiful. The pirates watched quietly from the back as the principal hesitated. The pine needles rustled in the breeze behind them. "There are seven of you," the man pointed out, looking crisp and clean in spite of the heat, his hair ruffling around his head, "and there are nine awards." Rolling his eyes dramatically, he breathed a deep sigh. "Will the Blue Cat kindly join us?" The twins grinned as the football players and the basketball players stood up clapping and calling out to them as they passed by, happily cheering them on with a well deserved standing ovation . They had been stars during their stint at Blue Bay High School. The glass cases inside the school halls held photographs of them and sports trophies, evidence of championships won as part of the school's history. And besides, they helped coach during the different seasons. So the nine of them decked out Xaira with all her medals won, Blue Bay High School's graduating class president, valedictorian, and sweetheart. As the principal turned to finish the ceremony, the audience watched as the lady pyrates approached the stage. Storm beckoned the principal to the edge and Rouge handed him a note. All eyes followed as they returned to the back, once again joining the pirates. The principal scanned the note quickly and reacted with shock. Everyone watched expectantly as a smile blossomed on his face. He looked at the pirates in the back, seeking out the older one. "You are very generous, sir," he informed him, inclining his head. Don Carlos returned the gesture with a smile. Covering the microphone, he winked at Xaira. "These people really love you," he told her softly, motioning with his head in their direction. At her nod and smile he grinned. Then he turned back to the people in attendance. "I have a surprise for all of you," he informed them. He hesitated, smiling once again as all eyes stayed riveted on him. "There is a gift for all the graduates and their parents." He paused once more to laugh in disbelief. "On behalf of the Gaitano family and the rest of the pirates," he looked at them, drawing out the suspense. "You all have been... are being... and will be..." The principal laughed again. "Captured by Caribe!" The crowd screamed.

The men smiled. Xaira and Reef were like children on Christmas morning. Ocean on the other hand was much more contained and relaxed, although his eyes seemed to sparkle with the intensity of a supernova. Their interest lay on a chest Change had emptied for the pirates when he had gone to pick Jesse up in the Cool Change.

Reef shook his head, his blond curls shining barely visibly in the cave's light. "Man, I am so going next time," he muttered.

Cool also shook his head. "I know, so am I," he smiled. "But for now, it's starting to rain. Let's go, buddy," he urged gently.

Reef sighed. "'Bye, Dad. Have a good time." Change Coltrane exchanged a hug and a kiss with his second son. Reef turned to his older brother with a scowl. "Bring me back something, Ocean, from your adventure." His eyes softened as he looked up at Ocean. "Please..."

Ocean laughed. He hugged Reef impulsively, kissed him on the cheek and ruffled his head. "I've got your back, Reef. Then it will be your turn, bro..."

Pablo turned to Xaira with a sigh. "Be good, Xairita, behave yourself. Please do not scandalize the inhabitants of Encantada, *mi amor*..." He laughed as she nuzzled him for a moment.

"I'll be good, Papi," she promised with a murmur.

"Be smart, *mamita*," Joe urged in a low voice. "Enjoy yourself, baby, Encantada is awesome!"

Xaira turned to him with a grin. "I will, Dad," she giggled.

Thunder crashed overhead making her squeal and jump into their arms in a goodbye hug. Her dads reassured her with smiles ad stepped back, making their way to the mouth of the cave. Another round of good wishes, and the ones who were not going were gone.

The ones on the way to Encantada remained, moving to the front of the cave to enjoy the storm.

Inside the cave all was quiet. The visitors had faced the storm head on, looking straight at it, absorbing every detail. Now they sat around in the cool darkness, waiting for God knew what. As they kept gazing at the cave's mouth a shadow crossed it before they could see what caused it.

Jamal jumped up and rushed towards the cave's entrance. "Manuel!" Everyone waited. The shadow moved and morphed until it became a man. A low rumble that sounded like laughter reached their ears.

"Jamal!" The man stood at the entrance, his features standing out clearly in the gray fading light. Dreadlocks, thick and graying, framed a very handsome black face. The face of an African king. The man's body was still straight and strong, his carriage proud, belying the hell he had recently gone through. His eyebrows shot up as he burst into a huge smile. "Caribe!" he called into the cave.

"Papa!" his son called back happily. Father and son embraced at the mouth of the cave. Caribe smiled up at his father. "Has Mama dreamt about my girl?"

Don Manuel chuckled and shook his head at his son. "Just every night since you have been gone." He lowered his voice in conspiracy. "She is crazy about her."

Caribe nodded, relief and happiness pouring over him like a cloak. "Good." He reached behind him blindly and found unerringly Xaira's hand. Bringing her forward, he smiled at her encouragingly. "Xaira, this is my dad, Don Manuel. Papa, this is Xaira. Jackson, Salomé, and Marina's youngest sister."

Don Manuel nodded, taking Xaira's hand from his son. "Pablo and Joe's baby," he winked at her, his deep voice rumbling soothingly from his chest. He kissed her hand and let it go after a squeeze. The rest of the party stepped forward, eager to begin their adventure and meet their first contact. Caribe's dad was cool. They were stoked.

Jamal made the introductions. "You know Rashawn of course. These are Change, Jesse's brother and his oldest son, Ocean, Pablo and Joe's lawyer and partner, Shane Butler and his sons Derek and Tyler." He turned to his friends and smiled. "Guys, this is Caribe's dad, Don Manuel." A greeting rumbled all around.

Don Carlos laughed and gestured to the lightening sky, urging them all to step outside. "Welcome to Encantada."

Xaira grinned. After her own moms, Leila was the coolest mom in the world. Caribe's mother had taken one look at her and brought her under her wing so to speak, putting an arm around her and clucking like a mother hen, teasing her about how she was so thin nobody must be feeding her. Xaira had giggled, taking to the woman like a duck takes to water. A couple of minutes later she was decked out in cutoff white sailor pants held at the waist by a length of rope, and a bright piece of flowered fabric tied around her chest. Dressed in that outfit she looked just like Salomé and Marina had during their stay on the island. "Caribe is doing really good in our world," she told the older woman. "He has his own business where he captures people's images. We call it Captured by Caribe. He is very popular and on his way of becoming very wealthy. It is awesome!"

Leila smiled back. She was so blessed that her son had found this divine young woman to help him and love him. "I am very proud of Caribe, Xaira, and very grateful you are in his life. I hope you two end up serious, married and with babies," she teased observing the girl blush. "For now, go," she ushered her out, waving her hand at the men standing around, looking around them in awe. They had been prepared for the sights and sounds of village life but nothing compared to the actual thing. "You only have a couple of days here," Leila reminded her sternly, but it actually came out gently. "Do not waste a single minute, *bebé*."

Larissa studied the younger girl carefully. Max was happily snuggled in Gaitano's arms, gurgling his little head off. John was busy chatting with the men and Caribe just stood to one side, watching closely. She finally locked eyes with the girl and sighed happily. "You are absolutely stunning," she informed her. "They mentioned you quite a few times. Always in worship." Larissa laughed softly. "Now I understand why."

Xaira smiled back. "I cherish my family," she admitted. "They rescued me from a life without love and hope. Took me in and made me theirs," she laughed softly, pride in her voice. "I have come to see Caribe's world. To see what Jax, Salomé and Marina lived for so long."

"Then you better keep going, baby, you have a few stops still before you can come back and relax with me and tell me all about it," Larissa told her. And once more Xaira was ushered on her way. This time, the raven haired Max of the green eyes accompanied them.

"Thank God!" Liana exclaimed dramatically as she spied the visitors filling her beautiful foyer. "I am grateful, Gaitano," she told the pirate hurriedly, smoothing back the baby's hair gently, "for the opportunity to own my own business and I will forever be in your debt. But I need help." The girl was as exotic as they came on the island of Encantada. Her disturbing gray eyes were almond shaped hinting at someone Oriental in her heritage, her skin was the color of cinnamon and lightly freckled, her hair straight and black as night, her curves round and generous, a beautiful flower printed fabric sliding on her hips as she moved. Everyone turned to stare at her. The pirates smiled knowingly. She didn't blink an eye. It was as if they hadn't even been gone. "I love having this place, especially since Dr. Richardson and I are getting married," she waved a hand in the air in the direction of her beau.

The cowboy grinned and snatched the hat off his golden blond head, bright blue eyes dancing merrily as he grinned at Xaira, taking her hand and kissing it. "Kyle," he assured her winking in conspiracy.

"But Gaitano, it has been overwhelming," Liana admitted, "and right now I need some help." Without missing a beat she turned once more to Xaira. "I know who you are," she informed her sweetly. "You are Xaira, Jackson, Salomé and Marina's younger sister, the Aguilar-Banks baby." She narrowed her eyes at her suddenly. "Salomé owes me. I need you to stay and work for a couple of hours. Please."

Startled, Xaira turned to the men around her. They just shook their heads in sympathy and nodded urging her towards the older girl as they raised their hands, slowly backing away. Xaira scowled at them for a moment and then rearranged her features, turning to smile at Liana. "Sure," she told her. "Just tell me what to do."

"Are you ready for this?"

Xaira turned to look at her boyfriend. Caribe had gone to pick her up at the dress shop, but they hadn't said a word as they ran through the streets of Encantada. Now they were standing at the entrance of the Sirens' Lair getting ready to go in. He was grinning, delighting in teasing her. She smiled back. Stepping into his personal space, she reached up, slipping her arms around his neck. Xaira pressed her lips against Caribe's, distracting him for a moment. She opened her eyes and dove into his for a moment, connecting way deep down inside as they had fallen into the custom of doing lately. When her voice finally came out it was teasing, a low warning growl. "Get out of my way." Laughing, they entered.

The place was busy. Xaira froze in her tracks and for the first few moments could not get past the entrance. It was like Caribe's sketches come to life. To her left the sirens sat in the corner of the room, gossiping lightly, mostly just having a good time together. Next to them by the door was a group of sailors. Big scary pirates. The girl swept her eyes over them and continued assessing the room with the wonder of a child. Straight ahead was the bar with its mirrored wall and crystal glasses and bottles. Xaira gasped as she recognized Silas and Jimmy. The old man and the Chinaman flashed her identical smiles, having already heard about her. Sitting at the bar was her crew. Catching sight of her they raised an assortment of beverages in a toast and waved for her to join them. At the far end of the bar sat her brother-in-law holding court, a line of sailors waiting patiently for their turn, talking quietly amongst themselves. Next to them by the door to her right was another table of men. Big scary pirates to match the ones across from them, on the other side of the entrance. This time she recognized the crew of La Gitana and the individuals she realized were Encantada's lawmen, Pedro Barbosa, John Hawthorne and the scoundrels. Taking a deep breath she plunged into the room, Caribe right by her side. "Hi," she sighed reaching her family.

Ocean's eyebrow shot up in undisguised delight. "Dude! Can you believe this?"

"Awesome," Xaira breathed.

"How was the dress shop, *mamita*?" Jamal asked tenderly, offering her a glass of freshly squeezed orange juice.

"Not bad," she admitted, taking a long sip of her drink. Smacking her lips in appreciation she offered some to Caribe. "It was pretty interesting, actually."

"So you're not sorry you had to stay?" Shane asked, blue eyes twinkling behind his glasses.

"No," she shook her head, drinking again from her glass. Finishing it she held it out shyly to Silas for a refill. Thanking him when he obliged her with a grin, she turned back to her family. "Truth, guys, I had a great time! Worked my ass off," she teased, "but it was really cool. I'm glad I did it," she accepted, raising her glass in a toast.

"Aye!" her companions exclaimed happily, raising their own glasses in return, toasting each other through the mirror.

Xaira slipped into the space next to Ocean, squeezing between him and Rashawn. Leaning with one elbow on the bar she searched his eyes. "What'd y'all do?" she asked in a low confidential voice.

Ocean met her eyes with a smile, his voice just as hushed. "Moved some treasure."

"Not!" she hissed.

He grinned, nodding slowly. "Totally."

Xaira bit her lip, thinking about it for a moment. "You get the location?"

Ocean made a sudden sound of disgust, shaking his head. "Couldn't see."

"What do you mean?"

Next to them Rashawn chuckled, not being able to help himself from joining in. "What he means is that we weren't *allowed* to see."

"Pirates blindfolded us," Tyler explained, taking a drink from his own glass of orange juice.

Derek laughed. "All the way there and all the way back." He sighed. "They want us only for our muscle."

Xaira shook her head sadly. "So not cool." She turned back to Ocean. "So did you move a lot of treasure?"

Ocean nodded. "Yeah."

"Nice."

"Yeah."

"Gaitano!"

Everyone turned to stare at the table of the big bad pirates which were not part of the crew of La Gitana or the lawmen of Encantada. The crew at this table stared right back. Carlos Gaitano seemed amused. His smile and an arched eyebrow gave him away. "Blake?"

"Where is Marina?"

Xaira laughed. "Who wants to know?" She didn't mean for it to come out loud but she was overheard nevertheless.

The pirate Carlos called Blake turned his attention on her. "And who are you?"

Indio pushed his chair back from his place at his table and went to her. Taking her hand with a smile he pulled her gently towards the curious men. Ocean rushed to stay at her side. Pencil flying over paper as usual, Caribe reached them with a smile. They joined the pirates at their table, sitting with them. Indio made the introductions. "Xaira, meet the crew of the Medusa."

"Medusa," she repeated softly with the wonder of a child. "I know who you are," she informed them, "Marina told me all about you. I am sorry that I am not sorry for your loss." She smiled to herself as the pirates exchanged glances, acknowledging her words.

"John Blake, former Quartermaster, Crazy Jim Mallory, Sailing Master, and Blood Red, Boatswain." Indio waved a hand between them. "This is Xaira Chang of the Aguilar-Banks, and Ocean Coltrane, Snake's oldest nephew."

The pirates nodded at them. Blake kept staring at Xaira. "Xaira Chang of the Aguilar-Banks," he murmured.

"Do you know them?" Xaira asked.

"We met the children, not the parents," he replied thoughtfully. "I just cannot explain how you fit in."

Xaira dug her elbow into Ocean's ribs as he snickered next to her. "Well, think for a moment," she suggested, eyes dancing with mischief. "Whose younger sister am I, Salomé's or Marina's?" The pirates smiled slowly.

"That is a trick question," Jim Mallory informed her.

Playing along Xaira gasped in mock outrage. "A trick question?"

"We know a little bit about the Aguilar-Banks," Blood Red rumbled, his gold tooth glinting.

"So which is it?" Xaira challenged.

"You cannot be either or," Blake intervened smoothly. "If you are related to the Aguilar-Banks, then you are younger sister to Jackson, and Salomé, and Marina."

Xaira sighed in defeat. "Okay, so you do know them." She smiled at them.

The pirates turned their attention to Ocean. "You are also related to the Aguilar-Banks?"

Ocean grinned. "Distantly but yes, related."

His father moved and came up to stand behind him. "If you met Snake, then you know he's married to Joe's baby sister."

The pirates now turned their attention on him. "And you are...?" Crazy Jim inquired.

"Change Coltrane. I am Snake's younger brother, and Ocean's father."

They nodded. Blood Red smiled. "Fine young man you have there, Coltrane."

Change smiled back. "Yes, he is."

Noticing Change's increasing uneasiness John Blake decided to let him off the hook. "It has been an immense pleasure meeting you."

Slapping his hands on the table with a laugh Ocean stood up and walked around it. Standing directly behind John Blake who was sitting at the center he put a hand on each of Blood Red's and Crazy Jim's shoulders. "Caribe!" he called out happily. Caribe's head cocked to one side as their eyes met. The island boy was weary. He had gotten to know the Coltranes a little bit, and well enough to understand they were a force to reckon with, not unlike the Aguilar-Banks. They were all impulsive. The lot of them. Ocean grinned. "Take a picture."

Caribe grinned back, hastily sketching in his pad. "You know your mother's going to kill you."

Ocean's eyes sparkled with mischief. "I know."

Blake drummed his fingers impatiently, the beginnings of a scowl on his face. "What are we supposed to do?"

Indio and Xaira glanced at each other and smiled. She turned her attention back to the pirates in front of her. "Just sit still for a few minutes while Caribe gets your images down on paper." She laughed softly as they breathed deeply and flowed into stillness, gazing at her boyfriend. Xaira giggled. "Act natural." The crew of the Medusa laughed. They were captured by Caribe.

"Jamal!"

The pirates had spilled around the foyer at Villa Azúl, spreading out over the courtyard, greeting the people already in attendance. The visitors had followed but now froze as they caught sight of the pirate headed straight towards them. This is what they had come for. Jamal stepped away from the pack with a laugh, his arms outstretched. "Juan!" he exclaimed with happy relief. The men met in a warm embrace giving a hug and patting each other on the back, giving each other a kiss on the cheek before stepping back to appraise one another.

"You look good, Blackmon!" Juan Gaitano laughed.

"My wife takes good care of me," the detective admitted. He frowned at his friend. "You don't look so good."

Juan Gaitano sighed, running his hands through his coal black hair as the Gaitano men were wont to do. His friend was right. He had caught sight of himself in a mirror. There was a dark shadow on his face and there were dark circles under his eyes. His hair had grown longer than usual and so neglected that lately he had just been tying it back with a cord. He had also lost some weight. It was visible. His clothes sagged on him. The gold cross that hung around his neck stood out against a pronounced collarbone. His cheekbones were even more carved in his handsome Gaitano face. "I know." His eyes blazed into his friends'. "I called you."

"I know." Jamal nodded. "I heard you."

The breath left Juan's lungs with a whoosh. His eyes widened. "It worked?"

Jamal chuckled. "Miguel was a nice touch."

This time Juan laughed again. "Of course you heard Miguel."

Jamal raised his eyebrows. "You don't know the half of it."

"Do I hear a Blackmon?" a voice boomed from the second floor gallery making all heads turn.

Xaira froze, her heart skipping a beat and then pounding steadily in her chest. She knew who this was. She had heard so many stories about him that a chill ran down her spine. It wasn't fear, however. Instead, thrill. A delighted smile spread slowly across her beautiful face. Reaching blindly beside her for Ocean's hand, she succeeded in taking it and pulling him next to her. "No way," she whispered glancing at him.

Ocean was wearing the same expression of awe, excitement and happiness. "Way," he whispered back.

"Tío Miguel!" Rashawn exclaimed, moving to meet him at the bottom of the stairs. He let himself be wrapped in the older pirate's arms, surrounded by his loving energy.

Don Miguel Gaitano coddled the younger Blackmon for a moment, holding his face affectionately and pressing his forehead against his before kissing him on the cheek. "Rashawn," he rumbled happily. "I missed you, son." He glanced at the new faces. "Jackson and the girls?" he asked hopefully.

Rashawn shook his head. "Not this time."

Miguel slid his eyes over him wickedly. "I guess you will have to do, then," he teased.

Rashawn laughed back, acutely aware of his companions' mixed thoughts and feelings. "I will do you better." He led the pirate to the group that had arrived with them. "I have for you Xaira Chang, the youngest Aguilar-Banks, and Ocean Coltrane, Snake's oldest nephew."

The pirate's face transformed with a genuine smile loaded with sheer delight. He looked from one to the other, peering into their eyes. Opening his arms, he called the children of the group to him. "*¡Niños!*" Wrapping his arms around each of them, pulling them closer, murmuring with a smile, kissing each of them as if he were their long lost uncle. "I am Tío Miguel."

"We know," Xaira giggled throwing her own arms around the enormous mass of the man.

Ocean gazed at him with awe. "Jackson and the girls are crazy about you," he breathed.

Miguel Gaitano raised his eyebrows at the boy and grinned. "I know. As you will be," he added, patting him on the cheek. Releasing them, he turned to the rest of the party. "Blackmon," he greeted, his eyes twinkling, "you came."

"As agreed," Jamal smiled back.

"How much time do we have?" the pirate asked impatiently.

Don Carlos laughed. "You have twenty-four hours. We leave tomorrow afternoon."

"Excellent," Miguel answered, shooting their youngest brother a look. "We will be ready." There was a pause when they all looked at each other, but there were too many of them for there to be any kind of private conversation.

Don Carlos nodded. "We will speak later." Laughing, he slid his eyes around the spacious courtyard. Then he caught sight of what he was looking for. "For now," he informed his guests, "come meet the Council." He smiled to himself as the visitors from Blue Bay moved closer. The rest of the pirates reached them. "Don Miguel Gaitano, Captain of La Gaviota," he began. "Jack commands the Black Mermaid and is currently our liaison, besides Don Manuel and Leila, between Encantada and Blue Bay. Jack is also Rouge's cousin. These three," he waved a hand in the men's direction, "have crossed the Sea of Darkness to find fortune and have joined us. Sultan comes from Africa and is Captain of the Kalahari; Suleiman has sailed to us on the Chymera from the Mediterranean; Jai-Ling has commanded the South Seas on his Ocean Wind," Don Carlos smiled, waiting for the two groups of people to meet and greet each other. "Missing from here is the beautiful Captain of the Sea Gypsy, Rouge, whom you already know. These sailors are former captives from the galleon La Diosa del Mar, taken by my son, Indio Gaitano, and the crew of La Gitana. Meet the Spaniards, Don Andres Segarra y Collazo, Captain, and his Quartermaster, Don Luis Vega y Ramos." Introductions were made all around and the two groups of people measured each other. The Gaitano men stood around and observed the Council with the visitors. It was fascinating for them to watch their two worlds meet.

Suleiman stepped forward, teeth flashing bright white in his dark face with a genuine smile. His eyes twinkled like black glass filled with kindness and curiosity. The sunlight sparkling on his earrings matched that which glinted off the curved sword at his hip. He turned to the older of the Aguilar-Banks visitors. "You are the Aguilar-Banks lawman," he said in a husky musical tone. "I recognize your name being mentioned."

Shane stepped forward, his hand outstretched. They shook hands. Shane smiled. "Well, Jamal and Rashawn are the real lawmen, I am the solicitor. Their friend and the one who protects them in legal matters. I handle all of their official business, their important documents and such. My sons and I took care of their home while they were here in Encantada visiting."

Derek grinned at the pirate, his curly blond hair shining like a halo around his head in the bright sunshine. "We live with Jackson and the girls back home," he offered with a smile, gesturing at his brother and himself.

Suleiman thought for a moment. "Is it a good thing?" he finally asked.

Tyler smiled at the pirate. "Yeah. It works out just fine."

"They all take good care of each other," Shane explained.

Enlightened, Suleiman smiled. "So you are brethren."

"Yes, we all are," Change laughed.

"It is an honor," Suleiman bowed.

Sultan laughed. He reminded the visitors of Mr. Clean. The difference was that the pirate wore a vest made of tiger skin instead of a white t-shirt, hemp cutoffs instead of blue jeans, his nipples were pierced as well as his ears, a lion's claw hung on his massive chest, and he looked like a linebacker instead of a genie. "So you know the Aguilar-Banks well. Are you all fighters also?" The visitors laughed.

"They are all fighters," Carlos said. He raised his eyebrows in amusement at his own brethren. "Be warned," he called out softly.

Quiet until now Jai-Ling stepped forward. He had eyes for one person only, however. "All fighters," he repeated. "It has been my luck that the accountant has denied me the opportunity to fight with her once and again." He shook his head with faked sorrow. "The accountant will not fight anyone but the Boatswain of La Gitana."

"The accountant will not even fight me," the Captain of La Gitana declared with mock disgust. "I am her husband and she will not even practice with me," he muttered shaking his head.

"Just Solomon," chuckled Indio, eyes sparkling.

Jai-Ling locked eyes with Xaira. The Oriental pirate was an imposing figure. He wore black loose-fitting pants tucked into soft leather boots. The belt around his waist was set with jade to match the sword at his hip. He wore no shirt, instead displaying the broad, strong, and firm chest and torso of a samurai. "With so many fighters among you…" he shrugged happily. Seeing where their friend was headed, the Gaitanos moved closer. "Surely someone will take pity on this poor pirate who only wishes to have one good fight with a visitor."

Xaira stopped breathing. The scary Oriental pirate filled her senses. Thrill shot through her veins at roller coaster speed on a steep drop, reaching the tips of her fingers, the soles of her feet, the ends of her hair. Her sight sharpened and her ears filled with a soft hum. At a distance she felt Ocean squeeze her fingers locked with his until currents shot through them. Xaira shuddered. Caribe prowled around them, his hand a blur as the charcoal pencil flew all over his pad. But his head shot up at Xaira's reaction. He had hung out with her long enough to know that as awesome as this may appear to his girl, it still may not be a good thing. Xaira was too much like Marina. Wild and reckless. But she was completely focused. Here was this pirate. And he was aching for a fight. Xaira thought the word. "Yes." It came out under her breath.

Carlos reached out with a hand. "No."

Xaira nodded, the smile on her face blooming like a flower. "Yes."

The men in her company stepped closer, Jamal's, Rashawn's, Shane's and Change's voices coming out in unison. "No."

Xaira giggled. "Oh, yes," she teased them.

Carlos frowned, going to her. He noticed Ocean squeeze her hand tighter. "Xaira," he murmured. "I didn't come all the way to

Encantada just to have Papi and Dad kill me when I get back to Blue Bay."

Don Carlos frowned for a moment but then his face cleared. "Actually, they will not."

Indio turned to his father. "What do you mean, Papá?" His eyes sparkled with silent laughter. "Of course they will." He watched as his father grinned and opened his mouth to answer then closed it as something caught their attention. They all turned to Xaira.

Xaira walked to the nearest thing available. It was a sturdy old weathered rain barrel. Having dragged Ocean along she made him hold it steady while she climbed unto it. Straightening up until she was towering over them, she commanded attention. "I have to do this!" she exclaimed, almond eyes sparkling. Her cheeks were flushed, betraying her contained excitement. "It's all about me!" She put her hands on her hips and tossed her head, her hair floating around her like a black velvet cape. "There is no way you guys really expect me to pass up this opportunity," she informed her companions. "Marina would totally let me fight Jai-Ling!" she insisted, knowing no such thing, stamping her foot and crossing her arms. The men stared at her. The Gaitanos chuckled and stepped back. Ocean took her hand once more. Caribe reached for her other one.

Shane sighed and turned apologetically to his hosts. "There are many ways to go about this, gentlemen, and arguing with Xaira about how this is such a bad idea is the least appealing of them all." He smoothed back the hair on his head and slid his glasses down his nose just enough to allow himself to rub his eyes. Repositioning them, his blue eyes sparkled with mischief from behind the crystals. "The only other option is to allow her to have her way. Xaira may be a teenager, but I assure you that she is not above throwing a full blown tantrum in order to get her way if she thought it appropriate." Shane smiled as the pirates laughed. "The truth is, spoiled as she is," he confessed, "Xaira Chang, although a brat, is more than qualified to fight the Captain of the Ocean Wind." He had to stop. The pirates roared.

"Aye!"

"Yes!" Xaira shouted, throwing her head back with laughter. Beckoning to Rashawn, she had him stand in front of her and turn around so she could sit on his shoulders, and they all headed towards the bamboo grove behind Villa Azúl.

"My sons will supervise!" Shane called out, hurrying to catch up with them.

The Gaitano men stood together. They had taken the opportunity provided by Xaira and Jai-Ling's distraction to finally talk in private. The two fighters were in the middle of a clearing, Derek and Tyler dancing around them as they refereed. Caribe prowled the perimeter, charcoal pencil flying over the paper, smile glued to his face. He was so proud of Xaira he couldn't wait to go home to Blue Bay and show and tell the Aguilar-Banks all about it. Marina was going to be absolutely thrilled. More so even than the pirates cheering and shouting encouragement at the fighters alongside the Spaniards, the Blackmons, the Butlers, and the Coltranes. The pirates watched closely, making sure that Xaira, indeed, did not get hurt. Not that any of them would jump between her and Jai-Ling for any reason. After a few minutes of close observation they were a little more concerned that Jai-Ling did not get hurt, a possibility that did not escape the rest of the people in attendance.

"What is it like?" All heads turned to look at Juan. Other than his haggard appearance he seemed to be calm but it was all an illusion. His eyes flashed as he spoke.

Don Carlos sighed. There would come a time, very soon, when he would have the chance to tease his brother about the marvels and extravagances of the modern world. "It is quite spectacular," he breathed. "You cannot imagine the wonders. Their means of transportation alone are the stuff of dreams."

"Or nightmares," laughed Carlitos. His father and brother chuckled.

"It is not a world for cowards, that's for sure," rumbled Indio.

"Put me up to date," Don Carlos demanded. His brothers looked at each other and respectively drew in deep breaths. He looked into

Juan's eyes. "What happened?" No one asked what he was referring to, they all knew.

Juan squeezed his eyes shut for a moment, smoothing his hands back over his hair slowly. When he looked at his older brother his eyes were haunted. "I recommended further investigation into the circumstances where the Spaniard, Don Gerardo, was found dead near the big river. In fact, the young taína girl was missing from the village," he admitted, sliding his eyes over his nephews for a moment. "When the authorities probed deeper into the facts surrounding her disappearance along with her baby, whom is presumed to be dead, the result was that indeed, Don Gerardo was more of a monster than even *Madre España* could have imagined." He sighed deeply and looked around at his brothers and his nephews. "That is the good news." The men sighed collectively.

It was Don Carlos' turn to smooth his hands over his hair in the same slow familiar gesture. "And the bad…?" All eyes turned to the oldest of the Gaitanos.

Miguel Gaitano stood straight and looked at each of them in return. From the grove next to them came an explosion of sound. All turned to look. The Council and the visitors were screaming their heads off, avidly cheering the opponents on. In the middle of the jumping men they caught flashes of Xaira and Jai-Ling as they fought earnestly, their skin shiny with perspiration, their focus exclusively on one another. Of the two, it was hard to determine who was winning. Neither seemed to be even breathing hard, instead, projecting energy and excitement. The breeze rustled among the leaves, making the bamboo stalks sway and creak like a ship on the ocean. The Gaitanos turned their attention back on themselves. Miguel nodded his head. "The Spaniards are screaming for Carlos Gaitano and the crew of La Gitana." He caught his nephews freeze even as they seemed to remain unaffected by his words. "As their luck would have it, however," he teased them, fighting back the urge to laugh, "La Gitana has just gone down."

"How did you pull that off, Tío?" Carlos laughed.

"Did they believe it?" Indio demanded.

"The Hawthorne scoundrels investigated the events and made the report. John drew up all the papers and delivered them to the Spaniards. They haven't even been able to get the fleet commissioned to retrieve La Gitana out of the harbor yet." Miguel sighed dramatically and rolled his eyes at Indio, making him smile. "The Spaniards are conducting their own investigation."

"So they do not believe it!" Don Carlos exclaimed, a frown settling on his face.

"They do not want to. They think it is too much of a coincidence although they have no explanation for the young dead taína found on the mountaintop and the missing baby. But they will believe it," Miguel added, appeasing his family. "No one messes with John and the scoundrels. Their word is law." They laughed. "The truth of the matter is that Carlos Gaitano and the crew of La Gitana will never be found."

"Aye!"

"All your pieces are in place," Juan said, his expression dark and thoughtful. "You have made your move and it is our turn to make ours," he added, glancing at the oldest Gaitano. "Pedro already has the paperwork for our demise ready. He is just waiting for the dates."

"Which will be…?" Carlos asked.

Miguel sighed at him. "First we must allow the Aguilar-Banks baby to finish her fight with Jai-Ling." His eyes crinkled at the corners as they all chuckled. "I imagine that she will want to dance with the natives afterwards?" He snickered as they all nodded.

"Aye!"

"They all will, then," the older pirate muttered. "I can see that the visitors are very close."

Don Carlos smiled. "As Suleiman indicated, they are brethren."

Miguel nodded. "So tomorrow we will announce our departure towards Carey and in a few days John will announce that we never made it there."

"What about when the Spaniards get here?" Indio wondered out loud. His uncles shrugged.

"Not our problem," Juan growled.

"The Council hides out here in Villa Azúl with our Spaniards from La Diosa. Hawthorne, the scoundrels, Pedro, John Kline…" Miguel waved a hand as if the thought of the imposing Spaniards not yet arrived getting information about the Gaitanos from any of these people were simply preposterous. Luckily the newly arrived Gaitanos agreed.

"Aye!"

Don Carlos clapped his hands and rubbed them together in his own familiar gesture. "So it is done. You, my brothers," he smiled, "go retrieve whatever you can carry." Throwing back his head, his wicked laugh matched the sparks in his silver eyes. "We shall invest. If you think you are well off here, wait till you arrive at Blue Bay." He raised his eyebrows and smacked his lips. "We are rich."

Carlos and Indio laughed. Juan and Miguel nodded, hope and trust shining in their eyes at their brother, smiling at each other. Don Carlos on the outside embraced his brothers and his sons. On the inside he breathed a prayer with a huge sigh of relief: *¡Gracias, Dios mío!*

"I can't believe she's doing this," Change muttered. His companions turned to glance at him. The brush they were sitting in was inviting. Insects whirred and chirped, buzzed, flew and scurried all over without disturbing them, engrossed in their own nighttime activities. It was comfortable there, the ground still dry, the breeze rustling through the leaves fanning them. The men laughed.

"What can't you believe, Change?" Shane teased him. "That Xaira is dancing with the natives or that you're even here in Encantada?"

Grimacing, Change shook his head and lowered it on the arms he had propped on his knees. His shoulders moved with silent laughter. Raising his head he grinned at his companions. "All of the above," he admitted.

"And are you ever expecting to come back to Encantada?" Jamal wanted to know.

Caught off guard, Change shook his head. "I don't think so."

"Then I suggest you go dance your ass off." Laughing, the black detective jumped to his feet and with a yell leapt into the clearing where room was quickly made for him.

Change sighed dramatically and dragged his hands down his face. Turning to the pirates he couldn't help but grin. "I suppose I must."

Miguel nodded solemnly. "Ocean is dancing his ass off," he pointed out needlessly. They all turned to look just as Ocean spun in the air and landed nimbly on his feet, arms thrust out for balance. The natives went wild. "You must."

"How did he ever learn to do that? He moves just like a pirate," Juan snickered. His brothers laughed. To be a pirate required to be acrobatic.

Change smiled. "Rain, Jesse's wife, is Joe's baby sister. She owns a studio named Rain Dance. Teaches my kids for free, so they can recruit their little friends," he grinned. The pirates rumbled with approval.

"Let's see what you can do," Juan challenged him.

Change laughed. "Peace out." And he too was gone.

Shane gestured at the celebration. "Derek and Tyler are dancing their dances off, I'm out of here."

Now the pirates were alone, everyone else was dancing. Don Carlos turned to his sons with a dramatic sigh. His eyes, however, gave away his amusement even in the torchlight. "Xaira got hurt." His boys chuckled.

"Xaira could be Marina's daughter," Indio teased his brother.

Carlos shrugged, understanding his brother didn't refer to age but to likeness. "Jai-Ling got hurt." Then he chuckled. "I think Xaira is more vicious than the accountant." His eyes sparkled with pride. He loved all the women in his new family. They all added to his life. And it made him love Marina all the more.

Miguel laughed. "Jai-Ling has been wanting to fight Marina ever since he met her. He is jealous of Solomon. Xaira just made it worth the wait," he added, eyes slit with amusement.

"So they both got their kicks," Juan snickered. "Now that they got that out of their systems, we can go on with our lives."

"You mean," Miguel's laugh was wicked, "our *deaths*."

"Aye!"

The Gaitano men laughed. Carlos and Indio went to join the dancers. After a short while their elders joined them. They were celebrating. Life. Death. It did not matter. They were celebrating. Dancing their asses off.

Xaira sighed happily, snuggling closer to Caribe. He gently pulled her arm around him locking his fingers with hers. She was trying to slow her mind down so she could sleep. It wasn't too hard. With her best friend at her back and her boyfriend in her arms, she felt at peace, safe and loved. Encantada was fantastic! She absolutely loved everything about it. The encounter with the crew of the Medusa had been exciting, fighting with Jai-Ling incredible, dancing with the natives thrilling. But Carlitos' Bat Cave…

It had actually been Don Carlos' idea. A gift. Once they had finished dancing with the natives he had instructed Caribe and Xaira to make their way ahead and go all the way up to his son's lair. Everyone else had to settle for cooling in the waterfall. Xaira had been enthralled by the cave. It was just as Marina had described it. Being officially his, Carlos Gaitano had not allowed his bride to break down his bachelor pad. Thus Xaira was witness to the opulent Persian rugs, the beautiful sketches, the awesome furniture. Don Carlos had instructed for one of the servants to clean up for them. They were treated to a couple of hours before bedtime when the place would be cleaned up again so that Carlitos could stay in his own place and sleep in his own bed. So with no thoughts of anything but having a good time, Xaira and Caribe enjoyed the hell out of the place. Secure in their privacy, they peeled off their dusty clothes down to their underwear and went on a rampage.

First they had a water fight under the waterfall. The hot water was stimulating. It felt great as they squirted with cupped hands pumping in rhythm, simulating fish shooting streams of water at each other. They howled with laughter, the loud joyful sound reverberating and bouncing around the cave walls. Finally, breathing heavily, they got out. Their skin immediately cooled off the instant they removed themselves from the streaming hot water. That was when they found the burlap bag filled with goodies left for the pirate women the day Marina killed Xavier. Xaira hastily dumped it on the ground and to her delight found that there was enough of everything left for both her boyfriend and herself. The first thing she did was put the blades to one side. Xaira shrugged. She would be home tomorrow where she could shave in her modern world, not that it mattered. She didn't need it, she had groomed before coming to Encantada. Forty-eight hours wasn't going to kill her. Then she dragged Caribe back under the waterfall where she happily shampooed his shorter dreadlocks. Caribe smiled and took it patiently with love in his heart as Xaira coddled him, sang to him, and played with him, all the while lovingly worked on his hair, letting her hands slip and slide all over him. He returned the favor once she was done rinsing him, and afterwards watched the bubbles disappear underground. Caribe loved touching her, holding her, but he was careful. There would come a time when they would have a more intimate relationship. Not just yet. He snickered at himself, making her smile. He needed to be very thorough just to spend half the time on her that she had spent on him. Xaira's hair was as smooth as glass as it was, imagine it wet. He bit back a laugh at the image of himself going over it strand by strand. She would never allow him to get started. Xaira had laughed him off, actually, urging him to finish so they could continue. Knowing what to look for since Marina had previously described the contents of the bag, she found what was supposed to be the conditioner. This they treated each other to, smiling into each other's eyes, and deciding to leave on for a while longer while they took a tour.

Caribe's sketches tacked to the wall were breathtaking to Xaira. She took her time with each one, her eyes caressing every line, every stroke of the pencil. Sighing happily she wrapped her arms around him, squeezed him, and reached up on tiptoe for a smooch. Caribe squeezed her back and pressed his lips against hers for a while before drawing back with a deep dramatic sigh, smiling into her black almond eyes. The bed only attracted their attention long enough for them to lay side by side, holding hands, gazing up at the mosquito netting that shrouded them. Then with a squeeze and a sigh they got out with a laugh and went to admire the gorgeous Persian carpets hanging on the walls. They raced to the natural hot Jacuzzi, better known as an underground hot spring, shouting with laughter. Quickly getting in they each claimed a side. Sighing happily they leaned back with eyes closed, arms outstretched on the ledges behind them. After a while of relaxing in the stream the couple drifted towards each other. Dissolving into each other's arms Xaira had closed her eyes dreamily while Caribe nuzzled her neck, his breath nice and warm on her skin. Until he blew on her. Tickling her. She squealed with a giggle and pretended to gnaw on his neck like a vampire. Caribe laughed and quickly twisted his head away, capturing her mouth with his. He took her arms and slipped them around his neck. Xaira faced him and wrapped her legs around his waist. Caribe responded by cupping her butt with his hands and holding her against his chest, high in the awesome swirling water so she wasn't sitting on his lap. The time allotted them was not enough for them to indulge themselves in intimacy. They were here to have fun. Now comfortable in each other's arms their kiss deepened. They were a couple. Best friends. Business partners. Playmates. Some benefits, not many yet. They were tight, committing heart and life, body and soul to each other, already knowing their destiny was together. They made out until they were ready to take it a little further. So they broke away and decided to play instead. Unwrapping themselves from each other's arms they drifted back to their own corners. Then, closing their eyes, they began a hysterical game of Marco Polo. Due to the size of the hot pool they were in, comfortable as it was for two, they decided to play keep-away instead. When one found the other they would stop to kiss for a while so they took some time playing. Done with the game they floated side by side, heads pointing in opposite directions, and rinsed the conditioner out of their hair, confident the water would recycle in minutes. Sitting up they indicated to each other that they were quite satisfied with the silkiness and smoothness of their respective tresses. This was followed with wild laughter. Relaxed always brought on silly. Sighing because their time was up they climbed out and stole a few more minutes making out under the shower. Reluctantly they decided their time was indeed up, got out and got dressed, and finally made their way down the hill, laughing and holding hands. It was pitch black by now but the Gaitanos' servant had left tiki torches spaced out in intervals so they could make out their way in the dark. They would later be extinguished so that enemies could not make their way to the pirate's lair. The trail was symphonic. Insects buzzed, crickets chirped, night birds sang. A soft breeze caressed them, making their skin respond. Being early summer it was warm so the hike downhill was comfortable. Besides, there were dry clothes in Villa Azúl.

Villa Azúl itself was awesome at nighttime, absolutely spectacular in fact. There were torches everywhere illuminating the beautiful courtyard home. Even the clearing before the bamboo grove was illuminated where servants happily barbecued steaks, a pig, and some chicken along with assorted vegetables. A veritable feast. The pirates mingled everywhere, thoroughly mixing with the visitors. They would group in certain formations and then switch around in different combinations. The unconscious collective goal was that everyone got to know everyone else. It was the blending of two brethren, old and new, outlaw and civilized, a mutual admiration society with genuine respect and affection towards each other. Finally they had been called to partake of a splendid buffet laid out by the servants. Sitting at a long table consisting of smaller tables joined together the friends toasted to old and new alliances with the finest wine. Xaira and Ocean had been stoked, absolutely thrilled out of their minds. It was their first totally grownup dinner. On a pirate island. And a fine one at that. Once the day's activities fell on them like a cloak, Don Carlos offered Xaira her choice of spare rooms. Smiling, Xaira had happily declined and expressed a preference to spend the night at Marina's tent instead.

Don Carlos had narrowed his eyes a little at her. But then he sighed. Were he a young girl he would not want to sleep surrounded by pirates either no matter how much family was with her. The Gaitanos agreed. The visitors jumped at the chance to stick together and have privacy. So, Rashawn claimed the hammock and Change the beautiful comfortable recliner. Caribe, Xaira, and Ocean made themselves comfortable on straw mats on the bare sand. Outside Derek and Tyler made themselves comfortable at either side of the entrance, and Carlos and Indio opted for where they could face the jungle behind the tent. Jamal and Shane preferred the comforts of Villa Azúl, albeit surrounded by pirates.

Xaira breathed deeply once more. Behind her Ocean's hand caressed her hair once, comforting her. In front of her Caribe snuggled her, moving back so that her breasts pressed comfortably against him. Xaira kissed his bare shoulder, her lips lingering briefly on the warm skin covering hard bone and flesh. Her mind went back to her favorite part of the day, her lips murmuring her gratitude. "Gracias, Dios mío," she murmured against her boyfriend's back what she had been taught to express faithfully for every single moment of her life. Smiling, she added, "Gracias, Don Carlos." A giggle escaped her. Exhausted and happy, Xaira drifted off to sleep.

Marina sighed. Her bedroom felt like an icebox. The air conditioner was cranking and she would leave it be until she got up in the middle of her night to go to the bathroom. Then she would turn it off, finishing the night in the slowly dwindling coolness of her room. She snuggled deep inside her comforter making sure nothing but her face was exposed. Dreamily she gazed at the fish tank at the foot of her beautiful Lucite sleigh bed. Above it on the big flat screen high definition television hanging on the wall played a surf movie on mute. It was her way of hypnotizing herself, a manner of dealing with the realities of her life and tackling and solving problems in her mind so she could do so for real. But that wasn't the case now. Accompanying the seductive gurgling there was soft reggaeton flooding the room, pouring from the speakers high on all four corners. Not the dancehall nor the street kind. Instead, the lyrics were seductive and erotic, the rhythm filling her veins and taking over her pulse until she throbbed with it. Marina felt like she was swimming underwater inside her own skin. Sinking into a seductive quicksand. Warm and fuzzy, it was her physical happy place. A kaleidoscope of images filled her mind. They were all, with and without her, of her outrageously incredibly hot husband, the pirate Carlos Gaitano. Her hand crept. Making herself comfortable Marina prepared to indulge herself. Her mind screamed for her guy but her voice kept silent. Instead, biting her lip, she whimpered a quiet thought, one that overpowered her since he left for Encantada. "God, I miss you, babe." The pictures in her mind became more erotic, more graphic. Marina made contact. She touched herself. Screaming senses blasted into turbo, exploding into full sensorial mode. She closed her eyes. Taking a deep breath she could sense her man. Behind closed lids she could see him in all his tall, dark and handsome glory, blue eyes sparkling like tropical lagoons in the stunning chiseled face, hair as dark as night, the tanned physique of a god. His laughter teased her memory. She licked her lips. Her tongue recalled the taste of his skin. Squeezing her eyes swimming in tears shut, Marina's back arched, legs quivering, thighs tense. Shivering she gave it her all. She could recall everything about Carlos. His smile, kiss, caress, grope, foreplay, penetration, pleasure, enjoyment, fulfillment, climax… Marina bit her lip opting to scream inside her head instead. A big rushing wave, hot and wet, overtook her, making her ride it until it let her go. Marina shuddered and willed herself to float down. Once the lust, pleasure and satisfaction had passed, Marina turned on her side and eyes closed she slipped a pillow between her legs and one between her arms. Sighing deeply she let herself drift off. Carlos was there again, this time taking her in his arms and kissing her. Kissing her husband back, Marina fell asleep.

"Coltrane!"

The party of people stopped. The visitors glanced at each other. They were facing pirates not of their crew at the entrance of the Sirens' Lair. It was a gray day, cloudy, not raining yet. Everyone felt happy. Some to be going back home after such an amazing adventure, others excited at the prospect of a promising new life in a new world. They had already said good-bye to the Council or what was left of it at Villa Azúl, the natives and Leila and Don Manuel at the village, the Klines and Max at the General Store, and were now at the Lair to meet Pedro Barbosa and John Hawthorne with his scoundrels.

Change stepped forward nodding at the man. "Medusa." His family moved closer around him.

The pirates hesitated, glancing at each other, until finally their new captain stepped forward. John Blake actually looked uncomfortable, shuffling his feet and clearing his throat. Finally, he looked Change in the eyes. "We have an offer to make you."

Change frowned, totally puzzled. What kind of offer could the pirate be making? "What's up, Blake?"

The pirate waved a hand helplessly. He looked much different from the man Marina had faced down when confronted. Gone was the bushy beard. He still had facial hair but was handsomely groomed. His wavy black hair had gone from matted and greasy to soft and shiny, flowing thick around his head when it wasn't tied back putting his face in prominence. His face had cleared up considerably, being taken care of with home remedies by the sirens. He had also lost quite a bit of weight and had gained muscle. The crew of the Medusa had actually stayed on in Encantada to train at Tae Kwon Do and had therefore benefited from the constant grueling exercise. "We each," he gestured at his Sailing Master, his Boatswain, and himself, "offer you a chest." He shrugged apologetically. "Not very large, but of a nice size," he took a deep breath and rushed on, "in exchange for a year. We promise not to go back on our word, we have put it in writing, but we would appreciate it enormously if you consider it seriously. We imagine you are on your way out so we have caught you just in time."

Change's frown deepened to a scowl. He didn't look like an angel anymore. He had a feeling he knew exactly what the pirate was talking about. His voice cane out deathly quiet. "A year of what?"

The pirate's eyes bored deep into the younger man's bright blue eyes now clouded. "Ocean's service."

Change lunged at the pirate. He hadn't even realized he had done so until he found himself farther away from the older man than he had originally been, restrained by the men who accompanied him. They had obviously caught him in mid-air, hoisting him back and containing him before he made a huge mistake, surrounding him in automatic protection. John Blake blinked but he didn't budge. Instead his face expressed concern. *"He is just a boy!"* Change roared at him.

The Sailing Master and the Boatswain of the Medusa stepped forward flanking their Captain. They looked just as concerned. "There is nothing to worry about, Change," Jim Mallory appeased in his soft cultured voice. Calling Change by his first name put him on equal terms, at a more intimate level, meant to put the impulsive visitor at ease. "We are not depraved like Xavier was. In spite of what he said to the accountant."

"The accountant killed Xavier!" Charlie seemed to come out of nowhere.

Without thinking Xaira moved forward, fists clenched, eyes glittering, and got Charlie in the ribs with a round kick. The unfortunate sailor stumbled backwards, eyes watering. Xaira pursued him relentlessly, kicking and punching him, muttering under her breath. Her voice was a soft growl dripping with menace. "Shut the fuck up, Charlie." Finally the miserable man was flat on his back, rebroken nose flowing bright red, passed out cold. Coming back to the pirates Xaira tossed her head and smiled. "I've been dying to do that."

Crazy Jim finished what he was saying as if nothing had happened. His eyes betrayed him, however, sparkling with newfound admiration for Xaira. "We just think the boy would be an asset to the Medusa and we would greatly benefit from whatever he could contribute to us."

"We will make a fine sailor out of him," Blood Red assured him. "We will not keep him, we just want to borrow him," he promised.

Breathing heavily Change glared at the pirates. Then suddenly and unexpectedly he was hit out of nowhere by the hilarity of the situation. Not being able to help himself he burst out laughing. Astounded, everyone just stared at him. Ocean and Xaira were a different matter, however. He snickered, she giggled, and soon both were laughing just as hard as Change was. The Blackmons and the Butlers chuckled. Something was definitely up. They all let go of Change. The Gaitano men looked on and smiled. The visitors were always so much fun. "I'll tell you what," Change finally gasped, bending over, shaking his head with his hands on his knees, trying to quiet his laughter so he could fill his lungs with air. Finally succeeding he straightened up and faced the pirate, blue eyes still dancing. "Ocean is my oldest, my firstborn," he explained. "I would miss him terribly. That's why he's even here with me in Encantada right now. He is also the oldest of five and another on the way."

The pirates chuckled. "You have been busy," Blake teased.

Change grinned back and raised his eyebrows. "You should see their mommy," he admitted with a heartfelt sigh. "As a family we would all miss him, so here's what you can do." Everyone seemed to hold their breaths as he chuckled. "Along with that paper you have there, write a letter to my wife, Jill Coltrane, the boy's mother, and ask her for a year of Ocean's service. Make sure you promise you are only borrowing him. If you go back on your promise and keep him longer she gets double the chests."

"Aye!"

"No!" All eyes turned to stare at Xaira. She was smiling as she shook her head, black almond eyes slit with amusement. "It won't work because Ocean and I are a team!" she expressed happily, lifting their hands joined together with fingers locked to prove her point. "Ocean and I train together," she explained, "so if he trains for pirate, then *I* have to train for pirate also."

Catching on, Change backed her. "Which means you must write a letter to her mommy also, requesting the services of Xaira Chang to accompany Ocean Coltrane for a year." He forced himself to keep a straight face as he heard the Gaitano men rumbling with quiet laughter behind him.

"And who is Xaira Chang's mommy?" Blake asked.

"Marina Aguilar."

"Gaitano," Xaira added with a smile.

The pirates stared. Blake frowned. "I have met Marina Aguilar Gaitano."

"Aye," agreed Crazy Jim. "Marina is not a mommy."

Blood Red seemed to growl as he raked his eyes over the young Oriental woman. "At least not Xaira Chang's mommy."

"I assure you, men," Carlos couldn't help himself, "Marina is not anyone's mommy." He sighed with a smile. "But Xaira Chang's, of course."

Xaira rolled her eyes. "Okay, so she didn't give birth to me," she admitted. Her eyes softened. "But she is raising me so that qualifies her as a mommy."

"Aye," the Medusa rumbled, not too happy.

The Captain of the Medusa turned to the Captain of La Gitana. "Gaitano…" he began hopefully.

Carlos cut him off with a shake of his head. "You're on your own, Blake. Marina adores Xaira. That's her baby," he laughed.

Indio chuckled. "Aye," he agreed. His eyes danced with laughter at the crew of the Medusa. "Good luck, men." Everyone laughed. They all agreed on the difficulty of the situation.

"We can only try," Jim Mallory laughed. He turned to his friend. "*You* write the letter."

Blood Red sighed deeply and slid his eyes at him. He scowled. "Why me?" Everyone turned to look back at Crazy Jim. They also wanted to know.

"Marina likes you," Mallory shrugged. "You are her Medusa black."

Blood Red's face cleared and he chuckled. "Aye."

Change frowned. "What do you mean, her Medusa black?" It couldn't be too bad, though. Behind him the Gaitano men were chuckling. Next to him the Blackmons laughed softly.

Crazy Jim turned to him. "When we met her the accountant explained that she had been raised by black men." He smiled, blue eyes twinkling. "Joe Banks is her father black, Jackson her brother black, Catamaran her godfather cousin black, Jamal like an uncle black and Rashawn her friend black." He stopped, distracted for a moment as Xaira began giggling. Change's face cleared with understanding. "Sultan is her Council black," the handsome blond pirate continued, laughing himself, "and Solomon is her fighting black. That makes Blood Red..." he drifted off.

Change nodded with a laugh. "Marina's Medusa black."

Shane nodded with a smile. "Marina should make up a drink with that name," he murmured to his sons with a chuckle. The brothers snickered.

"I will write the letter," Blood Red agreed with faked reluctance, sighing deeply. Before they all entered the Sirens' Lair he turned to Xaira. "I can only try," he winked at her, "Marina does like me," making her smile.

Inside the Lair the mood turned a little festive with the entrance of all the pirates and their visitors. The Gaitanos conversed with Pedro Barbosa and the Hawthornes while the crew of the Medusa sat down to write their letters requesting the joint services of Ocean Coltrane and Xaira Chang for a year. Of course it was never going to happen, but the visitors couldn't resist the idea of going back home with the Medusa's request. Someone in Blue Bay was getting pranked. Lady Jill Coltrane and Lady Marina Aguilar Gaitano were so in for a surprise. Yeah, the visitors couldn't wait. So they didn't dwell. They said good-bye to the sirens and collected assorted greetings and messages for Jackson and Storm. Silas and Jimmy got a little emotional so they didn't linger on them except to reassure them they would see at least some of them again sometime, and to accept some beautiful black glass bottles for the younger Aguilar-Banks, Jackson, Salomé, and Marina. When Xaira protested they came up with one more, making them four. Hushed quiet conversations were held at the corner of the bar between the Gaitano men and the lawmen. Finally extremely confidential papers exchanged hands and the Gaitanos bade their farewells to Pedro Barbosa and the Hawthornes. These went to join the visitors in a round of good-byes. The letters for Lady Jill and Lady Marina were collected and they left. Everything was captured by Caribe.

The wind whistled around the cave's ceiling making the candles flicker. Flames hovered around the wicks, trembling, getting weaker by the moment until they expired. The people in the cave smiled at each other. They hadn't been there long. They had just spent their time arranging and organizing their belongings, chest, souvenirs, and documents both written and illustrated. Now they were sitting quietly in a circle enjoying each other's company biding their time. Outside the gray had grown darker. Out on the ocean whitecaps stood out against the deep smoky teal of the water. Overhead thunder rumbled and there was some lightning. It was still daylight, early afternoon, but shrouded in deep dark colors. The wind gusted then, whipping frantically around the cave, looking for an exit.

Don Carlos broke the silence. He was the veteran of the group. The one who had come through the storm the most times. "It is here." With a laugh he got to his feet, heading towards the entrance. In a moment everyone scrambled behind him, joining him outside.

Carlos and Indio looked at each other and smiled. They didn't need to say anything. They had come on a mission, rescued their uncles, and secured their present life status which was defunct, as far as Encantada was concerned or at least the Spaniards that were hunting them. They had gone and retrieved more of their treasure to use and dispose of in Blue Bay, watched over and took care of their girls' little sister and basically had some fun. But now they were more than ready to go back to their girls. Miguel and Juan stared the storm in the face along with everyone else. Don Carlos stood protectively between his brothers, keeping his sons close. The visitors stood on either side of them, shoulder to shoulder. The wind whipped the hair around their heads making them smile.

Lightning flashed in the distance at first, slowly creeping its way closer. The intense tones of gray over the horizon seemed to blend into each other. The lead clouds drifted a little faster, beginning to spread out and dance around forming a bank. A thread seemed to drop into the ocean like a lifeline from a rescue helicopter. Fascinated, the people on the cliff could only stare as the thread strengthened, seeming to expand before their very eyes. Then as if caught on the gears of a merry-go-round both sky and water began to circle in opposite directions. The ocean grew choppier and lightning was overhead now. The wind blew a little stronger but not that they noticed because still they stared. In response to the growling sky overhead the ocean began to churn a little bit faster, seeming to froth and foam. Whitecaps shattered against their liquid source in majestic, moving works of art. And before their eyes, with the faintest of roars, the ocean rushed into the chrome canopy flashing and rumbling above them. Sound abandoned them for a moment as the sky took in the last drop. Heaven and Earth held their breaths as well as the humans at the portal. Parallel ripples of energy rushed at them through air and water. The elements settled again. Then the water just dropped out of the sky. The pirates laughed, knowing the exact moment they went through. They could feel it. The wind blasted with the speed of a freight train, rushing right at and past them, its intensity dwindling some but still keeping its presence known.

Don Carlos chose that moment to honor the Aguilar-Banks. Throwing his head back, competing with Nature's impromptu concert, the pirate howled. In a moment the whole cliff clamored in harmony with the thunderstorm's opus in a cacophony of baying from the new arrivals at Blue Bay.